THE LIGHTRIDER JOURNALS

ERIC NIERSTEDT

iUniverse, Inc.
Bloomington

FOR COLIN

The Lightrider Journals

iUniverse books may be ordered through booksellers or by contacting:

iUniverse
1663 Liberty Drive
Bloomington, IN 47403
www.iuniverse.com
1-800-Authors (1-800-288-4677)

ISBN: 978-1-4759-5610-8 (sc)
ISBN: 978-1-4759-5612-2 (hc)
ISBN: 978-1-4759-5611-5 (e)

Printed in the United States of America

iUniverse rev. date: 11/6/2012

Cover Art by Derrick Fish

PROLOGUE

He stared at the leather-bound book that lay on the table. The colors danced beyond the window above it. Though his eyes stared at the book, his mind saw the outside perfectly—the reds, yellows, and blacks flashed across the skies, a drunken man's view of a kaleidoscope. It was so unlike the plain blue skies of his birth world; he remembered that when he'd first come to this place, the skies alone had entranced him for hours. Now, he barely remembered the amazement that had bound him.

But the work was still there. It had dominated his life long enough to kill the joys he'd once felt at the things he witnessed here. Now, as he stayed in this home, this prison, his duty was all that kept him alive.

Duty. God, he had grown to hate the very word. After all these years and betrayals, he no longer knew what it meant. Hate it all he might, he also knew that the joys duty had brought him would always be there.

That was why he had taken up the book once again. When he'd looked at it, with its bare, unadorned cover and yellowing pages, he'd set it aside, thinking it unimportant. Now, in its pages, he thought he might find understanding of all that had brought him here. It had been so long since he had allowed the past to truly wash over him, to let it bathe him in its scalding waters. But what else was he to do?

Slowly, he walked over to the desk. He waved his hand, and a chair blinked into existence. He sat and waved his hand again, calling a small jar of ink to appear on the table, a white feather emerging from its open lid. He reached over and opened the book, seeing the empty pages, their blank eyes waiting to be colored by the ink of his words.

He let his mind drift, turning back to those early days, until finally, he came to that moment that would allow him to dip back into the past. He smiled as he remembered that long-ago time. She'd been lying there in bed, the sunlight outlining every aspect of her face. God, she'd looked so sweet and beautiful!

That moment had been so ordinary and yet so joyful. He couldn't have *imagined that things would change so much that watching the woman he'd never see again sleep would be his happiest memory. But that was what happened when a man died. And if such a man was like him and made it past being dead …*

He dipped the pen and started to write. He began not on his own story but just prior, on the day that had shaped his destiny.

BOOK ONE

SELECTION

I.

THE MAN IN GOLD looked into the crystal sphere. His expression was one of neutrality—no crease on his weathered, bearded face showed the slightest hint of emotion. The orb glowed as scenes of a man in a combat uniform flashed within it. As the man in gold watched, the soldier leaped across the fray, his gun blazing as he mowed down his enemy. He saw the soldier whirl around, turning his weapon against another enemy and taking him to the ground in minutes. The soldier holstered his gun and moved to the corpse before him. He paused only to spit on the dead man's face before he moved on.

And still, as the orb flickered on, the man in gold showed no emotion. He watched the soldier break into a building, brandishing his gun and shouting at the men inside, who ceased loading bombs with poison gas. He watched as the soldier stood at attention and as a medal was pinned to his uniform. But despite his intense study of the scene before him, the man in gold still sensed another presence entering his realm.

"You have found another?" said the woman in black, her dark hair falling across her eye as she spoke.

"I have," the man finally said, the orb going dark at last. "I have been observing him for several days now."

"And what do you think you have?"

"A strong man. A man who fights for high ideals. But not one who can bear my power."

The woman sighed then. "Which is what you have said about the last few candidates."

"This is a delicate matter. We cannot simply give power to those who are undeserving."

"It still has to be given!" the woman declared. "All of us have made our choices; only you remain, spending your time gazing at mortals while the threat to existence grows worse. Everything we have worked to maintain, wiped out because of your inaction!"

"I am fully aware of the consequences of inaction," the man said, finally turning away from the sphere. "But I will not rush my choice out of fear of what may be. For now, we have time."

"You have never listened to your fears. It has made you foolish."

"I do this out of knowledge, sister," the man said. "We both know the weight of our powers. In the wrong hands, it would be disastrous, especially with the threat we face. Is that not why I helped you—so that your choice could bear your power but not be consumed by it?"

The woman in black paused and then answered, "Yes, I will grant you that, brother," the woman said. "We have always worked best when we combined our wisdom. Perhaps I should return the favor then?"

"You wish to help me?"

"If only to speed the process. I know the dangers of your power, as you know mine. Despite the threat we face, I could not allow a poor choice on your part."

"Very well. There is another that has been brought to my attention."

"Another man of the law? Or a soldier?"

"Neither. One who seems to possess the qualities, if not the experience. Come see."

The woman nodded and walked to where the man stood. Together, they looked into the orb. They watched as another scene was drawn for them and listened to the voice that filled the air.

*   *   *

"Don't forget the milk today," Jeri Hashimoto said.

"Huh?" Joe asked.

"Don't forget the milk," Jeri repeated as she poured herself a cup of the black, herbal sludge that somehow worked like coffee. "Like you did yesterday."

"Yes dear," Joe Hashimoto muttered. He hated to make mistakes like that. Jeri always said that it was because he was Japanese; she often hid the knives when Joe forgot or failed to do something and then made him promise not to "go kamikaze".

Luckily, she'd forgotten this morning. Joe finished buttering his toast. Still, sometimes Joe wondered if he should add a scar or two, if only to accent his bland features—short black hair; slanted, dark Asian eyes in a slightly rounded face; moderately fit physique; average height. His plainness had made him work hard to get people to recognize him for his skills, although being able to one-up his wife wasn't always one of them.

"Come on, you deserved it a little," Jeri said with a laugh as she brushed back her hair.

"Believe me, dear, seeing that disappointed look on your face is motivation enough."

"Aww, look at the little suck-up," Jeri replied. She leaned forward and kissed Joe on the cheek.

"Well, that is why you married me, isn't it?" Joe asked.

"Sure wasn't the sex," Jeri said, sipping her tea.

Joe just shook his head and began to butter his second piece of toast. As Jeri picked up the paper and started to read, he took a look at her face. Even though she wasn't wearing much makeup, Joe still thought he'd married the most eyes-popping-out-and-leaking-into-your-lap stunning woman in the world. Her red hair framed her face and still looked as fiery as ever after all the years. Still, Joe was always drawn to her eyes above all else. They were a deep shade of green, almost the color of the rain forest in the pictures Joe had seen.

That was why he waited until Jeri finished her paper before he turned her face against him. "I almost forgot; Mom called last night."

"Oh ..." Jeri said in horror-laced surprise. "Joe, please don't tell me ... not after the last time. Don't tell me they're ..."

"Yeah. On Thursday."

"Oh God, and you said yes?"

"I know, I know, but I think she's coming around."

"Dear, she will never forgive me for being your wife *and* a cracker. All I ever hear is, 'in Japan we do this' and 'this is how we did it when I grew up.' She spent the last visit giving me 'suggestions' on how to decorate the house, how to cook our food, and even how I should defend a case!" she snapped.

Joe tried to hide a smirk. "I don't disagree with you. But Mom was never happy about having to leave home when my dad got transferred—"

"And she wanted to make sure you didn't forget your culture." Jeri sighed. "She barely even accepted giving you an American name. But it's been years since all that, and I'm always going to be the ignorant cracker-Mick to her until one of us dies."

"I know. Even my father is tired of hearing it. But she's my mother, and I don't want to become estranged from her. Your dad and I didn't hit it off either, but he and I worked it out. Doesn't that prove that maybe we can get Mom to accept you?"

Jeri was quiet then. Finally, she asked, "When are they coming over?"

"They aren't yet," Joe said. "I said I'd have to clear it with you first."

"I hate you," Jeri muttered.

"I know. But what was I gonna do? Let her come by unannounced and have you even angrier with me?"

Jeri gritted her teeth and then said, "Thank you. I'll try to make it work then. But I'm not making any promises if she goes off the deep end."

"Good. Now, they were talking about taking us to dinner on Thursday. Is that okay with you?"

"All right. But if she goes nuts, you owe me big-time."

"I promise, if anything happens, I will be your slave."

"We're married, Joe. You already are."

"Dad's already what?" another voice said.

Both Jeri and Joe turned to see their twelve-year-old son standing in the doorway, his backpack slung over his shoulder. Cody Hashimoto had the open look on his face his father used so well. But physically, he was his mother's child, with light skin, blue eyes, and an oblong face. Only Joe's jet-black hair had managed to establish itself, along with a slightly Asian slant to Cody's eyes.

"Nothing important," Jeri said. "You ready for school?"

"Yes, Mom," Cody said with a sigh.

"You have your books?"

"Mom, come on. One day I forget my books, and you don't let it go for a year!"

"You can complain later; you have to catch the bus in five minutes—which is all the time I have," Joe said, looking at the clock. Grabbing his coat from the nearby rack, Joe threw it on, put some of his toast in his coat pocket, and headed for the door.

"See you guys tonight," he said as he worked the doorknob.

"Later, Dad," Cody said as he headed for the front door as well.

"Have a good day," Jeri added, moving to grab her briefcase from the countertop.

*   *   *

"He seems rather … quiet, don't you think?"

"Perhaps, but he does show promise. He knows how to negotiate."

"One argument solved is not enough. Yours is the final piece, and we cannot wait forever to determine whether or not he is acceptable."

"Give him time, sister. I was led to this man by the One, and we both know such things do not happen without a reason."

"Just make sure you do not misunderstand the message. I agree that this man seems to have the moral qualities we seek. But is he a leader? If he cannot end the conflict between his wife and mother, how can he face the challenges we have for him? How can he lead anyone when he cannot lead himself?"

"Wait and see. I believe that our answer will be delivered."

II.

Joe drove his car through the streets of Chicago, allowing himself a mental pat on the back for his deft handling of the situation. Usually, whenever he came between his mother and his wife, he had all the decision-making skills of a blind man buying a TV. But this time, he'd actually managed to work out a compromise.

Of course, Mom wasn't actually there to influence me, he thought to himself as he turned the corner. Ever since he was a kid, Joe had never really been able to stand up to Miyako Hashimoto. He remembered times when his mother had tried to push him into something he didn't want to do, like joining the chess club or the Boy Scouts (which she felt would help him develop, ironically, more Japanese values). He had told her, "I just don't want to do it." But after that, Miyako would begin to cry. And the only time he'd ever really been able to blind his eyes to the tears was when he'd married Jeri.

Since then, Jeri had become the target for his mother's disapproval, through comments and criticisms that were *supposed* to be subtle. *Oh, is the ham supposed to be so pink? I didn't know that color was in style. Is that your relative that's going blind?* After each family gathering, Joe had to listen to complaint after complaint from Jeri about his mother's rudeness. And those gatherings had been more frequent since Cody was born. As the Grenwal store came into view down the block, Joe was thankful that at least Ken Hashimoto had always thought that his son had married a fine woman and not a potato-eating Mick.

I just hope Dad can rein Mom in this week, or she'll probably give Jeri more advice on how to clean the house or some other thing, he thought to himself as he pulled the car into the store parking lot. *I can't stand another rant about hand cleaning instead of using the vacuum.* He exited the car and walked to the store.

As the doors opened, he said, "Morning, Miro," to the employee working at the register.

"Morning, boss," Miro replied as he continued to ring up the customer.

"How are the classes going?" Joe asked the cashier.

"Oh, great. I like how all these six-hour classes eat up all my time. But at least they're for my major. The science requirements really suck, though. I mean, I'm studying graphic design. Why do I—"

"Something about a well-rounded education," Joe answered. "It could be worse; you just have the basic courses."

"Maybe, but it still sucks," Miro replied. He paused to take the customer's money and give her the change. She left, and Miro turned and said, "I mean, half my professors are old as hell and don't even understand what I'm studying. One guy thought I was studying fashion and asked me if I was gay—in class!"

"At least the semester will be over soon, and then you won't have to deal with him anymore. Anything to report?"

"There is one piece of *great* news," Miro replied, brushing his long hair out of his eyes. "We got a call from ... her."

"Her?" Joe asked. "Who is ... wait you don't mean—"

"Yeah," Miro said. "She asked about the Jell-O sale, and I said we had plenty. Man, I wish we could lie."

"We have to serve the public, even when the public shouldn't be served," Joe sighed. "Thanks for telling me. I'll be on my guard for her."

"Actually, she's been here for an hour," Miro replied. "She found the Christmas stuff on the clearance rack and well ...."

"I see. All right, Miro, you know what to do when she gets up here," Joe said.

Miro nodded and Joe started walking to the office, muttering to himself on the way, "But she's *Jewish*. Why would she want Christmas— Oh, who knows? Anybody can be crazy at that age," he answered himself as he entered the office.

"Morning, Joe," Ronald, a shorthaired and thin-faced black man, said from his spot at the office computer. "You hear we got a call from—"

"Yeah, Miro told me," Joe said, moving over to the clock and punching in.

"Sucks don't it?" Ronald asked. "I mean, we're just getting through the holidays, and then they decide on a surprise inspection—"

"What?" Joe asked, whirling around to face Ronald.

"Yeah, Muriel called. She wants to come down and see the setup— just the general look, really."

"But the store's a mess! We still haven't cleaned up from the holiday rush," Joe cried out.

"Well, that's what she told me."

"But it makes no sense. I mean ... Ron?"

"Yes?"

"Are you bullshitting me?"

"No, of course not. Not about something like this."

"So you're serious?"

"No, but it's fun to tell you that I am."

Joe let out a long sigh, and Ronald started to laugh.

"You know, I could fire you," Joe added.

"And who would take care of all this shit for you?" Ronald asked.

Joe thought briefly of saying more, but he just shook his head, knowing that it wouldn't matter.

"You know, you could get rich from comedy a lot faster without these stupid pranks," Joe said.

"Aw, c'mon. Even you thought the crazy Jamaican grandma call was funny."

Joe started to say something but then stopped and said, "Okay, that was good. I don't know how they didn't realize it was you calling."

"Skill, man. So what did Miro have to report for you this morning?" Ronald asked.

"The lady of a million and one coupons and no patience is back," Joe said. "Whose turn is it this time?"

"I did it last time, so ..."

"I could just make you do it."

"But then who would finish the paychecks?"

"Figures," Joe sighed as he moved over to the countertop, where a few stacks of papers and order forms sat for him to look over.

"Amazing," he said aloud as he looked over the forms. "I feel like I just filled out the orders for last week."

"Blame it on Christmas," Ronald answered. "People come in for the clearance stuff and then end up buying half the store on their way to the register."

"I thought it was supposed to get easier for us after the holidays," Joe muttered as he checked out the forms that the other managers had prepared. "Eggs, milk, microwave burritos, dehumidifiers—well at least it isn't too out of the ordinary."

"We've got another problem," Ronald said, swiveling around in his chair. "Debbie called out for Friday night."

"Oh, for God's sake! This is the third week in a row!" Joe said.

"You saw how pissed off she was last week," Ronald said.

"Half the cosmeticians are on vacation. What else am I supposed to do?"

"I told her the same thing, but she didn't care. What do you want to do?"

"First, I'm gonna call her and talk to her before I change anything. Usually, I can get a yes out of her."

But as Joe went to the phone to do just that, he was interrupted by an announcement that said, "Code 33, Main. Code 33."

"Oh great," Joe muttered. He turned toward the door.

"Good luck!" Ronald said as Joe left the office and walked through the store to the register, where Miro stood with a great look of exasperation, along with an old, blonde-haired woman wearing a red coat and holding a long receipt next to a cartful of items.

"Hello, Mrs. Schlove, how can I help you today?" Joe asked in what he hoped was a cheerful and upbeat voice.

Waving her receipt in front of Joe's face, Schlove screeched, "Your system is screwed up again, young man. And your cashier is wrong! He says my receipt is perfect, but I did the math! Everything I bought is on clearance or I had a coupon."

"Well, let me take a look at it, ma'am," Joe said. He took the receipt and viewed the items.

"Mrs. Schlove, I'm sorry, but I don't see anything wrong here."

"Are you blind? With what I bought, I shouldn't have had to pay all that."

"Well, how much do you think you should've paid?"

"Exactly $22.95."

"So then, what appears to be overpriced?"

"This Santa doll," Mrs. Schlove said, pointing at the item on her bill. "There's no way that's 50 percent off."

"Hmm … well I remember that the doll originally went for $4."

"So?"

"It's on your bill for $2. That's exactly 50 percent off."

"Oh. Well, what about the reindeer—"

"No, that's right too, ma'am."

"And the candles, they're rung up twice."

"And voided off right after, ma'am."

"Oh. Well fine, maybe I was wrong on that, but I've got a Jell-O problem. I wanted thirty boxes of Jell-O, and your cashier only let me have five."

"Miro, why'd you do that?" Joe asked, although he already knew the answer.

"The coupon's only good for five boxes, and the sale just started today. Mr. Brown told me to save some for the rest of the week."

"This is a store. You have truckloads in the back! I know you do," Mrs. Schlove snapped.

"Now, ma'am, please," Joe said. "Did Miro tell you this when he rang you up?"

"No! Do you think I'm an idiot?"

"All right then. Now, he's right about the limit, and we have to make our supplies last the week. But since you weren't told about the limit beforehand, I'm going to let you have some extra boxes. How do ten extra boxes sound?"

Mrs. Schlove was quiet and then muttered, "Fine."

Joe motioned for Miro to ring up the extra Jell-O.

As Miro put the boxes through the machine, Mrs. Schlove grabbed each one and shoved it into her shopping bag. Finally, he finished the sale and asked for three dollars.

Muttering angrily, she shoved the money into Miro's hand and then stormed out, yelling, "I'm never coming to this place again!"

"You know, just once, I wish it could be true," Miro said once she was gone.

"I know, Miro," Joe said. "Look on the bright side, though. Doing this every week, you shouldn't ever have a problem dealing with the dormitory board again."

"Eh, they suck pretty bad too," Miro said. "Ah well, I'd better get back to work. Mr. Brown asked me to put away all the new cigarettes this morning. Of course, that's if he didn't take the Black and Milds again."

"I'm sure you can deal with it if there's a problem. I have to go and deal with scheduling in the office," Joe said.

"Debbie again?"

"How did you—"

"It's not that big a store, boss."

"Fair enough," Joe said, shaking his head and turning back to the office.

*   *   *

"Don't try to tell me that's leadership."

"It is part of it. He knows how to mediate."

"Pleasing an angry old woman is not the same as what we would be asking of him!"

"Agreed, sister, but it is a start."

"What promise do you truly see in this one?"

"He has made a strong rapport with those under him. We need a leader who has the respect of those under him, do we not?"

The woman in black hesitated and then snapped, "Yes, but think about this. You have worried about the power he would have. What makes you believe so much already?"

"He was fair with the old woman, despite her ... temperament. He cares for his family and wishes to create peace between his mother and wife. His relationship with his friend is strong enough that their insults mean nothing to each other. He listens to the problems of others with sympathy and understanding. Thus far, I believe he could prove worthy of the power."

The woman in black held her brother's gaze, her eyes fiery, but her silence was enough for him to press the issue.

"Remember your choice, sister? Did I not question his morals, despite your belief in his qualities?"

"Fine, fine, but we still need to see more."

"Agreed. So let us keep watching."

*   *   *

"Mrs. Schlove happily sent on her way again?" Ronald asked as Joe reentered the office.

"Yep, and she swore that she'd never come back to the store again."

"How long you give her this time? A week? Two days?" Ronald asked.

"Who knows?" Joe said. He walked to the phone. "I'm just glad it won't be my turn to deal with her then. Now, I've gotta deal with Friday night."

"I don't know how you can deal with her. Whenever I try to talk with her, I keep waiting for her to try to strangle me," Ronald said.

"That's because I can compromise," Joe said. He dialed Debbie's number from the employee listing on the wall. As the phone began to ring, he mentally rehearsed what he was going to say when she picked up.

God, the crazies you find in this job, he thought as the ringing stopped and a voice said, "Hello?"

"Hi, Debbie, this is Hashimoto. I need to talk to you about Friday night."

"Oh, don't start again!" Debbie snapped. "I worked the last two Fridays for you! I'm not doing it again!"

"Debbie, if you had a problem, you should've told me before, and maybe we could've worked something out," Joe replied. "And I told you last month that with Yusra taking a vacation, I'd need to—"

"Oh, she's a lazy little brat!" Debbie answered. "She never does anything at night anyway. I always have to clean up after her in the morning."

"Come on, Debbie, if she was that bad, don't you think I would've fired her already?"

"I've told you about it, but you never listen to me. I told you that the shampoo display wouldn't work out. I told you to hire more people. I told you—"

"Hold on, hold on," Joe said, rubbing his temples. "Now look, Debbie, let's try to get back to the point here. Is there an actual reason why you can't work on Friday?"

"Well, yes," Debbie snorted. "I need to take my kids to the Winnie the Pooh show at the playhouse that night. He's so cute, and they love him so much."

And so do you, Joe thought. Aloud, he said, "Well, how about this then? Why don't I switch the day shift with the night shift? I don't think that's a problem for anyone, and you can take your kids to the show."

"Well, that sounds fair," Debbie replied, her mood instantly brightening. "Thanks, boss. You're always so understanding. That's why I love working for you."

"I know, Debbie, I know," Joe said with a weary smile.

"Oh yes, you always listen to me when I have something important to say. I'll be there bright and early Friday morning."

"Great, Debbie. See you then," Joe said. He put the phone back down. Sighing aloud, he again rubbed his forehead.

"Ronald," he asked, "is it wrong to demand that one of your employees take medication without a doctor's script? Do you think jail is involved?"

"After five minutes with Debbie, I don't see how anyone would blame you," Ronald replied.

"Neither do I," Joe replied, picking up one of the stacks of paper from the desk and beginning to look through them. Grabbing a pencil, he began to check off the items they needed to order this week; he also made a mental note to begin slipping tranqs into Debbie's Friday morning coffee.

Or he would have, if Ronald hadn't suddenly let out a yell. Joe whirled around to see Ronald raising his paperwork over his head, about to slam it down onto a spider that was crawling across the desk.

"Don't, Ron!" Joe said. Joe took two huge steps forward and grabbed the papers, holding them in midair as Ron stared at him.

"It's a spider! I hate spiders!"

"You still don't need to smash it," Joe said as he stretched a hand over to a nearby pencil holder. Joe dumped out the pencils, and placed the holder in front of the spider, who quickly crawled inside.

"See?" Joe said. "And now I'll take it outside."

"Why is it you have such a hard time killing pests?" Ronald asked. "You saved that mouse last month and God knows how many spiders. Why?"

"I don't know. I just think it's the right thing," Joe answered. He moved toward the office door to send the spider on its way. But as he opened the door, Joe looked out the office and suddenly pulled back, holding his free hand over his eyes.

"You all right?" Ronald asked, getting up from his chair.

"Yeah," Joe muttered as he blinked several times. "The light was … just really bright all of a sudden."

"Looks fine to me," Ronald said. "Maybe you need to get your eyes checked."

"Maybe," Joe said. He went back into the aisle, still blinking his eyes.

*   *   *

"You watched too closely there brother. You forgot how just a little of your power can affect the mortals."

"A mistake, true. But I wanted a closer look at his act of kindness. Small it may be, but it gave me a further look into his character."

"Perhaps. He does seem able to deal with difficult situations, and he has the quality of … mercy you desire. But this is not enough yet, brother. We are asking him to maintain cosmic order, not reschedule an employee or save an insect."

"You are always disapproving, sister. He has demonstrated the qualities that we can mold into an effective leader, with time and experience."

"What we can do with him is only what he will let us. There is still time before we will be able to choose him. Let us continue to watch him and see what happens."

"Agreed. Perhaps then he can be prove to be worthy in your eyes."

"Perhaps. But every man has a flaw, brother. This one has one as well, and we must just wait to discover it."

III.

The restaurant was large and spacious, and the atmosphere, slightly more than casual. Fine carpet covered the floor and expensive decorations covered the marble walls. But the waiters' uniforms, which consisted of a red shirt with the restaurant's stylized name emblazoned on it, and their lack of mustaches, upturned noses, and nasal accents helped make the customers feel at home, creating a calm, relaxed atmosphere.

The atmosphere was the single most important reason that Joe had chosen this place. The decor made it seem fancy enough to suit his mother, but at the same time, it was causal enough for Jeri and himself. Joe and Jeri detested most of the restaurants his mother preferred; they usually meant three hours of waiting for food that had been gathered from the inside of a volcano and drenched in sauces made from alien vegetables.

"Right this way, folks," the waiter said. He led the four of them to a large table. Seating each of them, the waiter passed out menus and asked if they wanted to choose a drink. "We have an excellent wine list if you wish to look it over," the waiter added.

"That sounds fine," Joe said, even as he thought, *Must not let Jeri get drunk.*

The waiter nodded and left, leaving the family alone. Joe reached under the table, squeezed his wife's knee, and then began the evening's conversation. "So, Mom, what did you think about Cody's science project?" he asked.

They had met the parents at home, giving them a chance to see their grandson, who had been constructing a school project that was due in a few weeks.

"He certainly seems to have a taken a lot of time to build it," Mrs. Miyako Hashimoto said from across the table. She was a thin woman, with gray hair tied into a bun and narrow cheekbones that gave her a somewhat sour expression. But her face softened a bit as she spoke about Cody. "I didn't realize he was so proficient with machines."

"Yes, he really seems to know what he's doing with that robot," added Kenta Hashimoto. In many ways, he was a much older version of Joe, with a similar face and hairstyle, though his hair was almost totally gray. He also shared Joe's gentle disposition.

"Refresh my memory, why exactly did he have to build such an elaborate project?" Ken asked. "When you needed to do science stuff, Joe, teachers were satisfied with a baking soda volcano."

"Yeah. Three days of you telling me how to sculpt papier-mâché and pour baking soda down a hole," Joe said. "And then you made me practice my speech a hundred times."

"It got you an A, didn't it?" Ken replied. "That's the important thing. But I'll admit; that looks like a lot of work for a kid's science project."

"Blame the advancement of technology," Jeri replied. "His science teacher loves to work with machines, and he thought it would be a good way for the kids to learn about them."

"Cody was thrilled though," Joe said. "I've never seen him get so excited about a school project. He went out and got everything he needed in a few days and then got right to work."

"I'm sure that was the work ethic you gave him, which I passed to you," Ken said. "And I'm sure Jeri gave plenty of encouragement as well."

"Don't you mean nagging?" Jeri asked with a wry smile.

"If it works, I'll call it successful," Ken replied. "After all, how else can you will him out of the house one day, with the drive to succeed and be his own man?"

"I suppose I could just call you for advice on that. Although I don't know about you making a 'real man,'" Jeri replied, the wry smile still one her face.

"I believe you married the result of my work?" Ken said with a grin.

"I'd like to think that Cody has some drive," Miyako said.

"So do I," Jeri replied without missing a beat.

"Oh, he must. I still can't believe that he was able to build it all by himself," Ken said quickly. "And you said all he did was take apart a blender and an old toaster?"

"That's all, Dad," Joe said. "Of course, I had to help him do some of the welding for the arm, but other than that, it was all him."

"Amazing," Ken said. "I'll be honest, though; when I saw how good that thing was, I wondered just how much help you were giving him."

"Joe would never do that," Miyako defended. "And Cody's a smart boy."

"Very true, dear," Ken agreed.

"And besides, with all the complex devices that robot must've needed, I'm sure you two would've felt like old fogies if you'd tried to help him. The advancement of technology and all that, right Jeri?" Miyako added.

"Right," Jeri said, completely ignoring the barb. "But I think we would've all felt that way if we had to help him."

"He's always been good with machines. Remember the time that he took apart the vacuum cleaner, Dad?" Joe asked, directing the conversation out of the danger zone.

"How could I forget?" Ken said, picking up the signal smoothly. "I still can't believe that we only left him alone for fifteen minutes."

"Wasn't there a wrench in the room too?" Jeri asked.

"Yes, remember how you were fixing the TV that day?" Miyako asked.

Ken merely shrugged and said, "Perhaps we should pick out a wine before the waiter comes back?"

"Good idea," Jeri said, picking up the wine list. Looking it over, she said, "Oh, this sounds good. Sherri over at work had this for her New Year's party, remember, Joe?"

"Oh yeah," Joe said, seeing the name. "It's very good—dry, rich taste."

"Sounds all right," Ken said. "Besides, I could try something new tonight. What do you think, Miyako?"

"I'll certainly give it a try," Miyako replied. "After all, we have the word of Jeri's friend to go on, don't we?"

Jeri nodded, ignoring the barb as the waiter came back for the order. The wine turned out to be excellent (a fact that Miyako admitted with some regret), and the food was just as good. The four of them talked on a variety of subjects, from Ken and Miyako's life in Springfield (which included stories about their neighbors and how parts of the town were beginning to change with the times again) to the Bears' chances this season to stories about Jeri and Joe's jobs. But unfortunately, Joe was so happy from the calm, he didn't anticipate the storm that was going to follow.

"So anyway, this lady takes another drag from her oxygen bag, and asks Miro for a carton of cigarettes," Joe said, miming sucking through a tube.

"You didn't have to—" Jeri began.

"Oh, I did," Joe said. "Miro was right about her needing to quit, but unfortunately, the surgeon general doesn't say you can deny cigarettes to an addict who's still able to walk into the store and buy them."

"That can't be right," Miyako said, shaking her head. "I don't understand why more people don't get help."

"It isn't always that easy," Ken said. "I think I read somewhere that cigarettes are harder to quit then heroin."

"I heard the same thing," Jeri said. "Plus, it sounds like she's been smoking for a long time."

"Still, to get into such bad shape and still be allowed to buy—You really couldn't stop her, son?" Miyako asked, shaking her head.

"Believe me, I wanted to. But it's not something I can do for her," Joe said, taking another bite of his dinner. "Still, that's not the worst of it, Mom. After she bought them, she started to have this coughing fit, the worst I've ever seen. She was leaning on her cart very heavily, and even the customers got worried. But she just shrugged us all off and took another swig on her tank. The coughing tapered off, and she asked for her cigarettes again. I asked her if she was sure about it, and she insisted that they were for someone else."

"I'm sure," Ken answered.

"Like I said, the surgeon general doesn't say she can't buy, so we just let her have them."

"That's really depressing," Jeri said. "But the sad thing is, sooner or later she won't be able to come in for them anymore."

"I doubt it," Joe said. "The way she is, I don't think she'll ever stop. Even if they remove a lung, she'll figure out some way to smoke."

"Maybe, but remember one important thing, son," Ken said.

"What's that?"

"Oxygen is flammable. So if you ever hear an explosion in the distance, you'll know that she's gone to the big cigarette store in the sky."

Joe gasped at that but soon found himself trying to hold back guffaws, while Jeri laughed openly.

"Dad … that's … that's j-just …wrong," Joe managed to sputter out, while Ken just smiled at his son's discomfort.

However, Joe was able to stop laughing a second later when he noticed his mother's disapproving glare. The laughter instantly died in his throat, and what was on the way to his mouth became a series of small coughs.

"You all right, honey? Not smoking behind my back, are you?" Jeri asked.

"Sure. Sure I'm fine," Joe said as the coughs subsided. "Still, I think I've told enough stories about the crazy, old people. Maybe we should move onto another topic?"

"Sounds good," Jeri said. "I don't think we've told your parents about Cody's new interest, have we?"

"New interest?" Ken asked. "I thought he had the robot thing going?"

"Oh, he still loves that, but now he splits his time between that and Judy."

"Judy?" Miyako asked, her head snapping up. "Who's this now?"

"Oh, she's this girl he met at school," Joe said. "They're just friends right now, but it's obvious that he likes her. He's had her over for what, three study dates this week?"

"Sounds about right," Jeri said as Ken chuckled.

"Has he actually said anything to this girl yet?" the old man asked.

"Not yet. If they aren't talking about something like robots or whatever's going on in Dragonball or whatever, he doesn't say too much."

"But there must be more that they can talk about, right?"

"A little bit. He's still really shy around her, but I think he'll come around soon," Jeri said.

"And where is this girl from?" Miyako asked in a clipped tone.

"I think she lives on the East Side," Jeri replied. "She's very sweet. She said she wants to be a lawyer when she grows up so she can 'help people.'"

"Jeri, come now," Ken said. "You shouldn't lie about your profession; I mean, helping people?"

"Oh, ha ha," Jeri retorted as Miyako opened her mouth once again.

"And what kind of girl is she other than that?"

"Excuse me?" Jeri asked.

"What is she like?"

"I told you; she's very nice. She even offered to come and show me this weaving thing she does with her hair. It may be hard since my hair's so straight, but—"

"Wait," Miyako said. "You don't mean—Is this girl—"

"What, Mom?" Joe asked, although he feared he knew what she was asking.

"Well … colored and all," Miyako whispered.

Oh crap. Joe thought as Jeri's eyes narrowed.

"Yes she is. I wasn't aware that it mattered," Jeri replied, her voice as brittle as the crystal on their table.

"Oh no, of course, it doesn't," Miyako said, trying and failing to sound unconcerned. "I just want to make sure my grandson isn't hanging around with the wrong people."

"Dear, Jeri just described the girl to you," Ken said.

"Yes, very nice. But what about her family? Her friends? What about where she lives?"

"I don't know," Jeri said, her voice growing colder with every passing second. "It isn't my place to pry."

"If you didn't know this girl, no," Miyako replied. "But she is obviously having an effect on Cody. You need to make sure he doesn't fall into a bad situation."

"Mom, please," Joe said. "Can you drop this? Cody's—"

"He's a smart boy," Jeri interrupted. "He knows what a bad situation is, and he knows how to avoid it. Besides, how else will he learn without making his own choices?"

"By having someone show him the right choices," Miyako answered. "My son never would've become the man he is today if I hadn't shown him the right choices in life."

"Oh, is that what you call it?" Jeri asked. "Well, I'm sorry, but I don't believe in having that kind of *control* over my son's life."

Oh dear sweet megacrap, Joe thought. His mother sharply inhaled, the sign that her limit had been reached and she was about to go on the warpath.

"I never controlled my son!" Miyako snapped.

People in the restaurant turned to take note of the family squabble. But Miyako continued. "I showed him all the best choices. I showed him how he could make his life better. Maybe if you cared about your son, you could do the same!"

"I do care!" Jeri yelled back, jumping out of her chair. "I care enough to let him be his own person and make his own decisions. I guide him, instead of trying to run his life. You should know that doesn't work!"

"Oh, I know," Miyako snarled. "I know it fails when you aren't strong enough to truly guide your child! I've known for the last fifteen years," she snapped at her daughter-in-law.

Jeri's eyes popped wide open at that crack. Her face went flush, and she stared in utter disbelief at Miyako; she looked like she'd been slapped. But slowly, expression came back into her face, until she was able to turn to her husband and growl, "Are you just going to sit there, or are you going to say something?"

But Joe just sat there, face aghast, unable to form any semblance of words. A part of him was so angry at his mother that he wanted to leap across the table and slap her for daring to speak that way to the woman he loved. But even as that part surged, the dutiful son kept yelling, *But she's my mother!* With a confused, stupid expression on his face, Joe attempted to make words come from his lips, but all that passed was a babbling mixture that went something like this. "Well ... It's ... Mom, you shouldn't ... Can't we just ... I ..."

Thankfully, Ken stepped forward to stop his son from digging himself an even deeper hole.

"Miyako, enough!" He grabbed his wife's arm and turned her to face him. "Look at this. We were having a perfectly fine dinner until you ruined everything again," he snapped. "Can't we go anywhere without you insulting Jeri like this? For God's sake, she's the mother of your grandchild; doesn't that count for something? And our son is more than old enough to make his own decisions about his life and the lives of his family. Now you apologize right now!"

But Miyako merely sat there, her lips pressed tightly enough to squeeze water from a stone and stared coldly at Jeri.

Sighing, Ken turned to his daughter-in-law and said, "Jeri, I am so sorry about this. I had no idea that she would—"

"It's all right, Dad," Jeri said, her voice still taut and clipped. "It's not your fault. But I think I should go now, before I say something we'll all regret."

"Of course. I'll take care of the bill," Ken said.

Jeri grabbed her coat and purse and made her way to the door. Joe watched for a minute, still in shock. Briefly, he turned to his father, who motioned for his son to leave. But as he picked up his coat and began to follow his wife, Joe couldn't help seeing anger and shame in his father's eyes. It hurt enough to drive out the shock, and as they left the restaurant, Joe could already feel the shame beginning to well up inside him.

$$* \qquad * \qquad *$$

"You see?"

"All men have a weakness, sister. This one's seems to be that he cares too much."

"Cares too much? His weakness is that he cannot decide," she snapped at the man in gold. "He cannot handle this sort of pressure and you expect him to be given—"

"If you had to choose between a husband and family, sister, who would you choose?"

The woman pulled back then, her anger abated for a moment. But then her face hardened again. "I don't know, but I would make a choice. This one cannot even do that! We are asking for someone to deal with situations of life and death. He will need to think of the balance above all else, and he is too indecisive to do that. You are letting your emotions and your softness blind your judgment."

"And you are letting your stubbornness and impatience blind yours. We cannot give this power to a being who does not care. This one does. He is not experienced, but he can learn. And as you said, we cannot search forever."

"Perhaps not, brother, but to do what we will require of him, he may change into what you fear."

"Or perhaps, he will emerge from it a stronger man who can overcome his weakness."

"You risk much on what may be."

"No. I risk much on what I believe. That is worth a risk. Now come, there is still more to see."

IV.

THE HEADLIGHTS WERE BLINDING as Joe drove home. The night had become a classic Chicago rainstorm, with winds and pelting rain that ravaged everything in their path. Joe kept his eyes on the road, focusing all his attention on keeping the car steady. And truthfully, the rain was easier to deal with than angry, smoldering, silent woman who sat in the seat next to him.

But even as he tried to focus on the road, a part of Joe's mind was still raging at himself for being such a fool this night. He could see and hear the whole thing in his skull, pounding like the sound of a fat, tone-deaf woman trying to sing opera.

What is wrong with you? his mind said as he made the next turn. *Why are you such a frigging dumbass? You honestly thought this could go well? Damn it, Joe, those two use subtlety like sword blades! All those times they cut each other and smeared poison in each other's wounds, and you still haven't learned?*

But how *could I have known it would be* this *bad?* Joe thought as he stopped at the light.

You couldn't have. But you should've known something would happen! Face it, Mom will always hate Jeri because she doesn't meet whatever expectation she had for your future wife. And Jeri will always hate Mom for trying to make her into that kind of woman. What's the point of trying anymore? Just accept it.

But I want ...

Yeah? Who cares? Face it, Joe, what do you think you could do about it anymore? Tonight it was all up to you. If you want me to shut up about it, here's all you have to do—just pick a goddamn side! They will never stop hating each other, and all you can do is make sure they don't kill each other because of it. And that means, Joe, you have to be willing to pick a side when shit like this happens.

Those last words stayed in Joe's mind as he drove the car up into their driveway. The only way he would succeed with Jeri and his mother would be to perform major brain surgery on both of them and eliminate their hatred of each other. And since Joe couldn't abide the sight of blood, he was going to have to put aside that dream, grab the giant two-by-four that was reality, and whack himself in the face with it.

As he put the car in park and cut the engine, Joe slowly turned in his seat and faced his wife.

She stared straight ahead, her eyes pointed enough to shatter the glass in the windshield.

But he spoke anyway. "Jeri, I … I want to say—"

"That you're sorry?" she finished for him, clipping the words from his mouth like a blade through grass. "Is that it?"

"Yes. I'm sorry about my mother. I'm sorry about what she said to you tonight and what she's said in the past. And I'm sorry for expecting you two to make nice when she hasn't gotten over anything. I just want to see you two get along, and I care too much about hurting you both.

"But I promise you, this is it," he insisted as Jeri continued to stare straight ahead. "I'm not going to let her do this to you ever again. I'm going to call her tomorrow and tell her that if she ever says anything like that to you again, that I will stop seeing her, and I won't let Cody see her."

He stopped then and looked at Jeri, hoping for a response, for her to give him some indication that his speech was not in vain.

Slowly, she turned to face him. "Joe, that's good," she said, her voice cold as a frozen piece of steel. "I like that you want to make this end. But why are you doing it tomorrow?"

"Well, I thought—"

"No, Joe," Jeri said, her voice rising now. "Why couldn't you do it tonight? Why couldn't you do it when your mother was throwing all those old barbs at me? Why couldn't you move to pull even one out?

"Your mother is what she is Joe, and it's not worth my energy to be angry at her about it. You're right, we do hate each other, and that will never, ever change. And you want us to get along, fine. But your way of doing that is to let us fight for all these years and never take sides? I'm your wife. I love you. I share your bed. I bore your child. I take care of him and your house and your needs. But you don't even have the balls to defend me when I'm being sliced open? You have to wait until an hour after the wounds have festered to say something? Do you have any idea how pathetic it is when your father-in-law defends you while your husband just sits there, babbling away?"

"Jeri, I … I …" Joe tried to say, but Jeri just snorted and cut him off.

"Save it," she said as she moved to get out of the car. Pushing the door open, she stomped out and then turned and snapped, "If you ever do that again, I swear to God I'll—I don't know, but you really won't like it!"

With that, Jeri tramped her way to the house, while Joe sat in their car, waiting for her to get inside and a distance from him before he ventured to go out himself. He waited through the brief quiet of Jeri making fake small talk with Cody. Finally, even through the car, he could hear her moving up the stairs, with all the quiet of a rabid rhino in an antique museum. It was only when that quiet ended that Joe unbuckled his seatbelt and dared to venture into the house.

As he got to the back door, he opened it to see Cody sitting at the table, his homework out in front of him, looking at his father with a rather dry expression.

"Did things not go well?" he asked.

"Whatever gave you that idea?" Joe sighed as he removed his coat and slung it over the chair.

"Well, Mom doesn't usually storm into the house like she did when the garbage man wouldn't take the trash."

"Yeah. Pity, he might still have a job if he had," Joe said with a small laugh.

"You do all right tonight?" he asked Cody.

"I had fractions to do. They really suck, Dad. Why do I have to learn this?"

"They're good for a boy your age," Joe said. "You work with them, you'll get into all the best places when you're older."

"Dad, you sound like an after-school special," Cody said.

"Sorry," Joe said with the ghost of a grin on his face.

"Did Grandma and Mom go crazy at one another?"

"What makes you think that?" Joe said, turning to face his son.

"Come on, Dad. Even I know they don't like each other."

Joe paused, trying to think how to best explain the situation. "Well, I'm trying to get them past it. Or at least I was," Joe said, slumping into a chair.

"So how long have you known?" he asked his son.

"I figured it out last year. You remember at Christmas when they were having that discussion about the video game one of Grandma's friends had to buy for her grandson?"

"Grand Theft Auto V, right? I can still hear her now—'Who could make such filth for a child?'"

"Yeah I know. And what was it that Mom said back? 'Somebody who knows that plenty of people buy whatever their kids want just to shut them up.'"

"And then the yelling. Your grandmother doesn't like to be corrected by anyone except your grandfather."

"And Mom decided to correct her again tonight?" Cody asked.

Joe looked at his son then and asked, "When did you get so inquisitive?"

"Because you just mope around when this happens."

Joe halted a moment and then sighed and said, "All right. We told your grandma how you have a crush on Judy and—"

"Dad, I told you, it's not a crush! She's just a girl I can talk to about … stuff and—"

"Don't stop. This is more interesting than my problems," Joe said.

Cody sputtered a moment and then finally regained himself and pointed out, "I thought we were talking about you."

"Well, your grandma started to ask about Judy, since you seemed to like her so much."

Cody sighed loudly.

"And she started to ask some questions your mom didn't think were appropriate."

"Like what?"

"You don't need to know. Anyway, they started to yell back and forth, and the people in the restaurant started to notice us."

"And then things got bad? Did you do anything?" Cody asked, staring at his father with rapt anticipation.

Joe tried to explain the feelings of anger, shame, and uncertainty that had been in him and then stopped and answered, "No, I didn't really say anything. Then your grandfather stepped in and stopped it. We left after that."

Cody sat still a moment and then leaned back into his chair, hands behind his head. "No wonder Mom's mad at you. But how can you choose between her and Grandma?"

"Thank you, son. I really—"

"I mean it, it takes you at least fifteen minutes to pick between Shredded Wheat and Frosted Wheat in the morning."

"Gee thanks," Joe grumbled.

Cody kept on. "But Dad, it looks like you're never gonna succeed."

Joe sighed, and said, "You're probably right, son. But I suppose if I can't teach myself that yet, I should try to get you a lesson from all this.

"Cody, there will be times when you'll do things your mother and I won't agree with. And as much as I'll wish you'd listen to us when those times come, I don't want you to think you always have to go by what we say."

"Can I use this now?" Cody asked.

"Let me finish first. Don't always let someone else decide what you should believe in. But you should listen to other people and understand what they have to say, because that's how you learn what's right and wrong. I guess what I mean is, whatever your views become, make sure it's because you decided that they were the right thing to do, not because someone told you they were."

"Don't worry, Dad. I already know what I think. But, Dad, if you really believe all that stuff, then you need to take what you've heard and pick your side."

Joe smiled wanly and then ruffled his son's hair and told him to get back to his fractions.

As Cody sighed and turned back to his books, Joe got up and turned to the living room. Walking away, Joe thought that he had given his son a fine speech. And his son had given him one right back, one filled with just as much truth; he was proud of the boy for saying it.

He just wished he could make himself believe his son's words.

*   *   *

"Weak, brother, weak. He is too softhearted, too entrapped by his divided heart to recognize wisdom when he hears it, or even when he says it."

"Agreed. But I still stand by him."

"And I still say this is foolishness!" the woman snapped. "Perhaps he is a good man, but he is not a strong one. He is torn by his emotions and his loves. And you desire to take all that from him and give him your power, when you know full well what it will make him do? Do you really believe he can handle what will happen to him when—"

"Sister, you know that both our charges will face that facet of our power and must both deal with it on their own. But it makes no difference to this man. Tomorrow, he will lose everything he cares about. We have seen many different men and women, and while many showed promise, they were being torn apart by lesser demons than this man. Now, we see a man nearing great loss, a man torn apart not by greed or anger but by his love for others and a wish to better himself. Can you tell me that such a man is not worthy to house my power?"

The woman in black looked at her brother, at his golden robes and determined face, and sighed as she nodded.

"My decision is made. This man shall be chosen."

"You speak highly, brother, but you and I both know you give him no real choice at all."

"Perhaps, but then again, even your chosen one will come to regret it, sister."

"Yes. Mine will regret what he could have had, and yours, what he once had."

"It is the cost of this cruel thing we must do."

"It is a just thing as well. But it does not make this decision easy."

"Nothing is ever easy."

"This will be no different. By this time tomorrow, we will see how well your choice is, brother. And despite what you may think, I hope that I am wrong."

*   *   *

That night, Joe Hashimoto slept on the couch, his head pushed against the hard armrest, a thin blanket pulled over him. In the time that was to come, he would look back on this night and wish he had gone to the bed he and his wife had shared. He would wish that he had stayed with his son and talked with him more. He would wish for many things, but none of them really mattered. Instead, Joe Hashimoto lay there and slept the last innocent sleep of his first life.

V.

"Dad."

"Uh."

"Dad."

"Huh? Wha—"

"*Dad!*"

"Ah!" Joe yelled, starting like a deer caught in the headlights. Too startled to think about what he was doing, Joe twisted to the side, thinking he would turn onto the other side of the bed. Instead, he ran out of couch and hit the floor with a hard thud. As his mind slowly began to awaken, he remembered where he was and what had happened. He also remembered that he had not yet gotten around to having the carpet ripped up and the floors changed to hardwood.

"Sleep well, Dad?" Cody asked as he watched his father struggle to disentangle himself from the blankets.

"I was," Joe grumbled. "What did you wake me up for?"

"Don't you need to go to work?"

"Huh … Oh crap, it's not Sunday is it?"

"No," Cody replied as Joe attacked the sheets with renewed energy. "But you still have time."

"How much time?"

"About half an hour."

"Half an hour!" Joe cried, finally getting himself out of the sheets. Rising to his feet, he said, "Why didn't anyone wake me up sooner?"

"Mom got a call from the office. They said something happened with her case and she needed to get down there right away. She left a note about it in my room."

"Great. She was probably in too much of a rush to wake me up."

"Well, Dad, how were you going to wake up anyway? You don't have an alarm or anything down here."

Joe noticed the lack of an alarm by the couch, but answered, "No time for that now, son. I've got to hurry!"

Joe bounded past his son and raced upstairs to his room. But when he got there, he saw that his work clothes had already been laid out for him on the bed. On top of them lay a folded piece of paper with his name on it. Joe cautiously took the paper, wondering briefly if Jeri had rigged it to a bomb somewhere in the room and then opened it and began to read.

> Joe,
> *I had a lot of time to think last night, after I cursed you and your mother out for a while up here. Don't think I'm going to forget what happened last night or that I regret making you sleep on the couch. But I do know it isn't easy for you to choose between me and your mother (even though she is wrong!), and the only reason you keep doing this is because you love us both and you want us to get along. It will never happen like you want, but maybe tonight we can talk some more and work something out. I really don't want to have to go through this again with either of you. But look on the bright side. At least your dad and I get along.*
>
> *Later, my little rice worker*

"Ah. A refreshing dose of racial humor to get me going," Joe said to himself, shaking his head as he began to change into his work clothes. Looking at the alarm clock, he realized he would still have time to make coffee before driving off to work. And maybe he could use that time to start thinking of what he was going to say later. Maybe this time, they could work something out without having to fear too much for their blood pressure. A night of being berated by his wife and sleeping on the couch had definitely knocked a few things loose in Joe's head. Before he talked with Jeri, he was going to call the old woman and give her a hard push off her tall chair.

As Joe pulled his work shirt on, buttoned it, and reached for his tie, he smiled and imagined telling his mother these things he'd held inside for years. As long as his anger held, he wouldn't have anything to worry about. Plus, telling Jeri that he'd told off his mother would be a great way to start off their discussion.

As that thought drifted through his mind, Joe finished with his tie and headed downstairs to get what breakfast he could. He walked down the stairs and heard a door swing open and Cody's voice ring out, "Dad, I'm off to the bus!"

"Have a good day, son! Learn fractions," Joe called back as the door swung shut with a bang.

Joe reached the bottom of the stairs; walked into the kitchen; and as always, saw a large pile of plates on the table, exactly where his son always left them.

"Why is it he can spend three hours playing Smash Bros. but he can't spare a minute to clean up after himself?" Joe muttered, as taking the plates and moving them into the dishwasher. Once that was taken care of, Joe moved to the cabinet and, after a few moments of deliberation, grabbed the Folgers. One coffeepot later, he took his first sip of hot coffee. But he was only able to get a few sips in before he put the cup down. Something just didn't feel right. It wasn't anything he could point at, just a strange, black feeling in the pit of his stomach. Everything looked the same; the walls hadn't begun to collapse, the refrigerator hadn't come to life, the knives were in their proper holders, and all was total silence.

The silence—maybe that was it. Normally, he'd be listening to Jeri read the paper and comment on how politicians were slowly turning the world into crap or Cody talk about how he was looking forward to math with all the truth of a double-headed snake in Eden. This was the first time in years that Joe had eaten breakfast alone.

"Aw, so what?" Joe said. He shook his head and resumed his breakfast. "Probably good for me to eat alone once in a while." But as he drank his coffee and continually glanced at the clock, all he could think about was the feeling in his stomach and how it wasn't going away.

Whatever the reason for this odd feeling, Joe pushed it aside and finished his breakfast, dumped his plates in the dishwasher, and headed out the door. As he approached the garage, he suddenly halted in his tracks and then shook his head. Turning around, he walked back to the door and locked it.

"That's a first," he muttered to himself, entering the garage and moving over to his car. Pulling open the door, he sat down and slid the key into the ignition. But when he turned it, nothing happened.

"Oh no. Not now," Joe muttered, turning the key hard this time, like a bully giving a kid an Indian burn. This time, he got a weak sputter out of the engine.

"What in the hell is this?" Joe exclaimed, looking at the dashboard like it was the control panel of a spaceship. As he ran through options in his mind, he began to feel the blackness in his stomach again.

"Come on, work you blasted thing. Please work for me, huh?" he begged. He turned the key again. This time, the car sputtered for a minute and then gave out a spurt that almost sounded like it was going to catch. Before it died, Joe thought he heard something from the engine, like a last oily gasp from the throat of the car itself.

But instead of frustration, he felt … relieved, like a huge gorilla had just gotten off his chest.

As the feeling of relief spread in his body, Joe briefly toyed with idea of forgetting work today, for the first time in his entire career. As crazy as it sounded, the idea of staying home began to gain weight in his mind. He could feel his negative feelings flow further and further away from him, unwanted turds flowing down the porcelain river of his mind …

As Joe mulled on this strange new urge, the morning light began to shine in from the garage window. It fell onto the hood of the car, and suddenly, the engine caught and roared to life. As Joe started and looked at the engine in wonder, he leaned forward, causing the light from the window to fall onto his face. As it did, Joe suddenly heard his previous thoughts echoed back at him and felt like a fool. What next—would he call off getting out of bed because the covers were warm? Joe started to smile and then to laugh as the dark feeling in his stomach began to evaporate.

Good Lord, what's wrong with me? Joe thought as he wiped his brow in relief. *Hell, it's probably just heartburn or something.*

"I must be losing it. Besides, how bad can it be out there?" he said, gunning the engine and pulling out of his garage, down the driveway, and into the road.

*   *   *

"C'mon. For the love of God, come on," Joe muttered angrily as he sat behind the wheel of his car, stuck in traffic. He'd been sitting in this same spot for nearly twenty-five minutes, along with almost half of Chicago's working population. Everything had been going fine; Joe had made his route the same as he had every morning, making every turn without so much as a hint of traffic. He'd gotten to a red light, and then, as if by some twist of fate, the traffic light had frozen in place, leaving one side red and one side green. Someone must've called the police at that point because, after ten minutes of nothing but solid gridlock (and yelling at the opposing drivers who still had working lights on their side), the city maintenance crew had shown up and were working to repair the light.

The only problem was that, apparently, no one had thought to send the police out to guide the traffic. And so, everyone else was still sitting in his or her car, waiting for the maintenance crew, which had parked its trucks on the side of the road, in order to get to work.

"This day just gets weirder and weirder," Joe said to himself as he looked over at the light. Ten years now, he'd been taking this route to work, and not once had he ever encountered something like this.

Thank God that I'm not the one opening up today, Joe thought to himself. *But Ronald's gonna be annoyed that I'm not there. And knowing him, he'll probably act like I've been dead for three years and then risen from the grave.*

Joe started to grin at that. But for some reason, the smile barely registered on his face. On second thought, it just didn't seem funny.

It's probably this whole mess that's got me annoyed, Joe rationalized, looking outside his window. Joe snorted under his breath and then started at the streetlight intensely, wondering if, perhaps, he could make it work by sheer force of will.

"I command this to end. I command this to end," he whispered over and over, as if the mantra had some power he could use. But after a solid minute of chanting, the streetlight still stood there uselessly, while the opposing traffic, which was congested but still moving, inched along.

"So much for the power of positive thinking," Joe grumbled to himself as he sat back in his seat. But just as he spoke those words, a sharp noise pierced the air like a spear through a roasted pig. Though Joe's ears buzzed at it, he was incredibly glad to hear it. He was even gladder as the Chicago PD finally arrived through the traffic. As Joe looked on, the officers quickly exited their vehicles and began to set up a perimeter around the broken streetlight. As some of them worked to block off the oncoming traffic, another cop stepped into the center of the street and waited for the signal from his fellow officers. After a few minutes, he got the word and began to direct the traffic, moving his arms around like a windup toy as he motioned cars to come forward and get on with their lives.

"Oh, thank you, kind and merciful God," Joe sighed as, around him, cars awoke from their slumber and rumbled through the intersection. As the air became filled with the sounds of engines and angry citizens critiquing the lateness of the police in a series of four-letter-word sentences and paragraphs, Joe just gunned his engine and sped out onto the road toward his job.

"Man, I hope this doesn't spell out the rest of my day," he muttered as the Grenwal sign came into view. Thankful to see it, he pulled into his usual spot right across the street. Shutting off the car, Joe stepped out, not bothering to wait to hear the engine die and then sighed as he looked across the street. Standing in front of the store, arms crossed and a look of don't-I-crap-pure-gold smugness on his face, stood Ronald. He looked across the street at his friend and then suddenly gasped and clutched his chest in mock disbelief.

"My God, it's finally here!" he cried aloud as Joe made his way across the street. "The Rapture; the dead have come to deliver us all!"

"Thank you, Father. All you need is an old lady with a fan in a purple dress and bonnet and you can be a Bible thumper in a Christian movie," Joe said as he reached the sidewalk.

"Hey, how often do I ever get to do this?" Ronald said with a laugh.

"Insult me? Damn near every chance you get," Joe replied.

"Tell you what. You lose all your major flaws, and I promise to stop."

"Riiiiight," Joe muttered as he reached past Ronald for the door handle. "I got enough of that from Jeri last night."

"I'm guessing the dinner didn't go well?" Ron asked as Joe pulled open the door and the two of them walked inside.

"If I'd have lit myself on fire and ran around the place naked, it couldn't have gone worse," Joe replied.

"Wow. And considering how you look unburned and with clothes—"

"Why are we friends again?"

"I dunno. Guess it seemed like a good idea at the time."

Joe snorted at that, and the two of them made their way past the register. Joe waved hello to Miro and then asked, "So anything to report this morning?"

"No, but I'm guessing you've got a pretty good story. You're late what, once every leap year?"

"Well yeah, but who said I was going to tell the story?"

Before Ronald could respond to that, the sound of high-pitched screaming filled the air. All three men turned to see a middle-aged woman with stringy, blonde hair and dressed in gray sweats, struggling to drag her young daughter to the register as she pushed a full cart along. Her face was stuck in an expression of perpetual exhaustion that screamed, *Dear God in heaven, kill me!* Her eyes were surrounded by crow's feet, her teeth were clenched together like an industrial press, and her makeup was beginning to run like black sweat as she pulled her daughter along. The child, about five years old with black hair and dressed in blue pants and a Kim Possible T-shirt, struggled against her mother as if she were being led to a long, squishy death and screamed as if she were having a blazing poker jammed in her eye.

"For God's sake, Samantha, will you just come on?" the woman gasped, pulling her daughter along as if the linoleum floor were made of quicksand.

But Samantha just yelled louder and continued to pull against her mother. "No!" Samantha yelled. "I don't wanna go to Gramma's; she smells funny. I wanna stay home!" she howled.

"I told you, Gramma's expecting us, so come on!" her mother yelled back.

At this point, Joe stepped forward and asked, "Need a hand, Sheryl?"

The woman turned and said, "Joe, thank God. Do you mind pushing this cart over there so I can deal with—"

"Not a problem," Joe said. He took the cart from her.

Sighing with relief, Sheryl grabbed her screaming daughter and held her up, even as the child writhed in her arms.

Joe quickly wheeled the cart over to the register and told Miro to begin ringing up her purchases.

"I'd ask how things are going, but I think I can guess," Joe said as he turned back to Sheryl.

"It's … ow … just the same … as always," Sheryl managed to

get out as she struggled to hold on to her daughter. "Sam's mad ... because ... she's missing Dora."

"I wanna go home! I wanna see the mermaid episode!" Sam howled at the mere mention of Dora.

"But my ... mom's been expecting us for ... a week ... and—"

"I get the idea. Well, at least you picked a good place to come and stock up," Joe said.

"You guys ... do a good job ... keeping ... *Oww!*"

As Sheryl had gotten distracted, Samantha had managed to snake her arm around and grab a chunk of her mother's hair. Once she had it, she pulled with all her might, as if to rip the whole thing off her mother's head. Sheryl screamed and, in her pain, let go of Sam. Once her mother's arms were gone, Sam immediately dropped to the floor and started running for the door. Ronald quickly moved over, standing in front of the door like a linebacker. But Samantha just slipped through his legs and headed out the automatic door.

"Ah, crap. I'll be right back," Joe swore as he moved past Ronald and headed out the door himself.

As he stopped outside the store, a bolt of fear shot through his heart as he realized he couldn't see her anywhere. The crowds were already walking the streets, and Joe could picture Sam running with them, only to get pulled into some alley by God knows what or who. But as his eyes looked around, it was his ears that picked something up. From his right, he could hear the needling screech of tires, could hear the gasps and screams of the people. He turned toward the sound as he heard metal being crunched like two steel elephants crashing into each other in all their high-octane glory. As his eyes adjusted to his position, he could see two cars, smashed together like a four-year-old's attempt at a PB and J. He could see the drivers, their newly flowing blood already coating their faces, either pulling themselves out or being pulled out of their cars. But most importantly, he could see Sam, standing there by the cars, her spoiled, snotty look replaced by one of sheer disbelief and incomprehension.

Not daring to even utter a sigh, Joe ran toward the wrecked cars. Behind him, the doors to the store opened, and Ronald and Sherry ran out, faces full of worry. Joe heard them but just focused on Sam. He would take the girl and bring her back to her mother, who would have temporarily forgotten her child's selfish behavior and hug her tightly. The yelling would resume again later.

He ran over to Sam, calling out her name. But the child just stood there, staring at the accident in front of her, the one she had caused. Joe reached out his hand to take her shoulder and lead her back to her mother. But as he stretched out his hand, Joe could smell something in the air, something that stank of earth and metal. He had enough time for one brief thought—*gasoline*—and then he acted. Grabbing Sam, he threw her hard onto the sidewalk, away from the cars and yelled out, "Get back! There's gas—"

But it was already too late. Without any warning, the entangled cars suddenly erupted, sending a huge belch of flame and shards of metal into the air. Joe felt the explosion hit him, sending him flying him through the air with the force of a tank cannon. A sudden burst of pain shot through his shoulder, and then he saw a bloody piece of shrapnel fly past him. He flew backward, until he hit the side of the building across the street, with a sound like a frozen tree branch being snapped in two. He bounced off and skidded like a discus, finally coming to a stop as the sounds of the explosion dimmed.

Then he heard the screams. For a second, he wondered what was wrong. He tried to wake himself up, to feel pain, something, but whatever connection he had to the rest of his body was gone. Even as he struggled to move, he could see the pool of red that was growing at his side, next to a big circular piece of metal. He suddenly noticed a blue-coated arm that sat next to it, an arm that was no longer his.

He stared at the arm, unable to look away, its revelation only starting to register in his mind. He heard footsteps and voices yelling for someone to get him help. But even as he heard them and tried to hold on, Joe knew those voices were getting dimmer and dimmer. He tried to fight it, tried to think of the people—*Jeri, Cody, Ron*—that needed him. He called their names and faces to him, yet they faded away like dead leaves being burned. Someone next to him yelled for him to hold on. He wanted to. But without those people, those beings that were leaving his mind as sure as his mind was leaving his body, why should he? Joe could feel himself falling, aware of a new feeling filling his broken body. It was the love of a woman, the joy of hitting a fastball, a grandmother's Christmas, and so many more things—so many that Joe couldn't identify them all. As the images filled him, the voices telling him to hold on faded away. Joseph Hashimoto let go of the world and succumbed to the warmth inside him.

*　　*　　*

"Joseph."

"Uh ..."

"Joseph Hashimoto, rise up. Stand before us."

"But I can't sta—" Joe murmured. He tried to turn over, to make the voices leave again. Hadn't they seen what had happened to him? All he wanted was to sleep and banish the aches that he could feel beginning to fade ...

His eyes popped open. He could *feel*. Joe shook his head, trying to banish the cobwebs, and slowly got to his feet on legs that obeyed the commands from his brain. He got up and looked down at his whole body, which was complete and uninjured. Joe stretched out his arm, and it was fully attached to his shoulder.

"But wasn't I just—?" Joe started to say and then stopped. The amazement at his healed body vanished, replaced by his disbelief at where he was. He stood on a huge, circular platform made of translucent glass, like a giant serving tray that floated in a place that looked like outer space. All around Joe, black and blue raced together as if the colors themselves were alive and pulsing within the sky. As he looked, white energy flowed through the black and blue; it looked like the stars had melted and were running across the sky like spilled milk.

As if in a dream, he slowly looked down through the platform, wondering what kind of ground a place like this would have. But his glance showed him nothing—only more black and blue and white, pulsing across the cosmos. Joe stumbled back and then he fell, as if he'd seen a demon rising up from the cosmos to destroy him.

Be calm, Joseph. Nothing here can hurt you.

"What is this?" Joe yelled. He remained in the center of the platform, as if any other movement would unbalance it. "Who are you? Where am I?"

A place of great importance Joseph—a place where you have been brought to be chosen for a sacred duty.

"Wha—? Is this heaven? Are you God?"

Look and see.

As Joe heard those words, he felt something stab into his eyes.

Looking down in shock, he saw that the platform was shining with light. The platform had been divided like a pie, and now ten sections glowed with light, all of a different color. Joe saw gold, black, blue, brown, red, white, green, silver, gray, and orange. He saw the lights start to change. He saw them bend and twist as pillars began to grow at their ends. Then without warning, the pillars exploded, scattering the light all around. Joe shielded his eyes from it, but within seconds, it had vanished. Slowly, Joe lowered his arm to see that, at the edges of the platform, stood ten beings, each dressed in long, flowing robes colored identically to their section of the platform. Each one was hooded and wore a medallion engraved with a different symbol. As he looked around the platform at each of the figures, Joe heard the voice speak again, this time aloud rather than in his mind.

"Look forward, Joseph."

Joe traced the voice to the gold section on which he stood and followed it out to see the golden-robed figure looking at him. A long white beard, nearly reaching the floor, sprouted from beneath its hood. As Joseph watched, the figure reached up and slowly pulled down its hood. The face beneath the hood was thin and pointed, as if Ichabod Crane had survived the Horseman and lived to a ripe, old age. The bones beneath the skin could be traced easily, and only the beard hid the outline of his jaw. But the man's nose was short and even, and his head was bald, destroying the Crane similarity. His eyes were a deep blue, and as he looked at Joseph and spoke to him, they became warm and open, like that of a father welcoming his son home.

"Hello, Joseph. We have been expecting you."

"Um, that's great, really, but who's we? And where am I? And why have you been expecting me?" Joe stammered out.

"Be at peace, Joseph," Golden Robe said with a warm chuckle, holding up his hands. "My name is Ralin. My fellows and I are known as the Architects. This is our plane of existence, where we watch over our creation."

"Architects? And what have you created?"

"Long ago, the ten of us shaped existence, filling it with life and substance and power. We also made this plane, so that we could watch over our creation.

"Each of us took power over one of the elements we used to make the universe. My power is that of light," Ralin explained. He held up his hand, and a ball of golden light appeared from nowhere. As it twirled in his hand, Ralin pointed to the black-robed figure that stood next to him.

"My sister Rastla, Architect of Shadow," he said as the black hood came down to reveal a woman with dark purple eyes, hair as black as midnight, and smooth but pale skin. Her face was much younger than Ralin's, devoid of wrinkles and crow's feet, as if she and the sun had never made contact. She looked at Joseph and gave a brief nod, her cool expression not changing an iota.

"Brothers and sisters, show Joseph those who have summoned him."

Joe watched as Ralin named each of the other robed figures, each one pulling down his or her hood in turn.

Blue Robe was Ruta, Architect of Water, a young woman with blonde hair that was stringy and nearly white, as if it had been soaked in saltwater. Dark blue eyes gleamed from her face, which was drawn with high cheekbones and a squat nose. Her skin seemed clammy and was as pale as Rastla's, as if she'd been under the water her whole life. Joe swore he could smell brine coming off of her, but she looked at him with gentle eyes, raising a hand in greeting.

Brown Robe was Chirron, Architect of Earth, brown-bearded and tall, his robes tight against his muscular body. His long brown hair fell back as he pulled off his hood. His skin was dark and tan, the color of dirt baked in the desert. His square face was dominated by a short, compact nose; a thin mouth; and spots of dark color that were splotched all around, like spots on a dog. He grunted and gave a brief nod at Joe, as if the mortal was barely worth his notice.

Red Robe was Darya, Architect of Fire, with a short white beard and shorter white hair. He was woefully thin, his robes hanging off his body like sails in the breeze. His long, narrow face seemed just as wasted. Crow's feet and wrinkles lined it deeply, and it looked like just standing would tire him. But his eyes, red as a piece of steel out of the forge, blazed forth, looking at Joe with a will and strength that the mortal could feel like a hammer blow.

White Robe was Aeris, Architect of Wind. A small white-haired woman, barely over five feet, she seemed almost a child, with her small hands clasped together as if in fear. Her face was shrouded in long white hair that kept her from looking directly at Joe. But she pushed her hair back, giving him a look at her young but sad face and her pale, near transparent eyes. She reminded him of a picture he'd seen of a child in a war-torn country.

Green Robe was Demtia, Architect of Forest. His long brown hair covered a rugged face that smiled as he looked down at Joe. He bowed slightly to the mortal before him. His face was well tanned, as if he had spent a hundred days traversing the woods. A crown of leaves and branches decorated his head, and his green eyes were bright and open, almost like a child's. His body was thin, but Joe could see through the robes that he was far more muscled then Darya was.

Silver Robe was Zeuia, Architect of Thunder, a tall man who was completely bald. Looking at him was like looking at a bird that had taken on human skin—his nose was long and curved, his mouth small and pursed, all set in a small, tight-skinned face. Steely gray eyes peered out at Joe, who could feel the power running through them. Still, he also gave a small bow of greeting and briefly smiled at Joe as he did so. His eyes stayed steely and intense despite his grin, as if the smile was a mask so he could inspect without incident.

Gray Robe was Hephia, Architect of Metal, a man whose body was even more chiseled then Chirron's, his square bearded face covered in soot and grease. White hair covered in gray dust framed it, and from behind his pug nose looked eyes so dark, Joe could not tell what color they were. Unlike the others, the arms of his robe were skintight and did not droop. A belt circled his waist, holding a hammer and a thick leather glove. He seemed like the kind of person who might declare Joe a puny weakling, but he kept silent and respectful as Joe looked at him.

Last was Orange Robe—Nabu, Architect of Desert. Her skin was brown and tan, her eyes dark, and her brown hair tied into a long braid. Joe was instantly reminded of several different desert peoples as he looked at her angular, pointed face. He saw dark Arabian eyes, weathered Navajo skin, and silky Mexican hair. She gave him a quick, dry smile, though her eyes showed what looked like admiration and an almost flirty curiosity as she looked at Joe.

"It's, uh, really nice, and uh, well, a little frightening to meet you guys, but I'm still not sure why I'm here," Joe said. "The last thing I remember was being in an accident."

"As well you should," Chirron said, his voice deep and gravelly. "It was your last act on the mortal place."

"What do you mean last act?" Joe asked, whirling to face the Architect. "But if that's … then how am I still here?"

"You are not still *here*," Rastla said, her voice barely a whisper. "I brought you here, at the request of my brother, though I still do not know why."

"But … but that's not possible," Joe insisted. "I can feel everything. I'm breathing." He took two long breaths to show them. "I can feel my heart beat in my chest."

"You feel those things because you are not truly dead yet," Ruta said, her voice soothing and gentle. "The dead do not lose all their senses until they fully cross over."

"You keep mortal form, but the things that bound you to earth have been taken," Rastla said. "Look at your finger—the wedding ring is gone. As the dead cross over, they slowly lose the things that bind them to life—shape, clothing, even love."

"And you stopped that?" Joe asked as he looked as his now bare finger. "Why?"

"Perhaps you mean, why would I stop death to aid the holder of light?" Rastla asked back, her voice still a whisper. "Does it seem strange to you that light and shadow would stand together? In all your religions, a force of light and a force of dark are forever locked in eternal struggle."

"A matter that is always presented incorrectly," Ralin said. "Though all the elements are important, it is Light and Shadow that give life to all things. They exist in the heart of all living things. And because of that, our efforts have forever been to ensure a balance in creation, so that neither side may upset that which both have made. Neither good nor evil, as you see it, can ever reign supreme."

"Why?" Joe asked, his curiosity overcoming his confusion. "I could see what's wrong with a world of evil, but a good world?"

"A question many on your world have," Rastla said. "Brother, if you would?"

"Behold," Ralin said, and with a wave of his hand, a circle of light opened in the air before Joe. The mortal backed away for a second and then slowly peered inside. What he saw were images of war—tanks rolling over houses, men killing each other with their bare hands, and bombs exploding. But he also saw priests taking money from a collection plate, politicians signing war bills with smiles on their faces, men and women turned away from a church, and then …

"Televangelists?" he asked as the circle faded away.

"Men who preach good yet take all for themselves," Ralin said. "These are the results of imbalance. Shadow turns on itself. Light becomes arrogance and self-righteousness. Long have we worked to keep these two in check, but now we fear that the worlds have grown beyond our means to control them."

"Well, that's terrible, but … well, I don't understand what this has to do with me," Joe asked. "I'm dead, aren't I?"

"Joseph, I had you brought here because I have watched you and have been impressed. You do your best to be a good man but recognize the flaws inside yourself. It is such a man I would want to help restore balance.

"You see, we cannot leave this plane. Nor can we use our power to affect the worlds directly, for they are protected by the power of what you call 'free will.' We have observed the world and done what we could to ensure the balance. But now, the scales sway, and great destruction may be rained upon your world."

"What? By whom?"

"Some of it is caused by the forces you think of as myth or magic. They are the result of our power touching the world and are willingly kept secret from humanity in order to preserve the world. But there are beings that would reveal that power through their own foolishness. And others still would intentionally cause greater destruction, which is why we began this endeavor. Thus, we Architects have designed to have our representatives on the mortal plane—Knights, who would bear our powers, police the mythic forces, and ensure the balance is kept."

"And you want me to be one?"

"We wish you to lead them, as my representative."

"I … um … wow … I appreciate the uh, the compliments, but I'm not a warrior," Joe insisted. "And besides, dead or not, I'm just one man."

"That is why I chose you," Ralin said. "You always seek to improve, but you have never sought to be a great man, or a powerful one. If true light has one attribute, it is humility—the knowledge of its failings and the desire to change them. And it is through that, Joseph—the simple desire to better oneself and the world—that true heroes are made.

"You fear what may come, but you will not face it as you are. You will be gifted with the full control of light itself. You will learn to control it and wield it against the forces of imbalance. And you will not be alone."

"We have each made our choice of representatives," Zueia said. "All we needed was a leader."

"But be warned," Rastla said. "There is a price. You shall be given immortality, with all its blessings and curses. Disease shall leave you. Life will be yours until the end of all days. But the worlds will change and change before you, and you shall forever be the same."

"And what if I—*Can* I refuse?" Joe asked, though he feared he already knew the answer.

"Free will is yours Joseph. This task is not an easy burden to bear, and many would understand your decision to refuse. But to do so will forever cast you down among the dead," Rastla said.

"That's it? Those are all the choices I have?" Joe spat out. "Great. Either I can be dead or I can live apart from everyone I knew until the world ends."

"Yes, Joseph. But you will do great things if you would choose us," Ralin said. "You could still better the world for those you left behind, as you have desired. I have seen that power within you. The choice is yours to make, but the life you had ends either way. I am sorry for that."

Joe listened and then turned away from Ralin. Looking down at the ground, he felt everything whirl around inside him, a tornado caught in a typhoon. How could this have happened? Everything that was happening felt like something out of a bad Tolkien rip-off. He was supposed to be some sort of magic-charged messenger boy for these robed lunatics? Great things? What great things? He was a frigging store manager. And if he said no, he got to be dead and rot.

Yeah, and that's what really settles it. Even with their crazy offer, I'm just not ready to die yet. And if I really could make things better back home, hell, beyond home .... Maybe the answer here was the simplest of reasons; there was no else, and it needed to be done, for the good of all. And Joe could even see a better world for himself, if he worked to make it happen.

With a sigh, Joe turned to Ralin and said, "This is not what I want.

But this is bigger than me. I accept your charge. At least I can make the world better for the people I left behind."

"Well said, Joseph. Now step forward and receive the power I would bestow upon you."

Slowly, Joseph Hashimoto moved in front of the Architect of Light. The old man shook out his robes, freed his hands, and then placed them on Joe's shoulders. He closed his eyes, and suddenly his hands began to glow with golden light. Joe watched, then his body stiffened as the raw power flowed into him like ice water shot into his veins. He fell to his knees as the light swirled around him, and he began to glow. As the glow grew stronger and stronger, Joe could feel a lessening of himself, a burning in his chest. His mind began to flood with memories, images of the things in his life he'd done in anger, things that had shamed him later.

Throwing juice on his mother's chair at four.

Not feeding his neighbor's cat and having her come home and find it dead at seven.

Leaving his friend alone so he could play at the arcade at twelve.

Buying a term paper at fifteen.

Going to a party and failing a test at nineteen.

Screaming at Jeri after a long day at twenty-one.

Forgetting to pick up his son from practice at twenty-seven.

All these and a hundred more memories flowed through Joe's mind, and one by one, they were burned away by the power. And as they left him, Joe felt his guilt and anger and resentment from them fade away. He could feel more and more of that golden power taking their place, until …

"It is done," Ralin said. He pulled his hands away. The other Architects watched as the being that had once been Joseph Hashimoto stood up. His clothes were gone now. Instead, he was dressed in gold and brown clothes that looked like a medieval tunic and pants. Thick, leather boots adorned his feet, and brown, leather gloves covered his hands, with gold and brown braces on his forearms. A long golden coat hung over him, and his face was wrapped in gold cloth, leaving only his eyes uncovered. A wide-brimmed hat sat on his head. As the Architects watched, he lifted up his hand and held it out before them. A ball of light appeared on his palm and then grew and stretched out. With a flash, the light became a long wooden staff, adorned with the carved head of a lion, its mouth wide open in a roar. It glowed slightly as he turned the staff upright and held it before them.

"Behold, my representative!" Ralin called out. "Behold the last of the Elemental Knights—Lightrider, Knight of Light!"

"We hear and acknowledge," the Architects replied, bowing their heads toward this new being.

The eyes of the Lightrider watched, and though he raised his staff in acknowledgement of them, his eyes remained cold and silent.

INTERLUDE

The pen scratched the last few words and then came to rest. He placed it on the table. His hand ached like a boxer's skull after ten rounds with a steel-fisted man. He slowly took the wrist in his opposite hand and rubbed it, musing on that day so many years ago. He remembered the feelings of euphoria as Ralin's power had run through him, burning away all the dark deeds from his heart. He'd felt as whole and joyful as if he'd been shot with a dose of concentrated sunshine and bluebird song. It had been better than all the sexual experiences of his life. It had been better than his one experiment with weed. It had been like being given the key to heaven by God himself.

But that same key had led him to this place and then locked the door on him. He could no longer come close to the euphoria he'd felt in those brief moments when it had been bestowed on him. Now his heart was filled with the memory of the deeds he had been forced to commit in his new life. He closed his eyes then as he thought of the lives he had been forced to ignore, another part of the balance that Ralin and the Architects had cared for so much—the balance he had chosen to serve, in exchange for any kind of a life.

Then again, what choice had he had? All he had was a life of servitude and heroics or a journey to the unknown of death. Perhaps some would call him a coward for choosing service and life over the freedom death offered. But he didn't regret his choice for that reason. He'd not been destined for the darkness, but he would've rather met the sun in his twilight years, his wife holding his hand as he left.

He stopped massaging his hand then, raising it up to flex it. Already, the aches and soreness had faded—one of the last gifts he'd kept from Ralin and the Architects. He looked then at the pages still left within the book. If time had meant anything in this place, he might've claimed the hour as reason to stop. But it didn't, and he had no reason to stop. He picked up the pen once again as he thought back to that moment when he'd made the choice that had shaped his second life. They thought he had chosen his Knighthood to do good among the worlds they had made. And he had. But there had been far more to it than any of them had realized.

BOOK TWO

TRAINING

VI.

THE MAN ONCE KNOWN as Joseph Hashimoto, now called Lightrider, looked over at the cosmic beings that had called him here and made him one of their vessels. One by one, he met their eyes, until he came to the being that had given him his name and power. As Ralin watched, the man put down his staff, and then, moving his hands to his face, his fingers came to the wrappings that covered his lower face. But as he touched them, the wrappings glowed with golden light and then vanished, leaving his face bare.

The Lightrider licked his lips and spoke the first words of his new life. "Well … that was … goddamn!"

"True, if not eloquent," Ralin said. "How do you feel, my Knight?"

"All right, I think," Joe said, glancing down at himself. Looking at his golden clothing, he asked, "If I'm a Knight, shouldn't I have armor or something?"

"A Knight is made not by the clothing he wears, Lightrider, but by the virtue he keeps in his heart."

"Wow. That's uh … Can I say it sounds cheesy, or should I just nod?"

"Both, Lightrider," Demtia said with a chuckle. "Our brother lets his mouth run away with him quite often. I believe such terms are called 'cliché' in your world?"

"That's one way of putting it," Joe said. Turning back to Ralin, he asked, "Okay, so no armor. But what happens now?"

"What happens to all soldiers before battle," Rastla answered. "You and your siblings must train, and learn to use the powers you have been given."

"Siblings?"

"Siblings in our service. Remember, Lightrider, I said you were the final Elemental Knight," Ralin said. "My fellows have already made their selections of Knights. But we had decided that my choice would lead, and so we did not finish building the Knighthood until a leader was chosen."

"Okay, that makes sense," Joe said. "So who are these guys? Did you pick them from earth like me?"

"They do come from your world," Ralin answered. He gestured for Joe to turn. "You will find them somewhat … unique, I believe."

Joe raised an eyebrow at that, but he turned nonetheless. What he saw was each of the Architects holding his or her hand over a ball of energy that appeared on his or her part of the platform. Each was colored for its specific Architect, and as Joe watched, the balls grew smaller and smaller. As they did, Joe could see arms and legs poking out of the energy. But as they emerged, he realized something was wrong. The appendages he saw were slim compared to those of humans, and many ended in paws. Two of them seemed to be wings.

And as the energy faded completely, Joe looked at the being closest to him and said, …"A lizard?

"You expect me to lead a lizard?!" Joe exclaimed in disbelief. He stared at the reddish-brown creature that sat on Darya's section.

"Of course not, Lightrider. Don't be ridiculous," Darya answered.

"Oh, thank God. I really thought that—"

"This is a Gila monster, not a simple lizard."

Joe looked at the Fire Architect for a moment, and asked, "Uh, you realize that it's kinda, well, unadvanced, right?"

"That may be true now. But such things can be changed."

"Right. That totally makes sense," Joe said. He glanced over at the other Architects and their selections. At the feet of each Architect sat a being encased in strange, multicolored energy, frozen in one position. But none of them was human. As Joe looked at each Architect down the line from Rastla, he saw they had chosen a bat, an orange cat, a German shepherd, the Gila monster, a falcon, a squirrel, a ram, a spider, and a wolf.

"Um, I'm a little confused here," Joe said, looking back at Ralin. "I thought I was going to be leading a Knighthood, not Noah's Ark!"

"You thought that all our choices would be human?" Ralin asked. "Remember Lightrider, we Architects have created all manner of life—many more species than humans alone and on many other worlds."

"Though Earth and humanity were our first successes, there are few humans on Earth that are able to handle this power," Rastla whispered. "It would be a tool for them, easily abused for material gain or power.

That is a large part of the reason my brother chose you instead of another. But the rest of us chose animals that we saw as symbolic of our elements."

"But what do you expect me to do with them?" Joe asked. "I can't lead a bunch of animals into the fray and hope for the best."

"Nor would we ask you to," Ralin said. "Your Knighthood shall be one comprised of the best of man and beast—one providing the primal body and the strengths therein and the other the developed soul and intellect. For yours is not the only human soul taken from Death's grip."

"You mean… you've taken other people away? Given them this choice?" Joe asked incredulously.

"Not exactly," Naru replied. "The souls we chose have been dead for quite some time. We offer them a chance for new life, new purpose. You would understand that, correct? We have seen you demonstrate belief in redemption. It was one of many qualities I enjoyed seeing in you."

"Well … I guess that's different," Joe mused. "But I still don't understand what it is you plan to do."

"You have but to watch, Lightrider, and all shall be made clear," Ralin answered. He pointed to Rastla.

Joe shrugged but turned his eyes to the Architect of Shadow. She raised her arms, her long sleeves draping down. Something began to glow inside them. Joe's eyes narrowed as Rastla began to speak under her breath, muttering strange words that were too low and foreign for Joe to understand. The glowing from her sleeves grew brighter, until the black of her robe had been changed into a blinding white. Despite the light, Joe didn't blink; instead he gasped as nine glowing spheres of white energy flew out of Rastla's sleeves. They floated and twirled around the dark Architect, as she continued her strange chant. Finally, she finished her words, and brought her arms down. The spheres shot off in nine different directions, coming to rest before the nine beings selected to fill the ranks of Joe's Knighthood.

This is some majorly weird shit, Joe thought to himself, watching as the spheres hovered in front of their respective chosen ones. The spheres moved closer to the animals. As each sphere touched the magic aura that covered its animal, the aura glowed briefly, fading as the spheres pushed through and entered the animals.

Joe's eyes went wide as he saw a new glow encase each of the creatures, each one the color of an Architect. He heard a creak, and then Joe gasped as the creatures inside the glows begin to move. Wings twitched, heads swung, and legs kicked—the creatures awoke from whatever slumber they'd been placed into. But Joe realized that the creatures weren't just waking up.

They were *changing*.

It was the lizard that grabbed his attention first. Joe heard the creaks and cracks as the creature's body began to shift and move, like its bones were changing under its skin. It started to grow bigger, its limbs becoming thicker and longer. Its scales started to become more pronounced and defined. It began to rise up, its shape stretching and shifting underneath its frame. For a minute, Joe wondered what was going on, and then he understood as he saw how its lower legs had stretched and how it was attempting to push off the ground with its now long front legs.

It was trying to stand up.

Caught between amazement and horror, Joe whirled around to see what was happening to the other chosen. He saw the spider, already five times its previous size, holding itself up with six arms that now possessed clawed hands and attempting to balance on its two back legs. He saw the bat, almost as large as the spider, its small body becoming tall and lean. The cat next to it was the same, its head and face stretching and smoothing out, becoming a strange mix of woman and feline.

Joe's eyes spun from creature to creature, as if each one wasn't some horrible, new life-form evolving before his eyes, but a beautiful woman with a sign that read, "Come get me, Joe." As the creatures continued to change before him, Joe realized the tremendous mistake he'd made agreeing to this. Creators of the universe? Oh yeah, they were creators all right—the kind that belonged in a movie, digging up graves to form their monster. Whatever magic, whatever power they'd given him, it wasn't worth it—not for beings that would do something like this.

Maybe I can still get out, Joe thought. *It might not be too late. Yeah I can tell Ralin, "Listen, this was cool, but the whole Dr. Moreau thing is freaking me out. I'll be happy to help you find another dead guy, but I think I'd rather see what's in the great beyond and ..."*

"Hey."

That one simple word snapped Joe out of his mental hysterics. Slowly, Joe turned his head toward the sound of the voice and felt his jaw come unhinged and fall toward his chest. The dog that Chirron had selected had finished its transformation. The creature stood upright on two legs, and Joe saw that, despite the fur that still covered it, its naked body had become very, *very* obviously human. Its front legs had become a pair of arms, ending in hands with furry fingers. The rest of its body might've passed for a very well-toned human, had it not been for the fur and tail—oh and the German shepherd head that was now staring at Joe.

"Hey," the dog-man said again, its voice flecked with traces of a New York accent. "You see somethin' green, buddy? What the hell's with you?"

"Oh sweet Christ on the Cross," Joe murmured. "I'm trapped in the worst B-grade horror flick *ever*."

"What're you babblin' about?" the dog-man snapped. "And what's with the draft?"

"It might have something to do with your lack of clothes, buddy," chimed in another voice. Joe spun around to see the bat, now as tall as he was, looking at the dog with eyebrow raised and a look of amusement as dry as a sandpaper rattlesnake.

"But judging by how you look, they're only the first step in solving your problem," the bat added. Noticing Joe, he nodded and said, "Greetings."

"Whoa! A rat with wings? I dunno what I was drinking, but I am done with it," the dog said in amazement.

"Rat with wings? Pal, you seriously need to get off that stuff," the bat said with a laugh. "If you're seeing things that bad—bad—"

The bat paused then as he noticed the black fur that covered his body. Slowly, he looked himself over. He raised his arms to feel the thin, fleshy wings that had folded back over his forearms. Looking at one, he shook the arm and the wing popped out, stretching out like a giant, see-through curtain of flesh. In utter disbelief, he shook it again, and the wing folded back up. Completely horrified now, the bat reached up and felt his face—the piggish nose that jutted forth; the jaw with the slight overbite and sharp teeth; and the two pointed, foxlike ears that shot up from his head of dark hair.

"Holy shit," he whispered. "What ... what happened to me?"

"Huh. And you thought I was crazy!" the dog snapped. "Toldja you was a rat with wings, didn't I, buddy?" he asked, letting out a laugh.

But that laugh died a second later as he felt a strange, very unwelcome sensation. Reaching behind him, the dog wrapped his hand around something and then screamed out a simple question of his existence. "When the *Christ* did I get a tail?!"

"This can't be right," Joe whispered. He turned to Ralin and asked, "What have you made here? And why don't they understand?"

"We have made what we said—a mix of beast and man. But we gave you a different choice," Ralin answered.

"But ... but ... what about free will?" Joe demanded. "How can you talk about free will and force them into servitude like this?"

"Free will applies to all," Ralin explained. "These beings may still choose to reject the Knighthood. But they had to be brought here like this to understand what that choice entails."

"But what happens now?"

"They are still your charges," Ralin said. "Speak to them. You do partially understand their situation."

"Yeah right," Joe muttered. But still, he turned to the two man-beasts and said, "Uh, hello?"

Both turned to face him instantly. "You!" the dog snapped. "Did you bring us here? Did you do this to us?"

"Will you calm down?" the bat said. "He might actually know something!"

"I'm not sure I know much," Joe said. "But listen, guys, this isn't as horrible as it looks."

"It isn't?" the dog spat. "I wake up with fur and a tail, and this guy tells me it isn't that bad?"

"Who are you?" the bat asked. "Do you know what's going on?"

"Kinda," Joe said with a shrug. "I'm caught up in it, too."

"But you look normal," the bat said. "Why?"

"I'm not sure," Joe said. He pointed behind them. "But trust me, you aren't alone."

Both creatures turned then and saw the others on the platform. Again, loud proclamations of profanity rang out as they looked over their brethren. The spider was standing on its—no *her*—back legs while her eyes stared at six arms in an almost detached curiosity. The cat was feeling around the contours of her new face with a growing expression of horror. The falcon was folding and unfolding its wings in a way that was similar to the bat, only he was grinning like the Cheshire cat about it. The wolf was just looking around through its long black hair and growling to it—*her*self—while the ram and lizard observed the situation calmly.

"This is not what I ever expected to see," the bat said.

"Oh really?" the dog muttered. "Got any solutions?"

"We might."

At the sound of that voice, all the man-beasts stopped and turned to notice the Architects for the first time. "Fear not," Ralin continued. "What has happened to you is a thing of great honor and dignity."

"Mate, maybe you can clarify that fer me," the lizard said in an Australian brogue as she held up her scaly hands. "Last time I checked, honor and dignity didn't mean turning into a lizard—or whatever this is."

"What … what did you do to us?" the cat whispered. "What did we do to deserve this?"

"This is not something to be feared," Demtia said. "You have been chosen to receive a great and wondrous power, to be used for the good of humanity and much more. Your new forms are a reflection of that."

"Sounds pretty good to me," the squirrel said, his voice caked in a Southern drawl. "But before you tell us about this power thing, can Ah ask for somethin'?"

"Of course."

"Ah think Ah speak for everyone when Ah say that clothes would be nice. Ah like being naked under the right people and all, but you guys just aren't it."

The Architects nodded, and save Ralin, each waved his or her hand. Flashes of light burst forth, and when they faded, the man-beasts found themselves clothed similar to Joe, except that each outfit was the color of its Architect. Other unique changes were made; the bat and falcon had slits up the sleeves of their coats, allowing their wings freedom, and the spider had six sleeves in her shirt.

"What the hell is this?" the wolf snarled as she looked over her new outfit. "This looks like gunslinger Power Rangers or something. Only a complete idiot would dress like this!"

"Oh man, this is *awesome!*" the falcon said, his voice cracking halfway through as he gleefully examined his duds like a kid who actually got the rocket to Mars for Christmas. "First wings, now this. I feel like I'm in *Zelda*. Frickin' awesome!"

"Kid, are you retarded or somethin'?" the dog asked.

"Oh, let him enjoy it," the ram said.

"If we might explain your situation," Rastla interrupted. Though she only whispered, everyone immediately snapped to attention.

"This is your induction into a force unseen in creation until now—an order dedicated to preserving the sacred balance in the universe and fueled by the strength of the Architects of Creation."

"You guys," the spider said in her thick, mushy voice, like she was swallowing molasses, as her mandibles twitched over her mouth with each word.

"Correct," Hephia replied. "You were chosen to act as our representatives on the mortal plane, charged with the elements we command."

"You mean earth, fire, wind, and water?" the spider pressed on.

"That and more," Hepia explained.

As Ralin had done with Joseph, the Architect of Metal explained the situation to the new Knights—who the Architects were, the power they commanded, and the task that was to be set before the Knights. The nine man-beasts listened to the tale attentively.

Then as Hephia finished his tale, the cat raised her hand. "But why not bring us back like Joe? And if I'm supposed to be water, why am I a cat?"

"I chose this form for you because there are few beings in my oceans that could survive outside of it," Ruta said. "I desired an animal that could represent the qualities of water—calm one moment and then angry the next, unchanged by and unconcerned with the outside world. Despite the irony, I found the cat fit those qualities quite well.

"As for your other question, there are few humans like Joe who are capable of handling such power and resisting their base urges. Your animal forms will help you repress and control many of the urges you had as humans."

"Urges?"

"The ones that ended your past lives prematurely," the Shadow Architect answered. "That is also why you have been given new forms. I took Lightrider before he could reach the lands of the dead. You have long been denizens there."

"So what you're saying," the spider surmised, "is that … we're dead? Or that we have been dead?"

"You were each chosen to fill specific roles in the Knighthood," Ruta said. "But you were also chosen because you each hang between life and death. Unlike Joe, you hang there because of the poor choices you had made in your past life; they have prevented your souls from truly moving on."

"That does it!" the dog snapped. "I'm gettin' off this crazy merry-go-round! First you gimme a fur coat and a tail and then you tell me I been dead for God knows how long?"

"What makes you think otherwise?" Rastla asked.

"Because I know who I am!" the dog snapped. "I know my name, my family, everything."

"So who are you then?" the spider asked.

The dog smirked and started to answer. But slowly, his smirk vanished as he went through the trees of his mind and found them barren of fruit. Frantically, he tried to find even one rotted plum, but he found nothing.

"I-I don't remember," he said.

"You're not alone," the spider said. "I noticed it too. And I'm guessing that none of you can remember anything either?"

The man-beasts each put his or her mind to the task, but one by one, they came up empty.

"I don't understand," the bat said. "I can remember words, phrases, who won the last World Series. But my name, my life—it's all a blank."

"I think I had parents," the falcon said, the happy expression finally gone as he rubbed his head. "I remember going to school, but I can't remember any faces or names. What the hell happened to me?"

"I think the shadow lady's right, mates," the lizard said. "I think we *are* dead."

"We removed your memories, so you would not again fall into the traps that claimed you," Ralin said. "You may have died there, but we offer you a chance for a new life, one far greater than your old."

Before anyone could answer, the wolf let out a growl and leaped to the center of the platform. Baring her teeth, she glared at each of the Architects as she spoke. "Is that what you call this?" She snarled. "Being summoned at your beck and call? Haunted by pieces of memory that *you* took because you say we screwed up? For what? Some make-believe balance? Phh! All I care about it is you people telling me who the hell I am and where I came from. Now!"

The Architects stood silent, their eyes focused on the wolf. Finally, Naru said, "The balance is as real as the rage you possess. But the choice to serve it has been yours since before your selection."

"She's right," Joe said. "They have to let you have free will. You make the choice to do this."

"Yeah? Well, I don't need a choice," the dog said. "I'm with the wolf-lady over there. I'm not gonna spend eternity bein' dead and some crazy old man's lapdog."

"No pun intended?" the bat asked.

"Shut up!"

"Well, you heard the man," the wolf sneered as she looked over the group. "Now, is there anyone else who'd like to help me make these guys rediscover our roots?"

"It would not be wise to attack us," Hephia said, his hands already moving to his hammer.

"We brought you here. We can send you back easily enough," Rastla whispered.

"Maybe," the wolf said as the dog moved over to her. "But I don't think that you'd go through the trouble of bringing us here if you'd destroy us on a whim."

As the duo began to advance on the Architects, the others stood back, still unsure of their own decisions. Even Joe was conflicted. On one hand, he agreed with the wolf that the Architects deal seemed cruel and unfair. But the other part of him thought of the things he could do if he was able to return to Earth. If the Architects were gone, he'd lose those chances. And damn it, he was sick of sitting on the sidelines.

"Hold!" he yelled as he sidestepped them and stood in front of Ralin, his staff held out.

"Out of the way, little man," the wolf snarled. "You don't have the *cajones* to mess with me."

"No," Joe said. "I made my choice, and I am going to stick by it."

The wolf raised an eyebrow and then shrugged. "Don't make a buttload of difference to me."

"Great. So what happens?" Joe asked. "You kill me and then fight them to the death?"

"No. Just till they tell us what we want to know and make us normal again," the wolf said.

"Open your eyes! They can bring back the dead!" Joe yelled. "Do you really think a bunch of Dr. Moreau rejects can hurt them?"

"So what else is there? Be their serving boy like you?"

"I'm nobody's serving boy," Joe said. "But I'm not going to waste what I've been given.

"Think about it," he continued. "What do you have to go back to? You don't know how long you've been dead. The people you could *possibly* remember, they might not even be alive anymore. You'd go back to nothing."

At that, the dog seemed to grow nervous. He wiped his forehead.

Joe saw his chance and kept going. "And besides that, look at you. Even if you could go back, how would you explain yourselves to the people you knew? For all you know the Architects can't change you back! You could be stuck this way, and I guarantee that'll make conversation back home weird. 'Hey guys, listen I know I've been dead for a long time, but a bunch of weird cosmic beings brought me back to life. Oh, and get this, I'm some sort of human-animal hybrid now. Cool huh? Wanna get a beer?'"

"They made us like this," the wolf answered. "If they did that, they can change us back. But I guess that isn't a problem for you, Mr. Humanity. You aren't the one with a muzzle or wings, are you?"

"You think I don't wanna go back to my old life?" Joe continued. "But think about it for one second—*we are all dead here.* I may not be like you guys, but I'm as barred from whatever life I had just like you are. Do you think I can just take this stuff off and go home and go to work tomorrow, after everyone saw me get blown up in the street?"

"Your problem. Not mine," the wolf snapped. "I told you, I'm not gonna be anyone's errand girl."

"For God's sake, they're offering you something a lot bigger than that!" Joe yelled. "If these guys exist, then maybe other things do. Maybe there really are monsters and demons and who knows what down there. Maybe they're the reason some of us are here. And we could be the ones to pay them back."

"Really?" the falcon said, his eyes as wide as if he'd walked in on his parents having sex. "I could be like, like Van Helsing? Cool!"

"I said it before, kid, this ain't a video game," the dog sneered.

"And how would you know?" the squirrel asked. "Ah'd like to be in the story where Ah get to save the girls and kill the monster, wouldn't you?"

"It isn't like we have anything else to do," the spider said. "Lightrider's right; we're all dead, with no memories. How can we go back to lives we don't even remember?"

"And think of the people we could help," the ram said. "We could do a lot of good in the world."

"But like this?" the cat asked. "I mean, I like being able to help people, but ..."

"Better to be able to help like this than not at all. And it sounds a hell of a lot smarter than trying to take on gods," the lizard said.

"And probably involves a lot less cosmic disintegration," the bat added.

The cat was quiet, looking at her strange new hands. But then she looked up at the others, and slowly, she nodded. The other man-beasts began to look toward their Architects, and Joe breathed a sigh of relief.

But it wasn't over yet. The wolf let out an angry howl. "Then screw the lot of you!" she snarled. "If you wanna stay like this, fine! The two of us will take on these robe-wearing dicks ourselves."

"You've got a chance here. Don't throw it away," the bat said

"If I wanna be a hero, I'll join the fire department," the dog snapped. "C'mon, Wolfie, let's just do this thing."

"Don't call me that. But you're right," the wolf said. She looked around at the Architects, baring her teeth at each of them. Finally, she stopped and focused her gaze on Ralin.

"All right old man, looks like you're the one in charge here," she said. "Let's see what these guys will do when I take you down."

"You may try," Ralin said. He stood motionless, not even raising his hands to defend himself.

"Oh, we'll do a lot more than that," the dog said. And he and the wolf started to advance on the Architect. The other animal Knights moved forward, but then each one stopped, each hearing the voice of his or her Architect in his or her head—*this fight is not yours.*

And it wasn't. As the wolf and the dog advanced on Ralin, Joe once again stepped in between them, his staff at the ready.

"You really must have a death wish, kid," the wolf said. She glared at the Light Knight. "For the last time, get out of the way!"

"No," Joe said, although he truly wished that he could. He'd been telling the truth before—he had only won one fight in his life, and that was he because he'd dodged and the kid had hit the wall and broke his fist. And fur or not, this was still a woman.

There has to be another way. Maybe if I talk to her, Joe thought. He opened his mouth. But as he did, the wolf drew her clawed fist back and shot out a punch. Focused on his speech, Joe was completely open as the wolf's fist slammed into his mouth and knocked him back. Joe tasted copper flowing across his tongue as his thoughts flew out his mind.

Okay, forget not hitting the bitch. He turned around, just in time to see another punch coming in. He was able to dodge it this time, but as he brought his body down, he left himself open to a kick in the stomach from the dog. Joe groaned as if he'd been trampled in a Black Friday Wal-Mart raid. He folded over, and the wolf took the opportunity to grab his hat and pull it over his head, while the dog ripped the staff away from him and threw it down. Before Joe could even react to the lack of vision, the wolf had wrapped the coat around his head and was using it to pull him forward. Unable to see, Joe couldn't defend himself from the wolf's upturned knee, which was rammed straight into his gut. Barely able to breathe, Joe struggled to stay upright, even as the dog and wolf began to rain punches down on his back. But it got harder to do once the dog drove his knee up through the cape into Joe's face. Joe cried out as he felt the knee snap something in his mouth and blood washed over his tongue.

The coat and hat were pulled off then as both the dog and wolf drew back their fists and delivered a blow to Joe's face that broke at least three teeth, with a sound like glass being smashed over a man's head. Joe moaned in pain as the wolf grabbed his collar and pulled him forward so that she and Lightrider were face-to-face.

"You brought this on yourself, little man," the wolf sneered. "I would've left you alone, but you got in my way. Now, are you done yet, or do we have to show you some more?"

"What ... do you ... think?" Joe wheezed out as he turned and spat out fresh blood.

"I was afraid you would say that." The wolf sighed and drew back her fist once again. But before she could let it go, the dog grabbed her arm and threw it down.

"What are you doing?" the wolf snarled. "I wasn't done with him yet."

"C'mon, he's had enough," the dog said. "He ain't gonna try nothin' else against us. You wanna kick the crap outta somebody, let's do this guy here." He pointed at Ralin.

"Good point," the wolf said, dropping Joe on the ground before Ralin.

The Knight groaned as the two man-beasts moved forward against the Architect, who still stood silent and unmoving. Joe groaned. He pushed himself up on his hands and began to crawl toward the Architect. The dog and wolf paused to watch. The dog raised an eyebrow, while the wolf just laughed. But Joe ignored them both and kept moving, hoping that maybe, he could buy some time for Ralin or for somebody else to act.

"You don't seem all that powerful now, old man," the wolf said as she turned back to the Architect.

"Then perhaps you need to look closer," Ralin replied. "I am not to be destroyed by one such as you."

"Then you'd better do something to stop me," the wolf said, "because your guardian is bleeding to death at your feet."

"As long as he is before me, I have nothing to fear."

At that, the wolf just laughed. "Please, old man. He didn't even last five minutes against us. He was a pathetic man, and now he's a pathetic Knight.

"You hear that?" the wolf asked, glancing down at Joe, who had managed to reach Ralin's feet and pull himself into a sitting position. "You screwed up royally with these guys. You could've gone back home."

"But you screwed up," the wolf said again.

Joe stared at her with eyes that could've machine-gunned her to death, as she kept talking. "You decided to play hero with a bunch of crazy old farts in robes. And now, you get to stay here in oblivion with them."

"No," Joe whispered, his voice tight and raw, "you screwed up. You decided to spit in their faces. And you decided to spit in mine."

"Oh, is that what you think?" the wolf replied as she knelt down to

Joe's level. "You think this is spitting in your face? I can do that a hell of a lot better when I get back. Maybe I can get these guys to tell me who you used to be, huh? Maybe I can find out where your family is?"

"You stay away from them," Joe rasped.

"Relax. I don't hurt people who don't get in my way. But who knows? Maybe if I can see them, I can get an idea of the people who'd be dumb enough to spend their lives with you. Your wife, how long she been sitting on your back porch, playing the six-fingered banjo? I mean, the inbreeding would explain how she ended up with you, right?"

"Wha—Dude, let him alone," the dog said.

"Shut up," the wolf snapped. "I'll decide what he deserves.

But as Joe had listened to the sickening words spew out of the wolf's mouth, he'd felt something build up inside him, something that felt like an egg on top of a furnace stoked with kerosene. He pushed down with his arms and felt himself stand back up on his feet. The dog and wolf stared at him in surprise, but not for the reasons that Joe thought. They were staring at the wounds and bruises on his face, which were slowly fading away as small pools of light covered them. His teeth bared, Joe stuck out his arms, getting ready to tackle the wolf. But as he held out his arms, the staff suddenly flew from the ground into his waiting hand. Feeling the staff, Joe wrapped both hands around it, pulled it behind him like a baseball bat, and swung it forward. In his rage, however, Joe hadn't noticed how the lion head had begun to glow brightly. He didn't even notice it when he brought the staff around and swung for the man-beast's skulls.

But he did notice when it made contact. The staff hit the wolf's head. A blast of golden light spread out from the staff like a mushroom cloud. The others covered their eyes, unable to look into it. It only lasted for a second, but the power behind the staff left its mark. The wolf and dog were thrown back, as if hit by a Mack Truck driving in the Daytona 500. They hit the ground with a massive thud, screaming in pain and clutching their faces.

"Sweet Christ!" the bat swore. "*That* was unexpected."

"How did you do that?" the spider asked. Her six eyes looked at both the fallen man-beasts and Joe at the same time.

"I-I don't know," Joe murmured. He stared at his dimming staff, his anger dissipated by his curiosity. "What was that you did?" he asked aloud as he looked at the staff.

"Not the staff, Lightrider," Ralin said. "The power behind that was yours and yours alone."

"But how? I mean, I don't know how I—"

"The staff is a conduit to my powers," Ralin said. "It sensed your righteous anger and channeled the power of light accordingly."

"Jesus," Joe whispered as he looked from the weapon to the writhing man-beasts. "Should I do it again? Or should I wait until she calls my wife an inbred freak again?"

"It would do no good, Lightrider," Naru said. "It was our power that merged their souls to these bodies. And it lives within them until they reject it."

"Hey, look!" the falcon said. He pointed to the two man-beasts.

The group looked on in amazement as the wolf and dog stopped screaming and pulled their hands away from their faces. Though they could not see the magic that was taking place on their faces, they could feel it. The dog's left eye and right check had been opened wide by Joe's light. But now, rock and stone from inside the dog's body were filling in the broken areas. It pushed out through the holes, as if the dog had been filled with it all along. For the wolf, it was sand that pushed from her broken nose, her missing lower jaw, and the long cut across her face. As everyone watched, the sand and earth continued to shift around, stretching out and changing its shape as it replaced what was gone. Within seconds, it had formed into perfect replicas of the missing pieces of flesh. Then it changed into flesh and bone, leaving the two man-beasts looking completely unharmed.

"Awesome!" the falcon exclaimed. "Healing powers! Can we do that too?"

"Ah don't mean to interrupt your happiness there," the squirrel said. "But Ah'm more worried about them havin' healin' powers and wantin' to kill us."

"I wouldn't be," Joe said. He moved over and stuck his staff between the two of them. "Now, do you two want to calm down and listen, or should I put on another light show for you?" he asked.

"How do we know you can do that again?" the wolf sneered.

"How do you know I can't?"

"I'd listen to him," the bat said. "If a man can burn part of your face off, he's probably not somebody you want on your bad side."

"You don't have to tell me about it," the dog said. He pulled himself to his feet. "I'm not in the mood to go through that kinda pain again, healing power or not."

"Coward," the wolf snapped.

"Hey, better a live coward then a dead crazy man," the dog replied. "Besides, if he can do that, imagine what his boss can do? What're we gonna do against that?"

"And what if I don't want to be a hero?" the wolf snapped.

"Oh, I think you're a long ways from that," the cat said.

"Like I care what you think," the wolf said. "You go off and play Supergirl. I'll stay here and watch. It'll be fun."

"I don't think you will," the lizard said suddenly. As everyone watched, she walked over to the wolf and knelt down so that she was face to face with her. "I'm not completely into this either, but what they're offering sounds like it just might be worth these bodies. We'd be fighting monsters, evil, things that want to rip the world apart. We're going to need to rip them back just as hard."

"She speaks the truth," Naru said. "There shall be much violence and destruction in the Knighthood, should you choose it. And every pack needs a wild dog."

"You wanna be angry at somebody? Be angry at the right people," Joe said. "You can tear apart monsters and demons just as easily as you could me."

The wolf's eyes narrowed as she considered the offer. She glanced up at Joe, her lips splitting apart in a wide, toothy grin that screamed *Jaws* theme so loud that the squirrel and spider actually moved forward to grab her.

But as they put their hands on her, the wolf just shrugged them off.

Joe braced himself, ready to fight again.

The wolf looked up at him and said, "You mind calling your guys off for a minute?"

"That depends. What did you decide?"

"You make a good argument. And there's a lot more monsters in the world than there are you. I'm sure of that much."

Joe looked into the wolf's eyes for a tell. Seeing none, he said, "I suppose that's better than nothing," as she slowly got to her feet. "So does that mean I can trust you?"

"Maybe," the wolf said.

"Big surprise there," the bat muttered.

"And what about you?" Joe asked the dog. "Are you going to turn on me down the road?"

"I'm a lotta things, but I ain't a welsher," the dog replied.

As Joe nodded his acceptance, Ralin spoke once again. "The choice is still yours, mortals. You may still reject the Knighthood, if you wish."

"Wow, you are terrible at building our confidence here, aren't you?" the bat said. "After all that, you wanna remind them they can still say no?"

"It doesn't matter all 'at much," the lizard said. "I know I'm in."

"She's right. I'm in too," added the cat.

"What the hell?" the dog muttered.

"Sure!" the falcon added.

"Ah imagine bein' a hero has its perks."

"Being a hero's enough for me," the ram said.

"It makes more sense than choosing to be dead," the spider stated.

"I'd just better get some monsters to rip apart," the wolf grumbled.

"Very well," Ralin said. "The choice has been made. Now come before your Architect and receive the full power of the elements."

The man-beasts looked at one another and then returned to the section of the platform where their Architect stood. Slowly, they walked up to the powerful beings, who looked down on them with varying expressions. The man-beasts kept their heads lowered, save the wolf, who made straight eye contact with Naru. But the Architect of Deserts took no notice of it, and as the wolf moved to stand before her, Naru gestured for her to kneel. The wolf bared her teeth a bit but did as she was asked as, around her, the other man-beasts knelt before their Architects. The cosmic beings stood still a moment and then held out their hands before their Knight. Lights of different colors burst forth from their hands, changing and stretching until they had achieved new forms. The Architects gestured for the man-beasts to look up. Obeying, their eyes widened at what they saw.

Floating in the air before each Architect was a weapon, all as finely crafted as Joe's staff, but each completely different from the staff and each other.

The bat's was an elegant, black, long sword, with a handle wrapped in leather and a hilt shaped like outstretched bat wings.

The cat received a long blue trident.

The dog had a stone hammer with a large, flat head on both sides, a carving of a snarling dog on either side.

The lizard saw a spear carved of steel.

The falcon's was a short staff, with a top that funneled around in a circle, forming a tall circular head with outstretched wings on either side.

The squirrel received an ax, covered in long green marks, with an elongated head that came to a point on the back end and a wide, vicious blade in the front.

The ram had a silver metal rod that resembled a thunderbolt, with curved edges on each end.

The spider was given a mace, attached to a long metal handle wrapped in leather. It was covered with hundreds of blunt ridges.

Finally, the wolf was also given a long, almost plain-looking, wooden staff. But unlike Joe's, hers was topped by a large dream catcher, from which feathers and beads draped down.

Slowly, each Knight reached for the weapon before him or her. And as each one took his or her weapon, energy spread through the weapon and into the bodies of the Knights. They each bucked and twisted as the power ran through them like an orgasm and a lightning bolt combined. Joe wondered if they were feeling the same kind of euphoric rush he had when he'd been given his power. But as he looked at their faces, he doubted it. Some of the man beasts did seem happy as the power washed over them. And others, like the bat, seemed almost in pain, gritting their teeth against screams.

I wonder what he's going through, Joe thought as he looked at the bat. *I suppose if he's shadow and I'm light, then it's the opposite of what happened with me. God, does that mean all the good in him is being burned away?* As the energy pulse stopped, Joe looked at the bat, who was slowly breathing in and out, warily.

"The choice has been made," Rastla whispered. "The Elemental Knights have been formed. Behold Nightstalker, Knight of Shadow."

Once again, the Architects went down the line, giving each Knight a new name, just as Joe had been given his—Wavecrasher, Groundquake, Firesprite, Windrider, Forester, Thunderer, Forger, and Sandshifter.

"You're serious about this?" the newly named Sandshifter asked. "I'd prefer my name not be something from Saturday morning cartoons."

"And what would you choose? Louise, Master of Sands?" Forester asked.

"Did I ask you, ferret boy? And why do I have a stupid stick?" Sandshifter sneered.

"Both of you knock it off," Joe said. "The last thing we need is more fighting."

"Hey, who died and made you leader?" Forester asked.

"He has done that himself, through his actions and designation," Ralin said. "Light and Dark are the most important elements, and therefore, Lightrider leads, with Nightstalker as his second. And do not doubt your weapons; they are direct conduits of our power. They can also allow you to communicate with each other; merely hold the weapon and think of another Knight, and you shall be linked to him or her."

"Whatever," Sandshifter said.

"Hey, wait a second!" Forester cried out. "Why can't Ah lead? The power of forest isn't good enough?"

"It is merely different," Demtia said. "Forest and the other elements represent the physical world and its power. But shadow and light represent the heart, from which all life springs and from which all choices, good and evil, are made."

"That makes sense," Forger said.

Forester muttered under his breath, "But even then, you can't possibly make them leaders just on that. What experience do they have?"

"Well, I was a store manager," Joe said.

"And I'm sure if I could remember something about my life, leadership would be involved," Nightstalker said.

"I'm gonna die," Groundquake moaned.

"Enough," Ralin boomed. "There is much to do before leadership will be tested. You must first undergo the training."

"Training?" the falcon asked.

"To learn the depths of your powers and the methods needed to control them. Even we cannot grant such control instantly."

"Cosmic army days," Sandshifter grumbled.

"Well, you didn't think they'd grant us all these powers and then just send us back to Earth, did you?" Forger asked. "So when does this training start, anyway?"

"Immediately."

The Knights looked at each other in confusion and then gasped as they began to wink out, one by one, until they had all vanished. Once they were gone, the Architects looked at one another, and they too vanished, leaving the platform and the realm itself, empty.

VII.

"WHAT IN THE HELL—"

"Hey, buddy, why don't you watch where you're going?"

"Dill weed!"

"Huh?" Joe exclaimed, looking around in disbelief. One minute, he had been standing on the Architects' platform. Now, he was standing in the middle of a busy street in some city he couldn't recognize. All around him, people walked and talked and bumped into him, but no one noticed that he had appeared from nowhere. Stranger still, they seemed to ignore the fact that he was still dressed in his raggedy golden clothes and still holding his staff.

"If this is supposed to be training, I'm really confused," Joe muttered to himself. As he glanced around, he asked aloud, "Is this even real?"

"It is as real as it needs to be."

"Ralin?" Joe said, whirling around at the sound of the voice. Standing before him was the Architect of Light. The people walked around him, past him, and as Joe watched in amazement, one man even walked through the Architect, who briefly shimmered like light through a prism and then regained solidity.

"What is this place?" Joe asked.

"Your world, in a way. This place itself is one of the pocket dimensions we Architects have access to."

"Pocket dimension?"

"A fold in what your people call the space-time continuum—not big enough to create a world in but suitable for many needs, nonetheless. The other Knights are in similar dimensions, though each one is different."

"And you created this place just to train me?" Joe asked.

"Yes. As much of your work will be done on Earth, I caused the dimension to take the shape of one of the cities in your country. I believe this one is called Seattle."

"Seattle?" Joe asked. He looked around him. A second later, he nodded, noticing the giant outline of the Space Needle in the distance. Turning back to the Architect, Joe asked, "So these people are?"

"Constructs. They exist because the dimension must seem as real as possible. They will fade when we leave this place."

"Okay, so what do we do first?" Joe asked. "Is Godzilla coming? Will I have to hit him with a light blast or something?"

Ralin merely chuckled at his Knight's questions. "I appreciate your enthusiasm, Lightrider, but we have not come here to learn such things yet."

"Then why are we here?" Joe asked. "Because I'm really not sure what else I'm supposed to do with these powers."

"Part of your work will be violent in nature, make no mistake about that. But a greater part, especially for you, will involve understanding of the world around you. For you carry the power of half the heart. And through that power, not only shall you obtain defense and battle skill but also depth and enlightenment.

"Look at the man yonder," Ralin continued, his hand emerging from his sleeve to point behind Joe.

The Light Knight turned and raised an eyebrow in puzzlement. Behind him, curled up on a park bench, was a man wrapped in a filthy green coat and covered with newspapers. His face was red and sweaty and covered by a thick, grimy brown beard. He was somehow asleep, despite the hardness of the bench and the noise of the street.

"What am I supposed to do?" Joe asked.

"Go to him. And listen."

"Listen for what?"

"Listen."

Joe shrugged but did as he was told, slowly making his way over to where the man lay. As he drew nearer, Joe noticed other details about the man. Lines marked his face, too many to have been made by time alone. He breathed through his mouth, revealing several brown and rotting teeth. The hand visible through the newspapers was covered in long, diagonal scars. But the thing Joe noticed most of all was the undeniable odor that rose from the man—an odor that could be bought for three ninety-five at any local liquor store.

The man seemed to stir as Joe approached, as if he could hear the Knight's footsteps through his sleep. But he never woke; he merely grabbed the newspaper and pulled it tighter around him, like a child with a blanket.

As he looked the man over, Joe tried to ignore the smell and wondered what on earth he was supposed to do.

Ralin said listen. I suppose I should start there. Leaning in close to the man, Joe strained his ears, trying to pick up any sort of sound he could. But all he could hear was the sound of the man's ragged breathing and the crumpling of newspapers as he moved around. Joe even listened to those sounds, trying to unlock whatever code it was he needed to hear. But whatever it was, it wasn't buried in the noises he heard. Stretching out his hand, he poked the man once in the chest and then again, a little harder. But the man merely snorted and then turned over so that his back was facing Joe.

"This is ridiculous," Joe muttered. He turned around and looked at Ralin.

But Ralin only stared at the Knight he had created, his lips pressed tightly. Joe sighed in frustration and turned back to the man on the bench, trying to figure out what the hell it was he was supposed to do.

Suddenly, a fresh streak of lightning stoked his brain, as he remembered Demtia's words.

Shadow and Light represent the heart, from which all life springs.

Ignoring the strong odor, Joe bent down, gently pulled the man back over, and put his ear close to the man's chest. He listened intently, trying to feel even one beat of the man's natural rhythm.

Ba-bum.

Ba-bum.

There it was. Joe could hear it as clearly as the buzzing guitars of a death metal band. But though he could hear it, it made as much sense as the singing of that band's battery acid-guzzling singer. Still, Joe kept his frustrations back. He continued to listen, hoping that he could hear the code this time and get it to make sense.

Ba-bum

Ba-bum

Ba-bum

Ba (I)-bum (wish)

Joe pulled his head back as if he expected a face-hugger to pop out of the man's chest and devour his eyes. But no such sci-fi evil came after Joe, and after a minute, he slowly regained his nerve and placed his head back on the man's chest. This time, he could hear the rhythm, but he could also hear words over it, moving in perfect time.

I-wish she-hadn't left-me.

I-wish I-could go-back to-work.

I-want my-house ba-ck.

I-need my-son.

I-want a-bed.

I-want more-whis-key.

I-want to-stop drink-ing.

Eyes wide behind his mask, Joe listened to the words that told him about the man before him. They told how he had been a partner at a high and mighty law firm in Portland, how he had become one of the city's wealthiest men. They told him how he'd suspected his wife of having an affair with his brother but had never been able to prove it. They told how, in his frustration, he had turned to drinking. They told him that the man had pissed away his money on alcohol as his frustrations grew. When his wife had called him on his behavior and spending, he'd snapped and begun to beat her, calling her a whore and a bitch. He'd only stopped when their son had walked into the room and screamed at his father to stop. And the words told him how everything had collapsed from there—the money and house lost in the settlement, his job gone, and the love of his faithful wife and son evaporated into the air.

Joe listened to it all, until finally, he could take no more and pulled himself back, away from the man. He stood there breathing and sweating as if he'd just finished running a marathon. Joe glanced over at the man and then put his head back down, unable to even glance at him without hearing the words in his head once again.

"You see now," Ralin said. "You see the power that light gives you."

"I heard it all," Joe whispered. "I saw everything that happened to him, everything that brought him here."

"You saw into his heart and saw the hopes he keeps there," Ralin said, "even the hopes that he himself does not recognize. And along with those hopes, you saw all the things that led to their creation. For such is the domain of the heart's light."

"Will ... will it always be like that? It was such a rush, all the details coming one after the other."

"You will learn to control it and hear only what you need. But as for what you hear, I cannot say. Some carry hopes full of joy and love and all the things you consider good. But other hopes are born from tragedy and sadness. Both call out for fulfillment, but as you know well, not everyone listens to the desires of his or her heart. Still, such things are not always your domain."

"What do you mean?" Joe asked. "Are you saying I shouldn't help people realize those hopes?"

"No. You must always do what you can to aid people in that way, for such is the way of the balance. But as for the hopes that are buried and ignored, the ones that become secrets, that become fears and shames, they belong to the other half of the heart,."

"The dark half—you mean Nightstalker?" Joe asked. "He can do this too?"

"The Shadow Knight can also look into a being's heart. He will see the secrets they keep there, about themselves and the things they have done. He will see their greatest fears and deepest regrets. But while yours is the power to make others realize their hopes and dreams, his is the power to make them acknowledge the things they ignore or are afraid to face. The results can be similar, but the methods are very different."

"This is some seriously heavy stuff," Joe said to himself, finally glancing back over at the man on the bench.

"And it will fall on both you and the Nightstalker to understand it. Another clue to that awaits you now."

"What do you mean?"

"You have learned to listen to the light side of the heart," Ralin answered. "And now, you must learn how to allow others to listen to it. Return to the man on the bench. Make him hear his heart speech as you have heard it."

"Well … I mean I'll try, but he doesn't seem too receptive," Joe said. "I heard him hope for a drink and that he could stop drinking."

"Then you must allow him to hear both and decide for himself which hope is stronger."

"But how—" Joe stopped, unsure how to ask for guidance.

But once again, Ralin gave him the silence of the early morning desert. Joe sighed, turning back toward the man on the bench and steeling himself for the smell of booze.

Fighting the urge to back away, Joe moved over to the man and gently tapped him on the shoulder. As before, the man grunted and then continued to ignore him. Joe sighed and opened his ears to the heart speech once again. Almost instantly, the litany filled his mind— son, wife, home, drinking, not drinking.

"Now how in the hell do I make you hear it?" Joe muttered aloud. "Well, I suppose you can't hear a thing if you aren't awake."

Joe reached over and again gave the man a poke, with a response identical to the previous one. Joe shook his head, got up, and backed away a little. He gripped his staff with both hands, quickly spoke an apology to the man, and then swung it forward, driving it into the man's chest without enough force to truly hurt him but hopefully enough to wake him up.

The result was instantaneous. The man let out a great whoop of pain and then sat up straight, scattering his newspapers to the four winds. Still shocked, he looked around in complete surprise, wondering who or what had struck him. But then, his eyes came across Joe, holding his long wooden staff and grinning sheepishly.

"Wha' the hell do you want?" the man snapped, glaring at Joe through his bleary eyes.

"Uh …well …"

"Oh goody, ya can make sounds," the man snapped. "Look if ya wanna sit here, just gimme a sec to grab my stuff, awright?"

"No, no, it's not that," Joe managed to get out. "I … just wanna talk to you."

At that, the man glanced over with an eyebrow raised. "And why's that? Ya a cop er something? Ya trying to get me outta *this* place too?"

"Well, in a way," Joe said. "But I'm not a cop, I swear. I just wanted to talk to you."

"Then what ya wanna talk about?" the man snapped. "'Cause unless it involves a bottle, I'm not much of a talker."

"I don't think you really need that," Joe said as he moved over and sat on the bench. "Look, why don't you just sit down, and we can chat, all right?"

The man glanced at Joe a moment longer and then sighed and plopped back down on the bench. He leaned his head back to look at the sky and then flipped it back and looked over at Joe. "So what are ya? Government?" he asked.

"I'm sorry?" Joe asked.

"Yer a social worker or somethin', right? They're the only people that wanna talk with me these days."

"No, I'm not a social worker."

"Oh good. So you're a religious freak, right?"

"No, I'm …"

"Look, buddy, I don't have a problem with you guys goin' and preaching yer stuff. That's yer right. But don't come and tell me about how awesome Jesus is and how I can work fer him in the kingdom, all right?"

The man leaned in closer as he spoke, pushing his liquored breath into Joe's face. "If you can get God to gimme my house and my job back, then I'll listen to whatever you gotta say. Otherwise, go back to waving yer Bibles into people's faces at six in the morning." The man slumped back on the bench, looking directly at the street before him.

But Joe thought about what the heart speech had told him and then started to speak. "I'm pretty sure this one's isn't on God, Ralph."

"Look, will ya just fu—How did ya know my name?"

"Oh, I know a few things about you," Joe said.

Ralph turned around to face him.

"You used to be a lawyer right?"

The man on the bench gave no reply, so Joe continued. "Yeah, and you were good too. Really good. Graduated top of the class at Princeton, moved out here to work right after college. You even made your way up to partner. You were happy about it, but that put a lot of pressure on you. You tried to ignore the stress, but it was always there. You kept wondering if you were good enough. You kept worrying that maybe, just maybe, you weren't ready, that you'd screw up and lose your credibility."

"I … They kept sayin' how they expected great things from me," Ralph said.

"Yeah, and you weren't sure you could do it. No matter how much you tried, the fear was always there," Joe said. "And eventually it had to come out. But it didn't come out at work, did it?"

"No, it … How do ya know all this?" Ralph asked, staring at Joe.

"Because those things are the source of your hopes," Joe said, turning to face the man. "You want things to change, and the reasons are always on your mind."

"Then I'm an idiot," Ralph said, slumping back down on the bench. "Things will never change back."

"No, you're a man who made some mistakes. There's nothing wrong with wanting to fix them."

"There is when they can't be fixed," Ralph snapped. "I screwed up my whole life. I brought myself down, and I deserve to stay here."

"You don't really believe that," Joe said. "That's why you keeping drinking, to numb yourself. You want to believe in change, but you're afraid to."

"No I'm not," Ralph snarled. "Look, did it occur to ya that maybe I mean what I'm saying? That I really can't fix the mess I made?"

"If I was just hearing the words you speak, yes. But I'm hearing another voice from you," Joe replied.

"Oh dear God, yer crazy, aren't ya?" Ralph said. He started to back away. "Ya aren't violent, are ya?"

"I'm not crazy," Joe said simply. "I have been through a lot, but despite that, I'm not ready to starting talking to Harvey the rabbit. What I mean is that I can … sense that you want things to get back to what they were, and part of you believes that can still happen."

"Sensing?" Ralph spat out. "Oh great, yer some kinda empathizer now? Is that it? Ya can feel what I really want? Well, here's a thought. What am I really feeling now, huh? It should be coming off me in waves."

"You're pissed off at me," Joe said. "I don't have to sense anything to feel that."

"Puh!" Ralph spat and stood back up. "Ya know what? I don't have to listen to this. I don't know how ya know all that stuff about me, but I don't care! I get by every day by not deluding myself, and that's exactly what I plan on doing now! So, fuck off!"

"You could change things," Joe said. "If you could just hear what I hear, I swear you'd understand."

"Well, then make me! Or does yer fancy power only work for you, and no one else? I'll bet it does, doesn't it?"

"Maybe it doesn't have to," Joe said, getting up. "There is a way; I just don't know what—"

"Well, call me when ya figure out how to be a transceiver," Ralph said. He whirled on his heel and started to walk off.

But as he walked, Joe's eyes widened at the realization the man had brought him. "Transceiver—can it really be that simple?" Joe said.

Joe took off, moving fast enough to sidestep Ralph and get in front of him. The man started to tell him off again, but before he could finish a sentence, Joe placed a hand on Ralph's chest and then another on his forehead and summoned the heart speech again. But this time it was different.

Joe could feel the words emanating from Ralph's heart as if his hand was on a boom box speaker. The sound traveled through his body and moved through his hand. First, Ralph started and struggled against the vibration, but then he went slack as the words filled his head. Joe held steady, letting the words flow through his body into Ralph's mind. As he let them go, Joe could feel the words of the heart speech grow in intensity, as if someone was turning the volume knob higher and higher.

But there was more than that. Not only were the words getting louder, they were getting faster, like a CD being put through the "Chipmunks treatment" on a mixing board. They started to bear down on Joe's mind, boring into his consciousness like hundreds of dentists' drills going at once. Joe gritted his teeth against it but tried to hold on, knowing that Ralph had to hear the voices of his heart and understand what they were telling him.

But once released from its confines, the heart speech continued to grow in intensity. Joe could feel his resistance grow weaker and weaker, and he felt Ralph tremble under his hand. The man let out a moan and wavered under his grasp. Joe let out his own gasp and felt his legs begin to fall underneath him. It was then that Joe realized that, if he didn't let go of Ralph's heart soon, the heart speech would drive him insane. He tried to move away, but he could feel something pulling him back to Ralph, like a magnet to a piece of metal. The heart speech kept surging between them, a living, electrical current that kept them attached to each other.

Dear ... God ... Joe tried to think under the strain. *I thought ... this was supposed to ... help ...*

Him/me

What? No, this is his/my problem. He's/I'm the one who needs this and—Why can't I focus?!

Something's wrong. It's like ... It's like I/he can't tell the difference between (my/his) hopes and his/mine. I … I have to focus. I have to remember. Must focus on my memories. On Jeri/Linda, Cody/Harry … Oh God, I can't! No! Make it stop! Please someone, make it stop before I—

But Joe couldn't make it stop; he felt Ralph's hopes and mind continue into his own, blending the two together. More and more of his memories were becoming overcast, filled with people he didn't know. And the people he did know were starting to become unfamiliar to him. It seemed that only moments before both sets of memories would become one, as would Joe and Ralph.

But even though no being moved to help Joe, something did. His staff, which he had left on the bench, rose up into the air of its own accord. As it had done in the Architects' realm, it flew to Joe. When it reached him, it hovered in the air before the two men, as if it was watching and observing the spectacle before it. The lion's head began to glow. A golden beam shot down from the head and struck Joe's hand. The impact knocked the hand away from Ralph's forehead, breaking the connection between the two men. Both of them stiffened, as if simultaneously having icicles shoved up their nether regions. Then both exhaled sharply and began to breathe rapidly.

Joe tried to catch his mental breath, hearing a clunk as the staff fell down to the ground. He turned to pick it up but then saw that it sat at the robed feet of Ralin. Joe looked on for a moment, and then his face contorted in a grimace. Grabbing the staff, he unsteadily used the weapon for balance, stood before the ancient Architect, and barked, "When in the name of Christ was that?!"

"The heart can be a dangerous place," Ralin answered. "You must learn to—"

"Oh no. You are not getting out of this with some fortune cookie bullshit!" Joe snarled. "It felt like our minds were being melted together!"

"The heart can be dangerous, Lightrider," Ralin said again. "It was the intensity of the man's hope that overwhelmed you and caused the 'merging.'"

"Well, you could've told me!" Joe yelled. "And will you please call me by my real name?!"

"I have been," Ralin said, his eyebrows narrowing. "You are not the man you once were. You made the choice to leave him when you accepted my power."

"Maybe that was a mistake," Joe muttered, rubbing his head.

"It was my power that saved you. The staff sensed your distress and came to aid you. Had it not broken the connection, you and that man would've been left as mindless vessels, overwhelmed by the need of his hope."

"That might've been better," Joe said, his voice beginning to calm. "He... was so desperate. I could feel so much need and want for those hopes to come true. But I could feel his shame too, pushing at him from everywhere. It was like a tar over his heart, blocking anything from coming out or getting through." Joe shivered as he said the words.

"These are things you will have to learn to accept," Ralin said, putting a hand on Joe's shoulder.

"You sense all that is good and true within hearts. And too often, they are overflowing with the things that forever weaken them. Fear, loathing, hatred, these evils dwell with all hearts, even the most virtuous."

"And I'm always going to hear them?" Joe asked.

"Such is the price of helping men and women hear the voices of their hearts," Ralin said. "But you cannot avoid them, for the heart cannot be whole without them. And with time, you will be able to push them back and hear only what is needed. You will learn to repress the rest."

"God, even a person's hopes are dangerous. I guess no one really is perfect, huh?"

"Only the—"

But before Ralin could finish, a moan issued forth from Ralph. The two beings stopped talking and looked as the man slowly rose to his feet. Slowly, Ralph's face rose up to meet Joe's. Joe expected a look of hatred and anger. But instead, he saw gratitude through watery eyes.

"I-I don't know ... what you did," Ralph said. "But you were right. I have to get my life back. I've always known that. And even if I can't, I can at least try to make up for the mistakes I've made. Thank you."

"Don't ... don't mention it," Joe stammered.

Ralph turned around and walked down the street.

"You have done well," Ralin said. "You have given that man realization of his hopes and dreams. With such a thing, there is little he cannot accomplish."

"I had no idea," Joe whispered. "Will he be able to do it?"

"Such is not for us to see. But his determination is an encouraging sign," Ralin said. "How does it feel to have had such an effect on a man's life?"

"I ... don't really know," Joe said. "I saw everything when we were joined. I saw how deep his sorrow and self-loathing were, how low his hope was. And I could feel the pain they had caused him, like it was my own. And now ... I guess this is like what AA sponsors feel when their charges get their lives back."

"It is that and more," Ralin said. "Many times in your new life you will need to reignite the flame of hope in a man's heart."

"I hope so," Joe replied. "I don't think I've ever felt this good before."

"Then I have indeed chosen well," Ralin said with a smile. "Now then, we have more training to do—training that will not require the power of the heart."

Ralin waved his hand, and the world around he and Joe began to swirl and shift, like a painting that had been caught in a blender and had its paints spun around. Joe felt sick looking at the spinning, but before he could close his eyes, there was a bright flash of white light, and then Seattle was gone. Joe blinked his eyes against the nausea, and after a moment, it did fade.

When he opened his eyes again, he found himself in a place far different from Seattle.

VIII.

"Where am I?" Joe whispered. He looked around. The pocket dimension had shifted into a world that was completely devoid of … well, anything. Joe could see no land, no people, and no signs of life of any kind. All around him was a gaping blackness that seemed to stretch for miles and yet still push right against him like a cold hand.

"Ralin, what is this place?" Joe asked.

But he got no reply. The Light Knight turned and saw nothing but more blackness before him.

"Oh great," Joe muttered to himself as he ran his hand through his hair. "I'm stuck someplace that looks like the Big Bang hasn't hit it yet. This is just gonna be one big party, isn't it?"

"Hey! Ralin!" Joe yelled out into the dark. "This place looks better suited for Nightstalker than me. Why don't you come down and shoot me to some nice, sunny place, huh? I hear that Mexico is great this time of year!"

But Joe got no reply, not even an echo. He kept yelling a moment longer and then stopped himself. Whatever was going on here, one thing was obvious. Just like before, he had to figure the way out himself.

"I should've picked death," Joe muttered. He pulled his mask and hat back on and, holding his staff out before him, began to walk forward into the darkness. "I was a good guy. I would've gone to heaven. I could be there now, chatting with Jesus or whoever.

"I wonder what we'd talk about anyway."

*   *   *

"Yeah, and I say, 'Sure, Jesus, but if that's true, why won't you let the Cubs win the series?'" Joe theorized, after what seemed like hours as he walked the endless darkness.

In all his time in this strange, black place, he had seen nothing that resembled life of any kind. Though there was air, he couldn't even feel a breeze as he walked. And Dear God, the silence. He'd tried to go it alone at first, but it had just been too much for him to deal with.

It was like having invisible needles pressing into the balloon of his subconscious, trying to poke a hole into it and let his mind leak out. He'd started talking to himself after that, willing to try anything to keep the darkness and the silence at bay. First, he'd talked about the positives of being dead. Next, he'd vented choice words at Ralin for dropping him here. Then he'd returned to the advantages of death, further exploring the contexts of his conversation with Jesus.

"Then He'd say, 'I would, Joe, but you see, I love the Cubs so much that I would want their win to be admired not only by Chicago but by the world,'" Joe muttered to himself. "'For the wine is sweeter when the grapes have grown well in the sun.'

"Then I'd say, 'Yeah, but c'mon, Lord. You can't make wine out of raisins,'" Joe answered himself as he leaned on his staff. "'They have to win eventually and'—Oh, fuck it!

"C'mon, Ralin!" Joe yelled, hurling his staff down in frustration and raising his voice to the black heavens. "I've been walking and walking around in this black hole where I'm guessing Jimmy Hoffa is buried! And you know what? I'd like to meet him. Because at least his moldering corpse would prove that something is actually here besides me! So, come on, gimme a sign!"

But if Ralin was watching his Knight, he gave no response. As the darkness began to creep back up on Joe, he snorted and said, "Fine. Be that way!"

Bending down to pick up his staff, Joe said, "I'm not going to let that crazy old man get the satisfaction. I will get out of this place, and I'm gonna keep all my marbles. And if he thinks anything different, he's out of his gourd!"

*   *   *

"No, Mr. Lion, we left off at seventy-eight bottles of beer," Joe panted to his staff as the two trudged along. "Now, if you can't keep track, we're gonna have to start talking politics again. Do you want that?"

Joe shook the staff gently, so that the head appeared to shaking no.

"I didn't think so," Joe said. "Now let's get back to work shall we?" And with that, he cleared his throat and began to sing the all-too familiar refrain:

Seventy bottles of beer on the wall
Seventy bottles of beer
You take one down
...
You take one down.

"Gee, what do you do next with beer?" Joe wondered. "I think it has to do with drinking, doesn't it? What do you think, Mr. Lion?"

Again, Joe shook the staff so that it shook no.

"Well, that's okay," Joe said. "We have plenty of time to remember how it goes, don't we? Yes, all the time in the world in this wonderful, quiet, peaceful, relaxing, dead, ungodly—

"Oh dear God, I can't do this anymore," Joe moaned as he came to a halt. "I can't stand this damn place. I can't even stand the sound of my own voice anymore. And I even wore out '99 bottles!'"

Joe fell to his knees and then fell back into a sit, shivering while his panic and fear ran through him.

"Why? Why did I have to choose this?" Joe whimpered aloud. "I could've ... No forget that! Why did I have to die in the first place? I had a good job. I had a good home. I had a family who loved me more than anything and who I would've died for. I was happy. Why did that get taken from me? It's not fair."

Joe wiped his eyes and then said in a trembling voice, "I wonder what they're doing now. Knowing Jeri, she's probably telling Cody that I'm still around, watching over them. I didn't even get to see him finish the robot. I wanted to see him take home the first place ribbon. I wanted to see it crush a can like he said it would. But I'm here, and it's my own damn fault."

Joe stopped talking. He put his head down between his knees and drew his arms around himself, his mind swimming with the images of his happy past. He saw the college common where he'd first seen Jeri. He'd been walking to the mess hall to get lunch when a flash of red hair in the corner of his eye had caught his attention. He'd blinked, thinking something had gotten caught in his eye. But it hadn't gone away, and then he realized he was seeing red hair that must've been colored within the sun itself.

The hair had been a thing forged in the fire of the sun, but the eyes, the eyes had been green ocean water bathed in moonlight. He'd felt himself sinking into them as the girl who owned them glanced around the campus, looking for some lucky soul that was able to approach her beauty without bursting into flame. Joe had wished it could be him, wished it with all his heart. But of course, she smiled and waved over to another girl who'd walked past Joe.

He remembered the envy he'd felt as he looked at the girl and how it had faded away into sadness and numbness. It was the same cold, heavy feeling that always came into his stomach when these things happened, as if he'd swallowed a cannonball-sized ice ball. It would stick there for a while and then melt as Joe found something else that would take the place of that brief moment.

But this time, Joe had been forced past his usual stopping point. It hadn't been some new desire to fulfill his urge or new determination. It had been a large oak tree that he had ignored in his lovesick trance. He'd met it headfirst, quite literally since he'd turned his face to the ground. It had rammed into his skull like a drunken man's fist punching a barstool to stop it from mocking him. Joe had staggered back, too stunned to even think about looking up or trying to figure out what had happened. Then the back of the bench had appeared.

Joe winced as he remembered feeling it behind his shirt and realizing what it was a second too late to stop it. He'd waved his arms for a moment, tumbling over it in a heap. He remembered the feeling as his legs had attempted to force their way inside his body and wondering if they'd be able to succeed. He also remembered how his back had felt like a paper clip being twisted by a bored child as he'd pitched backward onto the concrete.

But most of all, he remembered hearing laughter from the other students all around him as he'd groaned in pain. And then, he'd heard a pair of shrill-high voices coming from the direction he'd been staring in. He'd tried to curl up into a ball as the laughter cut deeper and deeper into him. Because of that, he'd missed the sound of a voice yelling at the two voices to shut up. He'd missed it when the red hair of fire had burned its way through everyone else in the common. But he hadn't missed the voice asking him if he was all right. He'd looked up then, proof that the ultimate being was a woman looking down at him with concern. He could've looked at that face for ages, had not some primitive reaction in his mind flicked a switch and reminded him to take the hand being offered.

Despite his current dark and uncaring circumstances, Joe managed to smile at the warmth of the memory. Now that he was probably going to spend eternity in this dark hell pit, it was good to recall it again, to have something to warm his soul with ...

*   *   *

Joe felt his eyes burn with pain. Shocked, he shut them tightly, blurring away whatever light he might have had to see with. But even through his lids, his eyes burned with a fiery red light.

Red light ... wait. That's coming from ... Joe couldn't place the source. With great effort, he reopened his eyes and tried to look for the source of the burning. It didn't take him long.

His staff, which he'd placed aside so causally, was glowing once again. But this time, the light was shining like a great beacon in this dark, starless night. Slowly, Joe reached out his hand for it. He felt his hand touch the wood handle, and then his fingers slowly closed around it and he drew it in close. He looked at the staff a moment before turning it toward the darkness around him, waiting for it to cut through the dark and show him the place in which he'd been entrapped.

But though the staff continued to give off light, it wasn't enough to show him anything. All Joe saw was a slightly gray version of the blackness in which he'd been encased.

"C'mon staff, work with me here," Joe pleaded. He held it, waiting for the light to show him the way out of this dark place. But the light stayed in its holding pattern, giving him enough light to see but no more than that. Joe's eyes narrowed as he tried to force his will onto the staff and make its light shine brighter. But if the staff could hear his will, it had all the listening power of the IRS after tax day.

"Goddamn it, what kind of powers are these if they won't work when I need them?" Joe spat out, glaring at the staff. Of course, the second he did, the light from the staff began to dim.

"No, no, no!" Joe cried out. He shook the staff and even slapped the lion's head in a frantic attempt to keep the light going. But it was all for naught, as the light grew dimmer and dimmer and then finally winked out, leaving Joe in the darkness once again.

"No!" Joe screamed out into the shadows. He slapped the staff once more, and when the light didn't come back on, he screamed and threw it into the darkness. He never thought about how the staff was his only hope; he only felt his anger at the thing.

"Great idea! Trap me inside a place as dark and empty as a college kid's wallet and gimme a wooden flashlight with about four seconds of battery left in it," Joe snarled out to the empty world around him. "What do you expect me to do with that, huh? Am I supposed to think at the speed of light too?

"And you know what else? I ... I ..." Joe stammered on for a few more seconds and then finally let out a long, tired sigh.

"Screw it. I'm not getting anywhere with this," Joe said, massaging his temples. "Maybe if I figure out what I did to turn the staff on in the first place, I can find it.

"So let's see here," Joe said, tapping his finger against his palm as he thought. "I walked around for a buttload of time, and didn't seem to get anywhere. Then I think I started to talk to the lion and sing about beer. Then I gave up and sat down.

"Was that it? Does it only work if I sit down and ... No, that's stupid," Joe said. "What else did I do? I thought about Jeri and ..."

Joe stopped talking then and slapped his forehead, as in front of him, the staff began to glow. Joe quickly ran over to where it lay and picked it up.

"You glowed for her," he said. "Why? What makes her special to you? She's special to me, so why do you care about—

"Wait! Ralin said that this power was a part of me. So if I think about Jeri, then that should—

Without even finishing his sentence, Joe put his plan into action. Holding the staff above his head, Joe closed his eyes and allowed the memories to wash over his mind like a cleansing detergent. He smiled as he remembered all the times he and Jeri had spent together.

Traveling to Italy together their senior year in college and seeing the Coliseum and taking a photo of Jeri mock throwing him to the lions.

Meeting each other after graduation and spending the night at a long, wonderful party that he could only partially remember.

Their trip to a moonlit beach where they'd found a deserted sand dune and created their son.

Then, he was running through the hospital, orderlies throwing a gown and gloves onto him—not that he'd noticed—as he pushed the doors open and saw his wife on the table, bathed in sweat. The doctor looked at her from the other end of the stirrups. He'd run to Jeri then, taking her hand and wiping the damp hair from her face, telling her that everything would be all right. Her response had been to crush his hand as another contraction hit and damn him to hell for putting this thing inside her. As Joe gritted his teeth and reminded himself that he loved the woman destroying his hand very, very much, the doctor called out for one last push. Jeri had told the doctor to fuck off, to which he'd answered that one more push would end this.

Jeri had grimaced in pain and borne down, screaming once again, as Joe barely restrained his own howls of pain. And then, a third voice joined in, one that immediately silenced the other two. Jeri finally let go of Joe's hand as the two of them watched the doctor pull a bloody, slimy, wonderful baby boy out the rest of the way and hold him up to his parents. A nurse had moved up to Joe and asked him if he wanted to cut the cord. It took about two more questions before Joe finally snapped back, and nodded. Moving over to the doctor, he quickly cut the cord through as the nurses then wrapped the baby and brought him over to his mother, who took him with open arms. Joe had looked over at the family, his family, and knew that for the rest of his life, he truly had a purpose.

Like a furnace being stoked during a dark Alaskan winter, a warmth grew in Joe's heart. And the staff grew brighter and brighter. Joe's eyes opened wide, unaffected by the brightness as he watched it spread all around him. And as it spread, Joe could see the dark all around him begin to peel and curl, like old wallpaper in a derelict apartment. He watched in amazement as something new appeared behind the darkness, something bright and strong and, most importantly, *alive.*

"Thanks guys," Joe said. Within seconds, the darkness faded away completely, leaving Joe in a new place, one that he recognized but didn't understand. But as the plastic chairs, Formica tables, and linoleum floors came into view and the smell of grease filled the air, Joe realized there was no denying where he was.

IX.

"WHY IS IT THAT I've been seen inside a guy's heart and been inside a black hole, but this is still the weirdest part of this training?" Joe muttered as he looked around.

Formica tables, tiled walls, people eating burgers and fries all around, and the smiling face of Ronald McDonald all made it very obvious where he was, unlike whatever it was he was supposed to do in this place.

"If Ralin wants me to do good by destroying the main source of heart attacks, I'm gonna need a bigger place than this," Joe said. He looked around, trying to see anything that might lead to a clue. But all he got in response to his search was a pair of elderly ladies in a booth looking at him as if he had a swastika cut into his forehead.

"Uh, sorry," Joe said sheepishly as he tipped his hat.

Their expressions grew even more puzzled, but they returned to their meal nonetheless. Joe wondered what was wrong, and then he remembered that no one in 'Seattle' had seen his outfit or his hat.

"Good thing they aren't real," Joe muttered. Looking ahead, he saw the line at the counter and decided that the best thing to do was to appear normal until he could figure out what was going on here. Moving to the line, Joe pretended to look at the menu while he gave the situation some thought.

All right, something's gotta be wrong here, something that I'm not seeing. But that's probably the point; I doubt the answer will show up with a giant sign around it that says, "Kill me, Joe, I'm the Antichrist."

God, those burgers smell good.

So what is it? Could it be the people here? Is something going to happen to ... Yeah, why not? They said that I'd have to use these powers for violence sometimes, and I've already used it for enlightenment.

Fries—can smell the grease.

Get a hold of yourself man! For all you know, the burgers in this place could turn rabid and begin to eat people! Do you want to die again because you wanted a burger?

But I'm hungry.

At that, Joe paused a moment in his mental battle. He actually did feel hungry. Apparently, resurrection didn't eliminate basic needs.

"Well, I suppose the chances of demon burgers are pretty unlikely," Joe muttered. He looked at the board. But he had barely read the drink prices before something bumped into him from the back. Joe felt his midsection pushed into the wooden barrier as something else moved his way past him and kept pushing through the line like Jeff Gordon behind a bulldozer. As everyone yelled and complained at the intrusion, Joe pulled himself back up and scanned the counter to see exactly who or what was causing the problem.

Joe saw an old man dressed in a tweed sweater and blue pants standing before the cashier, holding a burger container in his hand. His head was bald, but he had a full crop of liver spots decorating it. Though the man's frame seemed spindly as a bird's leg, the voice that came from him was as strong as an elephant's call. "What kind of crap are you people serving me?!" The man hurled his container down on the counter.

"I'm sorry, sir. If you'll just tell me what's wrong, I'll help you," the cashier, a teenage girl with black hair and glasses, said, speaking in a voice Joe recognized well from his old job—the keep-them-sated-until-you-can-pass-them-off-or-they-die voice.

"What's wrong? This burger is nothing like what I ordered! Look at it!" the old man yelled.

"So you mean you didn't get the type of burger you wanted? Or was there something specific you wanted on this—"

"Oh goody! Instead of a cashier, I get a girl-sized featherless parrot!" the man snapped. "Yes, girly, I didn't get what I wanted. Do you want a cracker for that Polly? Do you?"

Wow. And I thought I had assholes at the store, Joe thought

The old man continued to berate the poor girl. As his insults rained down, her attempts at fixing the problem became fewer, until she stood there silently, absorbing the man's words with trembling eyes.

However, this also meant that many more eyes were drawn to the confrontation; all those in line, behind the counter, and eating looked at the situation with disgust. Even Joe, who had dealt with all sorts of angry customers in the past, felt a new level of loathing toward the old man.

"After all I did to make the world safe for your goddamn parents to raise you in, and you can't even take a damn order right!" the old man screeched at the girl.

"Dude, let it alone," said a man behind the old man, a twentyish African-American dressed in jeans and a long shirt. Putting his hand on the codger's shoulder, he said, "It's a sandwich, for Christ's sake! Look at her. She looks like she's gonna cry and—"

"Hey, shut up!" the old man snapped, whirling around to face the black man. "I didn't ask for you for a damn thing, did I? Your whining and bitching may work on everyone else in this country, but it sure as hell doesn't work on me!"

The black man pulled his hand back immediately. Joe watched him glare at the old man, wondering if this was what he had been sent here for. It didn't seem all that hard to believe that the old man was some sort of demon, and if he was, he sure as hell was doing a bad job of hiding it.

But thankfully, the black man just glared at the codger, shook his head, and left the line, heading for the door. Joe breathed a sigh of relief as the other people in line breathed sighs that sounded like "asshole" and "douche bag." The old man was either oblivious to or ignored every sign; he turned his attention back to the counter and the girl.

But instead of seeing the young girl, he saw an older brown-skinned woman dressed in the black-and-white uniform of the store manager; meanwhile, the other employees moved the girl to safety, away from the old man.

Good old, us-versus-them camaraderie, Joe thought.

"And just who the hell are you?" the old man snapped as he glared at the woman. Noticing the pin on her lapel, he mockingly cackled, "Ooh, a manager! What are you gonna do, Missy? Throw me out? Oh, please try, little Ms. ... Patel. Oh, isn't that original?"

"Sir, I'm not even going to pretend I want to help you," the newly named Ms. Patel said, her voice as cold and brittle as the Arctic. "I actually want to throw you out. But I'm going to let you decide how. Either you can leave on your own, or I can call the police and have them drag you out."

"For what?" the old man gaped. "A burger?"

"Causing a disturbance for one thing," Patel said. "Also racist comments, which I believe everyone here will attest to?"

A loud murmur of acceptance moved through the people in line, Joe's voice among them.

The old man glared at them, but everyone could see his eyes waver just the tiniest bit. "Look," he began, turning back to the register. "I just want my food all right? If I can get it, I'll apologize. How does that sound?"

"Oh, it's too late for that, sir," Patel said.

"C'mon, man," said a young voice from behind the man. Joe peeked out of the line just enough to see the old man whirl around and face a young boy, about twelve-years old. He was dressed in a Pokémon T-shirt and jeans and had a slightly shaggy head of brown hair. From his position in the line, Joe could also see that this boy had a crop of freckles over his face and clear blue eyes set above a pug nose. In a way, he reminded Joe of his own son.

"Some of us want to get food too," the boy said.

The old man growled in response and then turned back to the register to resume complaining.

"You'd actually throw me out over a sandwich?" the old man continued.

"Well, if you'd cause this big a scene over a sandwich," Ms. Patel replied. "Look, sir, just go all right?"

"But I want my goddamn sandwich!" the old man yelled, pounding his fist on the counter. "Is that too much to ask for around here? What, is it offensive to you because there's beef in it? Didn't you think of that before you started working here?"

Joe let out a long sigh and glanced up at the ceiling as everyone in line began to mutter their impatience. In a split second, the mutters turned to screams. Joe's head snapped back as he heard the people around him trying desperately to move away. Joe struggled to stay where he was, but the line was moving backward fast. Reaching out, he managed to grab hold of the railing and slip under it. But once he was out, he wished he'd stayed back.

The old man still stood at the counter. But he was no longer there of his own will. He was pinned to it by a long, flesh-colored spike that had shot through his chest, staining the counter and the workers with blood. But what was worse was seeing where the spike had come from. The young boy stood there with an expression of relief on his face as he moved his right arm away from the counter, taking the old man with it. As his now spiked arm held the corpse place, the boy looked at the workers, and with his eyes glowing red, said to Patel, in a deep voice that sounded like Satan on a slowed-down cassette, "Well, that takes care of that. Now, how about a couple of burgers, bitch?"

But Patel just stared at the creature in disbelief and horror, as if he was a living combination of death and disease in a suit of flesh.

The creature looked back at her for about three seconds, sighed, and said, "Why is it every time I go out, I have to deal with these human retards?"

With that, he swung his spike arm to the side, which slid the body of the old man off. It hit the ground with a thud, splattering more blood all over the floor. The second it hit, Patel finally let out a scream and backed away from the bloodstained counter, pressing her back to the fryer. The creature's red eyes narrowed then, annoyed at the sound. Bringing its spike arm around again, it held it above its head. The arm began to shift and change, the flesh quivering over the bone. The entire arm moved like Silly Putty, until it had assumed a new shape—that of a large ax head.

"See, lady, I like burgers," the creature said, brandishing the weapon. "But it's obvious I'm not gonna get one now, even though I took care of that asshole for you. So I think I'll save your bosses the trouble and sever your ties to this place—along with a few other things!"

Grabbing his staff from its holder, Joe leaped over the railings to where the creature stood. It started to turn its head to face him, but Joe was moving too fast for him. He landed right behind the creature and slipped his staff under its chin, using it to hold the creature in a stranglehold. As he applied the pressure, the creature let out a grunt that sounded like a pig gargling battery acid and began to swing back and forth, dragging Joe's body along with every shake. Joe gritted his teeth as he held on to the staff and tried to plant his feet on the ground.

Finally, the creature decided another approach was needed. He suddenly snapped forward, both destroying the staff's grip and sending Joe flying overhead. The Knight of Light flipped over the creature's back and hit the ground. Letting out another grunt, the creature brought up his ax hand and quickly brought it down, aiming for Joe's head. Joe saw it coming, and before he knew what to do, his hands were up and holding the blade in place mere inches from his face, even as the creature struggled to push it down.

Joe pulled his lower body backward, swinging his legs up over his head. Before the demon could react, Joe locked his legs under the creature's armpits and then rolled forward, throwing the creature into the wall, which it hit with a thud and a large crack. As it slowly slumped down to the floor, Joe flipped up to his feet and turned to Patel and the workers.

"Are you all right?" he asked.

"I … yes … how did—"

"Never mind," Joe said; he saw the creature beginning to stir. "Everybody just get of here—now!"

The workers and customers moved instantly, heading for the exits; the cashier grabbed Patel and led her away. Joe watched them leave and then turned his attention back to the creature, which was shambling its way back to its feet.

"What the hell did you do that for?" it yelled at him. "All I wanted were some fucking burgers!"

"That's not enough reason to kill someone, especially here," Joe said. He bent down and picked up his staff.

"They don't have apple pies anywhere else," the creature replied as it got to its feet.

"Then come here and get one," Joe said, brandishing his staff. "So I can send you back to Daddy in hell."

"You can try."

Before Joe's eyes, the creature began to change again. The Silly Putty-like transformation began, spreading all over his body and clothes. The creature's body stretched out, the arms and legs growing longer and longer, even as the flesh and cloth on them fell away, leaving gray, almost scaly patches underneath. Its shoulders surged to the sides, growing bigger and wider as its now bare chest stretched out, going from child to bodybuilder faster than Barry Bonds. Its hands and feet began to curve inward, and the hands became scaly yellow and birdlike, with long talons sprouting from them. The feet just curved as more of the creature's weight became focused on its heels. The toes merged together into a pair of long claws on each foot, with another poking down from the heel. Its face inflated like a frog, the cheeks swelling outward as the hair on top fell away. The skin shifted from pink to gray. The creature opened its maw and showed Joe how its teeth were growing longer and sharper. Finally, the last transformation hit—the creature's ears withdrew into its head, leaving a hole on each side. Its metamorphosis complete, it gave a snarl that was almost orgasmic and glared at Joe, who dug deep for the eloquent words that followed.

"Oh, buggershit."

The creature gave another snarl, and then leaped at Joe, its long claws outstretched. Joe brought up his staff to protect himself. He heard the creature's roar grow closer and closer; he tried to shift to the side. A blur passed before his eyes, and he saw the creature hit the floor from five feet away, shattering the tiles underneath. It was only then that Joe realized that the blur was him moving to the other side of the restaurant.

He had no time to try to deal with it though, as the creature jumped up, and on all fours, began to charge at him, smashing aside the tables and chairs like they were paper decorations at a party. Joe held out his staff again, but this time, he gripped it with both hands and as the creature approached, he swung the staff like a bat, driving it right into the creature's face.

Joe had only hoped to stun the creature, but as his staff made contact with its skull, there was a huge burst of light, and the creature howled in pain and was flung back as if it had been hit by a hormone-crazed rhino. It flew backward over the countertop and into the cooking area, taking the screeching sound of falling metal along with it. But Joe knew that the creature wouldn't stay down for long. Moving quickly, he ran to the countertop and leaped over it, his staff at the ready. But when he landed, all he saw was an empty kitchen, with scattered pots and pans everywhere.

"I didn't realize things like you were so easy to hide," Joe said aloud, walking into the kitchen, his staff held out before him.

"And I didn't realize that little China boys held power like that," the voice of the creature replied.

"I'm Japanese. But glad to know that your kind is just as ignorant as the white man," Joe replied.

"Heh! Believe me, little man, he doesn't have a damn thing on us," the creature replied. "There are about seven hundred different versions of us, and we all hate each other."

"Surprising that you've all lasted this long then."

"Oh, we hate you guys more. But you make good food on occasion. And so do places like this."

"You must be a hoot at parties with that kind of wit," Joe said, moving past a large greaser pit next to the wall.

"Too bad I'm not joking huh?"

"Why doesn't that surprise me?" Joe replied.

But this time, all he got back was silence.

"What? Did I hurt the monster's feelings?" Joe chided. "C'mon, gimme something."

But nothing answered back. Looking around, he scanned for a sign of the creature's whereabouts. But all he saw around him were machines that produced unbelievably greasy foods.

As he moved, the Light Knight heard a harsh clang, like two metal plates being stuck together. He whirled around, expecting to see the monster behind him holding a large and spiny instrument of death. But all he saw was the greaser, still bubbling away.

Joe shook his head and began to turn away. But the second his gaze was averted, the sound filled the air again. Again, Joe whirled around and saw nothing but the greaser. He cocked an eyebrow at the machine and then slowly moved toward it, his staff held outward as if the machine would come to life and make him the world's biggest French fry. But the greaser just stood there, refusing to transform into an unholy killing machine. And the creature didn't pop from its greasy depths, waiting to drag Joe down into a cholesterol-soaked hell.

Joe reached the machine, keeping his staff out before of him. He stuck it out and tapped the machine, hearing nothing but the clang of metal. He glared at the lion head. It remained unlit. Joe nodded, withdrew the staff, and went over to the machine himself. He looked over the pits, seeing the grease bubble, warning labels written all over it, and the basket of frozen fries that had yet to be dumped in.

Joe looked at it a minute and then shook his head. Whatever he was looking for, this greaser had no part of it. As he turned to leave, he caught a second glance at the warning labels on the machine. Most of the labels were large and red, with the basic "do not touch when hot," "wear hairnets if needed," "beware of hot grease," and various instructions for dealing with burns. Anyone else looking at it would've nodded and said everything was all right. Except Joe saw one little problem with the signs—they were all written backward.

"What in the hell?" Joe whispered. An idea crept into his head. He slowly turned his head to the side, hoping that he wouldn't see what he thought was there. But Joe's thoughts proved right. Standing there, just a few feet away, was a second greaser, almost identical to this one. Joe could see the dents in the same spots, the fries that sat on it, and the stickers that were written properly.

He glanced down to see the light of the stone glowing brighter than it ever had before. But the light was not so bright that Joe missed the large, metallic arms that had sprouted from the sides of the greaser and were now reaching for him.

Joe's first impulse was to turn and jump out of the arms' reach—a plan he put into action instantly. He leaped away, but the creature's arms reached and grabbed his coat, pulling him back with a noise that sounded like a frozen stick breaking and a tremendous amount of pain that shot up Joe's neck. He grimaced and tried to struggle, but his body had gone limp.

"Took you long enough, dipshit," the creature's voice said.

Joe watched as the fryer's metal top began to shift and change, as if something was trying burst through the metal. Within seconds, enough of it had changed so that a metal version of the demon's head now stuck out.

"C'mon, man, even I could've figured it out before now," the creature laughed. "What finally tipped you off?"

"The ... the stickers," Joe said, managing to bring his left arm up just enough to point at them.

"Oh yeah," the creature said as it glanced over at its side. "I always forget not to change into something with words on it. It's like changing form based on a reflection. It's a real pain, light boy."

"Huh?"

"Oh, don't look so shocked," the creature said. "I know Light God power when I see it. And that staff of yours is brimming with it. So are you, now that I can see you properly—a fantasy nerd who loves the transient D&D wannabe look."

"Are you ... gonna kill me or talk me to ... death?" Joe managed to spit out as he wriggled under the creature's grasp.

"Hmm. You have a point," the creature replied. And with that, the greaser pit under the creature's head began to bubble furiously. Joe realized what was going to happen and tried even harder to shake the creature's grasp, shaking and twisting like an epileptic watching a lightbulb flicker. But none of it made a difference. The creature hurled

Joe's face under the grease, laughing as Joe first tensed and then erupted into struggles, his face broiled in the hot grease.

"Well, I think that's long enough," the creature said. It finally brought Joe's head back up from the fryer, spilling grease all over.

The second his head was above water, Joe let out a pain-wracked scream. The skin had been charbroiled to the texture of a flame-cooked steak—pink and tender and raw. It looked as if strings of new flesh had been doused in acid and then melted onto his face. A good chunk of his hair had burned away, which left an even more burned spot on the very top of his head.

"You know, if you can really take that kind of punishment, I think there's only one thing left for me to do here," the creature said

Joe continued to howl in pain.

The creature shoved Joe's head back into the hot grease and brought the temperature up even higher. It quickly became impossible to tell the bubbles of boiling grease from the ones caused by Joe's screams. But the creature just watched with an evil smile, until Joe's struggling body finally started to quiet and go limp. The creature dragged Joe out once again and examined his handiwork.

Joe's face had become a mass of blackened meat. His skin had been charred black and looked as if a single rub would push chunks of it off in a puff of black powder. His lips no longer existed, having been totally fused together, leaving only a small hole that air was passing in and out of. His nose had also been fused shut from the grease. But the worst were his eyes. Joe had shut them the second he'd been shoved into the grease, thinking that somehow, that would protect them. It had but at a horrible cost. Joe's eyelids were now melted shut, leaving blackened flesh where they had once been.

"Mm-mm," the creature said as it licked its metal lips. But that aspect began to fade as the creature shifted out of the form of the greaser. Only its head and arms remained unchanged as it returned to its large monster form. It tapped Joe's burned face; the response was a moan of pain.

"Still awake. Good. I always like it when they're alive to feel this," the creature said. He pressed his face close to Joe's and opened his mouth. The inside of it was pitch black, heightened only by a set of teeth that would've made a dentist run to begin his proctologist degree. They were black, the front two inhabited by a worm that crawled between two large holes in the teeth. Some of the others seemed to be rotting away even now, as little clinks of teeth falling on teeth could be heard. The creature breathed outward, and the air flowed into what was left of Joe's mouth; he instantly tried to spit it out. But the creature merely pulled him in close, giving him a full whiff.

Chuckling darkly, the creature laid Joe's body down on the floor, moving his grip so that he was pressing Joe's chest onto the floor. Holding up his other hand, the creature looked as the fingers began to shrink and retract and the palm and actual hand began to inflate. It grew bigger and bigger, like it had been replaced with a balloon under the flesh. Finally, it reached nearly four feet wide, and then distinct crunching noise could be heard underneath the flesh. After a moment, the crunching stopped as the bones underneath finally settled into a club-like shape.

The creature looked at its hand with approval and looked back to the being that would become its meal. Still chuckling, he raised the hand over his head and looked over Joe's body. His eyes went over Joe's head, his chest, and his arms, before finally coming to a halt at his stomach.

"You know, I'm pretty sure I heard your neck snap before," the creature said as it positioned its hand over the area. "So if that's true, you shouldn't feel this, right?"

With that, the club-arm snapped down over Joe's gut and crotch, crushing every bone with a crunch like a man biting into a bone to suck out the marrow. When the creature looked, he saw Joe's legs were connected only by thin pieces of flesh that looked like they would snap with a single pull. The creature looked upward and raised its arm once again, positioning it right above Joe's face. With a grunt, it jerked the arm up and started to bring it down. But before it had even gotten a few inches toward Joe's face, the creature suddenly brought it to a halt. It looked at Joe's face, puzzlement slowly overtaking its joy.

The creature bent down, getting closer and closer to Joe's face. It ignored the smell of burned flesh and the flaky texture of the skin and moved over to the spot where Joe's eyes had been. The creature looked and realized that what it had thought was true. Underneath this man's eyelids, a line of gold was growing, spreading across his eyes like a thread being woven through from the inside. The creature stared, not sure what this meant for itself or its meal.

But then, Joe answered those questions for the creature.

Joe's eyes suddenly burst open, the scar tissue splitting apart to reveal pools of gold behind them. As the creature gaped in amazement, the light spread over Joe's face like a liquid, bathing the charred skin in its warm glow. But the creature could still see through the light to Joe's face. He could see how it was changing. The blackened skin was lightening, returning to normal color and texture as the flesh reformed itself. The hole that had once been Joe's mouth stretched outward, splitting apart as his lips regrew. Even the hair on his head was coming back, powered by the light within him.

The creature heard a series of cracks and pops. Bringing its eyes downward, the creature saw that Joe's lower body was undergoing the same transformation. The light shone through Joe's clothes as his broken bones reknit themselves, puffing his body back up like an inner tube. The creature stared for another moment and then, realizing what would happen if this being completed his healing, brought his club-arm to bear again, this time aiming for Joe's head.

But as the club whistled through the air, Joe's eyes narrowed, and with another blur of motion, his hands came up and grabbed the club in midair. Joe didn't stop there. His body moving at superspeed, he spun the club hard to the right. At his speed, it resulted in not only a huge snap but the creature being hurled off into the countertop, crashing through the wall with all the force of a crash test dummy hitting the barricade. As the creature moaned and writhed amid the broken plaster, the light around Joe faded away. The Knight of Light got to his feet, paused to grab his staff, and then walked over to the hole the creature had created in the counter. As he approached it, the creature turned and gave a snarl of both pain and anger.

"You broke my arm!"

"You deep-fried my face and made me a paraplegic. I'd say we're even," Joe replied.

"You walk pretty well for a cripple," the creature snapped back, cradling its arm.

"You won't," Joe said. He raised his staff, aiming at the creature's head.

But as he prepared to fire, the creature's snarl suddenly became a smile. It whipped out its injured arm, now in the form of a chain and wrecking ball and hurled it at Joe.

Once again, Joe dodged the attack in a blur, moving to the other side of the counter.

"You think you're the only one who can heal?" the creature smirked as it got to its feet. "I'm a shape-shifter, dummy!"

It laughed again as it hurled its weapon at Joe. But this time, the Knight stayed where he was. Joe glared at the ball as it flew through the air, and the golden light filled his eyes once again. He felt the power grow behind his pupils, but he kept it back—until the ball was only inches away from his face, and then he let it loose.

The light exploded from his eyes in a golden flash, brighter than a diamond-coated smile. The ball and chain froze in the air for a second, and both began to darken, dissolving into dust. The creature let out a howl of pain as Joe withdrew the light back into himself.

"Well, I guess you can't regrow them, huh?" Joe said as the creature wept and clutched at the stump where its arm had been. "Looks like I got the better deal."

"You," the creature hissed. "You are gonna—"

"Oh no I am not," Joe said. "But you are."

And with that, Joe vanished in a blur of motion, circling the creature as it snarled and tried to slap Joe away with its good arm. But whatever power was flowing through Joe was letting him move faster than a crack-fueled Speedy Gonzales. The creature felt punches and kicks strike it from every possible angle. Just as one would hit, another would strike somewhere else. It grunted and sweated and cursed as it tried to move ahead of Joe, slicing through the air with its good arm.

But it didn't have to worry about the punches and kicks for long. As it swiped its arm just past Joe, the supercharged Light Knight suddenly whirled back around and shoved the creature in the back. At his current speed, this meant Joe rammed into the creature hard enough to send it flying through the air and through the Formica tables with a crash and a storm of plastic-covered wood. Joe watched the creature land and watched it moan and clutch its ruined arm in pain. Then he slowly began to walk over to it.

"You … you can't … do this," the creature wheezed.

"I can, and I did," Joe said.

"All this … for a … jackass of a man. You are … Light God … aren't you?"

"I don't need to be," Joe said. "People don't need power like this to destroy a thing like you."

But at that, the creature just laughed.

"Oh ... they need ... something ... a pair ... of somethings," it said, through in a half laugh, half wheeze. "You still ... think they're ... like you. They're not."

"And what would you know about it?" Joe demanded. "You thought of humans as nothing more than cattle."

"More ... like ... bulls," the creature spat. "Always ... running around ... goring each other ... until a bigger bull comes in—then they ... listen to him. That's what ... I was. That's what ... you are now."

"No," Joe said, shaking his head. "I'm not going to hurt anyone—no one except you."

"You do that ... and you prove ... me right." The creature laughed. "Take... my place ... in the herd. Be a big ... golden bull. Until another one of me comes and ... takes ... you down."

Joe started to speak, but then fell silent as the creature laughed.

"You see? You are ... like me ... and you ... just realized it."

"Oh yeah. You bet I realized it," Joe said. He raised up his hand. The creature watched with a smile as he curled it into a fist. But the creature's grin faded the second he saw the fist begin to glow with the same light that had come from Joe's staff.

"Well. Look at what I can do," Joe said.

"Wait ... you'll be ... like me."

"Yeah, I will, won't I?"

"No ... you're Light God. You're supposed ... to hate things like me—to be ... all noble ... and garbage."

"I might be Light God," Joe said. "But no one said I was noble. And no one tells me what I can or can't do with these powers—certainly not some punk demon freak like you!"

Joe released the power that had gathered in his fist; a stream of light shot from his hand toward the creature's head. The creature tried to crawl away, cursing its broken arm as it struggled to its feet. But all its efforts were for naught. The light ball moved forward, curving to follow the creature, as did Joe's eyes. The creature moved as quickly as it could, but soon it realized that it had no chance against the power that was after it. It threw its good arm over its face, knowing the action was meaningless as the ball of light streaked toward it … *and exploded next to the creature in a spark of light.*

The explosion carried no sound, no force, and no pain. The creature held its arm up a moment more and then slowly brought it down, looking up at Joe with disbelief. The Light Knight shrugged and then swung his staff around, smashing the creature in the side of the face with a wet thud like steel hitting raw meat.

"No one said I was noble. But I'm damn sure not a killer," Joe said as the creature's head lolled to the side.

As Joe spoke those words, he heard something behind him, something like a pop of a champagne bottle. Joe whirled around to see if the creature had escaped and then gaped in amazement. The creature had vanished. Before Joe could process that, he felt the floor under his feet begin to soften. Looking down, he saw that the linoleum tile had turned into some sort of polished quicksand that was dragging down him. Joe struggled against the floor, but as he did, tendrils of it began to reach up and suck him in farther, dragging him up to his waist and then his chest and then his neck. Joe managed to stick his staff out and brace it against the part of the floor that was still solid. Pulling up on it, he took a breath and then strained to pull his body out of the mess it was in.

And he might have, if the rest of the floor hadn't suddenly transformed as well. The staff fell into the goop, which dragged Joe down, until he became sure that the last sight he would see would be the dollar menu at McDonalds.

*   *   *

"Joe."

"Uhh."

"I know it sucks, but we need some help here."

"Uhhlll … awright, awright."

Joe shook his head, slowly opening his eyes to see what it was that Jeri needed now. He hoped it wasn't the sink again; he'd just spent enough time getting the damn thing fixed once and—

"So, what happened to you?" Nightstalker asked as he peered down at Joe. The Light Knight took one look at the bat's furry face and let out a scream. He backed away on his hands and feet, as if trying to prove the horror movie notion that such movement actually halted death.

"Joe, it's all right!" Nightstalker yelled, holding up his hands for calmness. "It's me, remember? Nightstalker, Shadow Knight?"

Joe continued his scream for about a second more and then bit down on it as his memories started to return.

"Good. I was afraid we'd have to gag you or something," Nightstalker said, extending his hand to Joe.

The Light Knight took it, and as he was pulled to his feet, he asked, "What kind of training did you have?"

"The weird kind," the bat replied. "Rastla took me into this big meeting place where they were having this huge argument about a bill. She … she told me to listen to them speak and tell her what I heard. I didn't hear anything at first, but then … it was like I could hear other voices under theirs. Every one of them was thinking so many things, things they couldn't say out loud. And I could hear it all in this weird rhythm, like—"

"Like a heartbeat," Joe said.

"You heard it too?" Nightstalker started in disbelief.

"I'm not sure. I heard what people were hoping for. What exactly did you hear?"

"It was pretty jumbled," Stalker said. "But I remember one guy. He was agreeing with another guy who made a speech, and the other voice was saying, 'Yeah, Tom, keep talking. It keeps you away from home when your wife and I are doing it.'"

Joe cringed as he said, "I see what you mean."

"Rastla called it 'hearing the dark places, the place where secrets are buried, but do not rest,'" the bat said. "All I know was that it was mostly nasty stuff."

"Then forget it," Joe said as he turned from the bat and finally looked around.

The two Knights stood on a rocky plain, empty of everything but gray rocks and crevices all around. Nothing was alive about them, save for him and the bat.

"I don't suppose you have any idea where we are?" Joe asked.

"Not a clue. And looking up doesn't help either."

"What do you mean?" Joe asked as he turned his gaze to the heavens. But the second he did, understanding hit his brain like the air at a Grateful Dead show. The sky above was like watching a hundred paintballs thrown inside a high speed dryer; colors flashed and twisted across the heavens through bolts of lighting and the crack of the thunder.

"Jesus," Joe whispered. He brought his head and down and looked back at the bat.

"That's about what I said," Nightstalker said. "I guess this is some sort of ultimate test or something. It's got that feel to it, doesn't it?"

"It does," Joe agreed. "I feel like I'm trapped in *Labyrinth* or something."

"You don't think we'll be fighting David Bowie then?" Nightstalker asked.

"I wish," Joe said as he looked around. "Still, if this is a test, I don't think you and I will be the only ones to take it, do you?"

"Yeah, Wolfie might actually come in handy here," the bat replied.

"Have you seen her?" Joe asked. "What about the others?"

Before Nightstalker could answer, an all-too-familiar voice yelled out, "Hey, leather wing! You got something or what?"

"Never mind," Joe said as Sandshifter moved over a nearby rock and came to stand with them.

"Well. I see the little light boy actually made it through his training," the wolf said, glaring over at Joe.

"And I see you didn't get yourself killed," Joe said back. "Kudos."

"Look, guys, maybe we should focus on getting out of the large, empty world instead of snapping at each other?" Nightstalker said.

"You're right," Sandshifter said. "But you aren't one to give orders."

"But I am," Joe added.

"Still got you thrown in this place with us," the wolf said back. "Doesn't that sound great? You should've let me kill them before. Then maybe we could be home right now and ..."

"Please cut it out," Nightstalker said. "We don't need this."

"What? The truth?" the wolf sneered. "Oh sure, let's go with that. Let's pretend that we're not here at the bequest of people who brought us back from the dead to be their servants and—"

The wolf's speech was cut off, transformed into choked words and gasps for air, as Nightstalker's hand was suddenly around her throat. As Joe looked on in surprise, the bat lifted the wolf off her feet and then brought her right in front of his face. "I'm really not in the mood for

— 113 —

this shit," the bat whispered, all the warmth and humor gone, replaced by a brittle, cold voice that seemed to shoot white mist out of his mouth as he spoke. "I'm only gonna say this once. I don't need to hear your bullshit. He doesn't need to hear your bullshit. The people back there don't need to hear your bullshit. So until we get out of here, you are not going to speak your bullshit. This is bigger than what you want; this is what we need to get out of here. And that means we need to you to do it. But I'm not afraid to try it without you. So if you speak one more word about how terrible all of this is, I will rip off your limbs, tie you to a rock, and leave you here for eternity while the rest of us leave. And I will not regret it; hell, I'll enjoy it. Do you understand me?"

Sandshifter gave out another choked gasp and then jerked her head in what could've been a nod. Nightstalker took it as such and relaxed his grip, causing the wolf to fall to the ground. Sandshifter took huge whooping gasps of air as the bat wiped his hand on his tunic and began to walk off toward the rock where the wolf had first appeared, giving a small gesture for Joe to follow.

"Where ... did ... *that* ... come from?" Sandshifter managed to spit out as she rubbed her throat.

"I'd like to know that myself," Joe said. He remembered how Nightstalker had seemed to be in pain during his transformation, during the part where Joe had felt the good memories of his life expanded on. And once again, he wondered what exactly had been done to the man Nightstalker had been and just who that man had been for the Queen of Shadows to choose him as her Knight.

But that was for another time; for now, Joe extended his hand to the wolf. Sandshifter looked at it a moment and then shrugged and pulled herself up. Moving past Joe, she followed the bat toward the large rock. Joe watched as the two man-beasts walked off and then sighed and followed.

X.

"Hey look, they're back!" Windrider yelled, leaping to his feet as the figures of wolf and bat and man approached the remaining Knights.

"Ah see you're not too worse for wear," Forester said as Joe approached the group. "Some of us had a rather unpleasant time gettin' here."

"I didn't have that much fun either; believe me," Joe said

"Well, the important thing is that we're all together and we can actually put together a plan to get out of this place," Thunderer said.

"We'd better," Wavecrasher added.

"Hey, I gave ya some ideas!" Groundquake snapped.

"Oh yeah. The 'let's just walk around till we find something' plan. Brilliant."

"Knock it off, you two," Joe said, putting up his hands for quiet. "We aren't going to figure out anything if we stand around arguing. Now, does anyone have an actual plan we can put into action or what?"

"I'd say our best shot might not be too far from what Groundquake suggested," Forger said suddenly.

"Ha! Toldja, fur ball!" the dog gloated.

"What do you mean?" Nightstalker asked.

"I don't know what you guys went through, but every part of my training so far has been me trying to do something, doing it, and then getting sucked into something completely different," the spider explained. "So logically, we should be doing some sort of task here."

"Makes sense. But we don't have any idea what we're supposed to do," Firesprite said.

"Maybe not, but I think she's right," Windrider said. "It's like a video game—we went through all those tasks so we could get strong enough to take on the big boss. So we just have to find him."

"Not necessarily. We might just have to get somewhere and do something," Forger said. "Of course, the kid might be right, too."

"Don't tell me you're buying into this?" Sandshifter snapped. "It isn't crazy enough that we've been sucked into some sort of nuclear test site gone bad. Now you wanna tell me we're supposed to play *Mario Bros.* for real?"

"Of course not. Do you see any turtles and mushrooms around?" Nightstalker asked.

"Pop culture aside, I agree with Forger and Windrider," Joe said. "We must be here to complete something for our training. It's probably to teach us to work together or something."

"Ah'd say we're screwed already," Forester said. "But at least Ah'm here to help out."

"Oh yeah. Ya can grow flowers for the monsters just before they eat us," Groundquake grumbled.

"Hey, don't you mock me, boy! Ah learned tricks that would leave you on yer back!" the squirrel shot back.

"Oh, and ya think I didn't?" Groundquake said as he reached for his hammer.

"Knock it off, both of you!" Nightstalker yelled. "We've got enough problems without this stupid infighting. Every one of us learned how to do something from this; you guys aren't special."

The two Knights looked at each other and then glanced at the bat. After a second of looking at his angry red eyes, they both backed away from each other.

"Well, now that that's over, what should we do, fearless leader?" Sandshifter asked, glaring at Joe.

"That's what we're talking about here," Joe said.

"Oh, but you're the leader. Surely you must have some idea of what to do," the wolf said.

"Well, we obviously need to get somewhere and do something," Joe began.

"Great. Simple as daytime TV. So where do we head?"

Joe started to answer and then stopped. Quietly, he began to listen for heart-speech from the wolf. It told him that giving any kind of answer was just what the wolf wanted. She'd be able to twist it around into an indictment within seconds.

This seeing the heart trick really is a useful little trick, Joe thought. *Too bad it's no good to me here—not in this rock covered wasteland. Oh wait!*

"Actually, I don't know where we're supposed to go," Joe

replied as Sandshifter smiled. "But I do know how to figure it out. Groundquake?"

"Yeah?" the dog asked.

"When you got your training, you learned how to work with the earth, right?"

"Whadda you think?" the dog said with a smile. He held his hand over the ground, and following a low rumble, a pillar of earth shot up, stopping at the dog's hand.

"Very nice. Now I want you to listen to it," Joe said.

"'Scuse me?" the dog asked.

"Yeah, Joe, I'm kinda lost here," Thunderer said.

"Do you remember how the Architects said that Stalker and I had power over the human heart?" Joe asked. "Well, when I was getting trained, I learned that I can actually listen to a person's heart and learn about the things he or she hopes for. And Nightstalker said he could hear the things people keep secret."

"Cool trick. But how does that help us?" Firesprite asked.

"Well, think about it. If Stalker and I can listen to the thing we have power over, why would we be the only ones? Why can't Wavecrasher listen to the ocean or Windrider the wind?"

"I think I get where you're going with this," Forger said. "You want Groundquake to listen to the earth and see if it can tell us if there's anything around here."

"Oh yeah, that idea totally makes sense," Groundquake snapped. "C'mon, man, it's earth! It's rock and dirt! How am I supposed to talk with that?"

"You'll never know unless you try," Thunderer said. "Besides, what can it hurt? Worst case scenario, we're no worse off than we were before."

"And it does make sense," Windrider said. "I mean, if we have power over these things, why can't we talk to them? Aquaman does it all the time with fish."

"I don't know what frightens me more," Sandshifter grumbled, "that I'm stuck with a comic book nerd, or that his suggestions are making sense."

"We don't really have anything left to try here. So why not?" Wavecrasher said.

"Fine, fine," Groundquake grumbled. "But if one of you laughs at me, I swear I'm gonna throw a rock at you."

"Try it first. Then we'll see about laughing," Nightstalker said.

The dog nodded. Kneeling down, he placed his ear on the ground, listening as if the earth was a giant seashell. The others all watched as the dog's ears strained to hear something. Seconds passed and then minutes as Groundquake knelt there.

Suddenly, he gasped aloud. "I-I think I hear somethin'."

"What is it? Voices?" Joe asked.

"Yeah! And they're all sayin' somethin," the dog replied. "They're sayin' 'Man this guy's an idiot for trying to hear us.'"

"You could be a little more open here," Forger said. "If what Joe and Nightstalker say is true, then there's every reason in the world this should work."

"Yeah, except for the fact they were listening to people, not a buncha dirt," Groundquake snapped, sitting back up.

"Maybe so. But until you get a better idea, this is what we're doing," Nightstalker said. "It worked for me because I concentrated on trying to hear the voices. Maybe if you try harder, you can get something."

"Try to hear the voices. Right," the dog grumbled. But despite his words, Groundquake turned back to the earth, sighed, knelt back down, and closed his eyes.

The other Knights stood quietly, watching as Groundquake put forth all his effort into communicating with the earth he represented. Seconds moved by, flowing into minutes like a stream into a river. And as the time bore down on the Knights, their faith in both Groundquake and the plan began to fade away.

Finally, after twenty minutes had passed, even Forger had shaken her head and opened her mouth to suggest a new plan. But before she could say one word, Groundquake's hands suddenly dove into the earth. The dog let out another gasp, much louder than before.

"Quake, what is it?" Nightstalker asked. "Did it happen? Can you hear the earth?"

"Do you know, if you're joking again, I'm gonna rip you apart?" Sandshifter snarled.

"I-I'm not," Groundquake stuttered. "I can hear it. Oh God, I can hear it. This is ... this is like hearing James Earl Jones on slowed down audio inside a dark cave."

"What's it saying?" Joe asked as he knelt down by the dog.

"I'm not sure. I could hear somethin' before; it told me to stick my hands into the ground. Now, it's like I've got cranked up headphones going *inside my goddamn head.*"

"It's all right. You'll be fine," Joe said.

"I-I don't know how long I can hold this," Groundquake said, his voice trembling. "There's so much power here. I feel like I'm gonna get crushed."

"Then I'd say we need to move fast," Firesprite said. "Ask it if there's anything here that we need to see."

Groundquake nodded and closed his eyes as he thought the question at the ground. As he did, the others saw his face grow placid, the strain and fear passing out until he was almost normal again.

"The earth says ... It says it knows why we're here," the dog said, his eyes fluttering under his lids. "It says that Chirron told it we were comin'."

"Then does it know what we're supposed to do?" Joe asked.

"N-no," Groundquake said. "It just knows ... that there's a place we need ... ta go."

"Where? Is it the way out? Some sorta temple or place like that?" Windrider asked.

"It says ... that it ... was a place ...of great importance," Quake replied, "a few miles due north. It won't say ... what it was ... only ... that it fell ... years ago. It's ... been in ruins ... since."

"Well, that's encouraging," Forester said. "Can't ya get it to tell us any more than that?"

"It says ... Chirron forbid it to tell more than that," Quake said. "But it can ... tell us ... about the journey there."

"Good. What does it know?" Forger said.

Quake's eyes fluttered faster as he spoke. "We ... must take ... the route ... past the great eyes ... and the ... dragon teeth. After that, we'll find ... the field ...and the place ... But ... but ..."

"But what?" Sandshifter snapped. "What are we getting into?"

"It says we ... won't be alone," the dog got out. "It says ... that we'll find ... the ... I don't know ...what it means—best I can do is ... tenants."

"So people live around this place?" Forger asked. "Someone indigenous?"

"No … not people," Quake said, his eyes fluttering around like two butterflies on Jolt Cola. "Somethin' else—something … that … that …"

The others waited as the dog struggled to grasp the words the earth was feeding him. He struggled a few moments and then managed to spit it out. "Somethin' … that is always waitin'—something that … is hungry."

"Hungry. Are you sure that's the word?" Joe asked.

"Yes …. always hungry; it ate … it ate the world … all worlds … and it's still hungry."

XI.

"Well. Ah don't know about you guys, but my enthusiasm has dropped considerably," Forester said.

"Knock it off," Nightstalker snapped as he knelt by Groundquake. "Can you get anything else—what this thing is, what it looks like?"

"How we can kill it?" Sandshifter added.

Joe turned and glared at the wolf.

"It's something we might need to know," Nightstalker said as he looked back at Groundquake. The bat started to repeat Sandshifter's question, but before he could get a word out, the earth around the dog's hands first loosened and then released his hands, closing up the holes they had left in mere seconds.

The dog's eyes opened wide as he took in a great whooping gasp of air. The others watched and waited as his breathing slowed, resuming its normal rhythm.

"What happened?" Joe asked. "Why did it let you go?"

"It said that was all it could tell me," Groundquake replied.

"But it told us enough," Forger said. "We know what we've got to do now."

"Oh yeah," Sandshifter snorted. "Just go and find a couple of monuments that sound like they're *Indiana Jones* rip-offs and then fight a giant, world-eating monster. No sweat."

"Ah recall you wanting a fight before," Forester said. "Sounds like you've got a good one here."

"I prefer fights I might actually win," the wolf replied.

"We're in training. They wouldn't send us here if they thought we'd mess it up," Firesprite added. "'Sides, you've got all that anger that yer supposed to use. What better thing to take it out on?"

"We could win this," Windrider said. "Maybe we're supposed to go to those places so that we can get something we need. Or maybe something we do there will help us fight this monster."

Sandshifter looked at Windrider with an almost pitying expression. "You really think it'll be easy, kid?" she asked the falcon. "You really

— 121 —

think that we're just gonna find a magic sword that's gonna let us stab the monster in the heart?"

"Well, maybe not a sword, but something," Windrider answered.

"Right. Whatever you say," the wolf said, stepping closer to the bird. "Keep pretending you're in some sorta video game. But have you ever actually put your real life on the line?"

"Well … no. But I might've … I mean … I could."

"Yeah, you probably could. But it's gonna be a lot harder than pressing X on a controller. You could see what it's really gonna take to kill that monster—our blood, our teeth, everything we have—and then find out it might not be enough. What're you gonna do then? Are you gonna run? Are you gonna stay and fight? Do you even know if you'd make it that far?"

Windrider looked at the wolf, his eyes blazing with fury. But as angry as he was, the falcon's beak stayed shut. And the longer Windrider stood there quietly, the more the fury in his eyes began to dim, to be replaced by uncertainty. Sandshifter saw it, but for once, she had no reaction.

But that didn't mean that someone else did. An orange paw grabbed Sandshifter's shoulder and spun her around before she could even finish forming a snarl at being touched.

"Why don't you take your speeches and shove 'em up your ass?" Wavecrasher hissed at Sandshifter. "If he wants to go do this thing, it's his business."

"Fine. But I'm telling him the truth about it," Sandshifter said. "Maybe you should think about what he's getting himself into—"

"I think he knows plenty," Wavecrasher snapped. "He sure as hell understands more than you. We all heard what they want us to do. Do you think anybody thought it wouldn't be hard? Did you think we all saw it as a walk in the park? But I'd still let him do it, 'cause I know he'd keep trying, no matter how hard it got. You know how?"

The wolf gave no answer, so the cat went right ahead and answered her own question. "Because he actually wants to do something with— Oh, why bother! That doesn't seem to matter to you. You say that you know what's gotta be done, but when it comes down to it, you won't do it unless it's what you want, you hypocritical bitch. You don't even try to believe that we could have a higher purpose. And you figure it's easier to do that if nobody else wants to help either.

"Are you actually that selfish? Are you so unhappy with how this turned out for you that you wanna bring everyone down with you? God, grow up! If you wanna get anything good outta this whole thing, then try to think about what you might be able to do if you dug your head outta the sand and started looking around at the people that need you!"

Sandshifter stared at Wavecrasher, the other Knights echoing the wolf's disbelieving gaze. She growled under her breath and pulled her lips back, flashing her teeth at the cat. But Wavecrasher stood there, unmoved by the sight of the angry wolf or her pearly chompers.

The wolf took a few steps toward Wavecrasher, moved her eyes right up to the cat's, and held them a moment. Then she dropped her growl face, gave a tiny nod, and said, "Hmph." She then moved off to the side. The others stared in complete disbelief, until Wavecrasher said, 'So Quake, the ground said our first stop is north of here, right?"

"Uh, yeah, that's what it said," the dog replied.

"Then let's get going." the cat said. "Who can figure out where north is?"

"I think I've got an idea," Forger said, walking up to the cat. Holding out one of her hands, the spider gave a grunt, and as Wavecrasher watched, the skin on her palm began to change. The flesh began to stretch up as the bone underneath began to rise up in a circle. But as it grew, the skin seemed to fall away as something underneath, something shiny that looked hard, emerged. Finally, the process ended, and Wavecrasher looked at the metal cup that had grown out of Forger's hand.

"Fill 'er up," the spider said, gesturing to the cat.

"Huh?"

"You're the Water Knight, aren't you? If we're gonna find north, you need to help me here."

"Oh … right, right," Wavecrasher said. Holding her own hand over the cup, the cat clenched it into a fist, squeezing as tightly as a gold digger clutches her husband's throat. Water began to pour out of the fist, streaming down into the cup until it was full.

"Very nice," Forger said. "Now, for the last ingredient."

Holding out yet another hand the spider extended one finger, the flesh on it parting as a long, thin, metal needle popped out. Forger waited until it had stopped growing, then snapped it off and placed it inside her cup hand. The spider peered intently over the cup, as the metal needle first sank to the bottom and then began to rise to the top. Holding the cup steady, Forger watched as the needle drifted from side to side and then locked in position to the left of the spider.

"North is this way," Forger said, pointing in the direction of the needle.

"And how do ya know that?" Groundquake asked.

"Iron points to magnetic north," the spider declared, as she started to move in the direction the needle pointed.

"What's she babblin' about?" Groundquake muttered.

"Scouts," Windrider said. "Even I remember that."

"It's basic stuff, Quake. C'mon, let's go," Forger said.

"I don't recall makin' you leader, eight-legs."

Forger sighed and said, "I didn't ask to be. *Avez-vous jamais de ne pas se plaindre?*"

"What?" Quake asked as all the others stopped and stared at Forger, who stood there with a look of complete shock on her face.

"*Ce que le ce que je fais?*" she said. The spider took a breath, closed her eyes, and slowly said, "Why … am I … speaking French?"

"Why are you asking us?" Thunderer asked.

"I don't know why I did that," Forger said.

"It's a delayed reaction," Windrider said.

Everyone turned to him as he said, "Well, I just mean lots of times in comics, when heroes or villains lost their memories, they'd have little things come out that would steer them to their identities. Like if the Flash had amnesia and saw a lightning bolt, he'd get a … well, flash of memory or something."

"This wouldn't be regular amnesia," Wavecrasher said. "This is source amnesia. Normally, this would mean confabulation, which would signify brain disease. But these … bodies are supposed to be immune to that so—"

"Um, Crash?" Thunderer asked.

"Hmm?"

"How do you know that?"

"Well, I—" the cat began, only to stop in midsentence, the same look of confusion all over her face.

"Looks like this could happen to all of us," Stalker said.

"But that's great! We might be able to remember who we are!" Thunderer said.

"Or we might just get bits and pieces back," Sandshifter added. "And how are we even supposed to make it happen? We still don't know why the spider started talking French."

"Well, Quake did annoy me," Forger said. "But Crash's reaction was because Windrider mentioned amnesia symptoms. The rest of us might need a specific trigger to get our memories, and who knows what they are."

"She's right," Joe said. "And we can't sit around here trying to figure out what they are."

"Says the guy with all his memories," Sandshifter growled.

"No, he's right," Forger said. "God only knows what's in this place. Best we get out of here and then try to figure this out."

"Good enough for me," Joe said. "Everyone follow the giant gray spider."

*   *   *

The Knights followed Forger's compass across the barren land, passing such "memorable" monuments as rocks, dirt, and more rocks. Through it all, Joe urged the group forward as the Knights made their way toward the great eyes that would mark the first leg of their journey. It worked for a while, until even those who had some allegiance to Joe needed to stop.

"No breaks yet, guys," Joe said, glaring at Firesprite and Quake as they sat down on a pair of rocks.

"Mate, I'm not disagreeing with ya," Firesprite said. "But we've been goin' fer at least a couple hours. I think we earned ourselves a break."

"'Sides, I'm startin' ta get hungry here," Groundquake said. "Ain't we gonna get any food doin' this job?"

"Okay, let's take a break. But what do you expect we do for food?" Joe asked. "I doubt we'll find a Burger King around here."

As Groundquake sat and tried to answer that question, Thunderer suddenly spoke up. "We've just gotta put our heads together and think. I'm sure that the Architects don't mean for us to starve before we figure this whole thing out, right?"

"Yeah, keep believing that, horn head," Quake said. "I'm sure they'll just whip up a White Castle outta nowhere fer us."

The ram ignored the comment and looked around. After a moment, his eyes stopped on Forester. "Hey man, do you think you could come over here a sec?" the ram asked.

"Why?" the squirrel replied.

"Listen, Quake's hungry. I think there's a way you might be able to help him."

"And what would that be?" Forester asked.

"Look, you're the Knight of Forest, so you have control over plants and stuff. I'll bet if you concentrated, you could make something grow that we could eat."

"Ah suppose," Forester said. "But then again, this boy hasn't been much of a team player so far. All he's done is slow me down. Why should Ah do anything for him?"

"Cause I'm hungry, you twit," Groundquake growled. "It ain't that much for you to grow an apple, is it, fluffy tail?"

"Ah wouldn't insult someone whose help ya need, ya rude little Yank," the squirrel shot back. "Why don't you lick your ass? Ah believe dogs usually get their nutrients from there."

"You little stuck-up hillbilly!" Quake snarled as he moved to get up. But before he could, Thunderer got between the two of them, holding out his arms to keep them apart.

"Look, guys, we don't need to argue about this," the Thunder Knight said. "I don't think anyone's asking anything unreasonable."

"Oh, maybe it started that way," Forester said. "But Ah believe it's changed direction now."

"Forester, he's just hungry. And he's not the only one," Joe said. "At least try to make something?"

Forester seemed to think a moment and then said, "Ah would enjoy the quiet. But Ah think Ah would like an apology for the fluffy-tail comment."

"Yeah? Well, you can take your apology and shove it up your—" Groundquake started to say, but before he could finish, a pair of furry hands, one black, one gray, grabbed his ears and pulled his head back, forcing him to look up at the annoyed faces of Sandshifter and Nightstalker.

"Congrats. You've actually managed to get us to cooperate on something." Nightstalker said.

"Look, mutt, I'm not having a great time either," the wolf snarled. "But a little food would help. And if your stupid mouth is the only thing that's keeping us from getting some, then you'd better smarten it up. Get it?"

"All right, all right," Groundquake yelled. "Now will you let go already?"

Both bat and wolf complied, releasing their respective ears with a snap. Quake grunted against the pain, rubbing his ears as he reluctantly looked over at Forester. "I'm—I'm soooo … rrrrr … yyyy … for calling ya fluffy tail," Quake managed to spit out.

"See, that wasn't so hard, was it?" the squirrel said, with all the smug tone of a man that can afford his own planet. "Now, why don't Ah try to whip us some real food?"

"I hope Demtia gave you a good lesson on this one," Firesprite said. "I'd prefer not ta eat an apple that tastes like a squash."

"Ah wouldn't worry," Forester said as he held his hand out over the ground. "He said this was one of the easiest things ta do."

"And you did do it, right?" Sandshifter asked.

"Nah, he didn't tell me to demonstrate. But he called it a skill that was inside me, one I could do without thinkin'," Forester replied. "Now be quiet and let me work."

The wolf grumbled at that but kept quiet as the other Knights watched Forester pull off his glove and attempt to force his will upon the earth. The squirrel's fingers twisted and moved as his face strained with the effort. As the group continued to watch, they saw a green glow suddenly emerge from Forester's hand and wash over the ground.

The glow got brighter and brighter, spreading over the ground. The other Knights waited, looking for the first signs of life to sprout from the earth and deliver them food. And then, the light from Forester faded, leaving the ground full of … absolutely nothing.

"Without thinking. I'd say that's a perfect description for that little trick," Wavecrasher grumbled.

"I'd like to rescind my apology now," Groundquake snapped, looking up at the squirrel.

"What happened?" Thunderer asked. "You were doing something. Why didn't it work?"

"Maybe the earth can't grow anything here," Forester said, his voice just as surprised as the others were disappointed.

"If that was true, then the earth would be dead. But with Groundquake being able to talk to it, logic seems to say otherwise," Forger said.

"Well, Ah know Ah could feel somethin'," Forester insisted. "Ah'll just try again. Maybe Ah just need to use more power."

"Uh, guys," Windrider said, pointing to Forester.

"Oh, great. The mighty power of the forest will once again fail to come to our aid," Sandshifter grumbled.

"Guys."

"Oh, and what would your power do, oh, master of sand?" Forester snapped.

"Guys?"

"Look, I'm just going on what I see—"

"*Guys*!!"

"Ya got somethin' to say kid?" Groundquake asked as everyone turned to face the falcon.

"Uh-huh. I think that Forester did it," Windrider said.

"I think the absence of fruit might disprove that theory," Nightstalker replied.

"It might. But if you look at his hand," the falcon said, pointing to the squirrel's right hand.

"What does that have to do with anythin'?" Forester asked.

"Let's find out. Let us see your hand," Joe said.

Forester looked confused but still did what he was asked, bringing his hand up for inspection. The second he did, both he and the others understood what Windrider meant.

"Well, I'll be," Firesprite said.

"Demtia did say that it was something from within," Forger said.

"He was serious about it too," Wavecrasher said.

Forester just stared. Right in the center of his palm, attached to the flesh and fur, was a perfectly formed apple.

"Ah … Ah…"

"Yeah, I'm thinking the same thing," Groundquake said.

"I just thought about what Demtia said, and then I remembered Swamp Thing," Windrider said. "He got drenched in swamp crud and then his body started growing the plants of the swamp. So, I guess I thought about what Demtia said and put two and two together and ... well ..."

"I never would've thought of it," Forger said, shaking her head in disbelief.

"Okay, the kid can think outside the box," Nightstalker said. "But what are we gonna do about this?"

"You don't know?" Sandshifter asked. Before anyone could respond, the wolf walked over to the squirrel, grabbed his arm, and then held it steady as she reached over, grabbed the apple, and ripped it off with the sound of a cucumber being broken in half.

"So, Quake, you still hungry?" the wolf asked, holding up the apple.

"Uh ... no, not anymore," Groundquake said, his voice quavering just a little.

"Your call," Sandshifter said. She brought the apple to her mouth and took a big, crunchy bite. "Hmm. You make decent stuff, fluffy tail," the wolf said between bites.

But Forester took no notice, as he stared at his hand. The flesh and fur had peeled back when Sandshifter had ripped the apple away. What was left was a green, fleshy patch with a large hole in it. As he kept looking at it, the hole actually pulsed once, then twice and then sealed itself back up as the green skin changed back into normal, fur-covered flesh.

"Why is it that, despite being reborn as a man-bat, being sent through weird dimensions, and learning how to handle shadow, *that* creeps me out more than anything else?" Stalker asked.

"Good question, but I don't think it matters now," Joe said. "Forge, that compass still working?"

"Yeah," the spider replied.

"Then let's keep moving. Maybe we'll find something to eat that didn't come out of someone's body. And Forester?"

"Um?"

"Just a suggestion, but if you try that again, I wouldn't grow anything bigger than your hand. No telling where it could come out."

The squirrel looked at Joe for a minute and actually smiled a little bit. Joe returned the smile and then gestured to Forger to start leading the way.

*　　*　　*

The group continued to trek for the next few hours, or at least that's what it felt like it to them. With no sun or moon or any kind of timepiece, the Knights were forced to go by internal clock. And when coupled with the exhaustion they felt, those clocks ran very quickly.

"How long do ya think we've been going?" asked Firesprite, as she leaned upon her spear a moment and then kept walking.

"I'd say at least an hour or so since you last asked," Forger said, the compass still held out in front of her. "Don't worry, we'll get there soon."

"Ah'm pretty sure ya don't know what this thing looks like," Forester said. "So how can ya be so sure?"

"Well, we've been walking for a long while, so it can't be much further ahead," the spider replied, her voice staying calm and even. "Besides, even if we don't reach it today, it isn't gonna make too much difference. We haven't seen anything here that can attack us."

"Anyone ever tell ya you'd be the perfect Spock stand-in?" Groundquake said with a weary grin.

"Probably. It seems a logical assumption," Forger replied.

"Heh," the dog sniffed back, though his grin didn't fade.

"You know, as long as the two of you are here, I'd like to ask something," Joe said. "Quake, you said that we're looking for giant eyes right?"

"Pretty damn sure of it," the dog replied.

"Do you have any idea what that might mean?"

"Yer thinking of this now?" the dog asked in disbelief.

"I figured that whatever this thing was, we'd recognize it when we saw it. The word giant usually has that implication," Joe answered back. "But then I got to thinking. If there are giant eyes, that means something has to be attached to them. Do you think that means some sort of giant monster?"

"How should I know? I just repeated what the earth told me," Groundquake answered.

"I don't think it would be a monster," Forger said. "If it was, we would've heard about more of this thing than its eyes."

"Yeah, but last time I checked, the Crawlin' Eye counted as a monster," Quake countered.

"I still don't know for sure," Joe said, running his hands through his hair. "Damn it, why didn't I think of this before we got started?"

"Yeah, why didn't ya?" Quake snapped.

"Oh, knock it off," Firesprite snapped. "You didn't think of it either."

"'Sides, it don't much matter," the lizard continued. "We had to come this way, so we probably have to kill this thing if it is a monster. It's a part of the test."

"Well, yeah, but I woulda liked to know if I was fightin' a monster," Quake muttered.

"So would I, but Firesprite's right," Joe said. "We had to go this way, so there's not much we can do about it. Besides, we shouldn't think that this thing could only be a monster. It could be anything."

"Yeah? You still haven't said any alternatives."

"Well ... I suppose ... it could be—"

"It could be a pair a big tall stone towers with big circular tops that made them look like lower case *i*s."

At that, everyone stopped and turned to look at Firesprite. "And how did ya pull that one out?" Groundquake asked.

"Simple. I looked over there," the lizard said, pointing forward.

Everyone turned and gaped at what they saw. Rising up out of the ground was just what the Fire Knight had said—a pair of large brownstone towers that stretched up as tall as a pair of smokestacks. But instead of a hole at the top, each one held a large, circular ball of rock, held up slightly by each top's curving sides, making it look like a pair of tall *i*s.

"Well. I guess we can rule out the Crawling Eye theory," Joe said.

"The Crawling Eye? Oh yeah. Too bad, that woulda been cool," Windrider said.

"Why is it that every time you talk, I keep thinking that we're gonna have to stop you from charging a rhino one day?" Sandshifter asked.

"So we're here. What now?" Wavecrasher asked.

"For now, I say we take a real break," Joe said. "Besides, I think we've got a few things to talk about."

"Hey, whatever involves a break," Firesprite said and immediately plopped down.

"It may not be that much of a rest," Joe said. "After what happened with Forester, I think we need a little demonstration from everyone."

"Demonstration?" Forger asked.

"Yeah. He was able to make an apple grow out of his hand. But he didn't know he could do that," Joe said, looking at each member of the group. "We might all have powers we aren't aware of. And they could be a lot more dangerous than growing fruit. So while we rest, I want everyone to demonstrate what they know they can do. That way, we'll all know what we're capable of. And maybe we'll even learn a few new things."

"Not a bad idea," Forger said. "Knowing the depths of each other's powers could be incredibly important in whatever it is we have to do here."

"All right then, leader man," Sandshifter said. "What did you learn to do? Be a human night-light?"

"Something like that," Joe said, as he held up his staff. As before, he concentrated on an image of Jeri, and the stone glowed bright.

"Not bad, but not all that useful," the wolf said. "What else ya got?"

Joe just smiled as he released his concentration, dimming the staff. Holding out his hand, Joe summoned the light to him as he had against the monster. As the light ball formed in his hand, even Sandshifter's eyebrows went up in surprise. But Joe wasn't done yet. Turning around, Joe took aim at a large nearby rock and hurled the light ball forward. It flashed through the air in less than a second, burning out of view. Then the rock suddenly exploded in a burst of golden energy.

"So. Is that more useful to you?" Joe asked the wolf as the rubble rained down.

"Hmm. I guess so," Sandshifter answered. "Hey, bat boy, you're supposed to be pretty similar to him, right? Did you learn how to do anything like that?"

"Sorta," the bat replied. He held his hand out, palm up. As everyone watched, Nightstalker closed his eyes, and then a burst of flame suddenly ignited over his hand. But this wasn't ordinary fire. It was blackish-blue, almost the color of a night sky. Windrider gingerly reached out to touch it, only to draw his hand back the second he came close to it.

"You burn yourself?" Wavecrasher asked.

"No. It felt … it felt cold," the falcon answered. He rubbed his hand for warmth.

"Rastla told me this is called shadowfire," Stalker explained as he tightened his grip on the fire. "She told me that this is the purest form of shadow there is, and the most powerful. It can't harm me though."

"Darya told me the same thing," Firesprite said. "He said fire couldn't ever burn me again."

"Immunity to our own elements. Makes sense," Forger said. "Did Rastla say what this stuff could do?"

"She said that it was a weapon, the same as that light ball Joe conjured up," the bat replied. He closed his fist over the flame, extinguishing it. "But she did say that there were other forms I could use."

"Such as?" Forger asked.

Stalker turned to look at the spider, who waited for a reply. But Forger gasped a second later, as the bat's features suddenly were overtaken by a blackness that spread over him like a shroud or blanket, covering him and then pulling his form down into itself and vanishing.

"Holy crap!" Forester yelled. "The shadow ate 'im!"

"Oh, come on, that's stupid," Quake snapped. "He said the shadow couldn't hurt him, remember?"

"Well … what else would you call it?" the squirrel asked.

"I'd call it a damn good question," Firesprite said.

"Wait a second, guys," Windrider said. "I know. He didn't get eaten by his shadow."

"What? Y'all wanna be technical and say he was absorbed?" Forester asked.

"No. He *became* his shadow," the falcon said eagerly. "There's lots of guys in comics that can do that. Why shouldn't he be able to do it?"

"Kid's got a point," Thunderer said.

"But then where is he?" Sandshifter asked.

"Closer than you think," the bat's voice suddenly said. The Knights whirled around, only to gasp as they saw the dark form Nightstalker had become rising up out of Sandshifter's shadow. It began to take shape and grow in detail and color, until Nightstalker stood before them again.

"How—Oh, why bother? I'm sure you've got an explanation," Sandshifter said.

"Rastla showed me that shadows are basically like water for me now," the bat explained. "She said I could enter it at any time and use it to travel to another shadow at a different point."

"Cool. Did she give you a limit on how far you can go?" Windrider asked.

"Um … no. She just said, 'Think of where you want to go and let the shadow take you there,'" the bat replied.

"Not bad," Firesprite sad. "What other tricks ya got?"

"Just one right now. Rastla told me that I … I had the power to look into people's hearts."

"Really? And the ribcage doesn't stop you?" Quake asked.

"Not literally. I can sense the secrets people keep buried down in the dark," Nightstalker explained. "Joe says he can do the same thing."

"Not exactly," Joe replied. "I can only see the things people hope for."

"Wait a minute," Sandshifter said. "You mean you two have these powers, and you didn't think of what they could do?"

"What are you talking about?"

"You morons!" the wolf yelled. "You can use them to find secrets in people's minds! Like, oh I don't know, our names! Our lives!"

"I … you know, she's got a point," Stalker said. "I mean, if I can see things that are hidden, maybe I can find something out."

"Oh hell, I'll volunteer for that!" Groundquake said, as he stepped in front of the bat. "C'mon, take a look in here!"

"No way; this was my idea!" Sandshifter said, growling at the dog.

"I don't care whose idea it was," Nightstalker said. "I've only done this once and I could drive someone insane going into his or her mind."

Sandshifter immediately backed off and said, "All yours, dog boy,"

"Hold on a second!" Joe said. "How do we even know this will work? He said he could see people's secrets, and none of you even remember your secrets."

"Maybe they're buried in there," Windrider suggested.

"And how are we supposed find secrets that we can't remember anything about?" Wavecrasher said. "I'm with Joe; this is a bad idea."

"But what if it did work?" Thunderer asked. "I mean, maybe he could just take a look or something?"

"Maybe, but why would I get a power that would allow me to find info the Architects wouldn't tell us?" Stalker asked.

"Let's find out!" Quake snapped as he grabbed the bat's hands and slammed them onto his head, holding them down as Stalker tried to pull away.

"You idiot! Let him go!" Firesprite snapped, grabbing her spear.

"Wait, look at his eyes!" Windrider said, pointing at Stalker.

The bat's struggles had lessened; his black pupils began to expand, the red vanishing under them. But it wasn't only the bat; Quake's eyes were already dark and glistening.

"Oh dear God; we've got to break them apart," Joe said.

"That's what I'm going to do," Firesprite said as she stepped between them and started to place the butt of her spear under Quake's hands.

"*No!*" Windrider yelled, causing everyone to stare at him.

"They're linked! If we break them apart now, we don't know what could happen," the falcon explained. "They could wake up insane, or maybe we'd send them into a coma."

"And how do you know?" Sandshifter asked.

"Because that's what always happens in mind reading."

"Knights."

All conversation ceased. The Knights turned to see Stalker and Quake, as the voices of Rastla and Chirron had spoken through them in unison.

"Your minds will hold no answers for you. Secrets cannot be held without memories."

"Told you," Wavecrasher whispered angrily.

"Do not attempt this again. Further efforts will only result in madness. Continue your training."

The voices faded away, as did the black from the two Knights. They stood still a moment, and then Stalker yanked his hands back from Quake's head.

The dog shook his head and snorted and then looked at the others and asked, "What happened?"

"Nothing," Joe said. "It was a dead end."

"But ... I heard Chirron's voice in my head," the dog said. "You mean even he didn't—"

"You heard Rastla too," Stalker said. "We aren't going to find anything this way. Just like I thought."

"Well ... what if Joe reads me?" Quake asked.

"I can only see hopes, not secrets," Joe answered.

"I ... aw crap," Quake muttered, getting to his feet and kicking the ground. Even Sandshifter didn't say a word; she just gazed ahead unhappily.

"Well, uh, at least we can use those abilities in the future," Forger said to break the tension. "You two could see if somebody was lying or not or figure out what we'd need to do help someone."

"And be useless for everything else," Sandshifter muttered.

"And speaking of being useful, why don't you stop sulking and show us what you can do?" Joe asked.

"Excuse me?" the wolf snapped.

"We're all giving demos, so show us what you can do. Use those sandy powers of yours if you can."

"If you insist. But it's your funeral," the wolf replied with a grin. As everyone watched, the wolf's body began to change; the flesh and cloth and fur became paler, as if the sun was beating down on her with all of its force. The fur withdrew into the flesh, as the skin and clothes began to be pitted and less solid. The transformation was complete in a few moments—the wolf's body had become pure sand.

As the others looked on, the sandy body before them suddenly broke apart, spilling down onto the ground and forming a man-sized pile of the stuff that sat unmoving, without any sign that it had once been a woman.

"What? This is it? She can turn into a big pile of dirt?" Quake asked.

"Give her a sec," Joe warned. "I doubt she'd choose such a quiet display."

"C'mon, she's a pile of sand," Firesprite argued, pointing at it with her spear. "What else can she do?"

"I'd say we're about to find out," Wavecrasher said as she suddenly began to back away.

The others turned to see what was going on, but before they had finished, the sandpile, which had begun to draw into itself, exploded outward, whirling around them and trapping them in a sandstorm. All around them, the grains of sand flew, blinding their eyes and pulling their coats in all directions.

"What the hell is she doing?" Nightstalker yelled.

"Showin' off!" Wavecrasher yelled. "And I don't think she's done yet!"

The cat's words sadly proved true. Before the Knights knew what happened, the sand swirling around them began to come together slightly, forming solid forms inside the sandstorm. The forms it chose were giant arms that reached out, grabbed the Knights and pulled them deeper into the swirling sands like cows into a tornado. At such close range, the Knights were forced to close their eyes and mouths, unable to speak or even see without being blinded or muted by the sands. The sands began to spread, traveling along each Knight's body, and as it covered their legs, each mass actually broke apart, half of it staying on the legs, and another half moving along the upper body.

The second half traveled along the Knights' backs, reaching their shoulders and then stretching out over their arms. Once they had covered over the muscles and bones, the sands somehow managed to pull the arms backward, dragging them to the small of each Knight's back, despite each Knight's protests. Then, the sands wrapped over their wrists like a pair of liquid handcuffs, while the sand on the legs formed a pair of manacles. Once each sandy trap was formed, it stiffened and then grew hard, forming an almost baked piece of sand that was clamped hard around each Knight's limbs, trapping them.

The sandstorm suddenly came to a halt. The arms holding the Knights up vanished back into the departing sands, causing the Knights to fall to the ground. Landing with a thud, Joe managed to look up in time to see the sands coming back together into the pile that was slowly rising up into the familiar form of Sandshifter. The Light Knight looked on angrily as the sand changed back into fur and flesh and cloth, growing until the wolf was finally back, staring at them with a very pleased grin on her face.

"So, you think I did all right, boss?" she asked mockingly.

"Oh, that was very impressive," Joe said through his gritted teeth. "I'd just like to say that if you need us for your demonstrations, *tell us*!"

"But it was just sand. It couldn't have hurt you," Sandshifter said as she looked over at Firesprite.

The lizard glared back, but said nothing.

"I wasn't gonna hurt anybody," the wolf continued. "I just wanted to show that I could do that. And I still can. Anytime I want to."

"Bully for you," Nightstalker said. "Now, can you please let us go?"

"Oh, of course," Sandshifter replied as she waved her hand.

Instantly, the sand manacles softened; spilling down over the Knights' limbs, the sand returned to its master and reformed into Sandshifter's body. Once the wolf was complete, each breathed a sigh of relief—except one.

"You know, I meant to ask. How many grains of sand does it take to make a wolf lady?" Groundquake snapped, as he brandished his hammer.

"Come and find out," Sandshifter replied.

The dog smiled back and then charged the wolf, his hammer at the ready. Sandshifter stood there quietly, barely concerned with the attack. And her apathy was rewarded, as Thunderer and Firesprite grabbed Groundquake, holding him back.

"What are you doing?" the dog yelled. "Did you miss what she just tried to do to us?"

"No, but fighting her won't help anything," Thunderer said.

"He's right, mate," Firesprite said. "Even if she is a bitch, we still need her."

"She don't seem to think she needs us," Groundquake snapped.

"She might change her mind. We've gotta at least give her that. Besides, how would we get rid of her?" Thunderer said.

Quake struggled a moment more, but as the words sank in, he stopped, nodding to the others to let him go. They did so slowly. Once they had released their grip, he didn't go after the wolf. Instead, he gave her an angry glare and walked off.

"Infighting won't help us here," Joe said as he walked up to the front. "But I swear to God, Sandy—"

"That's not my name," the wolf growled.

"I don't care. If you ever do something like that again, I am gonna make sure that all further demonstrations are taken out on you. Understand?"

The wolf growled again, but as Nightstalker moved over to stand by Joe, the growl died in her throat, and she gave a simple nod.

"Good. Now I'm tired, and I think we've gone far enough to camp for the night. Firesprite, would you mind if your demo was making a campfire?"

"Not at all," the lizard replied.

"Good. Forester, you get him the wood we need. Try to grow a little more food too, but remember to stick to stuff that fits in your hand. The rest of you, sit down and take a load off. Oh, and, Sandy?"

"What?!"

"Could you go with Forester and give him a hand? You know, just in case he does grow something in a space he can't … reach far enough into. Okay?"

The wolf growled once again but walked over to the squirrel, not willing to challenge Joe or Nightstalker for the time being. Joe watched her go off and then shook his head, wondering how in the name of God he was ever going to get the wolf to work with them.

XII.

DESPITE ITS TUMULTUOUS BEGINNINGS, the resting period was still good, and the Knights managed to enjoy it. Forester managed to grow an excellent pile of fruit for the others to enjoy, as well as firewood. He had also been able to happily witness the pained look on Sandshifter's face when he said he was growing a watermelon and wasn't sure where it would end up (it had turned out to be an orange in his hand instead). The group was currently sitting around the woodpile, awaiting Firesprite's demonstration of her powers. Holding her palm out, fingers splayed, the Fire Knight created a ball of flame that hovered just above the flesh of her hand. She held it there a moment and then threw it down into the pile, which instantly went up in a fiery blaze.

"Not bad," Joe said as he watched the fires burn. "Any other tricks you can show us?"

"Might have a few," Firesprite replied as she looked down at the fire pit. The lizard raised her eyebrows, and the fire suddenly erupted upward, shooting toward the sky like a volcanic eruption. The Knights' immediate reaction was to back away, but not a single spark broke free of the fire. Finally, Firesprite lowered her eyebrows, pushing them down like she was concentrating on her back taxes. The fire instantly fell back to earth, until it had reached the pile again. But it continued to fall, until all that was left of it were a few sparks on the blackened wood. As the others peered at it, Firesprite unclenched her eyebrows and the fire returned to normal.

"You know, I think I might actually like that one," Sandshifter said. "Anyone who could create a towering inferno and control it like that has to be useful where we're going."

"Glad you approve, mate," Firesprite replied. "But I was hopin' to use it for less dangerous things tonight."

"Such as?"

"Forger, think you can make a long metal pole, real thin, like for shish kabob?"

"*Oui*," Forger said. Holding up a single finger on one of her right arms, Forger caused the finger to stretch outward, growing long and shiny as the flesh became thin, sharp stainless steel. She grew the finger outward until it was at least a foot long, and then she causally reached over, snapped it off her hand, and tossed it to the lizard.

"Er ... won't cha' be needin' that?" Groundquake asked.

"She needs it the same way you needed a new face after Joe burned you up there," Wavecrasher said as liquid metal began to flow out of the missing finger hole, hardening as it reformed into a new finger. The spider flexed it as the metal slowly changed to flesh.

"So what exactly did we watch that for?" Sandshifter asked.

"Just be patient," Firesprite replied. She took large pieces of wood out of the remaining pile. Unsheathing her spear from her back sling, the lizard used the sharp tip to carve a hole into each log, making sure each was in the same spot. Taking the metal rod and some apples, Firesprite speared the fruit with the rod and then placed the wood on each side of the fire and stuck the rod into the holes, which held the fruits over the fire, cooking them as efficiently as an oven.

"All right, give that a few minutes, and we'll be chowing down on baked apples," Firesprite said as she sat back down.

"What if the logs catch on fire?" Forester asked.

"They won't,"

"Why not?" the squirrel questioned.

"Because I told the fire not to touch 'em."

"You told—Of course you did," the squirrel said, chuckling to himself.

"How'd you know to cook them like that?" Thunderer asked.

"I ... I dunno," Firesprite said after a moment's thought. "It just sorta ... popped into my head."

"Maybe that's what you did before," the ram suggested. "Maybe you were a chef or something."

"I wonder," the lizard said with a laugh.

"Or maybe you flipped burgers at Wendy's," Forester added.

"Eh. Wouldn't be too bad either way," the lizard replied. "After all, you'd still be coming to me when yer hungry."

"Point taken. It's too bad you'll never find out for sure," Sandshifter replied.

"Oh, you never know," Firesprite said. "I might find a few things out. Besides, it isn't that big of a deal."

"You aren't curious?" Nightstalker asked.

"Oh, a bit. But we were dead. Probably best we don't know anyway," the lizard replied.

"I agree," Windrider said. "This is probably the sort of thing where we sleep better not knowing."

"Or we might sleep better knowing," Groundquake argued. "I can accept it if my old life is gone, but I'd like to know what the hell it was."

"It's the past," Wavecrasher said. "No point in worryin' about it. Just focus on the future."

"Guess you're right," Stalker said as he looked out over the empty plain. "But I'd still like to know."

"Like the lizard said, you still might," Joe said suddenly. "But for now, why don't we focus on what we can learn at the moment? Thunderer?"

"Sure. But it's a bit limited at the moment," the ram said as he got to his feet. "Zeuia showed me a few tricks, but most of them work in different circumstances."

"Such as?" Groundquake asked.

"Well, he showed me how to turn into electricity and travel through machines," Thunderer began. "It was really cool. I ended up going through a computer. I was actually seeing the energy of the microprocessors connect and the motherboard sending out information to everything in the hard drive … but I don't know how I knew that."

"Looks like someone might've been a computer nerd," Windrider grinned.

"This from the comic book nerd?" Forester asked.

"Nerd factions aside, did he show you anything else?" Sandshifter asked. "The computer thing sounds pretty good, but I don't think we're gonna be fighting the Devil's robot anytime soon. And, kid, if that was a movie, don't tell me."

"There was one other thing," the ram said as Windrider closed his mouth. "He taught me how to harness lightning and use it. Lemme show you."

Everyone watched as the ram held up his gloved hand. There was a crackle in the air, and then the hand erupted in bluish white energy that crisscrossed and sparked across his palm. Thunderer grinned and then held his hand up high so that everyone could see.

"Cool," Windrider said as he stared at the hand. "What can you do with it?"

"Take a look," the ram said. He turned his palm toward the open plain before them. Extending his index finger, Thunderer gazed out at the open plain. As he did, the energy stopped crisscrossing and began to run together, moving toward his finger. It gathered there for a moment and burst out across the plains with a sound like a gunshot, a blazing line of white and blue that streaked through the empty space.

"Not bad huh?" Thunderer said as he turned back to face the others.

"Oh, I think we'll definitely have a use for that one," Joe said with a grin.

"And besides, the whole glowing electrical hand thing would be great on April Fool's," Nightstalker added.

"Yeah, long as they don't get electrocuted. I can see the headline now," Groundquake said. "Livin' Handbuzzer Fatally Shocking; April Fool's Death."

"Good way to start a career," Forester chuckled.

"Shockingly good," Wavecrasher added, which started them laughing.

After a few minutes, they stopped as they could smell dinner burning.

"Aw, shit!" Firesprite swore as she raced over to the fire pit. She stuck her hands into the flames and brought out the fruit, which had only just begun to burn.

"Well, it's a little more charred then I intended but still good," the lizard said, holding the metal stick up. "So, who wants what?"

"Isn't that hot?" Forger asked.

"Mm? Oh. No, not really," the lizard said.

"It was on the fire for twenty minutes. And you don't feel the heat?" the spider asked.

"Well, it's warm but nothing I can't handle," Firesprite replied.

"Glad to hear," Sandshifter said, pointing to the apple atop the pole, "especially when it saves my dinner."

XIII.

ONCE THE MEAL HAD been saved, the Knights were granted dinner and a show as the remainder of their ranks gave demonstrations of their powers. Wavecrasher showed how she could summon water from the air, control its form and shape, and liquefy her body. Groundquake turned his body to rock and willed the earth around him to shake and erupt upward. Windrider made small windstorms, flew, and though it took much concentration, created a tiny tornado in the palm of his hand. As for Forger, she turned her body to steel, created metal shapes from within her body, and then engaged in a theoretical discussion with Windrider on one aspect of her power.

"I'm not sure about this," the spider said.

"Aw, come on. It makes perfect sense," Windrider insisted. "You're a spider; you must be able to make webs somehow."

"Number one, spiders shoot webs from their rear. Number two, if that bit of information is still the case for me, then this is going to hurt tremendously."

"But it would be funny," Groundquake said.

"Forge, I happen to think the kid's got a good idea," Joe said. "Just try what he asks; it can't hurt. Besides, it worked for—"

"I am not going to test this based on a comic book!" Forger snapped. "Peter Parker should've died from radiation, not been given superpowers. It's the dumbest science ever."

"Look, we're all doing this to demonstrate the range of our powers so far. You've been able to control how the metal exits your body so far. Besides, if you're right about where the webbing comes from, don't you want to learn how to control it?"

Forger started to argue but then, seeing no logical argument against Joe's words, sighed, and said, "Okay, can you show me again?"

"Like this," Windrider said, turning his palm up and pressing his middle fingers into it.

Sighing again, Forger raised her middle right hand and imitated the pose. She opened her mouth to say, "See, nothing" only to gasp as a metal chain suddenly burst out of a hole in her wrist, shot forward, and hit Groundquake right in the jaw. The dog toppled over with a grunt and a thud.

"Whoa," Windrider said, as he gleefully turned back to the spider. "See? I told you it was like the comics!"

"Well, I suppose it's better than the alternative," Forger said as she stared at the chain coming out of her wrist.

"And it *was* funny," Forester said as Wavecrasher and Firesprite helped Quake back up, the dog's broken jaw already reknitting itself.

"So what are you gonna do with the chain?" Nightstalker asked.

"Well, I suppose if it's part of me, I can just will it back in—"

But before the spider could finish, the chain suddenly raced back up her arm and into her wrist, the hole sealing itself the second the chain was inside.

"Amazing," the spider said as she looked over her wrist.

"Not the word I'd use," Groundquake muttered. His jaw clicked all the way back in.

"Maybe we should hold off on the demos for now," Firesprite suggested, "unless anybody can do somethin' without causing bodily harm."

"Probably not," Nightstalker said.

"But Ah wanted to show some stuff," Forester complained. "Ah guarantee it woulda been amazin'."

"I think you've done that already," Sandshifter said. "But please, if you feel the need to pass a watermelon, I'd be happy to watch."

The squirrel just glared at the wolf. Sandshifter sat there grinning for a few more seconds and then suddenly yelped and jumped into the air as if someone had shot her from a cannon.

"Okay, that totally wasn't random," Nightstalker said as the wolf landed on her feet. Rubbing her backside, Sandshifter turned back to the spot she'd been sitting, only to see a small but thorny-looking bush poking out of the ground. Her eyes narrowed as she turned to the squirrel and growled at him.

"Like Ah said, amazin'," Forester said with a smirk.

"You wanna see something amazing?" the wolf snarled. "How about a squirrel man that bleeds green?"

"Ya dummy, Ah heal. There's nothin' you can do ta me."

"Oh, I'd be more than happy to try. And try. And try." Sandshifter snarled as she leaped at the squirrel, who rose to his feet immediately.

But before the two combatants could even come close to battling, a white mist suddenly sprayed over Sandshifter. There was a sound like tinkling bells and then the mist vanished, revealing the wolf frozen solid, small bits of ice and snow dripping from all over her body. Even her face was covered in ice, though her eyes moved around in utter confusion.

"Guess I forgot to show you that trick," Wavecrasher said as she stood by the fire, her outstretched hand still creating the white mist.

"Thanks for that. Now Ah can find out what frozen wolfie tastes like," Forester said as he drew his ax. He approached the frozen wolf, but before he could get close, a ball of light suddenly whizzed in front of his face. The ball then exploded in a wave of gold mere inches from his face. Forester cried out in surprise and pain, dropping his ax and clutching his eyes as he stumbled blindly in pain. As he staggered about, Forger stood up and pointed her hands at the squirrel. She flexed her palms and just as before, chains shot outward. They shot toward Forester's feet and wrapped around his ankles, binding them together. Once they were in place, Forger suddenly pulled on the chains, causing the squirrel to fall onto his stomach with a thud.

"How the hell did you learn to do that so fast?" Firesprite exclaimed.

"I figured that if I could retract them just by thinking it, it should work that way for other things," Forger said. "I just can't believe it was that easy."

"Don't knock it, mate."

"Uhlll—Which one of you bastards did that?" Forester moaned. "Ah swear, Ah'll—"

"Who do you think did it?" Joe said as he moved over to the squirrel.

"Oh … right."

"So what is it you're swearing to do to me?"

Forester muttered under his breath but said nothing clearly.

"That's good," Joe said. "Now then, I'd like to speak to you just for a moment. I can understand that you and Sandshifter don't get along. I'll be frank; I don't like her all that much myself. But we have to work with her."

"And what if Ah don't want to? Ah'm the one who can carry the ball here, boy, so you just give me the dang pigskin and lemme run it past that block for a touchdown so we can win the game."

"This isn't football!"

"Ah know it ain't! Why are you saying it is?"

Joe took a deep breath, and said, "You were just talking about it."

"Well, so what? Ah was probably right."

"See, this is why she doesn't get along with you and why I'm kinda fifty-fifty on you myself. I think you wanna do this thing, but you seem to have your priorities a little screwed up. *You* are not the one going through all this so *you* can save the world. *We* are going through all this so *we* can save the world. And if you keep pressing *you* over *we*, then I promise that these guys are not going to keep saving you forever. I promise that, one day, you will get eaten alive and *we* will not do a thing about it if you keep thinking about *you*. Do you get it?"

Forester gave no reply but just sat there clutching his eyes. Finally, he gave a slow, hard-pressed nod. Joe took that as enough and then turned to where Sandshifter stood, still frozen. He slowly walked over to the frozen wolf and looked at her with a look somewhere between disgust and exhaustion.

"Can she hear me?" he asked Wavecrasher.

"Hold on one second," the cat replied as she stretched out her index finger and made a circular motion. Instantly, two small holes appeared in the ice at the side of Sandshifter's head.

"She can now," Wavecrasher replied.

"Good," Joe said as he looked at the wolf. "So what was it? You decided that it was easier to pick on somebody other than me and Stalker? I know you don't want to be here. But as long as this is the way it is, you might as well try to deal with it like a grown-up and not a fifth-grade bully on a school camping trip, because, just like I said to your friend over there, sooner or later, these guys are not going to save you anymore. And I won't blame them for a single minute. So how much more of this crap are we going to have? Blink once for none, twice for less than that."

As Forester had done, the wolf didn't move for a moment (though it wasn't totally her fault) and then gave a blink.

"Good. Let her out," Joe said.

Wavecrasher nodded, and with a wave of her finger, unfroze the water. Sandshifter fell back to earth completely soaked as a pool of water dripped to her feet. She took in a few whooping gasps of air and then slowly got to her feet before Joe.

"You aren't gonna be able to tell me what to do forever," the wolf sneered.

"It looks that way," Joe said, folding his arms. "But tell me, is there any way to change your mind? Or will we keep playing out this scene until Judgment Day?"

"I'll tell you this much," Sandshifter said. "I'm still thinking about it."

"Uh-huh."

"But threatening the squirrel's not a bad start," the wolf said as she gave a small, slightly vicious grin.

Joe gave no response as the wolf walked away, toward Forester, who was finally beginning to open his eyes. The wolf glanced down at the squirrel but continued walking, eventually sitting down quietly at a rock just out of the firelight, as if she was putting herself in the corner.

*　　*　　*

That night (or what the group deemed as night), as the others slept, Joe leaned back on a rock, looking up at the ever-changing skies. Despite everything that had happened, Joe found himself completely relaxed as he gazed up into the strange, alien sky.

This must be what it's like inside a kaleidoscope inside an oil slick, Joe thought as he watched the various colors swirl and twist over the black canvas of the sky. *I could never get tired of this.*

"It is impressive, isn't it?"

Joe started and then turned his head to see Nightstalker walking over.

"Don't you wanna sleep?" he asked the bat.

"No. There's too much here to keep me awake," Stalker replied as he sat down next to Joe.

"The sky?"

"For one."

"Lemme guess about the rest—our new calm, peaceful friends?" Joe asked.

"How'd you ever guess?" Stalker asked.

"A hunch here and there."

"How did you keep your cool when talking with those two?"

"I've had to deal with a lot of angry people who can't get along," Joe said. "Believe me, I know those two very well. Forester isn't a bad guy, but he thinks that he has all the answers. And Sandy, well, she's just angry at the world. She wants what she wants and she can't think of anything else right now."

"And how did you deal with that sort of people before?"

"Well, I'd just talk to them and try to work things out. And after a while, I would just fire them if things didn't work out," Joe sighed. "But I don't think that's gonna work here."

"You're a more patient man then I," the bat replied. "I would've ripped their spines out through their mouth by now."

Joe raised an eyebrow at that, which the bat caught.

"Sometimes you need to be rough to get people in line."

"Sometimes," Joe said. "But I'll be honest, after that little stranglehold you had on Sandy before—"

"She needed it," the bat argued.

"Maybe. But it still surprised me."

"I'm not sure where it came from either," Stalker said. "I just knew she needed someone to tell her off and then—But I'll be frank, Joe, I did it because I knew you wouldn't."

"What do you mean?" Joe asked.

"You seem like a nice, reasonable guy. And after all that we've gone through, it probably takes a lot for you to stay that way. But that sort of guy can't always be the one to take charge in a situation, especially with someone like Sandshifter. She only responds to people that she's afraid of. And she may learn to respect you, Joe, maybe after tonight, but she's never going to be afraid of you."

"I wouldn't want her to be," Joe said. "Nobody who led out of fear ever did well with it."

"Not always. Some people need fear. Some people don't see anything else," the bat said. "And I learned something else when I was training, after I saw inside those hearts. I learned how to make people fear me. I can do that for you."

"Uh … thanks, then. But I hope it doesn't come to that."

"We'll see. Just remember, I don't mind causing fear for the right reasons," the bat said. "Maybe it's why I'm here."

The two of them sat in silence for a moment and then Nightstalker took it upon himself to speak. "So, what do you think of the rest of this crew so far?"

"Truthfully, I'm not sure yet," Joe answered. "But thus far, they're making a good case for themselves. And Forger is a good one to have around."

"Windy's not too bad either," the bat added. "Although I keep waiting for him to start telling us about comic books and anime that we could've died without knowing about."

"He's a kid. It's what they do," Joe said. "My son did the same thing when I … was around."

"What's he like?" Stalker asked.

"My boy?"

"No, the ghost of Elvis. Yes your boy. Good kid? Smart?"

"You bet your ass," Joe said. "He can take apart a blender and put it back together with the speeds doubled."

"Well, I feel inadequate now," the bat said. "I hear Windy talking about his PlayStation setup, and my head spins."

"Well, you're dead. Don't feel too bad about it. Besides, I couldn't understand half of what he did … back then," Joe admitted.

"Joe?" Nightstalker asked as the Light Knight fell silent. "Are you okay? I'm sorry if—"

"Naw, it's all right," Joe said, shaking his head a moment. "I … I guess I gotta start getting used to the way things are, huh?"

"You won't be the only one," the bat said, putting his hand on the man's shoulder.

"Thanks," Joe said, with a somewhat shaky grin on his face. Slowly, he extended his hand toward the bat. Stalker nodded and then stuck out his own hand. The two met, clasped, and shook but not without their hands glowing black and gold respectively.

Surprised, the two broke their handshake. Almost immediately, the glows dissipated, leaving their hands normal once again.

"I guess opposites do … something," Joe said, moving his hand about for emphasis.

"Looks that way," Stalker replied. "But I think that's enough male bonding for today. Night, Joe."

"Night," Joe said as the bat shambled off. Joe watched his new friend and then looked back up at the sky, his mind whirling and twisting as much as the colors above.

*   *   *

The next day, or at least the period after the Knights slept, saw them resume their long trek toward the dragon's teeth and then to the goal that awaited them. Forger led the way, her hand-compass pointing a perfect north the whole way. The others trudged behind, mostly together. Their time together was beginning to form the first semblance of friendship as Groundquake and Firesprite walked together, talking and laughing about what they remembered of the world they knew.

Wavecrasher, Windrider, and Nightstalker also walked together, though their discussion focused on the dangers that awaited them at whatever strange place their journey would lead them. As they walked, Windrider suggested that perhaps whatever horrible creature waited for them was some ancient beast, conceived at the beginning of time to destroy the world at the proper moment and that such moment had already passed. The cat asked him how it was possible for them to be walking on the world if the creature had destroyed it. Windrider, not batting an eyelash, replied that the Architects had sent them ahead in time to when the creature would destroy the world or created a place that replicated that very time. Stalker took a minute to go over the possibilities in his head, rubbed his forehead hard enough to bruise it, and then asked the falcon how many times he had watched *Back to the Future.* Windrider said he'd lost count after the last hundred.

Most of the other Knights walked together, with Thunderer doing his best to keep the mood light with words of enthusiasm, while Forester grumbled about the walk. Only two Knights walked alone—Sandshifter, which came as no surprise to anyone, and Joe, even though he was next to Forger. The Light Knight walked side by side with the spider, but he was focused on the conversation he'd had with Nightstalker the previous evening.

How can he seem so friendly and have such a grim outlook? Joe thought as he trudged along. But he knew the bat's words held some truth. Joe did have the advantage of his old morals and principles to guide him, while Stalker only had an uncertain future and the dark forces he was supposed to represent. And there was his power as well. When Joe had summoned the light to him, he'd felt the purest joy he'd ever felt in his life. Maybe the others had too, but he couldn't believe that Stalker had. The bat had seemed happier when he was done demonstrating the shadowfire. It was like taking a cold shower or

— 151 —

changing in a gym room filled with high schoolers; it was something he'd just wanted to get done.

What did Nightstalker feel when he used the power? Joe didn't know, but he wished he did. The bat was the first person that Joe thought of as a friend since he'd begun this crazy journey. He glanced over as Stalker let out a laugh at something Windrider mentioned. He briefly wondered what the joke was.

"Hold on!" Forger suddenly said, breaking Joe out of his mental quandary. This also meant Joe nearly ran into the spider, but he was thankfully able to stop himself.

"What is it?" he asked, as the others came to a halt behind him.

"I believe we have come to the end of the current stage of our journey," Forger replied.

"Oh, yeah? Any reason you're making that statement?" Groundquake asked.

"I actually have to ask the same question myself, Forge," Thunderer said as he looked around. "I trust your judgment, but I don't see any dragon's teeth around here."

"Like you'd actually know what they look like," Sandshifter muttered.

"They're likely giant teeth. They can't be that hard to find," Quake shot back.

"Giant, yes. But not actually teeth," Forger said. "Take a look at the rocks over yonder."

Everyone turned to face the large rock formation that had come up on his or her right side. Once they had seen it, they all understood just what the spider had meant. One large rock stretched out before them, supported by a series of small, long rocks placed in between them. Both sets of rocks were set upon a rock underneath that was nearly identical to the one on top. Together, they gave the image of a giant jaw, filled to the brim with sharp gray teeth.

"Well, why not?" Nightstalker said. "We've seen enough weird shit already."

"Point taken," the cat replied. "So how much further till we reach the end?"

"From what Quake told us, only a few hours," Forger replied.

"Thank God. I am sick of feeling nauseous every time I look up at the sky," Sandshifter said.

Everyone ignored the wolf's comment (a more and more frequent occurrence as the journey kept going) and prepared to continue the march to the last spot on their journey. But as the Knights started to move away from the dragon's teeth, Nightstalker suddenly paused and cocked his ears.

"Something wrong?" Wavecrasher asked.

"I dunno. I thought I heard something moving," the bat replied.

"C'mon. We haven't heard or seen anything since we got here," Firesprite said.

"Yeah, probably just your imagination," Thunderer said.

"I guess. But I could've sworn—"

"Don't tell him he's wrong."

Everyone turned around as Sandshifter glared back at them, her eyes daring them to say something back.

"Uh, Ah'm sorry. Did you just agree with one of us?" Forester asked.

"I don't have a problem saying somebody's right when they are," the wolf replied.

"So you heard something too?" Windrider asked.

"No. But I think that he did."

"And the reason ya think that is?" Wavecrasher asked.

"Because there's a smell in the air," the wolf replied, flaring her nostrils.

"I don't smell anything," the cat replied. "Anybody else?"

"I … yeah, I smell it too," Groundquake said suddenly, his own nostrils flaring. "Dear Christ, it's strong. How can you guys not smell this?"

"What does it smell like?" Joe asked.

"I dunno. One second it kinda smells like ripe fruit," the dog began.

"And then it turns into something covered in sweat," Sandshifter finished.

"Now it's turnin' into somethin' like garbage," Groundquake said, his face wrinkling in distaste.

"No, now it's like flower petals—fresh ones too," the wolf added.

"What is going on here?" Forester said. "Are you guys sayin' we're bein' stalked by a walking perfume case? A case that only you can smell?"

"It may be possible," Forger said. "Both dogs and wolves have incredible senses of smell. And maybe what we went through enhanced that."

"Like Wolverine," Windrider said. "Hey if that's true, maybe you guys can localize it, figure out wherever this thing is."

"I dunno if we can," Quake replied. "The smell keeps getting strong and weak every few moments, like something's getting closer and farther away at the same time."

"Well, that narrows it down, doesn't it?" Nightstalker said.

"Just everybody keep alert," Joe said. "Whatever this thing is, it seems to be staying around us, so maybe—"

But before Joe could finish, he heard a sound that made everyone believers. The unmistakable low rumble of rocks sliding down a dirt incline and crashing over each other as they moved filled the air. Joe's eyes glanced around as each of the Knights took in his or her own view of the scenery.

Whatever this thing is, it's real. And it is very close, Joe thought. The memory of the shape-shifting demon came sharply back into focus.

As the other Knights found their hands reaching for their own weapons, Joe felt his fingers brush the wood of his staff and then wrap around it. But he heard a scream shatter the air before he could draw the weapon—a scream that somehow managed to be low and piercing at the same time. Joe quickly drew the staff and whirled around toward the sound, but a spindly, jagged-looking figure suddenly leaped out into his field of vision and then landed on him, knocking him to the ground.

Joe struggled to push the creature off as the two of them rolled on the ground, the creature biting and clawing to get at his face. Joe managed to pull his staff up a few times to block the creature's attack, but that only seemed to enrage it further, as it redoubled its attack.

But before it could push through Joe's defenses completely, Stalker's black-gloved hands and Windrider's white ones managed to grab the creature and hurl it off their leader. Joe scrambled back his feet, to help his friends destroy this creature once and for all. But that plan fell apart as he saw both Windy and Stalker fall to their knees in pain. As Joe heard the other Knights engage the creature, he turned to check on his two saviors.

"Guys, what happened?" he asked as he moved in front of them. "Did you cut yourselves on it? Is there some kinda poison?"

"No, it burns!" Windrider moaned as he cradled his hands to his chest.

Moving over, Joe gingerly pulled the hands away and gaped at what he saw. The falcon's hands were raw and bleeding, covered in multicolored burns that were now oozing over his exposed flesh. But as Joe watched, he also saw the flesh beginning to heal, to seal up the wounds like candle wax.

"How bad?" Windrider asked, tears of pain already in his eyes.

"It's gotta be at least third-degree burns," Joe said, trying to remember the emergency chart he'd put up in the break room by the countertop stove. "But it looks like you're healing it up."

"Cool ... how fast?"

"Fast enough."

"Still in a lot ... of pain over here too," Stalker moaned.

"You'll be ok, Windy," Joe said as he moved over to Nightstalker. Like the falcon, the bat had his hands clasped to his chest. But when Joe pulled them away, he saw something totally unlike Windrider's injury. Stalker's hands were covered in white frost and ice, as if he'd stuck them inside a freezer for the last four hours. In the few exposed patches, Joe could see how the bat's fur had frozen together and the skin underneath had become gray and rough, as if from frostbite.

"This is impossible," Joe swore as he grabbed the folds of his coat and rubbed them over Stalker's hands, trying to warm them.

"Trying to ... warm a frozen ... bat's hand ... or this ... situation?" Stalker asked.

"What the hell is this thing?" Joe replied, as he rubbed as hard he could, feeling the cold even through the folds of his coat.

"Maybe if you ... take a look," Nightstalker suggested, gesturing behind him to where the others were battling the creature.

Joe looked over, half expecting to see a creature that leaked lava and ice from two different holes. Instead, he saw the other Knights dodging and trying to attack a tall, thin creature that looked like it was made out of some sort of living quartz. Its clear, crystalline body glowed with a strange, whitish light as it swung out at the Knights with its long, clawed arms. It was moving too quickly for its face to be visible, but Joe got a glance at what looked like long teeth and white, pupil-less eyes.

As he kept watching, he saw Wavecrasher dodge the creature's swipe and then bring her trident around, slamming it to the ground and pinning the creature's arm down. Joe mentally applauded the attack, but it didn't last long. As Joe watched, the creature pulled back on its arm, and it passed through the trident as easily as smoke. Wavecrasher stared in shock, an opportunity the creature took to bring its long foot around and slam it into the cat's face, sending her to the ground in a heap.

The creature didn't get time to enjoy its victory though, as a crack of thunder shook the air and a burst of white energy slammed into its back. It yelped in pain as Thunderer readied his rod for another burst. But he didn't notice Wavecrasher shaking off the kick. Stretching out her hand, already changing it into liquid, the cat released a blast of water at the creature, just as Thunderer released his second bolt. The creature, seemingly in pain, didn't react to the lightning coming its way—not until the last second. Just as the bolt was about to strike, the creature suddenly turned to the side and stuck out its arms, pointing one at the lightning and another at the water stream. As the two forces struck it, a burst of sparks and then gasps and howls erupted; the water, channeling itself through the creature's body, had leaped through its arm to strike Thunderer, while the lightning bolt had forced its way through Wavecrasher's body, causing her to writhe and howl in pain.

As both forces dissipated, the creature finally stopped long enough for its face to become visible, showing the Knights a pair of white eyes, a boar like nose, and a huge mouth with fangs coming from both the upper and lower jaws. It hissed through its teeth and glared at them, daring them to attack.

This time, it was Groundquake who answered. As he ran toward the creature with his hammer outstretched, Firesprite added cover behind him, throwing fireball after fireball at the creature. But the creature managed to sidestep everything the Fire Knight threw at it, except for two stray fireballs. Those two, it caught in its clawed hands and, before anyone knew what had happened, spun around and hurled them at both Quake and Firesprite. It struck the two of them dead on but without flame. Instead, Quake fell to the ground, his feet frozen to the earth while the lizard found herself flash frozen in a block of ice.

With six of its members already down, what remained of the Knighthood began an attack that was half plan and half desperation. Sandshifter pointed her arms at the creature, and they suddenly shot outward, growing long and huge as they transformed into sand. They wrapped themselves around the creature, trapping it within almost a half ton of sand. As Sandshifter held the creature steady, Forger added to the mix, shooting out chains from each of her hands. They dove inside the sands, whirling around inside as the two Knights created a prison of sand and steel.

But it wasn't to last. As Forger fed the chains into the sand, she suddenly found herself doubling her efforts; she felt something pressing against the chains, forcing them out. After a few seconds, she realized what it was.

"What are you doing?!" the spider yelled, as Sandshifter continued to force her will into her sandy fists.

"This thing is mine. If you wanted to kill it, you should've trapped it yourself!" she snarled back.

"Don't be stupid! We've got no idea if you can hold this thing by yourself. *Prenez mon aide!*"

But the wolf's only response was to pop a few of the chains out of the sand. Narrowing her eyes, Forger forced the chains back inside, as the two of them began their reverse tug-of-war contest, pushing out and inserting chains every few seconds. But by doing so, they forgot about what they were doing.

A strange yellow light began to emanate from inside the grainy prison as the chains tried to find their way inside the sands. It grew stronger, peering through the cracks in the sand, even as Sandshifter redoubled her grip. Still the light continued to push through, finally growing to the point where neither Knight could look at it. But that faded a moment later, leaving them with a brand-new problem.

The sandy hands were now gone. In their place was a huge pair of crystal clear, glass hands, in the center of which stood the creature, partially wrapped in chains. The glow around its body intensified, and it began to grow. Its spindly appearance vanished, as its body rounded out, stretching the masses of chains surrounding it. The crystalline look splintered, changing into one of scales and crevices, as its face became more insect-like, the eyes stretching outward and growing bulbous. But the most amazing change was the growth of two more arms that pushed from underneath the chains that held the creature.

Finally, the glow returned to normal, as the creature finished its transformation. It stood still for a moment, as if its mind was catching up to its body, and then its extra arms reached out and grabbed the chains that held it and pulled them apart as if they were made of deep-fried paper. It held on to the parts that were still connected to Forger, and before the spider knew what was happening, she was pulled into the huge glass hands. She hit them with enough force to shatter them as she flew toward the creature. But as with Wavecrasher's water blast, Forger flew through the creature and through the second wall of glass, right into Sandshifter. The two of them collided with a huge thud and rolled backward on the metal chains and broken glass. The creature looked at them and let out its strange, low, piercing laugh again.

"Aw crap," Nightstalker said as the creature turned its attention to the rest of them.

"I know," Joe said. "Are you guys ready?"

"Forget us," the bat said. "You've gotta … do this."

"But your hands—"

"Go help them," Nightstalker said, as he flexed his fingers under the coat.

"Are you sure?" Joe asked.

"Joe, just go!" Windrider yelled as Forester backed away from the creature, his ax held out like a shield of sorts.

That was all it took. Joe drew his staff and charged the creature. At the sound of his approach, the creature turned around to face him. But when it saw who was running toward him, the creature did something unexpected. It held up its arms and turned away, as if it didn't want to fight Joe. Joe took no notice of this, and with his staff, unleashed a huge burst of light right at the creature. It struck the thing like a battering ram, hurling it backward into a large boulder and then right through the rock.

As it lay there, Joe turned to Forester and asked, "You okay, man?"

"Ah could've taken it," the squirrel replied. "Ah just wanted to wait for the right moment."

"Whatever," Joe said, not in the mood for an argument.

"So ya think it's dead?" Forester asked, glancing at it with uncertainty.

"I hope so. The last monster I fought didn't go down that easily," Joe said.

"Then Ah hope this one is—damn it," Forester moaned suddenly.

Joe turned and saw that, just like the shape-shifter, this thing would not die. The creature was already slowly pulling itself out of the rock. It got to its feet, shook off the rubble, and then turned back to the two Knights. As it did, Joe realized that he had done more damage then he'd thought. The glow on the creature's body had diminished, as if it was running low on juice. The scales on its body looked dry and cracked, and its face looked partially melted, the eyes looking deflated and mushy.

"Holy God, ya did all that?" Forester asked.

"I guess so," Joe said, amazed at the damage his powers had done.

"Well then, Ah guess it's my turn," Forester said as he held out his hands before the creature. The squirrel concentrated, and the mouths on his palms opened once again. As the creature turned toward them, a pair of long, thick vines shot from the squirrel's hands, not unlike Forger's chains, and wrapped around the creature's arms. Forester then pulled down hard, forcing the creature to kneel.

"Okay, now what?" Joe asked.

"Now, Ah give this place some new fertilizer," the squirrel replied as he looked at the ground before the creature. As Joe watched, a small growth sprouted on one of the vines, budding outward. Within seconds, it had sprouted into a small flower, which leaned toward the ground and then dropped something into a small crevice within the dirt. Instantly, the rocky ground began to rise up, as the seed underneath grew and pressed toward the surface. Finally, a stalk popped out of the ground, which began to grow and spread, changing into a circular shape the size of a manhole cover. Joe kept watching as the plant grew larger and larger, spreading until it seemed large enough to cover the creature's body. But it wasn't until Joe saw small, teeth-like appendages growing on the circle's rim that he understood what was about to happen.

"A Venus flytrap? This is your way of dealing with this thing?" Joe snapped.

"It attacked us!" the squirrel replied.

"Yeah, but we don't know why!" Joe said. "You don't need to have something swallow this creature alive. We might be able to use it to get out of here!"

"Think of it this way. Ah'll be helping the environment," Forester said, as he pulled down on the vines again, bringing the creature ever closer to his deadly creation. But there was one thing that Forester, in his assuredness that he would kill the creature, hadn't taken into account. While it was still damaged from Joe's attack, the creature's glow had steadily resumed while the squirrel and Joe were arguing. And as Forester was lowering the creature toward the flytrap, it had returned to its normal state.

The creature let out a roar, and then suddenly wrapped its hands around the plant. The second its skin made contact, the plant began to die, its leaves and stems withering, the teeth growing flaccid and limp. Within seconds, the plant had become a mushy pile of compost, as Forester and Joe looked on in horror. The creature moved its hands over to the vines that held it, and with the slightest touch, they began to die rapidly. The creature shook free of its bonds, but the vines decay continued, spreading down the line toward Forester.

"Shut it off, man!" Joe yelled, as the decay crept closer.

But Forester didn't respond; instead he shook his hands wildly, as if doing so would knock the vines loose. As the decay came closer and nothing worked, Forester began to blubber and panic, shaking his hands harder as Joe looked for something he could use to cut the vines.

But just as it seemed that the decay would reach Forester, a long blade snapped down and cut the dying vines, just before they reached the squirrel. However, that did not stop his blubbering, which caused his savior to sigh and slap the Knight of Forest across the face.

"Dear God, man, were you this much of a coward when you were alive?" Nightstalker spat as the squirrel slowly turned his head in disbelief.

"Glad to see you're feeling better," Joe said. "Where's the kid?"

"Helping the others," Stalker replied, gesturing over to Sandshifter and Forger.

"Forester, get Wavecrasher and the others up," Joe said, "unless you wanna keep fighting this thing by yourself?"

The squirrel shook his head and moved off to where the other Knights lay, leaving Joe and Stalker alone to face the creature.

"You know, I think this would be a brilliant idea for a male-bonding program back home," Stalker said as he and Joe pointed their weapons at the creature. "We can let a bunch of guys loose in the woods, give 'em a demon to deal with, and see who survives."

"Let's make sure we can survive it first," Joe replied as the creature moved to face them.

It looked at the two a moment, as if it was unsure of what it was seeing. The two Knights stood together, neither dropping their weapons or gaze. The three of them stood there for nearly a full minute, waiting for the opposing force to make the next move. Finally, one of them did. The creature, as if it finally understood what was before it, let out its strange cry once again and turned and ran from the two of them.

"Oh, you get back here!" Nightstalker yelled as he brought up his sword. The blade suddenly glowed, as the shadowfire raced down its length and then shot off, racing toward the creature with all the speed of a thunderbolt. It struck the creature directly in the back, causing it to scream in pain and then fall to the ground, where it lay motionless.

"Whoa! I had no idea," Stalker said, staring anew at his weapon.

"Don't be surprised. It had the same reaction to me," Joe replied. "Come on; if it's not dead, I want to talk to it."

"Dude, you did see that thing trying to kill us?"

"Yes. But what did it want? And where did it come from? I want to see exactly what this thing is and figure out why it seems so afraid of us. It didn't run away from the others."

"And you think we can find this stuff out by looking at what seems to be a dead body?"

"Maybe we can tie it up and heal it. We'll learn more than we would otherwise. Besides, don't you want to make sure it's dead?"

Stalker nodded, and the two of them began to move toward the monster, keeping their weapons firmly in their grasp. They walked slowly, neither one having any idea what to expect.

"You know, I'm not a genius or anything, but I think the lack of breathing and movement might be telling us something." Stalker said, as he looked the creature over.

"How do we know it even breathed in the first place?" Joe asked.

"Maybe we should test it somehow?"

"How? Poke it with a stick?"

"Well, you do have a pretty big one right there."

"Point," Joe said. He turned his staff toward the creature. He gingerly poked the creature with the butt end of his staff. The wood made contact with the creature's flesh, and then the familiar cry pierced the air.

"Shit!" Stalker swore as the creature leaped back onto its feet, its face a mask of pain and anger.

Joe brought his staff around, but before he could use it against the creature, its arm snaked out and wrapped its gigantic fist around his head. In panic, Joe dropped his staff and started to beat at the fist with his hands.

Without a second's hesitation, Nightstalker leaped forward, his sword drawn behind his back. One of the creature's other arms snaked out to stop him, but the bat dropped down into his own shadow and vanished. The creature's head whirled around, trying to find where its foe had gone. It was still looking even as Stalker popped out of the creature's own shadow, right at the point where its arm was, and with a yell of rage, sliced through the creature's wrist, cutting off the hand that held Joe.

The creature howled in pain as Joe fell to the ground, its hand still wrapped around his head. As the creature cradled its wounded arm, Stalker ran over and grabbed the severed hand, pulling the fingers apart.

The second he could move, Joe sat up, taking in a gasp of air. "Dear God, it smelled terrible in there," he breathed.

"I don't think you'll be going back," the bat replied, gesturing to the hand.

Joe looked over at it, realized what the bat had done, and then felt a none-too-welcome sensation raising up in his stomach.

"Joe? Come on man, don't pass out on me," Stalker begged, seeing the way his friend's face was turning green.

"No ... I'm okay," Joe said. He scrambled to his feet as quickly as he could, desperate to get away from the hand.

"Good. Because I'm pretty positive it isn't dead yet," Stalker said, gesturing toward the creature. It was no longer clutching its wounded arm but instead looked at them with a big, angry, toothy grin, as its teeth grew even longer inside its mouth. It held up its stump as the skin and bones twisted and stretched outward, moving out until they had reformed into a new hand.

"We're gonna need more swords," Stalker said as the creature began to advance on them. The two Knights held their weapons at the ready, but suddenly, a huge burst of wind shot out from behind the two Knights. It hit the creature with full force, causing it to fly backward as if it had been shot and then pinning it to a large rock.

Joe and Stalker whirled around to see Windrider, supporting the near unconscious form of Groundquake, creating the winds as the other Knights looked on.

"Anytime you wanna shoot the thing!" the falcon yelled.

"You heard the boy," Stalker said, raising his sword.

"Make it quick," Joe replied, raising his staff.

The bat nodded and then the two of them sent streams of shadowfire and light toward the creature. As the two forces streaked toward the creature, the energies flickered as they pulled at each other, almost like magnets pulling at the same piece of metal. As the beams grew closer to the creature, they began to spark, until the two beams of light and dark fused together, forming one huge stream of black and gold energy. The creature saw what was coming and howled in fear and panic, but it was too late. The beam struck the creature dead in the chest, and the screams were cut off instantly. The two-in-one beam burst through the rock, exploding it in a shower of debris, just before Nightstalker and Joe were able to shut off their respective powers.

"Holy crap!" the two Knights swore in unison as they saw the result of their combined powers. The ground around the rock was covered with smoking rubble, the dirt scorched black. The creature itself was gone, vaporized in the instant the beam had touched its body.

"How did we—?" Joe began, but before he could finish, another voice suddenly broke in.

"Christ almighty, that was somethin' else!" Quake said in amazement as the others gathered around the two Knights.

"Did you guys know you could do that?" Windrider asked eagerly.

"Uh no. The ability to utterly destroy like that is fairly new. Right, Joe?" Stalker asked.

"Yeah," Joe said, still looking in disbelief. "Right."

"Well, whatever it is, I'm just glad to know we have that kinda power," Thunderer said. "Though I guess the better thing to say is that you two have it."

"Well, you know what they say," Forger said, glaring at Sandshifter as she spoke. "Two heads are better than one."

"Aw, is the spider upset 'cause I didn't like her plan?" Sandshifter said back mockingly.

"No, I'm pissed because we might've been able to hold that thing if you'd have let me help you!" Forger snapped.

"But then we wouldn't have learned about the little trick our 'friends' have," the wolf replied.

"I would've rather we didn't," Joe said, moving to face Sandshifter. "If we'd captured it, we might've been able to learn just what the hell it was. And I wanted to avoid killing it, threat or not. But now we can't. I agree with Forger; you should've worked with her."

"In fact, we all should've," Joe said, turning to face the others. "We need to think about this in terms of the group, not ourselves."

"Hey, we didn't abandon anybody!" Quake protested.

"No. Overall, you guys did okay. I'm saying this because we need to follow through with it. Combining our powers makes us stronger than any one of us alone. For God's sake, look what Stalker and I did! And you guys could do the same sort of thing if you worked together instead of individually. Forger and Windy understand that; I just want to make sure the rest of you do."

"He's right," Wavecrasher said. "If Thunderer and I had coordinated our attacks, I'll bet we could've electrocuted that thing."

"Yeah. Or Firesprite and Quake could've captured it in a rock and barbecued it," Thunderer added. "Not that I was hoping for it to come to that."

"It's a step in the right direction," Firesprite said. "Joe's got a good idea, and we ought to figure out ways to do it."

"It could be cool to try," Quake agreed. "Just imagine flaming rocks flyin' through the air."

"Good idea," Stalker said, turning his gaze to Sandshifter. "Maybe you could think about that too, huh?"

The wolf growled back, but Thunderer got between the two of them before anything happened.

"He's right, Sandy," Joe said to the wolf. "And you'd better think about it, because next time, it might be a lot worse than what you got. And we might not be around to save you."

Again, the wolf growled, but with Thunderer and Stalker blocking her path, she settled for flipping Joe the bird.

Joe didn't seem to notice though, as he turned to the others and said, "All right, guys, I don't know what that thing was, but I don't think we should stay around to find out if it has relatives. Forger, get the compass ready. We're moving out."

XIV.

THE KNIGHTS TRUDGED THE next few miles in silence. Some of them were still shaken from the battle, while others wondered about the creature and if they were going to find more when they got to the end of their journey. Joe and Stalker took up the lead along with Forger, watching the compass and keeping their eyes open for any sign of their destination or another breed of creature waiting to disembowel them.

But the oddest pairing was taking up the rear, assigned there by Joe to make sure they weren't being followed. Sandshifter looked around through angry eyes, her mouth moving silently as she cursed Joe for banishing her back here. Forester walked alongside her, mostly keeping his eyes to the ground, like a child traveling with a parent he'd angered. But unfortunately, Sandshifter did not have the love that tempers the anger those parents feel toward their child.

"Hey, fluffy tail, are you gonna watch, or are you looking for the damn worms to pop out of the ground and eat your boots?" Sandshifter snarled as she reached over and grabbed the squirrel's head, pulling it back up.

"Ah'm looking, all right?" Forester snapped back.

"Look, Mr. Green Thumb, if we're gonna be stuck here looking for monsters, then you might as well try doing it for real, eh?"

"Sure. Right," Forester spat out as he looked back at the ground. "Ah'm just so eager to go against somethin' else like that."

"Don't be a crybaby," Sandshifter sneered. "You didn't think that something we'd fight might come close to killing you? Grow up."

"Ah know. Ah just didn't think—"

"Didn't think what? That it would happen to you? *Por supuesto que no, idiota poco, lo que habría que usted no puede manejar.*"

Sandshifter stopped, a look of surprise plastered onto her face.

"What's with you?" Forester asked, as he came over to her.

"*No sé,*" Sandshifter started to say, and then she shook her head and shifted back to English. "I don't know."

"Say what?"

"I don't know Spanish. Do I?"

"It looks like you might. The spider knows French, after all."

"I hate this," Sandshifter said, putting a hand to her head. "How can I not remember what language I speak?"

"Maybe you should talk to the kid. He's probably read about weird things like this."

"Right. As if being in this group wasn't humiliating enough, now I have to consult with a comic book nerd."

"Hey, do you wanna keep speaking Spanish for no reason?"

"I … I don't know. I just hate this!" the wolf snarled. "I hate not knowing who I am. And now it's like I'm getting a little glimpse of it, but it doesn't make any sense."

"Maybe you will," Forester said. "And besides, we're all in the same boat."

"Right, and the minute I mentioned it, I'd hear light boy talk about the family he left behind. I think I'll pass."

Forester started to say something, but then he heard Firesprite yell, "Hey! Start moving back there!"

The squirrel quickly turned back to catch up, motioning for the wolf to follow. Sandshifter shook her head but followed all the same. As the two rejoined the group, she asked him, "When did you start listening?"

"Ah have to," the squirrel replied.

"Because the robes say so?"

"Because Ah won't let that bat think Ah'm a coward. Ah won't let any of them think that."

"And why do you care what they think?"

"Ah know Ah screwed up back there. Ah won't be looked at like a fool by them."

"Why? Why do you care what they think?"

"Because … because … because Ah just do!"

Sandshifter listened and then brought her arm over and grabbed the Knight's shoulder. She turned him around to her slowly, almost gently. Forester looked over at the Desert Knight in surprise as the wolf spoke to him. "You aren't the first person to be afraid," Sandshifter said, her rough, angry voice suddenly quiet and gentle. "Don't be ashamed of that."

"But Ah … Ah want to do better," the squirrel said. "Ah was

ready to kill that thing; Ah had everything perfect. But once things changed—"

"I heard about what you did. I liked the idea, but not the execution. Joe was right about one thing—you need to kill 'em fast. An elaborate death for an enemy doesn't mean much if you have to die to pull it off."

"Ah … Ah suppose."

"Right. Now listen, kid, I did like the flytrap idea; I really did. So I'm gonna give you a piece of advice right now. When we get involved in something like that again, you forget all that elaborate crap. When the moment comes, you take it and you kill whatever it is you need to kill. And if things start to change and go badly for you, then don't stand there like a baby that's lost its bottle. Deal with it. Think about nothing more than dealing with it and turning things back to your advantage. You understand?"

Forester stared at the wolf for a moment, and finally said, "Yes. Why are you telling me this? You've talked to everyone like crap. Why am Ah so special?"

"The others at least showed they know how to fight. And even if you did screw up, you had the right idea. I'm curious to see what you could think up when you have better understanding of your powers."

Forester looked at the wolf quizzically and then nodded. "Thanks. And Ah'll be curious to see what happens if you ever decide to talk with me about the whole Spanish thing."

"Listen, if you say a word of that to anyone—" Sandshifter began, but then stopped in her tracks, as did the rest of the Knights.

The squirrel just managed to stop walking soon enough to avoid running into Thunderer. As he came to a halt, he saw Sandshifter looking out before her with an expression between amazement and Dear-sweet-Christ-on-his-Cross-with-a-can-of-beans disgust. As he looked on, Forester noticed a strange feeling growing in his stomach, a feeling like ballpark hot dog nausea mixed with bachelor party hangover. And as he glanced over to the front of the group, he started to understand what that feeling was.

Before them was a huge field, filled with all manner of large plants and flowers. Some of the Knights could recognize roses, daises, tulips, and countless other flowers. Some of the plants seemed to be something other than the flowers of earth, bigger than any flowers they knew. Or at least they had been. For every single plant that stood before them was dead, their stems blackened, their petals gray and dead, mostly fallen off and littered on the ground. All around them, the Knights saw a place where the earth below seemed to have been salted and burned, filled with a cancer that had grown up into the plants, killing their roots and rotting them from the inside. But despite all this death, all that this horrid field set before them, the Knights could also see what lay beyond it—a single light, emanating from deep in the field, a light that sprouted from a structure, something large and black, as if the finger of death that had touched this field was still there.

*   *   *

"It's hungry. It ate the world, and it's still hungry," Wavecrasher said as she looked out onto the field. "Isn't that what the earth said?"

"This isn't what I thought it meant by eating the world," Firesprite said.

"I wish you'd been right," Groundquake said.

"What do you think happened here?" Thunderer asked as he looked down at the dead flowers around his boots.

"It doesn't matter how this happened," Nightstalker said. "What does matter is that we have to go in and take care of this thing."

"Oh yeah, really simple," Sandshifter said with a black chuckle. "We'll just walk through the field of dead poppies and go see Oz the Great and Plague-Carrying. Real simple."

"You have a better idea?" Stalker asked.

"Maybe. And maybe it doesn't involve you," the wolf growled back.

"Why wouldn't that surprise me?" Stalker replied.

"Don't start, guys," Joe warned, looking solemnly out at the field. "This isn't a place for arguing."

The two Knights looked onto the field and both nodded in silence.

"So what are we going to do?" Windrider asked.

"What we aren't going to do is go in there like Sandy says," Joe said simply.

"Well, you finally got some sense after all," Sandshifter said as the bat gaped at Joe.

"For one thing, we can't see Oz without a few special people involved," Joe said. "Forger could give us a tin man, but we don't have a lion or a scarecrow or even a pair of red shoes. So we can't go see Oz with just a man of tin and a surly Toto."

"So we're going to leave him alone in his field?" Wavecrasher asked, as Quake muttered about a Japanese Dorothy.

"Naw. We're just gonna forget the storybook crap and let whatever lies inside this field deal with the Elemental Knights," Joe replied. "Because that's a good plan."

"Sounds like a great plan to me," Nightstalker replied.

"Good. So let's get ready to do this," Joe said. "Sandy, you gonna come? I'm sure there'll be something there for you to rip apart."

The wolf just shrugged and turned to face the field. Looking out at the light that gleamed in the center, she said, "It hurts to look at that thing. Why is it that?"

Joe turned his eyes directly toward the light, the very thing he was supposed to have power over. But like the wolf, he felt his eyes begin to water at the sight of it. Within a few moments, he was forced to turn his eyes away, as they'd started to water. "I don't know. I don't think it is light," Joe said, as he wiped his eyes.

"Then we'll have an interesting time, won't we?" Sandshifter said.

"Maybe that's reason enough to fight it," Windrider said. "Didn't you have friends you were willing to do crazy things for?"

"How would I know?" Sandshifter replied coldly.

The falcon paused, his tongue twisting inside his beak. But before he could think of what to say, Forester let out a groan and fell to his knees, clutching his stomach in pain.

"Ah ... Ah can't go in there," Forester managed to get out.

"Come on, kid, couldn't you try somethin' more original than this—"

"Shut up, Quake," Joe said as he bent down next to the squirrel. "What's wrong?" he asked. "How long have you been feeling like this?"

"Ah felt ok ... till we got here," the squirrel groaned.

"Why? We all feel fine," Groundquake said.

"'Course we do," Firesprite said, looking back at the field. "We're not the one standing before a huge dead field of our element, are we?"

"She's right," Forger said. "The flowers are all dead, so he feels sick. It makes perfect sense."

"Will he be all right? Is he gonna die?" Windrider said.

"He can't die. We're immortal, remember?" Sandshifter said.

"But he can feel like crap, apparently," Forger said. "As long as he's by the field, he's going to feel it."

"Ah … Ah don't think … Ah can go in there," the squirrel gasped. "Not … without a shield or something."

"What kind of shield would work against this?" Firesprite asked.

"No, not a shield," Windrider said. "Something he's already got."

"And what would that be?" Joe asked.

"Look at our weapons," the falcon said, pointing to his staff. "Ralin said they were conduits to the Architects. Forester can draw power from his ax, like a plug from a socket. It might make him strong enough to block the feeling of the dead plants."

"Something else outta a comic book," Quake said. "But what the hell?"

"I agree. Someone get his ax," Joe said.

Firesprite nodded, knelt down by Forester, and drew the squirrel's ax from its sheath.

"You understand what you need to do, mate?" the lizard asked as she handed the ax over to her fellow Knight.

"Ah think … so," Forester sputtered out. Reaching out, he put his hand on the ax head, gripping it tightly.

"So what happens—" he began to ask, but before he could finish, the ax head began to glow green, the light poking through his fingers like spears of green glass. As the others watched, the pained look on the squirrel's face began to ease.

"That … feels much better," the squirrel breathed out as he slowly began to get back to his feet.

"So you're ok now, fluffy tail?" Sandshifter asked.

"I told you to stop calling me that, Sandy," Forester replied.

"Yeah, you're all right," the wolf replied.

"Hold on a sec," Wavecrasher said. "How do we know he won't get sick again once we get inside the field?"

"Let's find out," Nightstalker said as he reached into the field and pulled out a dead flower. Tossing it to the squirrel, he asked, "How do you feel now?"

Forester caught the flower in his hand and held it out to the group. The flower began to straighten up, as if a rod was being placed through the stem, and the plant began to turn green and bloom. "Ah think Ah'll be all right. Don't you?" the squirrel replied as the flower finished regenerating itself.

"Good. But tell us if you start to feel sick again," Joe said.

"Indeed. I'd prefer not to have to carry you," Sandshifter said. "I imagine you'd prefer walking on your own two feet, right?"

"Ah believe Ah would," Forester said.

"Good," Joe said. "Cause we got a hell of a lot of walking ahead of us."

"Then let's get started," Stalker said. He turned and stepped into the dead field. Joe followed him, hearing the crackle of dead plants and weeds as they stepped through them.

"It feels like walking through old, thorn-filled paper," Firesprite said. She pulled her hands back from the still sharp thorns of the plants on the outer border. "And it still cuts like a bastard," she added, looking at the fresh blood on her hands.

"Yeah. But the healing helps, doesn't it?" Forger said as she leaned over and saw the scales on the lizard's hands seal back up within seconds, leaving only the fresh blood.

"I suppose it does," the lizard said.

"You know what else helps? If you keep moving," Sandshifter added, though not unkindly.

"Point," Firesprite replied.

*   *   *

The Knights trekked through the field, trying to ignore the constant thorns and the smell of rotting flowers as they made their way through the huge field. They could feel their legs burn with exhaustion. Some of the Knights ignored the pain and continued to trek through the flowers without comment. But others felt the need to voice their thoughts, and how this situation could've been avoided.

"How much further do Ah have to go?" Forester panted. "We should be at this place by now. And that smell—"

"This is what builds character, kid," Sandshifter said, even as she managed to pant and wrinkle her nose at the same time.

"Screw character!"

"If it bothers you, why don't you just bring the field back to life?" Firesprite chimed in. "It'd be a lot more productive."

At that, Forester reached out and touched a plant. There was a spark of green light, but no change. He muttered something that could've been, "Ah'm not strong enough for that."

"Pardon, mate? Could you repeat that fer me?" the lizard asked.

"You heard him," Sandshifter snapped. "So why didn't you just burn the field down?"

"You got any idea how big a fire that'd make?" Firesprite asked. "Besides, it … it don't feel right."

"Don't feel right?" the wolf laughed. "It's a field of dead flowers. What could possibly be wrong with burning it down?"

"I dunno. I just don't want to," Firesprite said. "I did think about it, but—"

"Ah think yer right there," Forester said. "There's a reason for this place. Burning it would be just as bad as whatever killed in the first place."

"You two are nuts," Sandshifter said.

"If we're nuts, why didn't Quake have the earth swallow it? Or why didn't Wavecrasher drown it? Or 'ell, why didn't you bury it in sand?" Firesprite shot back.

"Big deal. We could still do those things," the wolf said.

"So do it," the lizard said, coming to a halt. "We all know you can do it. So c'mon, sand up and bury this place."

"If you insist," Sandshifter said. She held up her arms and closed her eyes, ready to start the transformation again. But before it could start, the wolf's eyes opened a crack and then a little more, until finally, she was looking out on the field once again.

"We're waiting," Forester said.

Annoyed, Sandshifter shook her head and tried to begin the process again. But once again, she found herself gazing at the field, looking at it almost sadly, as if it pained her.

"Well?"

"I … I don't know why, but I can't," the wolf said, bringing down her arms at last. "Every time I think about it, it feels like … I don't know, pissing on a grave or something."

"I thought the same thing," Firesprite said. "This isn't a place we're supposed to touch, no matter how horrible it is."

"And even though we should," Sandshifter muttered, as she took another sad glance at the dead flowers.

"C'mon. If we get to that light, maybe we can fix this," Firesprite said as she turned and began following the others again.

"Yeah. We'll kill the monster and everything will turn normal again. Sounds like something the kid would say," the wolf said.

"You sayin' you can't kill it?" Forester said. "Think of how much fun you'd have taking on something like that."

"True," Sandshifter said. She started to follow the group again. "And you might be able to try that Venus flytrap thing again. And get it to work this time."

"Ah doubt even our fearless leader would object to killin' this thing," Forester said as he followed.

"And if he does, that doesn't mean we have to listen to him," the wolf replied with a grin. "Now come on. Let's get to that building and bust some heads."

The squirrel nodded, and the two Knights began to walk a bit faster toward the building, thinking of the glory that awaited them. For a time, the fear that both of them held in their hearts, that this journey would lead to their death and destruction, was banished.

It didn't stay that way for long.

XV.

"So WHAT ARE YOU expecting to see when we get there?" Nightstalker asked Joe as the two trudged along, leading the others behind them.

"I don't really know," Joe said.

"Any idea what we're gonna do about it?"

"Not really."

"Thank God I'm the one hearing this. Sandy would've torn you apart in a minute."

"I know," Joe sighed. "But planning attacks against world-devouring entities was never a skill I had a lot of practice in."

"Who does, really?" the bat asked.

"I'd like to know," Joe said. "Thus far, I've only beaten two monsters, and I didn't even kill the first one."

"I'm sure things will work out," Stalker replied. "Who knows? Maybe you'll be able to reason with this thing."

"And how many times are heroes ever able to reason with the eaters of worlds?" Joe asked.

"Hey, nothing wrong with blind, idiotic …"

"Yes? I think the word is hope," Joe said as he plodded along. But then he realized that he was the only one walking. He also realized that the sounds of dead plants being trampled had stopped. Coming to a halt, he turned to see Stalker and the other Knights gazing stupidly like chickens caught in the rain. Slowly, Joe turned his head and took in the sight that had so transfixed his friends. The Knights had reached the light that sat in the center of the field. Or rather, they had come to what was left of its holder.

It had been massive once; they could tell that just by looking at what remained of its black, stone base. It stretched all around them, close to half a mile around, curving in a great circle. Part of the structure's base still reached toward the sky, high above the heads of the Knights. But whatever it had held had been torn away years ago, leaving a jagged top as unhealthy looking as naked bone after the ax. Parts of what it had been littered the ground around them, black chunks of broken stone spikes and black marble that had fallen inside the ring of ground where the flowers did not grow. It wasn't enough to be all of what had been destroyed. It was almost as if the remainder of pieces hadn't fallen, as if they'd been obliterated before ever hitting the ground. It was just as well, for their curse would be to forever look up at the jagged, broken stump that jutted up from the ground, a ruined arm stupidly held up to the heavens.

"Jesus," Sandshifter whispered, for once too shocked to complain about her state of affairs. "This is … this is wrong."

"I know," Windrider replied. "I feel like Charlton Heston when he found the Statue of Liberty."

"What do you think it was?" Stalker asked. "It couldn't have been just a building."

"It wasn't," Forger said. "Whatever this place was, it had to be important. Why else do we feel like this, even though we have no idea what we're looking at?"

"What do you mean?"

But before the spider could begin to answer, Windrider suddenly let out a yell and ran over to a large pile of rubble. As the others watched, he began to dig furiously, piling up the broken pieces as he looked for whatever had caught his eye.

"Should we be letting him do that?" Stalker asked.

"Probably not," Joe answered. "I can't imagine there's something good underneath there."

The bat nodded and moved over to stop the falcon, but before he could, the Air Knight pulled a large piece of rubble out, turning it around so that his friends could see. The dark gray piece was shaped like a diamond and was about the size of a basketball. It was pointed at both ends, and its body had been cut into sections that wove around it in equal shares.

"You were digging for that hunk of crap?" Groundquake said in disbelief.

"Don't you see?" Windy replied, as the others drew around him. "Look at it."

"I am lookin' at it. And I'm not getting anything outta it," the dog replied.

"Maybe you aren't. But I am," Wavecrasher said as she bent down and looked closer. Placing her hands on it, the cat slowly turned the piece around, moving it so that she could see each of the sections. She then turned it over so that the others could see. The section she held out to them had been marked with the image of a wave crashing down. And below it, was the carving of a flame shooting up.

"What the hell is this?" Quake asked.

"The medallions," Wavecrasher said back. "Don't you remember the medallions?"

"What medallions?"

"The ones the Architects were wearing," Forger said suddenly. "That wave was the exact image Ruta had on hers! And Darya had the flame on his."

"And look here," Windrider said, turning it slightly to reveal three concentric circles on another section. "I saw this one on Aeris's."

"Keep turning it," Joe said. "See if we're all there."

The cat nodded as she continued to turn the piece. After a moment, the Knights saw that all of them were accounted for through the symbols—a hammer striking an anvil, a tree, a thunderbolt, a silhouetted figure with wings, a silhouetted face with horns, a mountain, and a sand dune.

"All of us, all the way out here," Joe said. "And we were part of whatever this thing was. But why?"

"Better question is," Sandshifter replied, "if the Architects had something all the way out here, who or what was powerful enough to bring it down?"

"Weren't you trying to take them out yourself not too long ago?" Stalker asked.

"I knew they weren't powerless. Anyone who can bring back the dead—"

"Still wasn't enough," Joe said, as he looked down at the gray piece. "And now it's our turn."

"Do you think that's what this is?" Forester said. "Do you think they just brought us here to … to …"

"Fluffy tail, spit it out already," Stalker said.

But Forester didn't give a worded response. Instead, he pointed beyond the group, toward the remnants of the huge tower, his hand shaking as if he was a heroin addict.

The group turned to follow his direction and instantly felt those same shakes fill their own bodies.

A glowing florescent goo was pouring out of the broken base, spilling everywhere like the liquid of an overfilled cauldron. It oozed out of the crevices and holes of the black stone, covering everything around it. As the ooze poured out and hit the ground, it began to grow upward, stretching toward the sky as if there was some alien sun up there giving it life. As it grew bigger and bigger, the glow grew brighter and brighter, shining into the Knights' eyes like a 700-watt bulb. Instantly, they covered their eyes, shielding themselves from the light. Even Joe found himself in pain from this unnatural glow as the ooze began to form itself into a cohesive shape.

"Any ideas?" Stalker yelled.

"Not right now!" Joe yelled back.

"Of course not!" Forester yelled. "How can we fight it when we can't even look at it?"

Joe started to say something, but before he could, Sandshifter yelled out a reply. "We'll figure out a way, kid! Times like these are when we see just how much courage you got in your nut-smuggling belly!"

"But look at that—"

"Kid, just shut up and get ready to fight! We got something to do, and we ain't leaving till it's done!"

Did the wolf just help me out? Joe wondered to himself. But before he could formulate an answer, another unexpected thing happened. The light that was working to blind them suddenly vanished.

Joe gingerly opened his eyes and looked out before him. The goo had taken on a new form, one that was vaguely humanoid, but only in that it had two arms and two legs. Its body was wide and thick, almost shaped like a giant square block that stretched up for at least two or three stories. It stood on a pair of long, slender legs, one of which ended in a hoof, the other in a shape that looked like a fin. Its arms were just as thick as its body, looking as though they were as heavy as stone and steel and just as strong. The left ended in a hand, tipped with long, sharp-looking claws, and the right was a thick ball. The top of its chest surged upward, culminating in a head with two pairs of eyes, one insect-like and one that looked normal. A hole underneath them seemed to serve as its mouth. The glow still emanated from its body, which was covered in the scales that had dotted the previous creature.

"This is the eater of the universe?" Sandshifter said in disbelief.

"It looks like some sort of mutated amoeba," Forger said. "That could explain how it … feeds."

"So, do we attack it?" Windrider asked, as the creature looked down at them.

"I'm not sure," Joe said. "It's not attacking us."

"Maybe it doesn't think we're a threat," Nightstalker said.

"Well, we can change that, can't we?" Sandshifter said as she drew her staff.

"Hold on a minute," Groundquake snapped, pushing the wolf's hand down. "You wanna piss off something that might have eaten the world?"

"Gimme a break," Sandshifter snapped. "Look at that thing. A minute ago it was a pile of snot, and now you're afraid because it's standing on two legs? It's not even moving!"

"So what?" Quake snapped back. "I think the bat's right. It doesn't think we're a threat because we're like gnats to that thing! So forgive me if I don't think we should go and start shootin' at a creature that's fifty times our size!"

"Ah'm with the dog. Let's not piss it off," Forester added with a gulp as he looked over the monster. "Ah'm ... Ah'm not really in the mood to fight an eater of worlds."

"It's got the same scales as that thing we fought before," the wolf replied. "So it's the same sorta creature. And we took that thing down. So untie your panties and let's do this!"

"Nobody's doing anything," Joe ordered. "I'm not sure this thing is what we're looking for either. If it was some enemy of the Architects, I think it would've tried to attack by now."

"So, what's your plan?" Sandshifter asked.

"I'm gonna try to talk to it. Maybe that will start something," Joe replied.

"Famous last words," Sandshifter said back.

"Maybe. But going in with guns blazing doesn't have to be the only option," Joe said as he turned to face the creature.

Joe took a few tentative steps toward the creature, doing all he could to seem nonthreatening. "Um ... giant, glowing creature?" Joe said, as he came close to it. As he spoke, the creature's eyes glanced down at him, looking at Joe as if he really was a gnat.

"We're, um ... we're sorta unsure of what's going on here, and we'd like to talk to you about it," Joe began. "We're trying to find our way out of here, and we need to take care of something before we can go.

You, um, you might be able to help us there, and I was hoping … was hoping …"

But before Joe could finish, he realized that the eyes of the creature had totally focused on him and that it was somehow bending its upper body up and down, like it was trying to nod.

"Do you understand what I'm saying?" Joe asked.

Again, the nodding motion.

"Then you … you know what we need to do?"

Another nod.

"Great, then we can—*Arrrrrrrrrrrrrrrhhhhhhhh!*"

"*Joe!*" Nightstalker yelled. A huge tendril had shot out of the creature's chest and wrapped around Joe's body. Clouds of steam and the smell of burning flesh joined Joe's screams.

"We've got our answer!" Sandshifter said as she unleashed a torrent of sand right into the creature's eyes. It bucked a moment, and then raised its arm up, rubbing the eyes as the sand scratched inside of them. But the tendril did not release its grip on Joe, who kept screaming as the touch of the thing ate his flesh.

"Hang on!" Stalker yelled, drawing his sword and racing over to where Joe stood. Without a second's hesitation, the bat began to hack at the tendril, digging deep with every cut. But despite his efforts, the tendril wouldn't let go, healing itself after every slash. Stalker grimaced but kept hacking. Or he would have, if he hadn't felt something wrap around his sword and hold it up in the air. He tugged at it, pulling with all his strength, but as he looked up and saw another gooey tendril covering the sword, he could also see it moving down the blade to his hands.

But before it could reach him, the goo was suddenly ripped away, as if something had pulled it back. Nightstalker felt the sword being pulled away from him but managed to hold on to it. He pulled it free as Thunderer shot another thunderbolt into the creature's chest, while Groundquake shifted the ground under the creature, destroying its balance. The other Knights stood back, their weapons drawn and ready to strike. The bat nodded, and returned to slicing the tendril, which was still attached to the creature.

"Fall!" Nightstalker yelled, as he brought the sword up once again. But before he could finish the blow, a second blade suddenly whistled through the air, slicing through the tendril with a single blow. As Joe fell to the ground from the disconnection, Stalker looked up to see Forester standing there, his ax flying back into his hand.

"He's free, rat. Now let's get the holy hell outta here!" the squirrel snapped.

"Nice job Flu—Forester. Go help the others. I'll get Joe to safety."

"Boy, you run off, Ah'm coming with you. Ah ain't fighting that thing."

Stalker didn't give an answer; instead he grabbed the squirrel's collar and brought him in close. As black fire glowed in Stalker's pupils, he snarled, "You *were* this much of a coward when you were alive."

"Ah ... Ah was at least smart enough to know when to run!" the squirrel answered. "We have to get out of here!"

"No."

"You pointy-eared bastard! You're gonna get us all killed!"

The bat stared at the squirrel. Forester gulped in fear, as the bat brought his sword up to the squirrel's ear. Forester thought he knew what was next, but then a moan was heard. The bat glared at the squirrel and released him.

"You stay. You help. You fight. Or else I take you apart, piece by piece. Starting with your nonpointed ears," Stalker said.

The bat then turned back to Joe, who was still moaning with pain at the tendril's touch. He started to reach over to pull it off, but Forester pulled him back.

"If it's burnin' him like that, maybe ya shouldn't just touch it," the squirrel snapped.

The bat started to say something and then muttered "Good point." He looked down at the tendril, which was still squirming. "Any ideas then?"

"Ah don't know," Forester said. "Ah doubt it's a plant matter."

"Not if those black roses meant anything," the bat began, but then he stopped as a look of inspiration struck him. Turning back to Joe, Stalker placed both of his hands over the remains of the tendril. As Forester watched, the bat's hands suddenly erupted in shadowfire.

The effect was instantaneous. The shadowfire spread over the tendril like it was gas-soaked tissue paper, reducing it to ash within seconds. Joe let out a shiver as the flames came near him, but that faded as the shadowfire vanished.

"Joe? Joe, are you ok?" Stalker asked, moving to help his friend.

"Dunno. Kinda feel like I've been frozen and burned at the same time," Joe managed to get out as he clutched his midsection.

Stalker pulled away Joe's hands, and grimaced. The Light Knight's midsection had indeed been both burned and frozen. His clothes had been burned away, revealing flesh that was covered by black, crisp patches that were also caked in frost.

Stalker reached over and pulled Joe's staff out of its holder. Placing it in his friend's hand, he wrapped Joe's fingers around the staff and waited for the healing to begin. But the stone only glowed dimly, and the wound didn't begin to heal.

"What the hell?" Stalker said aloud. "Why isn't it working?"

"Maybe it needs a kick-start," Joe managed to say.

"And how are we supposed ta give you that? Especially with the giant monster on our backs!" Forester snapped.

"You're not helping here!" Stalker snapped.

"Oh, forgive me for not knowing an answer to the impossible question!" Forester snapped back.

"Just lemme think," Stalker said. "How would we give him a kick-start?"

"How the hell should Ah know? You're the number two; you figure out how ta give him some juice," Forester said as the screams of the battle raged above them.

Stalker listened a moment, gritted his teeth, and then turned to the squirrel. "You have to figure it out. I still have a monster to help kill," the bat said as he drew his sword and leaped back into the fray.

Forester glared at the bat, muttering, "Fine, dummy. Go die." But even so, he looked Joe over, trying to figure how he could loan him power. And as he thought, his eyes drifted to his ax. He moved his hands to its glowing head, feeling the power flow through his fingers. Forester could've let that feeling overwhelm him, but cries of pain and battle turned his attention over at the fight.

The other Knights had joined in with the efforts, but the creature was proving to be an equal match for them. As Forger let loose with a wave of metal spikes, the creature stuck out a gooey arm and absorbed them into itself. The spikes stayed in there a moment and then dissolved inside the goo.

Windrider tried next, summoning powerful winds that he collected into a single stream and then released at the creature. The winds struck the monster with the force of a hurricane, but it didn't move an inch. The falcon stared in disbelief and cried out as the creature suddenly sent out a wave of goo. Nightstalker vanished into the shadow, but the others were hit. The goo covered over their bodies and then hardened, pulling them down to the ground.

Pulling his hands away from the stone, Forester quickly placed them down on the burn marks on Joe's torso. Green light pulsed through the squirrel's hands and into Joe's body, flowing over it like Joe was inside a dance club on St. Patrick's Day. As the light spread over him, the wounds and burns caused by the creature's touch faded away as new skin formed over them. Even Joe's clothes were regenerating themselves, cloth appearing out of nowhere and stretching to cover him again. Finally, the treatment was complete, and Joe let out a gasp.

"Feelin' better? The monster is still here, ya know," the squirrel stated.

"A little," Joe said. "I seem to ... be able to speak ... nearly complete sentences."

"Great, but maybe you could be able to shoot light outta your hands? Ah think that could be more useful at the moment," Forester said. He turned back to see what was going on with the others.

The creature was already advancing on the Knights, its spindly legs somehow managing to support its huge body. Forester watched and gritted his teeth, wishing that he had run when he'd had the chance. The bat couldn't handle that thing by himself, not if it had already taken down all the others.

"What is that boy doing? Bug hunting?" the squirrel muttered as the creature stepped even closer.

"We've ... gotta do something," Joe said. He tried to pull himself up.

"Ah gave my idea, but your buddy shot it down—Oh, crap!"

Joe looked up and saw that the creature, having beaten the others, was now slowly making his way toward the two of them. Forester pulled out his ax with trembling hands and held it out, while Joe slowly reached for his staff. The squirrel glanced at Joe and then gulped as he looked back at the creature. As its glowing body approached, Forester slowly began to step back, though he didn't know whether he meant to get into position to fight or run. But before he had even gone two steps, he saw a huge black cloud erupt from the ground before the creature. The huge monstrosity stopped moving and stared as the cloud faded to reveal Nightstalker standing there, staring at the creature with anger in his red eyes.

The creature's eyes widened, and it actually stepped back, putting its hand up as if to shield itself just from the sight of the bat. Stalker paused a moment, his eyes going from the sword to the creature backing away. As the creature backed away, the bat wrapped both hands around the sword's handle, and the blade began to glow black. The shadowfire leaped forth from the blade, slamming into the creature with the force of a heavy metal riff hitting the ears of a Britney Spears fan. The creature let out a god-awful, scream caught somewhere between a cat in the garbage disposal and a man getting his arm loped off as the black flames struck the monster dead center.

Forester's hands went right to his ears; the screech tore at his ear canals. But Stalker didn't make a single motion, even though his face was a huge grimace of pain. He just stood there, turning the fires even higher as the creature let out its howl.

"Maybe Ah shouldn't be pissing him off," Forester breathed, as he looked on.

Behind him, Joe stirred and tried to pull himself up, only to fall in pain a second later. Forester heard him and, sheathing his ax, moved over to Joe (and away from the creature).

"You ain't ready yet," Forester insisted.

"I can't let him die," Joe said as he dragged himself up. "Besides, you did something to get me this far—" But that was all Joe got out before he fell again

"Apparently it wasn't enough," Forester said. But then he paused and turned back to his ax, willing the green light to stream from it once again. Joe saw this and tightened his grip on his staff as it began to echo with its own green light. The light washed over him, growing brighter and changing from green into gold. Joe let out a sigh of relief as his pain faded away. Within seconds, the light stopped, and Joe got to his feet, his body completely healed.

"Wow," Joe said. "Thanks for the boost. Go help the others while Stalker and I deal with Big Ugly."

"But what if Big Ugly decides it wants some squirrel salad?"

"We'll keep it occupied," Joe said. "Now hurry before something else comes out and tries to kill them."

With that, Joe ran past him and toward the site of the battle that was taking place. Forester held back a moment. He glanced toward the fallen Knights and then shook his head and groaned, "Damn you, light boy!" and started moving.

Stalker was continuing to pour the shadowfire onto the creature, which was now on its misshapen knees in pain. As Joe looked on, the bat finally cut the shadowfire, bringing his sword down at his side. He looked at the creature, its scales barely glowing, its transparency now marred with what looked like chunks of black and blue energy trapped inside. It huddled there, its arms wrapped around its body as if it had been through a snowstorm and was only now beginning to warm up. But it managed to pull its head up and look down at the small creature that had caused it so much pain.

Joe watched as Stalker looked up and met the creature's gaze. The Light Knight saw no expression on his counterpart's face as Stalker looked at the creature. As he watched, Nightstalker's gaze briefly shifted to the sword he held and then over to the creature once again. But he still made no move; he simply continued his staring match with the creature, as if he was waiting for something to happen.

Suddenly, Stalker's eyes began to darken, and a new emotion began to fill them. It wasn't anger this time, but a dark, horrible-looking joy. And if there was any question what that joy was about, it was made clear as he lifted his sword once again, pointing it right at the creature's misshapen face.

Joe saw the bat's face and took off running toward him, his hands outstretched as he called out, "*No Stalker! Don't do it!*"

But if the bat heard his friend, it didn't matter to him. The first sparks had already begun to fly off the blade when Joe reached him. Without a second's hesitation, Joe pulled out his staff and knocked it into the blade, forcing it down onto the ground.

"You don't need to do this," Joe said.

The bat's eyes lost their focus a moment and then turned over to see Joe. For a second, Joe thought he saw shards of black in the bat's eyes, but then Stalker started to speak. "Huh? Joe? You healed already? How?" Stalker asked.

"Never mind that. What are you doing?" Joe demanded, pointing at the creature.

"Killing the destroyer of worlds. It sounded like a good idea," the bat replied.

"How do you know that? Maybe we aren't supposed to kill him. Maybe this isn't even it," Joe retorted.

"Joe, it's trying to kill us. We have to deal with it as such," Stalker said. He raised his sword again.

"No, you don't," Joe said. "I'm not going to let you do it. Do you have any idea what you looked like a minute ago? Dear God, man, you shouldn't look that happy when you're about to kill something!"

"Joe, if this thing is called the destroyer of worlds, and it seems to have made good on its name, is killing it really so bad?"

"Well …"

"There's nothing wrong with punishing someone who deserves it. And I'm going to do it with or without your say-so."

The bat brought his sword up once again, and before Joe even noticed it, the blade was engulfed in shadowfire that shot out toward the creature. It struck the creature straight in the face, and it let out another cry of pain. Joe watched in horror as the creature began to burn again. Despite whatever this thing might have done, that screaming was enough to break whatever hardness Joe had. He turned, ready to take down Stalker if need be. But when he turned to face the bat, he realized that he didn't need to.

"I … think we're … in trouble," Stalker spat out as he struggled to hold on to the blade. The shadowfire still blazed from it, but now Joe saw that it was beginning to change, to brighten and lose its dark hue. The brighter flames were flickering against the bat's hands, and he gritted his teeth against them.

"What in the name of God?" Joe swore. He turned to face the creature. That's where he got his answer. Joe saw that the chunks of black and blue in the creature were fading away, becoming transparent once again, as the creature started to stand up.

"Shut it off!" Joe yelled.

"I … can't!" Stalker yelled back. He grimaced against the touch of the flames.

"Try, man! I don't know what's going to happen if it finishes, but it's going to suck tremendously!" Joe snapped.

"It's not … working. The sword … isn't … listening to … me!" Stalker screamed.

"Hang on," Joe cried out. He drew his staff. Holding it high, Joe activated it, turning the lion's head into a glowing orb of light.

"What … are … you doing?" Stalker breathed.

"Just hope we don't die," Joe said as he brought the staff down onto the sword. The instant the staff touched the blade, the golden energy began to crackle and hiss, sparking out like a wet cat licking an electrical socket. The pale shadowfire grew even more intense, and as it spread out, it began to regain its black color once again. The creature howled again and hid its eyes from the new fire. The pained looked on Stalker's face began to dissipate, and Joe started to relax. But then, he noticed how the staff and sword were now glowing even brighter in their respective colors.

"I don't think—" Joe began. But then the two energies exploded in a huge wave of gold and black light. Both Knights were thrown back, skidding across the ground. The two finally came to a halt nearly twenty feet from the spot where they had started. The creature gave another howl and began to limp forward, its body tarnished and smoking from the attack. It looked from Knight to Knight, as if unable to decide whom to go after first.

But before it could make a decision, the ground under its feet begin to rumble and shake. The creature looked around in confusion and then anger as a series of huge vines suddenly shot out of the earth and wrapped themselves around his body, holding it in place tighter than a teenage girl holding Daddy's credit card. The creature began to struggle against the vines as Forester ran out from his hiding place and began heading toward Joe. Grabbing the semiconscious Light Knight, the squirrel started to pull him upright, just as the bat was pulling himself up.

"Uh … that was fun." the bat muttered as Forester came to him.

"Hurry and wake up; Ah've only got so many vines!" Forester snapped, as he pulled Joe up.

"Okay then," Joe said, pushing Forester's hand away. He wiped the dirt and gravel off his clothes.

"Joe, that had to be the craziest thing I've ever seen you do," Stalker said.

"I thought so myself," Joe said.

"Any chance we can do that again?" the bat asked.

"I have no idea. But I think we should try," Joe replied.

"And Ah think now would be a great time for it!" Forester yelled. He glanced over at the creature, which was stretching the vines to their limit.

"What about the others, plant boy?" Stalker said.

"Ah already tried to free them. Whatever's holding 'em has 'em tight."

"Then we need to add to the recovery effort. Stalker, go with him." Joe said.

"You want us to leave you alone against that thing?" Stalker said in disbelief. "Joe we don't even know if you can hurt it."

"We didn't know if you could do anything either," Joe said. "Besides, if the two of you work fast, we can go after it with all guns blazing."

"You're gonna have to fight to kill, Joe. That thing's not gonna let you go any other way," Stalker said.

"Let me worry about that," Joe said. "You just make sure I'm not fighting this thing alone."

"Ah've got no problem with that. C'mon, boy," Forester said, slapping the bat's shoulder and running off toward the others.

Stalker hesitated a moment, looked at Joe, and then turned to follow the squirrel.

Joe watched them go off and then heard a roar that turned his attention to the creature. There was a snapping sound as it tore the last of the vines to pieces and stretched out, ready to fight. Joe swallowed, tightened his grip on the staff, and leaped into the creature's view. It looked down at him and glared with rage at this small nuisance. Joe looked back at it and then held out his staff, the head glowing brightly.

As it had when Nightstalker brandished his weapon, the creature looked down at him and its eyes widened in surprise. But this time, it did not back away. Instead, it focused its gaze and brought its arms around, looking like it was about to crush its small foe. But Joe didn't move; he just held up his staff and prepared himself as the creature moved to strike.

*   *   *

"C'mon, you wanna get outta this alive, don't you?" Forester said as he and Nightstalker raced toward the prone bodies of their friends.

"Don't worry about me," the bat snarled as the two of them reached the others. "You're good at that, aren't you?"

"What's your problem?" the squirrel snapped back.

"With a giant monster attacking our friend and me being stuck with a coward? I can't imagine," Stalker replied.

"Hey he volunteered. And as Ah recall, that thing thinks you two are Freddy and Jason," Forester snapped.

"And if it was you down there, you'd be saying something different, wouldn't you?"

"Hey, Siegfried and Roy! Mind puttin' yer little domestic problems aside and getting us outta this?" Groundquake snapped.

"C'mon, guys. We need to get down there and help," Thunderer said from his casing.

Stalker nodded and, without a word, placed his hand on Forester's ax. The ax head glowed for a moment and then began to darken, until it was almost black.

"What the hell did you do?" Forester snapped.

"I loaned you some power—the same way you loaned Joe yours. Now use it. Or I'll come back and rip it out of you," the bat said. He moved away from Forester over to where the ram lay, drawing his sword. The squirrel glared at the bat angrily for a moment and then turned to the other side and drew his ax, heading for the casings that held Groundquake and Sandshifter.

"Took ya long enough ta remember we were back here, eh?" Quake snapped as the squirrel turned his ax and began to hammer at the casing with the blunt end.

"Oh, didn't you notice the giant monster?" the squirrel shot back.

"Shut up!" Sandshifter said. "Just get us outta this so we can get down there."

"What, you're actually in a hurry to save Joe?" Forester asked.

"I'm not stupid. Ten stand a better chance against that thing than one. Besides, if anyone's gonna put that guy in his place, it'll be me!"

"Your funeral, *senorita*," Forester grumbled as he continued to hack away.

But then, the creature's roar filled the air again, causing everyone to pause and look over at the battle unfolding.

The creature let out another roar as it prepared to bring its fists down onto Joe. But as the shadow of the creature's fists began to overtake him, Joe glanced up and then held his staff up higher into the air. There was a flash of golden light, and the creature pulled back, howling as it held its smoking hands.

Joe held the staff out again and swung it out before him, creating a wall of golden light. As Joe watched, the wall shot forward, slamming into the creature's chest. It let out another howl of pain and then fell back into the ruins of the building, sending up a huge cloud of debris.

Joe paused briefly as the creature begin to pull itself out of the ruined building. Suddenly, the creature whipped around and pointed its clawed hand at the Light Knight. The claws shot off the hand and sped toward Joe. But again, Joe pointed his staff and a large square of light suddenly appeared before him. The claws struck the light and vanished into nothing; the creature screamed in pain once more.

But Joe wasn't done yet. His eyes filling with golden light; he gripped the staff with both hands and then brought them apart, holding them at either side while the staff stayed suspended in midair. As he did this, the square broke down the center, becoming two long golden rectangles. Joe closed his fists, and the rectangles folded into two small balls of light. He then unclenched his fists, and the balls began to straighten, becoming two long, pointed tendrils of light. The creature saw this and began to back off, but before it could move away, Joe brought his hands back together with a clap, sending the two poles of light directly at the creature. As they impaled themselves in its chest, and it howled in unbelievable pain, the monster stumbled out of the wreckage, too pain-racked to even consider pulling them out.

"'Bout time we saw something like that from you."

"Huh?" Joe said as he turned toward the voice, the gold in his eyes fading away.

"I said it's about time," Sandshifter said, as she and the other Knights approached.

Stalker stared at the creature and then looked back at Joe with disbelief.

"I guess I didn't have to worry about you after all," the bat said.

"What are you talking abo—" Joe began to say as he turned around, but then he saw the creature collapsed on the ground, grasping the light spears in pain, and stared in amazement.

"I ... I did *that?*"

"Either you or somebody else gifted with power over light," Sandshifter replied.

"I-I knew we had to stop it, but I ... I didn't think ... I didn't want to."

"It's awright," Firesprite said gently. "You did what you had to do. And we gotta take this thing down."

"Agreed," Wavecrasher said. "Forger, Thunderer, you guys thinking what I'm thinking?"

"I believe so."

"I guess."

"Good, then let's get started."

"I'll go first," Groundquake said. He knelt down and dug his hands into the earth. As the group watched, there was a rumble and then two giant arms suddenly rose up out of the earth near the creature. It briefly looked up as the hands at the end of the arms tightened into fists, and then it howled again, as the hands grabbed the spears and began to twist them, driving the light further into the creature's body.

"How's that feel, ya world-eating jackass?" Quake said with a grin and continuing to work the earth.

"Stop it! You ... don't ... need to—" Joe began to say but then stopped as a bolt of pain and pressure burst through his head. Grasping his forehead, he rubbed it, trying to relive it.

"Joe? What's wrong?" Thunderer asked.

"Don't ... know. It feels like ... like something's being pulled and pushed ... inside my head," Joe replied.

"Wait a second," Forger said. She pointed out toward the creature. The others turned and instantly understood. The light spears embedded in the creature had begun to flicker and wink out, growing dimmer each minute as Joe continued to rub his head.

"You think—" Sandshifter began.

"Yes," Forger replied.

"He must have to concentrate on them. Like telekinesis," Windrider said.

"Um. Has anyone thought about what will happen when those things are gone?" Forester asked.

"*Oui*," Forger said grimly. She turned and ran toward Groundquake. Grabbing the dog by the shoulders, she pulled upward, dragging Quake's hands right out of the earth. The second they were out, the stone arms froze and then released the light spears and retreated back into the earth.

"What're ya doin'? I had that thing!" Groundquake yelled.

"Yes, you had it. And you were destroying the only thing keeping it pinned down!" Forger snapped back.

"Actually, Ah think you're going to have to rephrase that last part," Forester said as he pointed back toward the creature.

The light spears were flickering even more now, becoming every suburban house at Christmastime. As the Knights watched, the spears gave one last burst and then winked out, leaving two giant holes in the creature that instantly began to fill back up.

"That's bad, isn't it?" Quake said, a note of panic in his voice.

"What do you think?" Sandshifter snapped.

The creature got back on its feet.

"Okay, who's got a plan?" Forester asked as the creature slowly turned its gaze back to them. "Anyone at all?"

"I say we ... we ..." Forger began but then stopped as she began to cough uncontrollably.

"Are you—*hakk*," Stalker tried but was unable to speak, as he was caught up in his own fit.

Within a few seconds, the rest of the Knights joined in, each coughing uncontrollably.

"What ... what's wrong?" Windrider managed to get out. He sensed a bitter smell invade his nostrils.

"Something's ... something's in the air," Sandshifter coughed out. "That ... smell ..."

"Oh, God." Forger said. "It's ... poison."

"Where's it ... coming from?" the wolf hacked back.

Forger couldn't reply, but she was able to point back to the creature, which hadn't moved but was now standing there, staring at them with a fiery intensity.

"How can—"

"I ... don't know ... but ... we've—" Forger tried to say, before the lack of air drove her to her knees. She knelt there, trying to get in a single breath as the creature continued to stare its death knell at them.

But it didn't get the chance, as a golden beam suddenly shot forth and struck it directly in its four-eyed face. It howled again and staggered about, clutching its eyes as the Knights slowly found themselves able to breathe again.

"You guys all right?" Joe asked, one hand holding his staff, while the other pressed his coat against his mouth.

"We are now," Stalker said. He took in great breaths of air. "But we still have a monster to deal with."

"We can take him down," Joe answered. He helped the bat to his feet. "For whatever reason, you and I seem to be able to hurt him. I think we need to do that merging trick we tried before."

"Good idea, but it's not gonna be all that easy at the moment," Sandshifter said.

The creature finally pulled its hands away and looked toward them with rage once again. But this time, it held up its huge arms as its sides began to ripple under its watery skin. Slowly, two more growths began to grow out of the creature's sides, stretching out like a pair of transparent tendrils. The transparency then began to fade away as the new arms became silvery and metallic. No hands formed, but the ends of the arms began to pull into themselves, leaving large holes as the silvery color spread over the stumps, until they had finally formed into a pair of cannon-like appendages.

"Holy crap. We're fighting evil demon Mega Man," Windrider said, this time without a trace of awe or worship in his voice.

"I don't know what the hell that means kid, but I know what those things are," Firesprite said. "*Everybody duck and cover!*"

"Shit!" Sandshifter spat out as the space inside the new arm began to glow with a purple light.

The Knights began to scatter as the light was suddenly released in a burst of energy that scorched the ground where they had been standing. The shots came faster and faster, forcing most of the Knights back behind a large rock. But two of them managed to move past the rock and keep running.

"Damn it, I officially hate Mega Man!" Firesprite yelled, as the creature continued to fire on them.

"We've gotta shut those things down before we can attack," Windrider said, running alongside Firesprite.

"Great idea! Any idea how we're gonna do it?" the lizard asked.

"Do you think you can get some fire up there?"

"Yeah, but it won't burn fast enough to do any damage."

"It doesn't need to."

Firesprite looked at the falcon, started to say something, and then just shook her head and turned back to the creature. Facing it, she took a deep breath, put her hands together and pulled them up to her chest. As the creature turned its "guns" on the two Knights, Firesprite suddenly pulled her ignited hands apart and with her eyes glowing red, she unleashed all the flame she could muster at the creature. The huge steams of fire struck the creature's weapons dead center and began to catch, burning the silver all around. But just as Firesprite had feared, the flames weren't working fast enough to destroy the "guns" or even cause the creature real pain. And worse still, she saw the energy begin to gather inside the guns once again.

But before the weapons could fire, some kind of miracle happened. The flames suddenly burst into new life, burning almost twice as big and spreading just as fast. The energy inside the weapons held for a moment and suddenly faded, as the creature howled in pain, shaking its extra arms in an attempt to extinguish the flames. Watching the creature burn, Firesprite wondered what she had done to boost the firepower. But then she heard a sharp whistling sound and turned to see Windrider standing there, directing a huge gust of wind at the creature, fanning the flames with all his might.

"Good shot, kid!" the lizard called out gleefully.

The creature had finally begun to retract its arms to escape the fires. The flames vanished the second the arms reentered the creature's gooey body, and Windrider quickly stopped the winds. As he did, Firesprite's grin vanished. The creature turned its gaze on them, raising its remaining arms upward as it began to advance on them.

Both Knights took a step back, but as the creature began to bring its arms down, a series of green vines suddenly wrapped around its club arm, while a huge sandy tendril wrapped around its claw arm. The creature roared in protest as it struggled against its constraints. It tried to take a few steps forward, but before it could even take a step, the earth suddenly grew and clamped down on its feet, locking the creature in place. It let out another howl and continued to struggle. Behind it, Forester, Sandshifter, and Groundquake each held his or her own bond tight against the creature.

"Awesome, guys! Don't let up!" Windrider said.

"C'mon, we gotta get another attack ready," the lizard said.

"No need guys," a voice said from behind the duo. The lizard and falcon turned to see Wavecrasher, Forger, and Thunderer standing there.

"We saw you guys had the right idea," the cat said. Standing before the creature, she brought her hands together much like Firesprite had. Her eyes glowing blue, the cat brought her hands up, flipping them palm upward but keeping them together as a huge torrent of water shot forth from them. The water struck the creature directly in the chest, causing it to yelp again, though it wasn't clear if the cry was one of pain or annoyance.

"Uh, maybe I'm unclear here, but what good does giving it a bath do?" Windrider said.

Wavecrasher continued to move her stream around, soaking the creature's imprisoned body.

"That's only part one," Thunderer said.

Wavecrasher broke off the stream and stepped back, while Forger moved up. The spider brought up each of her six hands, pointing them toward the creature as she pulled her fingers in, just like she had at the campsite. Six chains immediately shot forth from the spider's palms toward the creature. But this time, with her eyes glowing just like her companions, Forger tried a new trick. As the chains streaked toward the creature, she sent her thoughts out to them, giving them an image to conform to.

The chains obeyed instantly; the ends suddenly reformed into spikes just as they struck the creature and embedded themselves in its liquid body. The chains then exploded out from inside the creature, spreading out like germs from an infected needle. The new chains crisscrossed each other as they infected every pore and crevice. Finally, Forger willed the chains to halt their progress, and she gripped each chain. The holes in her hands closed up, breaking the link to her body.

Thunderer came up to her. Forger handed the chains over to the ram, who gripped four in each hand. His eyes glowed white, and the air began to crackle around him. The monster heard the crackles and turned its attention to him, but it was already too late. The electricity crackled and sparked in his hands, until Thunderer could contain it no longer. It shot through the chains in a flash and then right into the creature. As the metal and water conducted the energy through the creature, its body glowed like a Christmas tree on electric crack. The creature screamed and howled as the power raced through its body, burning whatever passed for nerves.

Finally, Thunderer halted the lightning and dropped the chains. The creature fell to its knees, its body smoking. As it knelt there, barely able to move, it heard footsteps. Somehow pulling its head up, it saw Joe and Nightstalker standing before it, with their weapons ready.

"You ready?" the bat asked.

Joe paused a moment and looked at the creature, seeing it kneeling there in pain. Then he turned to his friend and saw the cold, uncaring look in Stalker's eyes as he glared at the creature. It was only then, that Joe sighed and said, "Just make it fast."

Stalker nodded. They both pointed their weapons at the creature. The sword and staff glowed black and gold almost instantly, the energies sparking outward. The creature knelt there, taking in whatever breath it could, as the energies of light and dark shot out from the Knights' weapons, combining into one gold and black beam. They struck the creature head on, and as they hit, the light from its scales began to intensify, glowing brighter and brighter, surrounding the broken building, the Knights, everywhere until none of the Knights could see.

*　　*　　*

"Open your eyes, Lightrider. You have reached the end."

"Wha—" Joe said. He slowly opened his eyes, briefly thinking that he had failed and the monster had destroyed him. But instead, Joe found himself inside a huge gray room made of bricks. The other Knights stood around him, and they too slowly opened their eyes and looked around in surprise. But eventually as they found their focus, they saw the Architects assembled before them.

"Congratulations, Elementals. You have passed the final stage of training," Ralin said.

"Wait a sec. That thing was the last step?" Quake said. "That was the final thing you guys decided to test us with?"

"Is that not what you desired?" Darya asked.

"No, I'm just glad that's the last of it," the dog snapped.

"That creature was the ultimate test we could give you," Rastla whispered. The early tests were for you to learn how to use your powers. The final test was for you to learn how to use your powers together, for that is where your strength lies."

"Alone, the elements are powerful," Naru said. "But together, they are unstoppable."

"Like the way Joe and I merged our powers," Nightstalker said.

Naru nodded.

Ralin took up the conversation. "That is the greatest strength of the Knights, the power to merge light and dark," Ralin said. "But if it is not controlled, it can destroy all around you."

"Makes sense," Stalker said

Sandshifter came to the front. The wolf looked at the assembled Architects, paused, and then briefly spoke. "I have three questions that you're gonna answer. Number one, where are we?"

"A sacred place," Ralin replied. "Do you remember the broken building you saw when you fought the creature? That place was a world we created for your training based on this one. We showed you that world when this place had fallen. You stand in the linchpin of the universe."

"Does it have a name?"

"In truth, it has many names and many forms," Ralin replied. "You see it as a building of stone, but that is the only way your minds can perceive it. To others, it is a pyramid, a skyscraper, or even a man. But regardless of its shape, it has one function—to be the anchor that shines from within the darkness."

"From within the darkness?" Joe asked, his curiosity awoken once again.

"The skies you saw on your travels were unchanged from the true ones," Aeris whispered. "This is a force of light buried within the purest darkness. The two mix together and travel into the universe, filling the worlds with their power."

"Why in their right minds would anyone build a place like this inside a giant cloud of dark?" Groundquake asked.

"Can you think of a better way to protect something than to hide it in the dark?" Forger asked.

"Yeah, man. The good stuff is always hidden in the dark," Windrider added. "The princess is always at the top of the dark, evil tower."

"*Ahem*," Sandshifter coughed. Looking at the Architects, the wolf asked her second question. "Why are we here?"

"This is to be your home now," Nabu answered.

"You're serious?" Forester said. "You're asking us to stay in a big, empty room inside something that looks like a giant stone ... Ah dunno, obelisk or something?"

"You know, that's not a bad name for this place," Nightstalker said thoughtfully.

"Ah mean, couldn't we at least have some throw pillows or something?"

"What you see is the entrance—the lobby, in other words," Nabu replied. "There are many levels to this version of the linchpin, as many as you would wish."

"But there aren't any stairs or anything," Forester said. He gestured out to the empty walls. As soon as those words were out of his mouth, though, Forester noticed a spiraling staircase nestled in the right side of the room.

"This place is however you imagine it," Aeris said softly as the other Knights chuckled behind Forester.

"It is from this place that all elements sprang, not only light and dark," Zueia explained. "That is why it is the perfect place for you to dwell."

"Yes ... that's why we found that thing by the wreckage," Forger said, "the one with all your symbols on it."

Zueia nodded. He gestured to the medallion around his neck. "But these are no longer just our symbols. Now they are yours as well."

"You have earned the right to represent us in the mortal worlds," Ralin said. "You shall wear our colors and use our powers as an extension of our will. I would speak more, but I believe you had a final question for us, Sandshifter?"

"Yes," the wolf replied, keeping her voice tough. "Those things we fought—the monster, that huge thing—why did you create them for us?"

"Mate, they were just random monsters," Firesprite said. "Don't bug 'em with that."

"Random, huh?" the wolf sneered. "Is that why they both had those glowing scales? Is that why they both seemed able to do anything?"

"Firesprite's right. Let it be," Joe said, stepping up to the wolf.

"No, Lightrider. She has the right to ask that of us," Ralin said. "And it is well that she should."

"What do you mean?"

"The creatures you fought were our creations. But they were based on beings that are very real—beings older than us that you will deal with for the entire length of your Knighthood."

"What? That giant monster—that's real?" Joe said in disbelief.

"Yes. But with luck, your efforts against its spawn will prevent you from ever having to truly face it," Ralin said.

"What are they then?" Joe asked.

"They are the one thing that opposes all the elements and the safety of the balance—chaos."

"Chaos?"

"Yes, Lightrider. They are called Chaos Demons. Long ago, before the universe as you know it came to be, there was nothing. From that eventually came the Chaos Demons. They existed in a realm with no rules, no order, nothing to organize them. Nothing was permanent; everything could change—friendships, morals, even their own bodies changed at random, to no one's whims but theirs."

"Then order came, didn't it?" Forger asked.

Ralin nodded. "We came. And we fashioned a solid, unchanging, ordered universe. The demons saw it as everything they knew and loved fading away. They hated all the aspects of the new order—it's solidity; its constants; and most of all, the decree that they could have but one form. Enraged, they waged war against us, to destroy what we had created and return the universe to nothing once again. But they were driven back, trapped inside a pocket dimension along with their leader, the monster you saw."

"It calls itself the High Chaos," Ruta said with a shiver. "We did not know it, but it possessed the power to cut holes in our pocket dimension and allow its brethren to escape. Thought it cannot escape itself, the High Chaos waits for its brethren to bring it freedom."

"When a plane explodes in midair for no reason, the Chaos Demons have been there," Ralin said. "When a hardworking man loses a promotion to an inexperienced coworker, the demons cackle with glee. And when a cruel man has a brief spell of kindness, only to fall back into his true nature, they have been there as well, working to upset the balance through both good and evil. And should they succeed and create enough chaos in the world, then the High Chaos shall be able to escape and bring about the return of the nothing."

"And we're supposed to stop them?" Joe asked. "But ... all due respect, we barely made it against them today."

"Inexperience fades. You will learn, and you shall send them back to the nothing they spawned from. For that is the nature of order—to vanquish chaos."

"Then ... then that's what we'll do," Joe said.

Ralin nodded, but behind him, Rastla's eyes narrowed as she looked at Joe. After what had happened, she no longer believed that this man was unfit to wield the light. But as she heard the words of his heart, she wondered what would happen when the time came for him and his brothers to truly fight the Chaos Demons. Rastla could feel the reluctance within him as he thought of the pain he had endured. She felt his disgust at being forced to kill, despite the evil the creatures represented.

He is worthy for my brother, Rastla thought as she listened to his heart, too *worthy. And if what I fear about him proves true, what will happen to the world we have created?*

Rastla did not receive an answer to this question; she already knew it. And that was why she turned her eyes from Joe as he swore to uphold the order and destroy the Chaos Demons, not wanting to watch him lie.

INTERLUDE

As he finished the last words on the page, he remembered how long it had taken for Rastla to admit that to him. Nearly a hundred years of earning respect and doing his duty before the great Architect of Shadow had admitted that she had once doubted him. He had been angry for a moment, but it had passed quickly, for such had been his nature then.

And now? He mused on it as he put the pen down a moment. As with so many things that had mattered back then, he found it no longer mattered now. Besides, she had been right. He had been a man of principle, taught a code of right and wrong. And that code had told him that killing was wrong no matter the reason. He had believed that until the time he'd died, and he had planned to continue to believe it as a Knight.

Thank heaven, he'd stopped being so naive.

He shook his head at the thought of his past foolishness. That had been another man, one who did not know that the brightest light creates the biggest and darkest shadows. He had learned to see the truth of all things. But it did not tell him the truth of his duty. Not yet.

As he picked up the pen, he remembered how it had felt when doing the right thing was enough. As he continued to write, he focused on the time just before he'd been forced to put that belief to the test against the desires he'd had.

BOOK THREE

THE REAL WORLD

XVI.

JOE WATCHED AS SHE left the building, the doors quietly revolving behind her. He had watched her long enough to know her habits—how she liked to leave to eat at the bistro on Fifth on Thursdays, the exact time she left for her lunch, the direction she headed toward the bistro. He turned that way now, observing from his vantage point how she paused a moment as someone called out her name. She turned toward the voice, a smile spreading across her lips as she recognized the person behind it. He watched as the man came up to her, waving his hand in greeting as he approached. The two conversed quickly, he noticed, as the man spoke words to her, which she apparently took to like a Southern belle receiving an empty compliment, turning her face to the side and letting her hair shield her from the sight of the dashing gentleman. Not that that stopped him; he continued to speak, smiling as she twisted in embarrassment. Finally, he finished speaking and offered his hand to her, flashing a smile as bright as starlight reflecting off the sun. The woman shook her head in one last show of embarrassment and then finally took the man's hand. They began to walk down the avenue, just another two businesspeople on their lunch in the busy city.

Watching them walk off, Joe found himself admiring the man's choice in women. A crop of long, blonde hair, curled ever so slightly, framed her face, which was supported by strong, Swedish cheekbones and intense blue eyes. Her body was perfectly proportioned—neither fat nor thin but blessed with curves that any sane man graced with the sense of touch would love putting his hands on again and again. As he watched her walk off, he saw how her short dress suit managed to hug each part of her body in just the right way, enough to cause a dreamtime expedition to see what lay beneath.

But she wasn't the best woman in Joe's mind, and it hadn't been her features that had put her under Elemental notice. Like so many others, this woman had been brought to their attention because of what she represented. Her name was Cheryl Evans, Miami's newest city council member. She had been in the position only a few months, but she had proven herself more than capable of her job. Evans had been responsible for creating hundreds of jobs, partially by updating the city's technology but largely by cracking down on the unfair rates that many business owners placed on Miami's Cuban immigrant population. She was also putting forth several motions to the city council to create a job center within the city, where the immigrants could go and be hired with fair and agreed upon rates, instead of standing on street corners, waiting for jobs. Moreover, the center would also help these immigrants become full citizens, without fear of deportation. To many, it had seemed like a pipe dream, but Evans, through careful and intelligent negotiations, had managed to convince many of the council members and businesses to help contribute to her cause, saying the center would help to create a Miami that "was associated with fair and equal jobs for everyone."

Of course, many said that Evans was simply pandering to the city's Cuban population, but that same population was thrilled that a white woman was working so hard to help them and their families. Joe knew the truth of course—that Evans, who had watched her immigrant parents work themselves into early graves to give her a better life, wanted everyone to have her chances, without going through the humiliation and backbreaking work her parents had endured.

And that was precisely why he watched Ms. Cheryl Evans. He knew that the chance for a fall was coming, sooner than Evans thought.

Evans and her friend walked past an alleyway, so caught up in conversation they failed to notice the hands that reached out, grabbing Evans's arm and dragging both her and her friend inside. The alley was wide and perfectly situated within the shadows of the buildings. They'd be silenced quickly and then dragged further back into the alley for the rest of the job.

But that was only if he did nothing. Taking a brief glance toward the alley where everything was happening, Joe closed his eyes and then vanished from sight.

*   *   *

"What are you—"

"Shut up!" the man snarled, his hoodie keeping his face shielded as he dragged Cheryl and Jeff into the alleyway. He pulled sharply on her arm, slamming her into the wall and away from Jeff. Jeff spun around, only to come face-to-face with the barrel of a gun. The man in the hoodie barked at him to stay still, even as he pushed Cheryl against the wall.

"Look, there's no need for this," Jeff said, holding up his hands. "We'll give you whatever you want. In fact, let me get my wallet—"

"Fuck that!" Hoodie snapped. He turned back to Cheryl. "I'm here to take care of her."

"Wha—"

"You cost me my job, bitch! I got laid off because of those goddamn Cubans you keep getting hired. Sure, they gimme some bullshit about me having a drink or two on the job, but I'll tell you what it really is. They wanna look all nice and multicultural for you, Miss White Queen of the Brownies."

"I-I'm sorry. I—" Cheryl began, only to stop and struggle for air as the man's hand found her throat and began to squeeze.

Jeff let out a gasp and started to move toward her, but Hoodie just cocked the gun at him.

"Don't try it! She's gonna die for what she did to me and everybody else," Hoodie said, tightening his grip.

"P-Please," she rasped.

But Hoodie just looked on, grinning like a dog that's found a fresh piece of meat.

"She did say please, you know."

Hearing the new voice, Hoodie actually loosened his grip a bit as both he and Jeff turned to see a man standing on the other side of the alley. He was dressed in a long gold coat and brown clothes, with a wide brimmed hat and a cloth wrapped around his lower face. He carried a long wooden staff in his hand.

"Wha—beat it! This don't concern you, shithead!" Hoodie yelled.

"I'm gonna have to disagree there," the golden man replied. He took a step toward the scene. The minute his foot came down, Hoodie moved the gun from Jeff to him and snapped the trigger back three times. The golden man jerked as each bullet struck him and then tumbled back, striking the wall and slowly falling down. Cheryl could see the blood stain the wall as he fell, and she started to scream, only to have the man point his gun at her.

"Shut up or I'll kill you both right now," Hoodie snapped.

Cheryl gave a sudden, nervous nod as Hoodie turned back to Jeff.

Hoodie opened his mouth to say something, but then a gloved hand grabbed his collar and pulled him back. Hoodie started to move the gun toward his attacker, but before he could, a wooden lion's head crashed into his face. A sound like glass and china exploding filled the air and then a scream of pain from Hoodie as he clutched his broken face.

"I didn't want to do that, you know," the golden man said, moving to stand in front of Hoodie. "So would you like to end this, or do you want to keep going?"

"But … but … I shot you," Hoodie managed to spit out.

"I noticed," Golden replied. He reached inside his shirt, pulled his hand back, and opened it to reveal three empty shells, red with blood.

Cheryl and Jeff froze in shock. But Hoodie wasn't so easily startled. Even with the pain of his broken mouth, he pointed his gun at the golden man, hoping the rest of the round would be enough to take him down. But before he could even put his finger on the trigger, the gun suddenly jerked to the left and then flew out of his hand entirely. Hoodie looked with disbelief as the gun soared through the air and was caught by another figure in a coat, this one feminine, tall and dressed in gray. She held the gun in her hand, looking at it with something almost like curiosity and then held it, palm open with the gun balanced on top. It sat there a moment and then its metal framework seemed to ripple. The shiny metal suddenly began to shrink, losing the shape of the gun and becoming liquid as it vanished into the crevices of the woman's gloved hand. Finally, the gun was gone completely, and the woman flexed her hand and then pulled it back into her coat.

"How … how did—" Jeff said. Both he and Cheryl stared at the gray-clothed woman.

"I wouldn't worry about it," the golden man said. He moved over to Hoodie, who looked back at him, his broken teeth glistening, his breathing a pained whistle of air through his broken nose.

"The important thing is that you no longer have a weapon," Golden said, leaning in close. Looking right into Hoodie's eyes, he said, "Not that you ever needed one, right? You just needed to play the part. You couldn't do her in the usual way, not without too many questions being asked about it. I know what you had planned, and I know why you planned it. It was basic really. But something like that isn't supposed to happen here. Not yet."

"That's what you think," Hoodie whispered back. "Even if you know, so what? If you know about me, then you know that you can't kill me."

"That still leaves plenty of options," Golden replied. He took a step back.

Hoodie, seeing a chance, suddenly moved forward, but he didn't get far. Before he could even take more than two steps, a pair of arms suddenly rose up out of the concrete and grabbed his shoulders, pulling him down.

Jeff and Cheryl, who'd been entranced by the spectacle, now backed up against the wall. As they continued to watch, something else began to rise up out of the concrete, something that slowly took the shape of a man built of stone but dressed the same as the other two in the alleyway. This stone man rose up out of the ground, only to stop at the waist. But that was still enough to hold Hoodie down at his level as Golden knelt down before him and placed both hands on the sides of his head.

Hoodie's eyes darted from side to side as Golden stared at him intently. Suddenly, Hoodie's darting eyes stood still, and the hands on his face began to glow. Golden light pressed against Hoodie's skin, and his eyes went wide in terror. As they froze in place, staring blankly ahead, a hacking sound began to emanate from Hoodie's throat, like he was trying to cough up a dishrag soaked in motor oil. His throat started to bulge, as if the dishrag was actually there. The hacking noises grew stronger. Hoodie's eyes began to cloud over, a golden sheen coming over them as if they were being painted. Golden held on through it all, even as green liquid began to pour out of Hoodie's mouth and he began to convulse. The stone man held him still, and Golden's light didn't fade. The hacking noises began to grow thicker and nastier, as if a herd of frogs had taken up residence in there as well. The noises kept on, until finally, Hoodie threw his head back and a green light suddenly shot out. It hung in the air for a split second and then fell back to the ground right behind the stone man. Golden instantly released Hoodie, as did the stone man, who pulled himself completely out of the ground, turning to flesh and brown cloth in the process. Both they and the gray woman watched as the green light began to fade away, revealing a new form underneath it.

It wasn't huge; it seemed just over four and a half feet tall. Its body was thin but strong, with ropey muscle under the skin. It was dressed in baggy black pants and a sleeveless shirt. But any resemblance to humanity ended there. The creature's skin was green and scaly and, in some places, oozing green sludge. Its arms ended in three fingered, clawed hands that looked sharp enough to cut all the way through a fat man's belly with a single swipe. As the light finished disappearing, the creature let out a snort and then got to its feet. It arched its back and turned to face them. Jeff's face contorted in disgusted shock while Cheryl just stared in utter horror.

The face was the worst. It was stretched out; bones poked out from beneath the skin, creating two lines of small spikes that ran from the forehead down the cheek and met just at the chin. Its mouth was filled with two rows of broken teeth. But the forehead was worse still, long and sloping over the eyes, as if it was trying to form a shield around them. Lack of visibility wasn't a problem, though, as it looked at its prey and attackers with anger.

*   *   *

"Light God. I should've known," the creature sneered, it's voice sandpaper after being pitted with acid.

"And we should have known a gremlin would be dumb enough to pull this stunt," Quake said. "None of the other demons would be stupid enough to do it themselves, Nerb."

"Don't you dare mock me!" the newly named gremlin snapped. "I am Nerbino, Prince of Gremlins."

"And we are three of the Elemental Knights," Forger replied, brandishing her mace.

"You know the rules, Nerbino," Joe said. "Your kind wrecks machines and occasionally possesses others to bring out mischief and light destruction to keep the balance. Murder is out of your jurisdiction."

"How do you expect my kind to do our job with people like her around?" Nerbino sneered, pointing at Cheryl. "Things keep improving every five minutes. People are feeling so secure about it that they don't care about our mischief. We had nothing!"

"There was plenty for you to do," Joe said. "And even if there wasn't, you know we'd never allow murder of an innocent person."

"Like I care," Nerbino answered back. "I'm taking back my territory and no do-gooder human sow is going to stop me!" Nerbino's arm snapped up, and he released a bolt of green energy right at Cheryl.

But before the bolt had gotten close to her, there was a crack of thunder, and a bolt of pure white met the bolt of green. The two held in midair for a moment and then canceled each other out. Nerbino stared in shock and then let out a yelp as a second bolt shot into his chest, knocking him into the wall.

"Wha—What the hell?" Cheryl managed to stammer out.

"Sorry if I startled you. Are you both all right?" a voice said.

Cheryl whipped around to see another strange man, this one dressed in silver, his hands actually smoking as he rubbed them together.

"Yes ... yes. But who ... what are you people?" Cheryl asked. "And what is that *thing*? And how did it get inside that man?"

"Er, kinda hard to explain all at once," the silver man said sheepishly. "Let's just say we are the good guys, and we wanna make sure that he doesn't hurt anybody else. Sound good?"

Cheryl didn't answer right away, and the silver man shook his head with a small laugh. "I know it's a lot to take in, but ...*Hulph*!"

"Jeff? What are you doing?" Cheryl yelled as her friend tightened his grip with the arm that he'd wrapped around the silver man's throat.

The silver man gasped and choked, beating at the man's arms, while Cheryl moved forward and grabbed Jeff's arms, trying to pull him off. But Jeff just drove his elbow into her stomach and doubled his grip, even as the air around him began to crackle. He noticed it all but a second too late; the silver man's body suddenly erupted with electricity, shooting into Jeff with all the force of an electrified cat leaping out after a ride in the dryer. He flew off into the wall, his clothes burned and smoking. But the impact didn't stop him; instead, he rode it and then fell to his feet and bared his teeth at the silver man, the same acid-sandpaper growl coming from his throat that had come from the gremlin.

*   *   *

"Aw crap! There's another one of them!" Groundquake said. But Groundquake had barely gotten the words from his mouth

— 211 —

before a burst of green energy exploded around them. The three Knights were hurled in all directions, as Nerbino cackled and continued to unleash his demonfire on them. Green energy burst all around them, but after the first attack, the Knights sprang into action. Joe held out his palm, calling the light to him. He hurled it at Nerbino, who was too caught up in his attack to notice until it was too late. The light exploded in front of his face, blinding him but not injuring him. Stunned, Nerbino halted his attack and tried to clear his eyes, but those few seconds were all the other Knights needed. Quake pulled out his hammer and slammed it down onto the ground, creating a shockwave that ran through the concrete, cracking it faster than veins crack the eyes of a stressed-out parent. The shockwave reached the gremlin and blasted him up into the air. He hung there a moment and then two large pieces of metal shaped like huge staples flew through the air and connected with his arms. The impact forced him back and into the wall, where the staples buried in deep, pinning the gremlin prince to the wall.

"Nuhhh! Let me go!" Nerbino screamed, struggling against the barriers.

"I think you're better suited there," Forger said.

Thunderer held his staff out, keeping Jeff at bay while Cheryl stood and watched as Jeff growled, his body swaying back and forth as he waited for the moment to strike.

"Let the guy go. We can end this without anyone getting hurt," Thunderer said, keeping his staff trained on Jeff's movement.

"I don't think so," said the gremlin inside Jeff, its voice creaking out from his mouth like a spider from the mouth of a corpse. "We won't let our world be taken by some cow in a bad office dress."

"Look, we both know something like this isn't the way. So why don't you just let that guy go and we can try to figure this thing out?"

"You're terrible at stalling," the gremlin said. "I know why you really want me out. You can't use that thunder crack of yours without hurting this body. And I have no reason to leave. What can you offer anyway—a 10 percent increase in mischief?"

"How about nothing, jackass!" Groundquake snapped as he and the other Knights advanced on the gremlin.

The creature turned Jeff's body toward them and snarled again, holding out Jeff's hands as green energy began to crackle across them.

"You're done here," Joe said, holding another light ball. The others cocked their own weapons. "Just let the humans go, and we'll take you and your prince back to the gremlins. Maybe the king won't destroy you if we talk to him."

The gremlin looked at them and then back to Thunderer and Cheryl, like a caged animal fearful of zookeepers ready to deliver an enema. Joe and the others watched intently, not letting their gaze or weapons down for an instant.

Cheryl stood by, wishing there was something that she could do to end this mess. Looking right at Jeff, she cleared her throat and said, "Look, I don't know what you're all talking about, but I can't believe that all this crap is happening because I wanted to help some people. Isn't there something I can do to work this out?" She looked at Jeff intently. "I know there has to be a sane way for us to let you do your ... well whatever you do and—"

But she never got to finish her statement; another roar issued from Jeff's throat, and the creature leaped at her, his hands glowing green. The Knights instantly started to move as the creature's shadow fell onto Cheryl and Thunderer. But just as he came close to hitting Cheryl, a black-gloved hand suddenly stretched out of the creature's shadow on the ground and grabbed him. Jeff's body seemed to halt in midair as the hand slid through his chest, sinking in like it was a tub of butter. But then Jeff fell forward, the energy on his hands dissipating as he flipped over onto his back and let out a groan.

"What the—Oh, dear God!" Cheryl said. She looked to where the hand still stood inside a pool of black shadow, holding the fat green gremlin in the air. As she and the others watched, the hand began to grow out of the pool, revealing another man, this one dressed in black. But unlike the others, this one gave Cheryl the biggest case of the creeps she'd ever had. He had a long sword hanging from his side, encased in a black sheath. And as he held the gremlin up, Cheryl could see that even his eyes were glowing black. She moved closer to the silver man as the black one began to speak.

"Couldn't have just gone through the usual channels, huh? Had to break the chain of command and try the crazy way?" the black man said. He tightened his grip on the creature's ugly neck.

"We ... shouldn't ... have to ... use channels," the creature managed to get out.

"You're not better than anyone and you damn well know it," the black man said. "You and the prince screwed up here, and you are going to deal with the punishment."

"We're taking you two back to let the king deal with you," the golden man said.

"Now doesn't that sound like a fair treatment?" the black man asked.

"No ... I ... won't go back—not until I—"

"I was afraid you'd say that," the black man sighed. His free hand moved to his waist. There was a hiss of metal as he drew the sword and then held it in front of the gremlin.

"I hope this goes smoothly," the black man said. The gremlin glared at the sword with mounting fear. "I have to use my bad hand here."

"But ... you said ... I had ... to face—" the gremlin stammered as he began to struggle.

"I can see it all there in your heart," the dark man said. "You thought the whole thing up, but you knew the king would never approve it. So you turned to the young, stupid prince and got him to listen to you. And you'll do it again if we let you go. But if you can't talk to anyone else—" The black man released his grip, and the gremlin fell to his feet. But before he hit the ground, the bat swung his other arm, his sword gleaming in the split second it moved across the air. The gremlin stared in disbelief, as a line suddenly opened up in his neck, oozing black blood. The line began to spread, until his entire neck was awash. As the blood touched the ground and began to hiss and bubble, the creature stood there, staring stupidly at the black man, until the latter stretched forth a finger and tapped the gremlin's forehead. The creature's head immediately fell back, falling off his neck as the rest of the body collapsed.

Cheryl's hands flew to her mouth as the black man turned from the body, looked at the golden man, and asked, "Is that all of them?

Joe stared at the dead gremlin, slowly trying to remember how to speak. "Yes," he finally said. "But that was—"

"That was frickin' awesome!" Groundquake said with all the joy of someone watching a winning touchdown. "I mean, with the speech, and the *swish* and the—I mean, *damn!*"

"Your eloquence amazes me as always," Nightstalker said. He

sheathed his sword. Turning to Cheryl and Thunderer, the bat asked, "You all right?"

But Cheryl didn't give an answer; she just stared at the bat. Stalker just shook his head and said, "He would've come back for you if I'd have let him go."

"It really was something we had to do," Thunderer said, helping Jeff to his feet. "But believe me, killing isn't out first option."

"But … it wasn't … I mean … Goddamn it, what just happened here?" Cheryl finally said, looking around. "Guys in primary colors, monsters, weird powers, and decapitations. This is like some sort of twisted version of *Power Rangers*!"

"Pretty good analogy," Stalker conceded.

"Will someone just give me some answers here?" Cheryl said.

"It wanted you dead," Jeff said suddenly, turning to face her. "I could hear everything that the thing wanted when it was inside me. It hated that you were doing so much good around here. So it convinced the other one to go after you, and it used me to get to you."

"Jeff, I—Are you all right?" Cheryl said.

"I am now. But I swear, Cheryl, these guys are a godsend. You wouldn't believe the hatred I felt coming from that thing when it was in me. If they'd have let it live, it would've kept coming back until it had done its job."

Cheryl was quiet a moment as she absorbed that and then asked, "Okay. So do you know who these guys are?"

"I'm not sure. When they showed up, it said something about Elemental Knights," Jeff said. "Is that what you guys—"

"Wrong question," Nightstalker said. He stretched out his hands and placed them on the two humans' foreheads. They started to protest and then stopped as the bat's eyes began to glow once again, and their own eyes began to cloud over with black. He waited a moment, and then leaning in between them, whispered words to them as the others watched. After a few moments, he backed off and said, "Okay, you kids go have fun now."

The blackness left their eyes, and Cheryl and Jeff nodded and walked out of the alleyway to rejoin the flow of humanity.

"So, what did you tell them they were doing?" Joe asked.

"They deserve a nice lunch and romantic conversations," the bat replied. "He does like her, you know."

"Yeah, I got that," Joe replied. "And they won't remember anything?"

"At best, they'll think it was a dream—a really nasty and weird dream."

"Very nice," Thunderer said. "She's done a lot of good around here."

"That's great, guys, but I think we gotta deal with the gremlin prince here," Quake said.

"Agreed," Forger said. She finished chaining together the gremlin's hands and then ripped him from the wall. "Think that the others had any luck with the king?"

"We'll find out soon enough," Joe said. "Don't forget the body."

"Wish Firesprite was here. We could just burn it," Thunderer said. He helped Stalker pick up the dead gremlin, placing the head on the chest. Joe nodded and then vanished in a flash of bright light. One by one, the others followed, disappearing into shadow and thunder, cracking into earth and vanishing, and melting into liquid metal that evaporated into the air, leaving no sign of their presence but some black stains on the wall and the ground that no one would think twice about.

*   *   *

They reformed a second later (or so it seemed to them) inside a large, empty cave, the walls caked with dirt and only a few torches and glowing crystals embedded in the walls to provide light.

"Lovely," Stalker said.

"You sure this is the right spot?" Thunderer asked.

"The gremlins make their home deep under the city, a little bit above sea level," Forger said. "They use magic to keep the water out and have about a million passageways to get to the surface."

"So where are they then?" Thunderer asked, looking around in confusion.

"Let's ask the prince about it," Forger said. She jostled the gremlin's handcuffs.

"Like I would tell you," Nerbino sneered. Stalker began to reach for his blade again, causing the prince to give a second reply. "I don't know where they are."

"That's somewhat comforting," Joe said. "But there should be something here, especially after the others came to talk with the—"

"*Eeeeeeehhhhhhhaaaaaaaahhhhhhh!*"

"Holy Christ!" Stalker cried out as the unknown scream echoed through the cave. He reached back for his sword. But the bat had barely wrapped his fingers around the hilt when he was hit in the gut with a hard, cold missile. He grunted and looked down to see a huge glop of green slime trailing down his tunic and onto his boots. His face contorted in disgust as a second gob of slime struck him in the face. The bat tried to wipe the slime away, as more and more of it rained down on him and his friends, who let out howls of revulsion and stumbled around.

Nerbino just laughed. But after a few minutes, an all-too-familiar voice rang out. "All right, they've had enough!"

The second those words were spoken, the rain of slime stopped, leaving the Knights in their fresh coats of nastiness. They looked up as the gremlins shimmered into visibility around them on the walls, and Sandshifter sauntered in from the side pathway.

"I see you've made some new friends," Joe said. He wiped the slime from his face.

"Naw. I guess I just forgot to warn you about the gremlins' way of dealing with intruders," the wolf replied. "Of course, no one warned me about it either," she added, pointing to the dried slime stains on her clothing.

"Not that you're bitter," Groundquake snarled, slime dripping down from his hat. "Not like you could've made them understand we were coming."

"Hey, I told you I was better at fighting then negotiating," Sandshifter said. "Of course, some people think I need to learn it. And besides, don't they have a lovely war cry?"

"Please tell me you didn't kill the king and take this place for your own," Stalker said. "I'd be happy to be rid of you but—I can't actually finish that sentence."

"Sorry to disappoint, but Wavecrasher took over the negotiations," the wolf replied. "The king is waiting for us and the prince. Weren't there two of them?"

"There were," Thunderer said. "But Nightstalker took care of the other one. Apparently, he was the one who started this."

"Did he now?" Sandshifter asked. "Good for you, Bats."

"Just doing my job," the bat replied.

"Then follow me, and we'll keep you doing it," Sandshifter said. She turned and headed back down the pathway.

The Knights glanced at each other and then put their slime-covered boots to the floor and followed, dragging Nerbino as the gremlins watched.

XVII.

THE KNIGHTS TRUDGED THROUGH the deep caverns of the gremlins' lair, the torches and crystals their only light as Sandshifter led them through the twists and turns. They passed through large stone houses, cut into the rock itself and covered in the grime that the gremlins loved so much. The Knights saw more than a few of the creatures wallowing in the mud and moss of the caverns. And they saw just as many eyes glaring at them, sending daggers, axes, and probably some semiautomatic rounds their way. But not a single gremlin made any move past stares; they knew who the Knights were, and they knew what their presence here, with their prince in chains, meant.

"We're here," Sandshifter said, pointing to the large stone wall in front of them.

"Uh, and where exactly is here?" Groundquake asked.

"Look for the door, rock head," the wolf said, pointing to the large doors carved into the wall. Next to the doors stood two large, armored gremlins holding spears.

"Whatever," the dog muttered.

The group made its way to the doors. The guards glanced down at them and nodded; they stretched out their arms and pulled the doors open. The group made its way inside, dragging Nerbino with them. As the doors swung shut behind them, the Knights found themselves inside a small room made completely of rock and devoid of any kind of decoration. Sandshifter pushed them past that and into the next room. This room was also made of rock, it was but far larger and filled with barrels of rotting food and many other guards, all armed to the teeth.

But what the Knights paid attention to was the large throne in the very back of the room. Windrider, Forester, and Firesprite stood at the sides of the throne, their clothes covered in slime and looks of restrained disgust on their faces. Around them sat barely dressed (and slightly less ugly) gremlin women, hanging around the throne as little more than decorations. And sitting on the throne, was Nerbino's father, Hexeba the VI, the gremlin king.

This Hexeba was a king who had lived well; his fattened body pushed and stretched at his clothes. In the case of his belly, they gave up completely, and it surged past his filthy pants and filthier shirt to rest on his knees. He did resemble his son in some ways, but his bloated face had ruined much of the resemblance, taking Nerbino's features and buried them within folds of flab. A slime-covered robe had been draped over his shoulders and hung to the ground.

Despite his disgust, Joe knew enough about protocol to know he needed to show some respect. Removing his hat, the Light Knight bowed to the gremlin king; the others took the cue and repeated the gesture.

"We thank you for allowing us into your kingdom, King Hexeba," Joe said.

"I have no choice in the matter," Hexeba replied, his voice sounding as if he was gargling compost. "I'm not stupid enough to challenge the power of the Architects. But I do offer thanks for retrieving my son. What happened with the mortals?"

"We found him and another of your court possessing humans and attempting to kill a councilwoman of the city," Joe said. "We both know this is beyond the limits your people were given."

"Indeed I do," Hexeba said, his voice rising in anger. "Bring forth my son."

"With pleasure," Forger said. She dragged the young prince in front of the throne.

Nerbino quickly fell to his knees before his father, who glared at him in anger. "Father, please. I only wanted to improve things for our people," Nerbino stammered. "It is so difficult for us to do our work now and—"

"And this was your solution?!" Hexeba roared, suddenly standing up before his throne. "You have brought the Elemental Knights to our door. Do you have any idea how serious a crime you have to commit to bring them? *Do you*?!"

"I ... I—"

"What put this idea into your head?" Hexeba snarled.

"More like who," Nightstalker said. "Your son was acting with another when we found him."

"And who, pray tell, was this person, so that I might devour him?"

"Oh, I saved you the trouble, sire," Stalker said as he held out his hand. There was a small burst of shadowfire and then the gremlin's decapitated head appeared in the bat's grasp. Hexeba looked at the head and then narrowed his eyes in annoyance.

"Rikino. I shouldn't be surprised. And now, I have even more shame at my son." Hexeba glared at Nerbino.

"He was a fool and you should've been smart enough to know that. Your punishment will be swift and strict, once I decided upon it. Until then, you will be locked in your chambers. Guards!"

Two of the large gremlins quickly came over and took the prince, dragging him out of the room as he twisted and howled in their grasp. Hexeba watched them leave and said to the Knights, "My son will not trouble you any further. I will deal with him myself."

"I'm glad to hear that, sire," Joe replied. "We'll tell the Architects of your compliance. I'm sure they'll appreciate it."

Joe motioned for the Knights near the throne to return to the group. They came fairly quickly, and then Joe continued, "Majesty, I believe there was another of my group down here as well. I was told she negotiated with you."

"Yes, the Water Knight," Hexeba said. "She did quite well in convincing me of my son's stupidity. And in thanks for saving me from unknown shame, I offered her gremlin hospitality."

"Oh, let me get her," Sandshifter said gleefully. She walked over to a large door in the rock. The wolf quickly pulled it open, revealing a long, dark room, in which one could see only mud and rags. However, it was easy to smell the odors from inside and to hear the laughter.

"I think she enjoyed your dining hall, sire. And your harem," Sandshifter said as Wavecrasher stumbled out, her clothes and fur covered with rotten food.

Seeing Joe, the cat stumbled over to her leader. "All … all things … properly … dealt with," the cat sputtered out.

"That was my private hall, Water Knight," Hexeba said. "I do not even let my own son enjoy such finery."

"It was … unforgettable, your highness," Crash gasped.

"Thank you for your understanding, sire," Joe said as he held the cat up. "We will leave the kingdom in your capable hands. Please inform us of any other problems with your son."

The king nodded. As the Knights moved to leave, Wavecrasher

drew in close to Joe and whispered, "We need to talk later. I may have found something."

Joe said nothing but gave a subtle nod.

The Knights turned, gave a final salute, and then vanished in bursts of multicolored light.

* * *

"So, that went well, didn't it?"

"That depends on a few things, horn head," Quake answered. "Your tolerance for pain, your enjoyment of walking through shit, the stench of gremlin that is never going to come out of our clothes—"

"That'll do," Joe said. The light faded from his eyes, replaced by the gray of the Obelisk. Joe wiped the green slime from his clothes and then removed his hat and tried to wipe the gunk off his face. "Why do they insist on doing that?" he asked.

"It's how they treat outsiders," Crash said. She pulled her slimy coat off. "It's how they determine if you're worthy to enter."

"Besides, watching you guys get slimed made up for our little trip," Sandshifter said, chuckling under her dried slime-covered clothes.

"I told you, someone had to go and tell the gremlin king what was going on. And I figured he'd be afraid of you," Joe said.

"And they were," Wavecrasher said. "They scattered away from you in droves, Sandy."

"Yeah. But that changed when they found out *somebody* said that I couldn't kill anyone," the wolf said, glaring at Joe.

"Oh, knock it off. We've had enough trouble with the gremlins already," Nightstalker snapped. "Pointlessly killing them won't help matters."

"Oh, like you can talk," Forester said. "Ah suppose you were humming the words to 'Imagine' when you sliced that demon's head off?"

"He was trouble. If we'd have left him alone, he would've stirred up more trouble. I knew the king would see it that way," the bat replied.

"Sure, you can say that," Sandshifter sneered. "But if I killed him, it would be 'mindless' and 'horrible.'"

"Exactly. Like everything else you do."

"Oh, you shut up!"

"Both of you shut up!" Joe snapped. "Look, we're just tired and pissed because we had to tread through demon shit and be covered by slime from God only knows where. So how about we just knock it off, shower, and try to focus on the fact that we were able to save a person's life?"

The Knights were quiet a moment and then Wavecrasher nodded. "Yeah, at least we helped do that. Almost makes the slime worth it."

"Almost," Groundquake said. He watched the ooze slide off his coat and onto the ground.

"Now let's get this crap off," Joe said.

The Knights quickly turned and headed for the stairs that led up to the other rooms of the Obelisk—except for two.

Once the others had gone, Joe turned to Wavecrasher and asked, "What was it you saw?"

"I'm not sure of it," the cat replied. "But something in that place is wrong."

"I think we established that."

"No, it's more than the gunk. I-I'll need to check things out and make sure. Let me have some time, and then we'll talk in the library okay? I can give you a better report then."

"Fine. Just clean off first," Joe said.

The cat nodded and then headed up the stairs. Joe followed, grimacing at the feel of the goo on his clothes. But even with that and Wavecrasher's cryptic and undetermined "something," he supposed that he shouldn't complain about how things had gone. True, they had been humiliated, but at least the gremlins were taken care of and a good person had been saved. But the slime ...

Joe shrugged. He had saved someone's life. Still, he was getting tired of playing peacemaker. Even after six months in "real-world time" (time moved differently here) most of the Knights' early problems were still there. Sandshifter was still angry, and Forester was still self-righteous and sharp-tongued. They got Wavecrasher mad because she was convinced that all their efforts had to be for the balance. They got Groundquake mad because he wanted to do things himself. And Nightstalker, well, he just couldn't stand the two of them. The others, thankfully, weren't getting ready to kill them for it. But they were getting close.

How did this happen? Joe thought as he turned his gaze toward the door that appeared on his left. Joe turned off the stairs and stepped through into the level that served as his room. The Architects had been right about this place; it altered itself to suit their needs. The stairs, for example, worked in a very special way. All anyone had to do was to climb the stairs up to a door, which would open onto the level that they desired to be on.

Joe pushed the door open and stepped into the room he had created for himself. The Obelisk had shaped this room into a mix of several familiar things for Joe, so much so that Joe had had some difficulty staying at first. There was a large bookcase, filled with familiar texts that Joe had taken from the Obelisk's library (which contained nearly every book ever written and whatever new ones the occupant might desire). There was a large wooden desk, like the one he'd had in his old study, along with an old Planters container filled with pens. The room also contained a bed; a closet, which contained a few pairs of clothes; and even a shower and a battered Maytag washer and dryer that looked like the ones he'd had.

At the moment, those two items were the ones that called Joe's attention. He immediately pulled off his slimy clothes, and once he'd gathered them together, he dumped them into the washer, grabbed the bottle of cleaner, and turned it on full. As the washer ran, Joe turned to the shower, stepped inside, and turned the hot water on full blast. As Joe felt the hot water soothe his skin, he thought about all the other showers he'd taken after missions. The gremlin slime was bad, but Joe had had a few bloody showers as well. Not all the creatures they'd had to deal with were as (relatively) harmless or understanding of the balance as the gremlins.

His mind flew back to one of their last missions, concerning a young white magic user who had been exiled from his coven. The boy, Sam, had aided an imprisoned demon in the hopes of gaining greater power for himself, so that he might better the world. Sam had been a fool, but Joe had worked to help him. Sam had realized his mistake and tried to help them. But during the fight, the boy had attempted to send the monster away. And then …

*   *   *

"What the hell is happening?" Windrider yelled as, behind them, a black hole began to open.

"I'm sending this thing away!" Sam yelled, his hands still glowing with the energy of the spell he'd cast. "And I'm sucking out its power to do it!"

"You idiot! That means you opened the door this way too!" Wavecrasher cried out as the hole began to pull at everything, Knights and demon included. The portal even began to suck away the area, along with everything that wasn't nailed down. Only Sam was unaffected, and as they watched, he began to glow as the demon grew smaller.

"I don't care! I need the power!" Sam yelled.

The demon, a red monster with a horned face and scaly goat legs, tried to keep itself in this world.

"No, Sam! Look!" Joe screamed. He pointed to the hole. Behind the shadow of the demon, other forms could be seen—large, deformed shapes that were moving closer with every second.

"I need more power!" Sam screamed. "I won't close the portal until I get it!"

"Then I will!" Joe said. He managed to pull up his staff and fire a light beam at the demon. It struck the creature hard, throwing it back into the void. But just as it began to fall into the portal, it managed to grab the edges of the circle, standing just between the two worlds.

"Joe, hit him again!" Sandshifter yelled.

"No!" Wavecrasher cried out. "Joe's power would be infused into the spell! There's no telling what can happen with that much power!"

"Then what the hell do we do?" Groundquake demanded as the other demons got closer.

"The spell isn't strong enough to suck him in all the way. If we—"

"No!" Sam said. "My magic will be strong enough once he is drained. I can stop him and then fix everything!"

"Not without destroying it all first!" Groundquake screamed.

Sam gave no response, but the portal began to draw even more into itself as the pressure increased

Still the demon wouldn't let go; still, the others grew closer.

"Get back! I will stop you!" Sam kept screaming, even as the demon grinned, and the others began to step out of the portal.

"I command you to—"

But Sam said no more as he looked down and saw the end of a blade sticking out of his chest. He turned to see a black-coated figure standing behind him, his red eyes glaring. The weakened demon gasped and then grimaced as the portal started to fold in on itself, devoid of its spell caster.

The monster tried to hold it open, as did its fellows, but it was no avail. The portal folded up, taking the monsters back to nothing.

Joe looked over at Sam and watched as Stalker withdrew his sword from the boy's body. As the boy collapsed, Joe glared at the bat. "You killed him. Why? You could've just knocked him out."

"That wouldn't have stopped him," Stalker said. "The spell was infusing him with too much power. This was the only way this could have ended."

"No it wasn't! There was no need for that!"

"Joe, the boy was a rogue magic user. He was arrogant and would've sacrificed the world to reshape it as he saw fit. He had a chance to prove me wrong, and he failed. Can you say letting a person who posed this much danger to everything around him, and to the balance, deserves to live after failing a chance at redemption?"

"Yes, I—"

"I don't," Groundquake said. "The kid was a menace. If we'd let him go, he would've found something else to screw up."

"I ... I don't like it, but I can't disagree," Crash said.

"I do like it," Sandshifter added. "He got what he deserved."

One by one, the Knights agreed, though most were reluctant to admit it. And as they spoke, Joe felt himself understanding their logic more and more. And he hated himself for it.

*　　*　　*

Joe had been forced to accept that day, but he had added it to a growing collection in his mind of Stalker calmly doing horrible things for "the balance" that Joe had to accept. The problem was, as dark as he was, Stalker was also one of the pillars Joe needed. Stalker stuck up for him at every opportunity and always did his best to help out. Joe also found him to be a good listener, often helping to bring Joe out of the dark patches and help him get refocused on the task at hand.

Hell, why not just say it? He's the closest thing to a best friend that I have here, Joe thought. But that didn't erase the other half of Stalker's being. The bat was an extremely efficient and extremely willing killing machine. Stalker would take his blade to any human, demon, or angel that was upsetting the balance. Joe remembered the ease with which he had cleaned the blood from his sword after killing Sam and the coldness when the bat had called the boy "beyond our help."

He sure as hell is now, Joe thought. *How does he do it? How does he just kill them so easily? He says he doesn't like it, but how can I believe him when he's so calm about it? How am I supposed to keep the balance like this? Killing everyone that screws up? I mean it can't be part of it, right?*

Joe just shook his head as he reached up and shut off the water. He'd already been forced to accept that some demons and monsters were necessary in the world; maybe this was just something that he needed to accept. Sometimes, things on both sides just had to be killed.

But that wasn't all of it. Joe wasn't just worried about Stalker; he was worried about himself. The strange blacking out in the training, when he'd used his powers but couldn't remember it, still frightened him. Joe didn't want to have a Hulk problem on top of everything else. And despite the lack of a relapse, he worried that it might go come again and go too far one day. Having a berserker side might get the job done, but ...

"It ... it's so *wrong*," Joe muttered to himself. He got out of the shower and reached for a towel. Drying himself off, Joe turned his attention back to Stalker and wondered if maybe he needed to talk to the bat about his ease with killing. But he immediately threw the idea away. Nothing he'd tried before had worked; Stalker had listened and then politely told Joe that, while he understood what Joe was trying to do, he had accepted his role in the group, and there wasn't much more to it than that.

Maybe I need some outside advice, Joe thought.

The ding of the washer told him his clothes were done. Joe plodded over to the washer, pulled out the clothes, and threw them into the dryer. The battered machine buzzed and hummed, but ten minutes later, it was done. Joe marveled at the speed of the machines (though he figured it was magic-induced) and pulled out his clothes. He quickly began to step into them, enjoying the warmth of the freshly dried clothes. He had some other clothes in the closet that were more ... "normal", but for what he was about to do, Joe felt it was appropriate to dress up.

As he tightened his coat and pulled on his hat, Joe turned his gaze to his staff. Picking it up, Joe placed his hand onto the head. He called his power to him, and began to whisper Ralin's name. His hand began to glow, causing the staff to shine. It was only then that he pulled his hand back as the light left the staff in a sphere and began to gather into

— 227 —

another shape. Within a few moments, a golden, transparent being stood in front of him. Joe knelt before it.

"Thank you for coming," Joe said.

"It is never a burden to help one who needs it," Ralin replied. "What troubles you, my Knight?"

"The same thing, I'm afraid," Joe said with a sigh. "I know that you've heard me talk about Stalker before, but—"

"I have spent most of creation trying to understand Rastla. I know well your confusion," Ralin said. "But you must remember that there is a balance in what the two of you do."

"Maybe. But then, why I don't I believe it?" Joe asked. "I've seen things doing this job that I never thought anyone would see. And yet the idea of him being so accepting of death—it's so foreign to me."

"That is the nature of your relationship, as is mine with Rastla," Ralin replied. "And remember, he asks her the same questions of you. But there can be acceptance."

"How?"

"There will come a time, Lightrider, when you will see that there are many answers hidden away in the darkness that the light cannot reveal, as he will come to find answers in the light that shadow cannot see. Both of them can be right; balance is knowing when they are right."

Joe started to ask what that meant, but before he could, Ralin raised a hand and gestured behind him. Joe nodded, knowing that the Architect had many other duties to fulfill. Ralin's image began to fade, but before he vanished completely, he said, "Seek the answers in the dark."

As the words faded, Joe fell back onto his bed and put his hands over his face.

"Answers in the dark. *Riiiiiiiiight.* Now, if I was home, I know I could get a straight answer. All I'd have to do is—"

But the words turned into a sigh before Joe finished. Pulling himself up on the bed, he reminded himself that his days of asking Jeri for advice were gone. Despite his efforts to adapt to his new world, he was still catching himself yearning for home, the old ways, and old comforts.

"C'mon, Joe. You can't fall apart now," he said to himself. "After all the work it took to get everyone to accept this, can you imagine going back now? You're dead. And Stalker would be in charge then."

Joe kept going, naming logical, sensible reasons. But even if the sense they made was going into his head, Joe knew it wasn't going into his heart.

"I'd better go meet Wavecrasher, take my mind off this," Joe muttered. He got up from his bed. Grabbing his staff, Joe made his way to the door and focused on the level of the Obelisk he wanted to visit. He stepped out, but then paused a moment and retraced his thoughts.

He took a few steps up, and came to a door with a small hole in it. Glancing inside, he watched the scene in the sparse little room unfold.

"Can't we do this later?" Forester asked, clutching his ax.

"We had a schedule. You agreed to it. Fighting a few gremlins doesn't change it," Sandshifter said. She spun her staff in front of her. "Besides, I did most of the work."

"Hey, I—"

"Attacked at random, instead of using your powers like I taught you to," the wolf replied. "And I'm not going to let that happen again. When you can use your powers correctly, you can take on anyone. Now, use them!"

With that, Sandshifter stopped spinning the staff and unleashed a wave of sand at the squirrel. Forester gulped but still managed to spin the ax around, creating a circle of green energy that solidified into a wooden shield.

"Good!" Sandshifter said as the sand passed over the shield. "Now use—"

But the wolf didn't get to finish, as thick vines shot out of the shield. They went immediately for the wolf, first wrapping around her arms and then her legs. They lifted her up and shook her left to right, forcing her to drop her staff. It clattered to the ground as the vines quickly dragged her toward the shield. The wood of the shield twisted around, until a huge mouth of wooden teeth emerged from its center.

Sandshifter's eyes went wide, but she otherwise showed no reaction as she came closer to the mouth. The vines started to push her in, but suddenly there was a flash of orange and then the wolf exploded into a mass of sand. It fell about the room as Forester looked out from behind the shield. He watched as it piled up and sent out the vines to disperse it. But as the vines came close, the sand itself reared up in tendrils of its own and forced the vines down. The shield vibrated as the sandy tendrils pulled and tugged, until finally they were ripped from the shield, falling dead to the floor.

Forester saw his vines die but quickly grew more vines from them, in an effort to batter the sands away. But the tendrils reached out again, and caught them. They pulled the squirrel's arms taut, even as further tendrils wrapped around his legs, locking him into place. More of the sand spread out and pulled his ax away from its sheath, dropping it on the ground. The squirrel kept struggling, his efforts growing more and more intense as, in front of him, the sandpiles recombined and reformed into the shape of Sandshifter. The wolf looked at him a moment and then picked up her staff and walked over. She tapped him in the chest, and said, "You're dead now. Why?"

"B-Because—"

"Because you did what you've been doing since we started," Sandshifter sighed as the sands holding him in place fell away. "You came up with one idea, and when it didn't work, you panicked. Damn it, fluffy tail, you had a perfectly good shield! Why did you leave it?"

"You … you broke the vines. Ah didn't want you to damage the shield further so—"

"*Usted podría haber arreglado! Al igual que podría haber…* You could've fixed it! Just like you could've grown more vines from behind it!" the wolf snapped. "You can use your powers in more than one way! It doesn't have to always be the damn flytrap. Poison thorns on the vines? Calling the ax back to you? Did that ever occur to you?"

Forester was quiet and then muttered, "No."

"Of course not! Because you only think one step at a time. Look," Sandy said, her voice getting calm again. "You weren't being too elaborate there—it was a good, simple attempt without any boasting. And sometimes you can do a quick strike, and you were at least close to doing that. But there are also times that you can't kill things in one blow. That's when you have to be creative and think on your feet. It might mean a multistep attack, but then that's what you'll have to do. Panicking because your one idea didn't work is going to get someone killed. Okay?"

"Yeah."

"I need more than that. I'm not trying to teach you this for my health."

"Ah understand, all right?"

"Good. So what are we going to work on?"

"But you just—"

"Tell me!"

Sighing, the squirrel said, "Not panicking. Having more than one kind of attack. Having backups. And learning multistep blows."

"Good. Then let's do this again."

Joe turned away then. He heard the sounds of the battle beginning again. He'd found out about these sessions a few months ago, when he'd been looking for the wolf. He'd watched the session and a few more after it, with Sandshifter always coming up victorious against Forester. Joe let them think no one knew about their lessons because he thought it was a good idea for both of them. It gave Sandy someone to take out her aggression on, and hopefully, it would teach Forester better use of his powers. Even Joe had to admit that the wolf was making a lot of sense with her statements. And if they worked, he might have two people that were a little easier to deal with.

With that behind him, Joe refocused his attention on his original destination and, after a few steps, came to a door. Grasping the handle, Joe pulled it open and stepped inside the room. He paused a moment to take in the old musty smells of the great library. He'd come across this room by accident one day, during the initial explorations. He'd found himself trying to remember, for whatever reason, the title of the Robert Frost poem about a tree. He'd racked his brain, trying to think of it, and then he'd come across the door that led into the library. Joe had gone inside and then stopped in disbelief at what he'd discovered. The library was massive, as if it had been designed to hold every single book ever written and every book that would be. The room itself was a giant circle, with bookshelves that ran all around and seemed to stretch up to infinity. Despite the amount of shelf space, there was still plenty of room to move around.

As Joe had looked around in amazement, he'd heard the sound of something rolling toward him. Joe had whirled around, only to see a large metal ladder, attached to the walls of bookshelves, wheeling itself over to where he stood. Joe had looked at the ladder for a moment and then cautiously stepped onto it. The second he was on it, the ladder moved, whipping him around the room as the shelves seemed to rise up before his eyes. Finally, it had come to a stop, bringing Joe at least fifty feet off the ground. But as he looked ahead to counteract the vertigo, he'd noticed that the book right in front of him was *The Complete Works of Robert Frost.*

Since then, Joe had revisited the library many times but not only for leisurely reading. He'd quickly learned that the library also contained books on magic and demons that had been essential for the job.

Coming back to the moment, Joe said, "I should try to find that book on the Cyclops," as he walked inside. "Ever since that one that was hiding out under Athens—"

"The book's on the seventh shelf up."

Joe turned toward the voice to see Wavecrasher and Firesprite sitting at the table. The lizard was sitting causally, her legs up on the table, as she paged through a white paperback. But the cat was intently looking through a thick tome of demon text, with two more on the table next to her.

"You wanted to talk?" Joe asked as he made his way over to the table.

"Just a sec; I'm doing some research," Wavecrasher replied, not taking her eyes off the page.

"What else is new?" Firesprite asked. "No offense, but all you ever do is research."

"And what are you reading again?" Wavecrasher asked.

"*Tom Sawyer,*" Firesprite replied with a sigh. "It's a classic, without any facts to memorize. You might enjoy it, you know."

"I'll remember that when we're unprepared for the next demon attack."

"Look, I'm just saying you've already been obsessing over demons and that glimmer—"

"*Glamour.* And once I figure that spell out, we'll have the perfect disguise. We'll be able to walk around anywhere we want without sticking to the shadows."

"Yeah, that's great. But spending months trying to learn it, along with reading every other book in this place, is way too much to take in."

"I take my job seriously. And the glamour's complicated. I need to learn more about it."

"It's not that important. It isn't like we hang out on Earth unless we have a mission."

"And it could be useful when we do!"

"If you ever get it to work."

"Oh yeah?" With that, the cat suddenly called out a series of words. Her image shimmered before Joe's eyes, and when it cleared, both he and Firesprite stared in disbelief. Then the lizard started laughing.

"What's so funny? I look human now, don't I?"

"Oh, sure," the lizard said between giggles, "except Abe Lincoln's been dead for over a hundred years."

"Humph," the sixteenth president said, as he stroked his beard. "Well, when I get it down, it'll be great."

"Sure. If the Hall of Presidents at Disneyworld breaks down."

"Why, you scaly—"

"That's enough," Joe said, stepping between them. "Firesprite, you know the glamour could be useful to all of us, if Crash can get it to work. We need as much magic as science in this line of work. And speaking of which, Crash, would you shed the glamour and share with me what it is you think happened down there?"

The cat nodded and quickly spoke another set of words, changing back to normal. She then said, "After I check things. I wanna be sure I'm right."

"Look, I know you had a bad time with the gremlins today, but that doesn't mean that you saw something that shouldn't be there. They aren't exactly normal anyway," Firesprite said.

"No. But it could've been something," Wavecrasher replied.

"What did you see?" Joe asked, putting his hand on the book Wavecrasher was reading. "And why didn't you tell me there?"

"I saw some weird stuff with the ... concubines," Wavecrasher replied. "I think it means something big."

"What weird thing—well, more weird than usual thing—were they doing?" Joe asked. "And again, if you thought it was such a problem—"

"I didn't know if I was seeing it or imagining it," Wavecrasher said. "I just thought it was unnatural for them."

"Look, why didn't anybody else see anything like it?" the lizard argued.

"That's why I'm checking," Wavecrasher said. "And as soon as I find what I need, I'll prove it."

"Look, here's an idea. Instead of checking and rechecking, why don't you tell me what happened and I can judge for myself?" Joe asked.

"After I can back it up," Wavecrasher said.

"No. Now. Please."

The cat looked through another page and then, looking up and seeing Joe's stern expression, sighed and began to tell her tale. "The king invited them into the hall. The girls were apparently very interested in everyone ... and ... in me for some reason ... and they started ... touchin' me."

"Okay. Thus far, I'm inclined to think hysteria," Joe said.

"Listen. One of them started ... dancing by the torchlight."

"Oh dear God," Joe said, shivering with the words. "How bad was—"

"If you had seen your grandparents in the shower, it could not have been more disturbing."

Joe shivered and said, "Just keep going."

"Anyway, while she was dancing, I was trying to keep my eyes on the ground, when I noticed something about her shadow. It was ... well, flickering."

"Flickering?"

"In and out. One second it was there. Then it would vanish, and then it would come back."

"Couldn't that have been your imagination?"

"That's what I've been saying," Firesprite said.

"I know. But then, just before you guys let me out, she glanced at me, and I saw a weird light flash in her eyes. I wouldn't have thought anything about it—their eyes are always dilated when they're down there—but with the shadow too, I knew I had to check it out and make sure before I got everyone worried."

"What did you remember?" Joe asked.

Wavecrasher started to answer, but as she did, she glanced at the book, and suddenly let out a yell of "Ah-ha!" She stabbed the book with her finger.

"See? Right here, scale belly," the cat said triumphantly.

Both Firesprite and Joe made their way over to the cat and then glanced down at the page to read the text:

"As the Chaos Demons existed before the creation of natural laws, they do not normally follow them. Nor are they bound by them. This fact can be essential in tracking the Chaos Demons while they are in a mortal form. Though they are capable of duplicating any form flawlessly, their hatred for natural law causes them to have small 'flickers' or momentary breaks in their following of the natural law. Some examples can be a slight change in height or weight, a change in skin color or texture, or even failing to cast a shadow. However the most common 'flicker' is a brief view of the demon's 'unlight,' the glow it casts from its scales. This glow can come from many openings in a mortal form, but is most commonly seen in the eyes."

"You see? This proves it," Wavecrasher said.

"Oh, dear God," Joe said.

"Wait a second. We still don't know if this is real or if she imagined it," Firesprite said.

"Think about it," Wavecrasher said back. "This whole thing stinks anyway. You know the gremlins have about as much balls as a castrated snake. So what would possess a lowly royal lackey to think up a scheme like this and present it to the prince? And what would make the prince crazy enough to accept it, knowing the sort of cosmic shit it would bring down?"

"Well … she does have a point," Firesprite said. "They don't seem like the type to make a move like this."

"And when I did see the light, I was reminded of the demons we fought while training," Wavecrasher said. "I thought it might be something else, but now …" Her voice trailed off.

"I wish you were wrong," Joe said, rubbing his head. "But I agree with you, Crash. I think that we might be dealing with our first real Chaos Demon."

XVIII.

"Wait, wait, let's not start panicking just yet," Firesprite said. "You said you were distracted in there. And besides, why would they go after the gremlins? They're the lowest rung on the demon ladder."

"For the same reason they do anything—to screw up the balance," Wavecrasher said. "Why else would the prince suddenly be crazy enough to go after a human like that? And why would another one get the idea to suggest it to him?"

"Even if you're right, these books can't give us all the answers," Firesprite said. "We need to figure out what to do, not argue back and forth."

"Joe?" Wavecrasher asked.

"I'll contact the king, tell him we need a full search of his realm," Joe answered

"No. That might tip off the demon, if it is there," Firesprite countered. "The answer is for one of us to go down there covertly to watch and look for any signs."

"That would be trouble if we were caught."

"But it would avert tipping off the demon."

"I should do it," Wavecrasher said.

"No," Joe said. "I think we all know who should go."

"Oh, he's not gonna like this," Firesprite said.

"Do you really think he's the best choice?" Wavecrasher asked. "He hates them, and he doesn't always listen to you. And he isn't exactly quiet."

"Earth is the most abundant element down there," Joe said. "He has the best shot of anyone of us."

"What about Windy?"

"He's underground; there wouldn't be as much air for him to use."

"Joe's right. Quake is the best choice," Firesprite said.

"Thanks. But before I do anything, I want a second opinion. Crash, do you think this would work?"

"Well … if no one knew, it would be an advantage," the cat said. "And it—Yes, I think it would work."

"Good. Because I do too," Joe said. "But there's still one thing left."

*   *   *

"No. Friggin'. Way. In. Hell."

"Quake, please," Joe said as the dog turned to face the wall of his room. "You're the best one to hide down there."

"Their whole realm is a giant hole in the ground," Firesprite said. "A guy who can become part of the earth could hide out perfectly."

"Yeah, that's true," Groundquake said. He glanced at the poster he'd stuck on the wall of the NY Mets. The dog had gravitated toward almost all things New York in his room design; the room looked like a NYC city block had thrown up on it, especially with the "Stop" and "One Way" signs on the walls. Joe wasn't bothered by it, but he felt like he was walking into some kind of bad theme restaurant every time he came in here.

"So, you understand why we need you to do this?" Joe said.

"Oh, completely," Quake said. "But I still ain't gonna do it."

"You know how bad this could be," Wavecrasher said, "if there really is a Chaos Demon—"

"You jump at everything, fur ball. I am not spending days at a time down with those things on a weak hunch," Quake said, turning to face them. "Dear God, did you notice the smell when we were down there? It was like sweat socks and shit mixed together."

"Groundquake, I know it's a sacrifice," Joe said. "But if Wavecrasher's right about the demon, we might be able to stop this with minimal bloodshed. Does that appeal to you?"

"Sure. If the gremlins were somebody that would make a difference," Groundquake replied. "C'mon, Joe, they're mischief makers with poison blood. Are we really that concerned with them?"

"You know we need to be," Firesprite replied.

"Why? In case little Nerbino decides to go after somebody else he ain't supposed to?" the dog snapped back. "If the demon's there to take care of the gremlins, I say let 'em. We'll deal with it when it comes to something important."

"My God, how can you be such a douchebag?" Wavecrasher said in disbelief. "There's something that could destroy the world as we know it down there, and you don't care because it's hiding among gremlins?"

"Yeah, pretty much," Quake replied.

Wavecrasher snapped back with a few more choice words, to which Quake had a few retorts involving the cat's mother, a goat, and a long night alone in the field. The two instantly began to argue back and forth, louder and louder as Firesprite and Joe tried to get things back on track. But no matter what words the lizard or the man had to say, they were lost as the cat and dog bickered back and forth.

But then something happened that relieved Joe of the need to settle the argument. The door leading to the room creaked open, and a black, furry head said, "I heard arguing on the way to the kitchen. Is everything all right in here?"

"Keep outta this. It don't concern you," Groundquake sneered.

"It concerns everybody," Wavecrasher said back. "Stalker, can you come in? Maybe you can help us solve this."

"Wavecrasher believes she saw evidence of a Chaos Demon in the gremlin realm," Joe said.

"Are you sure?" Stalker asked, looking right at the cat as he entered the room.

"Not entirely. But I saw enough to make me think that we need to watch the situation," Wavecrasher said.

"We wanted to ask Quake because of his earth powers, but he's not willing to help," Firesprite said.

"I see," Stalker said, stroking his chin in thought. "Quake, exactly what is your reason for refusing to do this?"

"Do I have to spell it out?" the dog sneered. "It's *gremlins*. They don't even matter to evil and they're just a nuisance."

"So you would let everyone else in the world die?"

"No, but—Look the cat isn't even sure that—"

"I don't think you understand that this isn't a matter of choice anymore," Nightstalker explained. "If one of the demons has escaped, we need to keep an eye on it. And you are best qualified to do that right now."

"And what if I say no?"

"You can do that. And if this *is* real, and we have to go deal with it, then we can feed you to it first."

"Like you'd have the balls," Groundquake snapped. "Why don't you go down there then, you flyin' rat?"

The bat stared a moment and then let out a chuckle, shaking his head in amusement. Quake sneered at him, while Joe glared at the dog. But the glare changed a second later as a black-gloved hand wrapped around the dog's throat, pulled him up off the ground, and pulled him in close to Nightstalker's burning red eyes. "Lemme make this clear for you, Alpo boy," the bat said, his voice quiet but vibrating with anger. "This is something that could mean the end of the world. We need to check it out. You are the best person to do it, but you *don't feel like it* because you don't like the *fucking gremlins*?

"You stupid little mutt, do you ever think of anything other than yourself?!"

"Stalker, calm down," Firesprite said as Quake struggled and choked in the bat's grasp.

"I have put *up* with your *shit* for *too long*," the bat said, shaking the dog with each raised syllable. "You complain about *every single job* that you don't like. Well, guess what? This is bigger than you, bigger than the rest of us. So whatever you think about the gremlins means precisely *jack shit*! So here's what's gonna happen. You're *gonna* go down there. You're *gonna* watch for the demon, if it is there. And if you do find one, then you are going to do your job and help stop it! Do you get that?! *Do you*?!"

Even with the bat's fingers tight around his throat, Quake managed to squeak out something that sounded like "yes,"

Nodding, Stalker dropped him and then turned on his heel and walked out the door, his coat fluttering behind him. The others stared in shock, especially Groundquake, his face twisted between disbelief and rage. Slowly, he pulled himself up, his face working and twisting, until he stood and spoke. "Joe?"

"Uh?"

"When do ya want me down there?"

"As … as soon as possible."

"Not a problem."

"Good," Joe said. He slowly began to head for the door. "Sprite, why don't you get him ready? Wavecrasher, you too?"

"Sure—" the lizard began.

But Joe had already reached the door and pulled it open. Without a word, he stepped outside and shut it behind him.

*   *   *

Joe turned on the stairs and began to move up, focusing his thoughts on the kitchen as he walked up the stairs. After a moment, the wide door appeared before him, and Joe stepped through without a word. The kitchen was actually a huge, ceramic tiled room, filled with cabinets containing silverware, plates, and whatever food the person might desire. There were toasters, microwaves, a stove, and even a huge freezer for the special meals. Firesprite had been spending a lot of time in here, trying out her apparent talent for food.

Stalker was by the refrigerator, getting what looked like cheese and turkey.

"Nightstalker?" Joe began. "What was—"

"Oh, hey, Joe," the bat replied, as casually as if the whole incident hadn't happened. "You want anything? There's some pretty good roast beef in here."

"Stalker, can we talk about what just happened?" Joe interrupted.

"Sure. What part of it do you wanna talk about?" Stalker replied as he pulled out some mayo.

"Well, for starters, the fact that you nearly strangled him?"

"Joe, we can't die, remember?"

"That doesn't make it right. And it sure doesn't make it our first option," Joe asked.

"No. But you had been talking to him with no success, so I felt another course was the best idea," the bat replied. "Besides, you know how stubborn he is."

"Stalker, no one deserves that," Joe said.

"Not everyone does," Stalker replied. "But if I hadn't done it, would he be so eager to help now? He'll do everything in his power to be invisible down there and spend all his time watching the king. It's perfect."

"Stalker," Joe said and then stopped. He rubbed his head, trying to think of how to proceed. The bat was making a lot of sense, but it was wrong. It had to be. Thankfully, Stalker sensed his friend's anguish, and putting down his food, he came over to the Light Knight.

"Obviously, this bothers you," Stalker said.

— 240 —

"Of course it—I mean … Damn it, Stalker, I don't like manipulating people into doing what we want!" Joe finally said. "Letting you kill that gremlin was bad enough, but scaring and threatening someone like that makes this whole thing feel wrong. Do you know how fast I would've been canned for pulling shit like that when I was on Earth?"

"Ahh. Now we've got it," Nightstalker said. "Look, Joe, I never said I liked doing that to Groundquake. But it needed to be done. He would never have gone down there of his own free will. And even if he had, he would've done a shitty job of it, come back, and then whined about how horrible it was."

"How do you know?" Joe asked. "I agree he would've been unhappy, but I'd like to think he knows enough about the demon to take it seriously."

"If he did, he would've gone down there right away," the bat replied. "I've seen Quake. He goes with what he thinks is best. And he didn't think that going down there for so long on a hunch was the best thing. So I just gave him some incentive."

"By forcing him into it!" Joe yelled. "Is this how we're gonna do things? We're gonna twist people into doing what we want?"

"No," the bat replied, a hint of annoyance in his voice. "We're going to twist people into doing what we *need*, when we *don't have a choice.*"

"How about not twisting them?" Joe asked. "Goddamn it, we're supposed to be the good guys! This is what the demons do. This is what evil people do—"

"Gee, thanks," Stalker said, folding his arms across his chest.

"Wait, no, Stalker, I didn't mean—"

"No. But you said it. And you know what, Joe? Sometimes it has to be what we do too."

"Why? I mean, can't there—"

"I hope there is. But we aren't always gonna build trust or win people over like that," the bat said, his voice rising as he spoke. "But lemme make a few things clear for the moment.

"Number one, we are fighting off monsters on both ends of the spectrum to keep the universe in balance. Number two, we are currently a bunch of inexperienced creatures that haven't been doing it all that long. Number three, not everyone here is committed to that goal just yet. Number four, until everyone here does agree on that goal, we may have to twist some arms in order to get things done.

"And number five, *you are our leader, and you can't do that! So I have to do it for you! And if I didn't, we wouldn't get anywhere! So don't cry to me about it, okay?*"

As the bat finished, Joe found words bubbling up his throat toward his tongue, bitter words that tasted like the sole of a homeless person's foot. They would've spewed from his mouth, if the door hadn't suddenly swung open followed by Sandshifter entering.

"Oh, sorry to interrupt. I heard some yelling outside," the wolf said. "Is the odd couple finally having an argument?"

"Not one that concerns you," Stalker said coldly. He turned and placed the food back into the fridge.

"Oh, didn't you want that?" Sandshifter asked.

"I'm not hungry anymore," the bat replied. He shut the door and turned toward the exit, marching past Joe without a word.

The second the kitchen door shut, the wolf turned to Joe and said, "That was loud, you know. I heard it all the way in the training room."

"Not now," Joe said.

"You know, he's got a point. You really shouldn't bitch to him."

"How much of that did you hear?" Joe said, facing the Desert Knight.

"Enough," Sandshifter replied. "And like I said, you really shouldn't bitch to him. Stalker does all the mean and nasty shit for you."

"I do plenty on my own."

"Really? Do you think those Minotaurs in Greece slit their own throats when we couldn't stick them back in the labyrinth? Do you think those Iraqis begged us to save them from some other 'dark demon?' And do you think that Quake and I would even remotely care what you think, if we didn't have someone dragging things out of our nightmares to make them real?"

"No. I don't believe it would go that far—that *he* would go that far."

"Oh, he does. And it's the only reason things get done around here. Face it, sometimes your way doesn't work. He does the things you don't want to do. And the only thing you can do about it is accept it. Of course, that's just my advice."

"And why are you giving me advice?" Joe asked. "You constantly complain about the choices I make. You do everything you can to make it clear you hate me. And then you come in here and try to make sense of things for me? Why don't you just sit back and watch us tear each other apart, *amiga*?"

Sandshifter started at that but quickly refocused, and said, "I may not like you, but I know that it's better to have you around when I need you. And if that means you have to be a good leader, then I'm gonna make you listen to this. I didn't like you back in the beginning, and I don't like you all that much now. You've done some growing, but you are a long, long way from being the leader you need to be."

"Then what do I need to do to get there then?"

"It's simple—stop making me think I was right."

"That I'm not cut out for this?"

"No. That you talk, but you don't really buy into any of it."

"Huh?"

"This Architect 'balance; stuff. This big belief we're supposed to have."

"I'm here fighting for it, aren't I?"

"Yeah. But that doesn't mean you buy it. If you did, you'd understand why what the bat does is important. Violence and fear are as essential to this job as understanding and compromise."

"No surprise to hear that from you."

"I may like a good fight. But after all this, I know talking is sometimes the only option. I like seeing people come out of things alive because of us. I like that things keep turning because of us. And those things happen because we know how to talk and how to fight. But you still can't see both sides of it. You still want to keep things the way you think they should be—the way they were when you were Joe Hashimoto."

"So what?"

"You can't do that anymore! You have to make hard choices now—choices that will sting your heart like your ribs were a beehive. And you complain about a little manipulation? The only way you are going to be able to deal is to accept what you are now, what it means, and then do what the rest of us don't have a choice about—forget about what you were and what you knew."

Joe looked at the wolf as she finished her speech, and slowly spoke his reply. "And you think that's easy? That I can just forget?"

"No," Sandshifter said. "But that's what's going to get things right around here, Joe. When you accept everything about who you are now and what all that really means, then maybe you can start being someone I'd listen to, without threats. But right now, you're just reading words from a Bible. And we all know it."

When those words hit, Joe felt as numb as if he'd been wrapped in cotton and dumped into the Arctic Ocean. He couldn't feel a single emotion, just a strange, cold numbness that might have been recognition.

"Nothing to say, huh?" Sandshifter asked. "Just think about it then." She patted him on the shoulder and then walked to the fridge to get some food.

Joe stood there, his mind trying to unwrap the cotton it felt like it was buried in. But before his mind could do it, his staff began to glow. Joe noticed it, took a deep breath to calm himself, and then held it up. As he looked into the stone, he could hear Wavecrasher's voice speaking in his head, telling him that everything was ready and they wanted him to come for some last-minute instruction. Joe mentally replied that he would be there and then started walking out of the room, away from Sandshifter. It didn't make the numbness or the thoughts that came with it go away though.

* * *

A few minutes later, Joe opened the door into the Obelisk's most important room—the room that he and all the others believed might very well be the top. It wasn't as easily named as the kitchen or library; unsurprisingly, it had been Windrider who had named it. After about five seconds of thought, he'd choose to call it the Nexus of Worlds.

It was a good name.

This room of the Obelisk was covered in crystalline glass, into which images and symbols had been carved with painstaking effort. A large spire ran down from the center of the room. When the Knights had been sent upon their first mission, they had been told to touch the spire and think of where they wanted to go. Joe had been the first, and after a second of touching it, he had (according to eyewitness accounts), transformed into golden light, been sucked into the spire, and then sent up through the ceiling. All Joe had known was that there had been a flash of golden light and then he had been in Cairo. Forger had since theorized that the symbols each represented a different world or time and that the spire would automatically transport them to any place or period they needed to go. Joe wasn't sure what to make of it yet, but there were more important things at the moment. He looked ahead and saw Quake, Firesprite, and Wavecrasher standing by the spire, waiting for him.

"So, is there anything else you'd like to tell me, before I go down in the muck?" the dog asked.

"Yes," Joe replied, doing his best to push Stalker and Sandshifter out of his head for the moment. "Watch carefully. Let us know the second that there might be a demon, and for God's sake, stay hidden. We don't want anybody to know you're there, not even the king."

"Staying hidden in a kingdom of dirt and stone. Shouldn't be too hard," Groundquake said. "You'd better be right about this one, cat. I ain't in the mood to watch these things for nothing."

"Don't you worry about that," Wavecrasher replied. "Worry about what you'll do if you do find a demon."

"Right," the dog muttered back. Turning to the spire, he stretched out his hand toward it, still muttering as he reached it. His fingers touched the crystal, and the spire pulsed for an instant. Then his body dissolved into brown light, flowed into the spire, and then shot up toward the ceiling, vanishing into the unknown.

"You know, I keep thinking we should be doing something special with this," Firesprite said. "Maybe saying 'energize' or what not."

"You've been hanging out with the kid too long," Wavecrasher replied, shaking her head.

"It's still a good idea." the lizard argued. "What do you think, Joe?"

"Mm? Yeah, sounds great." Joe said halfheartedly.

"You all right?" Forger asked.

"I just need to think for a while. Gonna head back to my room."

"Okay," the Knights replied.

Joe turned and headed for the stairs.

Once he had shut the door behind him, Wavecrasher turned and asked, "You think he's worried 'bout the demon?"

"Not completely," Firesprite replied. "I'll bet it's the thing with Stalker. Sometimes I think Joe's too nice a guy for this."

"Joe'll pull through. But he'd better be careful," Wavecrasher said. "Wolfie hears about it, I can only imagine the crap she'd try to pull."

But as Joe entered his room and sat down on his bed, the idea of Sandshifter pulling shit was the farthest thing from his mind. Still, the wolf remained a presence as Joe heard her voice over and over again in his head.

You're just reading words from a Bible.

Joe knew that the words stunk to high heaven. Because they smelled like the truth. He wanted to keep his easy, black-and-white morality whole, even as he sat working in this world of unbelievable gray. He wanted there to be absolutes—all demons were bad, killing was wrong, people needed to feel remorse over it, and it should be something that you never forgot. But instead, he sat here, working to save a demon king, while he suffered for the murderous acts that Stalker committed.

"Why am I the one with the conscience?" Joe moaned as he fell back onto his bed. "It's not fair. I tried to be a good person. Why I am here protecting demons and trying to rationalize somebody else's killing of monsters? I can't deal with this. ..."

And there it was. The honest, simple truth sprung out of Joe's mouth at long last, like a tiger that had been waiting to pounce on a gazelle. Joe was used to talking things out, to finding the best solution for everyone. But discussion and compromise didn't always exist here. Sometimes, action had to be taken. And Joe Hashimoto was not now, nor had ever been, a man of action. Trying to be one had been a mistake, and it had taken him this long to realize it. He wasn't the man to lead this group. He was the man who should be running a supermarket. That was the kind of morality he could deal with, the kind of life he could understand. That was where he belonged.

But instead he was here.

There had to be a way back. It could take some work, but it could happen. He could go back to Chicago, make Jeri and Cody understand. And ... and then they'd leave the city. It'd be perfect—they could be away from Joe's mother! They'd find a new place, somewhere to settle where no one had ever heard of them. Joe could get another job, and there had to be people that could make him a new identity. It was perfect.

"No," Joe said. "After everything that's happened, how can I go back?"

Another argument started to form in his mind—that he could put it all behind him, that it was as easy as changing clothes. But this time, Joe pushed it aside. How was he going to come back from the dead? Ralin and the others would never let him go. And even if they did, there were too many on both sides that resented him now. He'd never be safe.

The only way out of this was to stop complaining and start doing. Joe was going to have to start doing something to keep Stalker and Sandy and Quake in line and let them know when things had gone too far. And if they didn't like it, then that was just too bad. As of right now, Joe was going to make things run the right way.

And as that thought took root in his mind, Joe heard a noise, like the jingle of a bell. He recognized it within seconds. It was a signal that said that the balance was being threatened and that it was time to go to work. And this time, Joe was more than ready. Grabbing his staff, he strode toward the door and flung it open, eager to face whatever awaited him when he got there.

He all but bounded up the stairs as he concentrated on the Nexus. In seconds, the door appeared before him, and he walked inside the Nexus, seeing that the others were already there, looking toward him as he marched toward them.

"And to think, I wanted to finish that book today," Forger grumbled.

"It's not gonna go anywhere. We got work to do," Forester said.

"Does anyone know what that work is?" Joe asked as he reached the group.

"Not yet. We wanted to wait till everyone was here," Wavecrasher replied.

"Speaking of everyone, where's dog breath?" Sandshifter asked.

"He's working another mission for me right now. We'll call him if we need him," Joe said. He took his staff and touched it to the spire. As the staff began to glow, Joe closed his eyes for a moment and then opened them again; they shone with enough gold to forge a hundred rings. The others watched as the spire spoke to Joe, filling his mind with the information about what was happening. Joe stood still, receiving all the data. For a brief moment, his eyes widened, as if in surprise, but then went back to normal. He pulled his staff away, and the golden light left his eyes.

"What is it?" Nightstalker asked as Joe turned to face them.

"You wouldn't believe it," Joe said. "It's the Hyelia."

"The what?" Forester asked.

"Dream demons," Wavecrasher answered without a second's hesitation. "They float around in the astral plane, causing nightmares and feeding on the fear and panic they cause."

"Not anymore," Joe said. "The spire says that a bunch of them got out of the astral plane and are running rampant."

"Can they do that?" Windrider asked. "I mean, the astral plane's for dreams and stuff. Can they still exist outside of it?"

"I read that some of them have been given physical form on occasion," Wavecrasher said. "But it required extremely complex magic and skill, and as far as I know, no one has ever been able to replicate it since the last attempt three hundred years ago."

"Looks like somebody did," Joe said. "And now they're running loose in Chicago, going after everybody they can find and scaring them all the way to the grave."

"Seems like a waste of food," Forester said. "Way Ah see it, they'd do better just keepin' a few of 'em alive for snackin'."

"Can you name a stronger fear then knowing you're about to die?" Nightstalker asked. "That kind of fear's like cotton candy-flavored crack to them."

"Then we need to go and shut down the carnival," Sandshifter said, marching up to the spire. Before anyone could stop her, the wolf placed her hand on the spire and vanished in a burst of orange light.

"Well, she's got the right idea," Stalker said. "Come on, we gotta get going."

"Shouldn't we call Groundquake too?" Forester asked.

"Why? You scared of going in without him?" Wavecrasher said as she moved up to the spire and teleported away.

"No, I just think a guy who can make earthquakes would be useful," the squirrel shot back.

"We'll call him if we need him. Now let's move," Joe said.

Thunderer and Forger stepped up to the spire and were sent off.

"Whatever," Forester grumbled. But he quickly made his way up and vanished into the spire. The others followed, until only Joe and Nightstalker were left. The bat advanced on the spire slowly and then paused and turned to Joe.

"Something else you wanna say?" Joe asked.

"Are you gonna be okay with this?"

"Killing the demons? I think I'll be okay with that," Joe said.

"That's not what I meant," Stalker replied. "This is your home. People might get hurt—maybe even people you knew. Are you okay with that?"

"I used to know them. But even if I didn't, I don't plan on letting anyone get hurt if I can help it," Joe said. "That's why I bring you guys along, isn't it?"

Stalker nodded his reply.

"Then let's get to work. I'm worried enough that something would bring the Hyelia out of the astral plane."

"Indeed," the bat nodded. "But there's still one more thing."

"What?"

"Are we okay?"

Joe took a half second before he nodded and said, "Yes. And I think things will stay okay this time," Joe said. He walked over and stuck his hand on the spire.

As he vanished, Stalker watched him go and then shook his head as he touched the spire and vanished into it.

XIX.

JOE SAW THE LIGHT wash over his eyes, and then it was gone, leaving Joe and the others in the back alley of a city street. The sky was dark around them, though it had been daylight in Miami (an expected event—the Obelisk existed outside of time). Joe shook off the transport dizziness and then began to look around for signs of trouble.

"Ah, I think this might be harder then we believed," Forester said, pointing out to the street.

Joe turned and looked. The scene before them was a mess of broken pavement, flipped cars, smoke, fire, and a tremendous amount of screaming. Joe could hear the roars of the Hyelia as they pounced and the fear-filled howls of the victims.

"What's the plan, boss?" Thunderer asked. "Boss? Hey, you all right in there?"

But Joe didn't reply; he just stared out into the broken mess before him. He knew this street. He remembered stopping in the little record shop some days after work, the one that was currently on fire with its windows smashed in. He saw the bodega that the Shahs' had run, its chairs now stained with blood.

"*Joe*!" Stalker yelled, shaking Joe as he brought the Light Knight out of his doldrums. "What's the plan?"

"Plan?" Joe asked.

"Yes. About the monsters that are currently wiping their ass with the city," Forester said.

But Joe didn't say anything else. Instead, he looked out as the creatures that were attacking came into view. This place had once been home—despite everything that had happened, *still was* home. Joe felt all vestige of thought leave his mind. Grabbing his staff, he held it high over his head, let out a scream of anger, and then charged the scene as the Hyleia turned to face him.

"My, what a master stroke," Forester said.

"So what? I'm in the mood to listen to our glorious leader, for once," Sandshifter said, baring her teeth.

"Then that's what we do. Split up and take as many as you can," Stalker said. He drew his sword.

*　　*　　*

The two gremlins walked down the cavern, their high, reedy voices echoing off the stone walls.

"So what's the king going to do to Nerbino?"

"Last I heard, they were supposed to chain him to the wall and have the Water Knight force clean him."

"Ehh, not so bad. I heard that the king was going to bar him from the mortal world forever and have him do the royal tax work."

"What tax work?"

"You know—how much mischief is allowed, how much carelessness can be tolerated, and all that junk."

"Heh. With Nerbino's head for numbers, we'd be screwed in about an hour."

"Then I wonder—"

"What?"

"I don't know. ...I could've sworn just now I saw ... eyes in the wall."

"You mean like a spy?"

"No, more like actual eyes, like the wall itself was looking at me."

"*Riiiiggghttt*. You been into the cave juice already?"

"No! I swear, I—"

"Yeah, right."

"Why, you little ..."

As the two of them argued, high above them in the cave's rock ceiling, part of the stone began to shift and crumble slightly, and a pair of eyes did indeed poke through, followed by a lupine face, all made of rock. The face looked down at the two arguing gremlins, who had now begun to claw at each other, and muttered, "They send me down here for this?"

Still, Groundquake knew he had to make it to the palace and check on the king and prince for his report before he could go home. Thankfully, his power over earth allowed him the perfect cover in this stony kingdom. But being part of the scenery in a gremlin boxing match, in the name of protecting their fat, crusty, I-fart-cyanide-and-burp-mustard-gas king did not fall under good use of his powers. And the idea of a Chaos Demon in this place was like a grown man getting into politics by running for third-grade class president.

Quake withdrew back into the earth and started heading toward the palace, swimming through the earth like an Olympic swimmer in a pool. As he moved through the cave, he reminded himself why he was doing this—not for the king or the demons or even Joe. No, he was here to be able to have one over that goddamned bat. To shove those words back down his throat. Quake relished the thought of it and began to move faster through the rock.

*   *   *

"Get off you bastard!" Stalker howled as the Hyleia clamped its jaws down on his arm. The Shadow Knight growled deep and pulled as hard as he could, trying to get the creature off him. But the monster was relentless.

"Fine," the bat snarled. He took his free hand and shoved it onto the creature's face. Shadowfire blazed forth, spreading over the creature's face like water down a canal.

The Hyleia let out its screech once again, spat out Nightstalker's hand and jumped back, keeping its distance.

The Hyleia, as its name sounded, did appear vaguely hyena-ish. Its lupine body was covered in gray spotted fur, and its face ended in a muzzle and piggish nose. But no hyena had ever had a jaw that stretched out for a foot and a half and was filled with enough teeth to give a dentist early retirement. The Hyleia's legs also grew into long spines at the joints, spines that grew up past its body. And from under the fur, several long spikes also popped up.

Stalker stood patiently, waiting for the creature to make its move. After a few seconds of pacing, the Hyleia snorted and then turned tail and ran in the other direction.

"Some nightmare demon," Stalker snorted. But then he saw where the creature was running. A woman was kneeling by the wreckage of her car under a streetlight, her clothes tattered and dirty, and a long bloody cut on her face turning part of her blonde hair strawberry red. She was reaching underneath what had been the front window, pulling at something. As she dragged it out more and more, Stalker saw that she was pulling at a pair of hands, hands that couldn't be more than five years old. She was so involved, she didn't even see the Hyleia running toward her as she pulled and cried and yelled out for help in a panicked, terrified voice.

Stalker began to run after the creature, his coat flying out behind him, as he called out to the woman, trying to get her to see the danger. She did pause a second and turn to see the Hyleia, but by then, there was no time to do anything but scream. Stalker held out his sword, hoping that his shadowfire could reach the creature instead.

But it didn't need to. As the Hyleia raced toward the woman, a burst of white suddenly spread over the ground before it, covering it like new fallen snow. A series of cracks filled the air, and the Hyleia found itself slipping and sliding as its clawed feet tried to find a foothold on the suddenly icy ground. But it had built up too much speed to stop, and so it found itself sliding along the now icy ground, following the path of the ice until it crashed into another wrecked car, just a few feet away from the woman.

Stalker kept running, past the downed monster, until he reached the woman. She looked at this black-coated figure holding a sword with disbelief and horror.

"You all right, lady?" Stalker asked. The woman stared out at the Hyleia. She gave no reply, so the bat asked again. This time, she started and then turned toward the bat, her expression unchanging as she saw him there with his black clothes, mask, and sword.

"Who ... what the hell are you?" she stammered out. "And what the hell was that thing?"

"I don't think you want to know," Stalker asked.

The woman just gaped at him, so the bat replied, "Easiest thing to say is that something got out of the zoo, and I happen to be animal control."

"But where did ... and how did ... I was just driving home from my mother's and..."

"Don't worry. We've got it under control," another voice said from the side. Both Stalker and the woman turned to see Wavecrasher coming toward them.

"It's okay. She's with me," the bat said.

"Lincoln was a she?"

"Linc—Damn it, Crash, do you have the glamour on again?"

"Yeah, I was trying to—"

"Blend in, I know. It doesn't help."

The cat sighed and muttered, "Man, I thought I had it that time."
Then she muttered a few words, the air around her shimmered, and the
woman calmed as she saw the cat's blue-coated form.

"At least you can still fight with it on. Nice trick with the ice, by
the way," the bat said as the Water Knight approached them.

"Nothing special," the cat replied. She tugged her mask as if it was
loose. "And it's not—Oh dear God, why are you just standing here
man?! There's a kid in there!"

Wavecrasher all but leaped between the woman and the bat, moving
to the wreckage of the car. Looking inside, Wavecrasher quickly reached
in and grabbed the hands, pulling with all her might. As the woman
watched in horrible anticipation, Stalker moved over to the spot as well.
But instead of reaching for the hands, he motioned for the cat to move
away. Wavecrasher gave no reply, so the bat yelled, "Move!"

Wavecrasher looked up at him with an angry and puzzled look,
but she did what she was told. Once the cat was safely out of the way,
Stalker took his sword and jammed it into the wreckage of the car. He
then looked down and yelled, "Kid, move back as far as you can!"

The bat pulled his sword to the side, slicing through the car's metal
framework as easily as Sweeney Todd slit throats. He pulled the sword
around in a circular pattern, creating a large hole in the car. After a
moment, he came around all the way and then stepped in front of the
hole, grabbing the left side. Wavecrasher quickly came over and grabbed
the right, and then, together, the two Knights pulled until, finally,
the metal circle came loose, creating a much larger hole that showed a
young girl in a Dora the Explorer T-shirt and blood on her face, looking
absolutely terrified.

"Samantha!" the woman yelled. She reached inside the car and
pulled out her daughter. But as she did so, the child let out a yelp of
pain.

The Knights saw one of the child's arms twisted and limp at her
side and the large bulge that had sprouted under the shoulder of her
shirt.

"Mommy! My arm!" the child howled as tears of pain began to
fall.

"Lady, give her to me," Wavecrasher said. "I can help."

"You're doctors too?" the woman asked.

Stalker rubbed the back of his head and said, "She was. Maybe."

The woman hesitated a moment and then slowly handed the girl over to the cat, who took her carefully, not wanting to jostle her arm at all. Moving carefully, she knelt down, sitting the child down on her knee and looked at the arm.

"Who are you guys?" Samantha asked as she reached for Crash's mask with her good hand. "Why are you dressed like that? Are you like the Power Rangers or something?"

"Really can't tell you, honey. And I knew we needed to stop the primary colors thing," Wavecrasher said. She gently pushed the girl's hand away and checked the girl's arm over.

"Mm," Stalker said, keeping eye contact with the girl. "You like the Power Rangers?"

"Uh-huh," Sam answered. "My big brother's got the toys. He won't let me play with them though."

"After today, you can say you saw something even better. Did anyone ever come and cut your brother out of a car with a sword?"

"Yeah, I—*Oowww*!"

"Sorry," Wavecrasher said. "Listen, Sam, your arm's dislocated. I need to move it again so we can fix it."

Samantha immediately looked doubtful, so Stalker said, "You gonna tell me you can't take a little pain after everything else you've been through?"

Samantha considered that a minute and then said, "Mommy, can you come here?"

"I'm right here, honey," her mother said, taking her child's good arm in her hand. "Just hold on tight and let the lady do her work."

"Here we go," Wavecrasher said. She grasped the girl's arm.

Samantha gritted her teeth and then yelped as the cat gently twisted it, shifting the lump in her shoulder around. Stalker even grimaced as he watched the lump twist.

"Okay, it's ready," Wavecrasher said as she gently laid her hands down on the lump.

Samantha moaned at her touch, but she stopped a moment later as she watched the blue light suddenly emanate from the cat's hands. As both Stalker and the mother watched, the lump began to shrink, and they could hear the sounds of bones reuniting under the skin. Within a few seconds, the lump was completely gone, giving the girl a functional arm once again.

"There we are. Good as new," Wavecrasher said, taking her hands away.

"How … how did you do that?" the mother asked as Samantha gingerly flexed her arm.

"For now, I would just take it as it is," Nightstalker replied as he gently took Samantha off Crash's knee.

"Fine. But I wish some of this made sense."

"Don't worry ma'am. I can help with that," Stalker said. He reached out to put his hand on the woman's forehead. But just as his fingers brushed her skin, Samantha suddenly yelled, "*Look out!*"

Both Knights turned then as the downed Hyleia leaped through the air at them. They moved in front of the mother and child, grabbing the creature in midair and pushing it back. It landed and snarled at them. The two Knights pulled out their weapons, and the creature charged them.

Stalker and Crash held their ground, but just as the Hyleia was about to hit, a blur of gold suddenly raced in front of them, knocking the creature off its trajectory and into a nearby signpost. As the gold faded, they saw Joe standing before them, his mask pulled down as he looked at the creature with rage in his eyes.

"Thanks, man. We—" Wavecrasher began.

"Get them out of here," Joe said. "I'll deal with this thing myself."

"Are you sure?"

"Let's go," Stalker said. "He wants to do this."

The cat paused but then nodded and moved away as Joe drew his staff and watched the Hyleia. As the creature rose to its feet, the staff ignited in a burst of gold, and Joe leaped at the creature, holding the staff over his head like a giant war club. The Hyleia saw him and turned to meet him, its clawed hands outstretched. But Joe leaped through them and slammed his staff into its chest, causing the Hyleia to scream aloud.

"Is he insane? Taking it on by himself?" Wavecrasher swore as the creature toppled over, with Joe still pummeling away.

"It's not like it can kill him," Stalker said. He turned to the mother and her child. "C'mon, we'll get you someplace safe."

But she didn't give a reply. Instead, she watched Joe fight the creature, her face a strange mix of emotions. But after a second, Stalker saw them for what they were, and he knew there was still more to do here. Because written on the woman's face was confusion … and recognition.

Groundquake pushed forward, swimming through the cave ceiling and into the section that served as the ceiling of the gremlin palace. Briefly, he looked down to see a couple of guards standing at loose attention. The dog then got to observe one of them pick his nose in sheer boredom. He sighed and turned toward the throne room.

But just as he was about to go, the guards suddenly snapped to attention, putting weapons at post and drawing fingers out of noses. The dog paused, wondering what would have caused such a drastic change. He got his answer when the king walked in from a room to the side of the guards. He watched from the ceiling, and as he did, he sent his mind out a little more into the earth, to hear what is was that was going on down there.

"Majesty, the majordomo has said he wished to speak with you," the guard on the left said.

"Has he now?" the king replied.

"Yes. He wishes to discuss the punishment for your son. But we would not let him in until you had enjoyed the riches of your harem."

"Well done. But what the domo thinks is best and what I know is best are not always the same. I will remind him of that."

"He waits in your chambers, sire," the guard replied.

The king nodded and then waddled off toward his rooms. As he did, the guards exchanged a brief look and shook their heads. And even from his high post, Quake knew why. The king he'd met before had been an angry, pissed-off sort, who was ready to chew his son's bones to teach the boy not to go against him. And now he'd barely reacted to the news about the majordomo. And the fact that this happened after a visit to the harem—Quake could feel Wavecrasher's theory growing heavier in his mind.

*   *   *

"Dear sweet Christ!" Wavecrasher yelled as Joe landed another blow, slamming his lighted staff into the Hyleia's exposed chest. As the smell of burning flesh filled the air, the cat whispered, "I didn't know he could—"

"Well, now you know he can," Stalker replied, watching the woman look at the scene before her. For the last few minutes, she had stared without even blinking as Joe had fought the Hyleia. The monster had gotten in a few blows, but Joe hadn't felt a single one. His eyes solid gold, Joe had unleashed blast after blast of light at the creature. Its fur was burned and smoking, and two of its leg spikes had snapped off, hanging on only by tendons. It was still growling and snarling at Joe, but even a blind and deaf man could see and hear that the Hyleia was on its last legs.

Stalker was neither blind nor deaf. He watched as Joe brought his arms out and formed two large spears of light in his hands, just as the Hyelia made a last leap at him. Joe just brought his arms back and hurled the spears forward. They flew through the air in an instant, flashing toward the Hyelia. For a second, the two forces hung in midair, and then the creature was flung backward. It flew back a few feet and then stopped, having slammed against a wrecked car. It hurled its head backward and let out a howl of pain but not from the impact. It howled from the two light spears that had gone through its shoulders and pinned it to the car.

The Light Knight watched it struggle. And then he drew his staff. He took the first few steps forward, the head of the staff already glowing. As it did, the spears glowed brighter, the creature's howls increasing along with them. But he kept increasing the light, increasing the pain the creature was feeling. And he might've kept going, if the woman hadn't stepped forward and yelled out, *"Joe! Stop, please!"*

The Light Knight stopped moving forward then. The light held a moment, and then faded away as the spears regained their normal luster. Slowly, the Knight turned toward the woman, her child, and his fellow Knights. And as the gold faded from his eyes, he looked out at them, and saw, truly saw who stood before him. And then, Joseph Hashimoto spoke.

"Sheryl?"

"Joe?" the woman said. He took a step closer to them. She stared at his face, at the mouth that had smiled at her, the eyes that had always been sincere and helpful. And then she saw the gold clothing, the hat and mask, and the glowing staff.

"My God. What happened? I thought you were dead!" she said in disbelief.

"Sherry, I … I can—"

"Who did this to you? Where did they take you?"

"I … It's okay. I'm okay," Joe tried to explain.

"Then what was that?" Sherry demanded pointing to the Hyleia.

Joe turned, and then saw his handiwork. His eyes went wide, and his jaw almost landed on the ground in shock. As the creature moaned and howled, Joe clapped his hands to his mouth, barely muffling the scream of horror. He started to sway then, but just as he began to fall, a pair of black-coated arms caught him.

"Easy, Joe," Stalker said as he held his friend up.

"What … what the hell did I do?" Joe stammered. "I remember fighting and being angry, but this …"

"I don't know," the bat said. "But if you hadn't, that thing would have taken out me and Crash and hurt your friend."

"But look at it!" Joe howled. "How can I do a thing like that and not remember?"

"Maybe it's for the best," the bat replied. "Do you think you can stand now?"

"I … I guess."

"Good. I'm gonna go put it out of its misery. You stay here."

The bat gently removed his arms and turned to the Hyleia, drawing his sword as he walked toward it. Joe swayed a moment more and then balanced himself as he watched the bat walk. But a hand on his shoulder caused him to turn, right into Sherry's face.

"Joe? What is this?"

"I … I can't tell you," Joe said. "I'm not allowed."

"Mr. Hashimoto?" Sam asked from the sidelines. "But the car hit you. How?"

"Let Mommy handle this," Sherry said, not turning her gaze from for a second. "Did you fake what happened? Was there someone else in that coffin?"

"No. I was dead then."

"And yet you're standing right here?" she asked, an angry tone growing in her voice, one Joe recognized instantly.

"I couldn't come back. It's complicated. I can't be that person anymore."

"I can see that," Sherry said.

"I didn't know things would turn out this way," he said as Stalker drove his sword into the Hyleia, and it screamed loudly enough to wake the dead and make them think they were in the midst of a bombing.

The others turned and watched. Its body faded away into nothing, back to the dreamworld it had come from.

"So what? So all this was an accident?" Sherry asked as the monster faded.

"No ... no, it's just ... just ..."

"What Joe? Tell me!" Sheryl yelled. "Tell me what the hell you disappeared for. Tell me what brought this nightmare down on us!" she demanded, gesturing at the damaged city.

"Lady, he can't," Wavecrasher said. "This is way bigger than what you think it could—"

"I'm not talking to you!" Sherry yelled. "I'm talking to the one person here who might actually be able to explain why this city is being overrun by monster zoo animals, who apparently came back from the dead to get involved after all this time, and ... and ..."

"And that's all," Nightstalker said as his eyes went black. His hand gripped Sherry's head tightly, and her own eyes went black. Samantha saw what was happening and yelled out, running to her mother. But Wavecrasher grabbed her and held her in place as Stalker finished coating her mother's mind with shadows.

Pulling his hand away, the bat motioned for Wavecrasher to bring Samantha over. The girl struggled, but the cat managed to hold on and bring her over as the bat knelt down to face her. And once she was close, he asked her something.

"Think you can keep a secret?"

"What did you do to my mommy?!" Sam yelled back.

"I made her forget," the bat replied. "We can't let people know about us. Otherwise, it'd be a lot harder to do our job. But your mom will be fine. And she won't remember what's happened. And since I don't want to do the same to you, can you keep quiet about what happened today?"

"But what about Mr. Hashimoto?"

"We'll watch Joe. I know what you saw was scary, but he was angry about what those animals did here. But we'll help him. Just like we helped you. You trust us after that right?"

Sam was quiet and then asked "My mom'll be okay? And Mr. Hashimoto too?"

"Promise."

Sam looked at the ground and then turned to look at Joe. The Light Knight looked at her and said, "It's okay, Sam. You can trust him."

The girl stared at Joe a minute more, and gave her answer. "Okay."

"Good," Stalker said. "Now go to your mom. She's gonna wanna get out of here soon."

Samantha nodded and went over to Sherry, just as the blackness left her eyes. Sherry looked around, as if unsure where she was, going pale as she saw the destruction. She glanced down and saw Sam and then scooped up her daughter and ran off, without noticing the Knights or Joe at all.

"Nice work," Wavecrasher said. "I thought you'd wipe the girl too."

"Kid's not old enough to be a loose end," Stalker said. "No one will believe her, and that'll be enough."

"Maybe you should wipe me instead," Joe said, staring at the spot where the Hyleia lay. "I don't know," Joe said. "Dear God, I don't really know."

"What? Our next move?" Wavecrasher asked. "I think we go after—"

"Not now," Stalker said. "Joe, I know this is hard, but now isn't the time for soul-searching. We need to keep going before more people are hurt."

But Joe stayed silent and likely would've done so for longer, if a familiar howl and shattering glass hadn't suddenly broken through the air. The three of them whirled around to see Sandshifter battling a Hyleia inside the broken window of one of the stores.

"Damn crazy wolf. If she'd just work together with us," Wavecrasher began, but she was cut off as Joe howled, "*Noo!*" He pushed past the others and ran toward the broken store.

"What's with him?" Wavecrasher asked. "It's just a store."

"It's more than that," Stalker said grimly as he read the name above the door. "He used to work there."

*   *   *

The majordomo was much like the king—fat, dirty, dressed in ugly robes, creator of a stench that deserved its own planet so that it could be far away from Earth. But from his spot in the ceiling, Quake could see how timid, even weak the gremlin looked. He continually glanced around, as if something from the wall was about to leap out, bite his crotch, and then vomit acid down there. His clawed hands bounced on his knees as both he and the dog awaited the arrival of the king.

Suddenly, the great doors swung open and the king walked in, causing the majordomo to leap to his feet.

"Your Highness, forgive me for bothering you after your constitutional, but I felt it was imperative to speak with—"

"I'm sure. Now, what is so important?"

The majordomo seemed surprised at the king's reaction but continued. "Well, sire, um … I heard from the courts … that your son was punished—"

"Yes. I dealt with it. Is that why you brought me here?" The king asked impatiently.

"It's just … well do you think it was wise, sire?"

"Explain."

"Well, after what he has done, shouldn't there be something … well safer for all of us?"

"The boy must learn to respect the boundaries. I can't think of a better punishment."

"But, sire," the domo insisted. "His last actions brought the Elementals down on us. And now, you expect him to guard our most dangerous relic?"

"It is under my care. I will decide who guards it. My son must learn respect for things bigger than himself."

"But, sire, after his last actions … none of us would be able to repair … and if he was so easily influenced by …"

"I am aware of my son's weaknesses," the king said. "And I am prepared to deal with them."

"Sire, we have always entrusted guardianship to our strongest and most understanding of the task. Nerbino is strong, but he still had much to learn and—"

Whatever the majordomo might've said was lost then as he gargled and sputtered, his green face growing darker as the skin swelled and stretched. Finally, the tension grew too much, and the gremlin's head exploded, spreading his superheated blood all over the walls. The king looked at the mess around him and on the walls and then shrugged. Looking at the domo's body, he said, "I know all about his weakness."

Quake watched the stone absorb the blood and corpse like sponges, but he did nothing to stop it. Because he saw the sparkle in the king's eyes, the sparkle that told him everything Wavecrasher had feared was about to come true.

*   *   *

Joe leaped through the broken window frame of the Grenwal store, not even noticing as a broken shard of glass sliced through his pants and skin. All that concerned him was the battle going on in the front of the store as Sandshifter wrestled with the Hyleia. The two of them rolled on the ground, the Hyleia clawing at the wolf's face, while she snarled and clawed back. All around them, customers screamed and ran, some going through the doors, others even going through the broken window through which Joe had entered. Joe only stood there, watching as the blade of his new life sliced through the remainder of his old life, while Sherry's voice rang in his ears all the louder.

He saw Sandshifter pick up the gumball machine that got quarters jammed in it every week and throw it at the Hyleia, who promptly got a mouthful of glass and gum.

He saw the wolf grab the cash register on the left desk, the one that always seemed to run out of change during a line of more than five people and slam it into the side of the monster's face, adding quarters and dimes to the items jammed in the thing's mouth.

He watched as the Hyleia let out a howl and then bit into Sandshifter's coat, using it to hurl her into a display of ice tea and soda, which Joe had always found to be a big seller, no matter the time of year.

He saw ...

"Miro, get the back door open. Start moving people out if there's anybody left, and then get the holy hell out of here!"

"Oh, God!" Joe whispered pulling up his mask, just as Ronald appeared at the back of one of the aisles looking down at the scene before him with complete disbelief.

"What in the name of Christ Almighty!?" he spat out as he looked at Sandshifter and the Hyelia.

As the wolf brought up her staff and used it to loose a sand blast at the creature, Ronald turned and grabbed a packet of knives and began to tear it open. But he had barely gotten into the plastic when another voice filled the air, one filled with anger and annoyance and loud enough that everyone—human, Hyleia, and Knight—stopped and turned toward it.

A woman emerged from the door in the wall that led into the stockroom. Joe took a look at her and, even with everything else, the first thought that ran through his head was, *Wow, how hard did the mule kick her?* He looked at her slack face and eyes that held all the life of a bottle of bleach. He also noticed the iPod in her hand and the headphones in her ears.

"What the hell is this mess? I told Jamal to clean up, that lazy brat!" the woman yelled. "Damn it, don't they know I'm busy researching beats?"

"Julie, get back in the stock room!" Ronald yelled, returning to his struggle with the knives

But Julie didn't even notice as she looked at the mess with growing anger. "Now I have to stop and clean this up? No way, not when I'm almost finished with my first hit!"

But the woman's act of stupidity was about to be dealt with. As Julie stood there ranting, the Hyleia suddenly crouched back on its strong legs and then leaped forward, covering the distance between itself and the woman in seconds, even as Joe, Sandy, and Ronald began to move toward her. Julie continued to rant, even as the creature's shadow fell over her and then, in the last seconds, she finally noticed and let out a scream of terror as the Hyleia came into view, only to be blown away by a light burst from Joe.

"*Holy crap! Holy crap!*" Julie screamed stupidly as Sandy ran over and grabbed her.

"Lady, shut up and get back there!" the wolf snarled, throwing the woman behind her, into one of the aisles. She then turned her attention back to the Hyleia, which was slowly bringing itself up.

"If you've got another one of those, now would be a great time!" Sandshifter yelled to Joe.

"Way ahead of you," Joe replied. He aimed the glowing staff at the creature. But this time, the Hyleia sensed what was coming and leaped out of the way of Joe's blast. It bounced off the wall and bounded back onto Joe, knocking him to the ground.

"Goddamn it, can't you shoot straight?!" Sandshifter snapped as she started to move over to Joe. But before she could, a hand wrapped around her shoulder and pulled her back.

"You've got to get me out of here!" Julie cried, her face filled with panic.

"Planning on it, but I have a problem here," Sandy snapped.

"Please, just get me away from that horrible thing!"

"I can't right now, so get back to the stockroom."

"But ... but ..."

"Just shut up and run!"

Julie stood stunned a second. Then she turned and started to run back down the aisle, toward the stockroom. But it was already too late. The Hyleia had stopped attacking Joe as its nostrils flared with the scent of fear. Joe realized what was coming and tried to grab the creature, but it was too late. The monster sprang out, over Ronald and Sandy, and right over the figure of Julie. She turned in its shadow and raised up her hands in defense as it knocked her down, chewing and tearing.

"Julie!" Ronald yelled. He finally pulled a knife out of the plastic. Bringing it behind his back, Ronald flung it forward with all the straightness of a pitcher in a movie version of the World Series. The knife buried itself deep in the Hyleia's back. It pulled away from Julie and let out a howl and then growled and turned to face Ronald, who was already pulling another knife from the plastic.

But the creature didn't make it past growling; Joe, back on his feet, let loose with a light blast that slammed into the creature, knocking it into the nearby display of cameras. Ronald spun around to see the Light Knight standing there, with his staff still smoking from the blast.

"Nice shot," he said.

"Thanks," Joe said, thankful for the muffling effect of his mask. "You'd best step away from that thing now, sir."

"Not yet," Ronald said. He moved over to the body lying on the floor as Joe followed. The two of them knelt, and Ronald looked down at Julie, only to grimace in disgust. The creature had ripped out most of her throat, leaving only part of the spinal cord and some flesh holding her head to her body.

"Jesus Christ," Ron muttered. He took off his vest and covered her head with it. "God, why didn't I fire her sooner? She was a bitch, but she didn't deserve this."

"It wasn't your fault," Joe said.

"No, but I should've been able to do something. I got promoted to do that. She was a major problem to everybody, but she shouldn't die for it."

"I know and—You got promoted? Great!" Joe said and then immediately cringed.

"Well … um … yeah … I'm just …" Joe sputtered.

But then he got a reprieve as Sandshifter yelled, "Watch out! It's getting back up!"

Ronald leaped back to his feet and pulled out another knife as the Hyleia struggled to its feet and began to shamble toward them, its gait slow and unsteady.

"I think we can take it," Ronald said, brandishing the knife.

"No, it's too dangerous for you," Joe said. He held out his staff, waiting for the creature to make the first move. "Lemme go first. I can—"

But suddenly the creature roared and leaped at them, all traces of slowness and pain gone as its claws reached for Joe's head. Joe barely had a second to react, but he still began to create a light field around himself and Ronald. Thankfully, it proved unnecessary, as a pair of sand balls suddenly flew through the air and struck the creature, knocking it back to the ground with a thud. The Hyleia flipped back over as it hit the ground, landing on its legs.

This time, Joe was ready for it. He took back the energy from the light field and changed it into a burst of light that he sent toward the creature. Instead of letting it striking the creature, however, Joe gave a mental command, and the light exploded before it, blinding it in a burst of gold. The Hyleia shut its eyes and howled, throwing its front legs over its eyes as it lay on the ground in pain. It was then that Ronald took his chance, running toward the creature with his knife in hand. He reached it, pulled up its head and with a single motion, sliced the creature's neck wide open, dousing the floor and his shirt with dark black blood.

"Get back to hell, you murdering bastard," Ronald said. He dropped the dead creature's head back onto the floor, where it landed with a smack into a growing pool of blood.

"Very nice," Joe said as Ronald got back up.

Ronald nodded, and then turned to see Sandshifter approach the two of them.

"Everybody okay here?" the wolf asked and then stopped when she saw the body.

"I took care of that thing," Ronald says. "But if you or your friend would like to tell me what in the hell is going on, I'd love to hear it."

"You don't want to know," Sandshifter replied. "Trust me on that."

"That thing killed one of my people, and I'd like to know why!" Ronald snapped.

"Don't try me," Sandshifter growled. "I'm the one who's working to save your ass, and everybody else's."

"Is that why I killed that thing?" Ronald yelled back.

The wolf growled again.

But this time, Joe stood his ground and yelled, "Don't start this now!"

"So what if I do?" Sandshifter said back. "Not all of us are happy to have someone else do our job. But you're still gonna be sitting in your room tonight, having one of your oh-was-it-the-right-thing discussions with yourself, right?"

At another time, Joe might've been calm and restrained about dealing with the wolf. But after seeing his city attacked and so much of his old life being destroyed, the rage part of Joe's brain overtook everything.

"I have had enough of you and your griping!" Joe screamed. "You tell me that I'm not committed—that I don't wanna do this shit? At least I'm trying to keep some kind of moral code while we do this job. All you're committed to is trying to undermine me or rip something's head off; God, no wonder you frigging died! Everyone in whatever godforsaken hellhole you lived in probably beat you to death. I am through listening to your bullshit and your complaining when you can't do any better than me. So for the last time, you flea-bitten, whining snit, *back the hell off!*"

Sandshifter's eyes went wide as Joe finished, and she stared at the Light Knight with an expression somewhere between anger and surprise. The wolf started to open her mouth.

But before she could say a word, Ronald let out a long "Oh shiiiiiiiiiiiiiiittttttttttttttttt" as he looked past them.

Both Knights turned to see three more Hyleias entering the store through the broken window.

XX.

"I REALLY DON'T KNOW what your problem is, but maybe we can deal with this first?" Ronald demanded.

The two Knights didn't answer. Without a word, they turned to face the creatures, their weapons drawn and ready.

The Hyleias leaped through the air at the trio, their claws outstretched. Before they made contact, Sandshifter held out her staff, and a wave of sand burst out, catching the creatures in midair and hurling them into the nearby wall. They hit with a thud. Sandshifter recalled the sand, and she and Joe advanced on the creatures, while Ronald searched for another weapon.

The Hyleias groaned as the shadows of the advancing Knights fell on them. But unfortunately, rage and anger was fuel enough for the Hyleias, and the creatures crouched and leaped at the Knights again.

Joe and Sandy pulled their weapons, but then a third creature leaped out from behind them, landing on both Knights and sending them crashing to the floor. As their staffs clattered across the floor, Joe and Sandshifter put all their energy into pushing off the huge claws that were pinning them to the ground. But that became more difficult a second later as the other two Hyleias landed and began to snap and bite at them. It took everything the two Knights had to hold them off. Jaws snapped and crunched, while the Hyleia holding them down took his own bites. Joe could feel flesh being pulled off his arms, and he heard enough yelps from Sandshifter to know the wolf had the same problem. He tried to call on the light, but with the biting and chewing sending fresh pain through his arms every few minutes, he couldn't concentrate long enough to summon it.

Joe frantically tried to formulate a plan. Suddenly he heard something whistle through the air, and the head Hyleia toppled over, taking its heavy claws along with it. The other two stopped in disbelief, giving Joe and Sandshifter just enough time to call on their powers. The sand and light shot forth, knocking the creatures into the sidewalls. As they slowly fell down, the two Knights looked up to see Ronald standing there with a heavy golf club in his hands.

"C'mon, all I've got is a driver, and I'm doing better then you two," Ronald said.

The two Knights got to their feet.

"Whatever," Sandshifter said. "Either of you got a plan of attack?"

"Yeah, but I don't think we've got much time to discuss it," Joe said. The Hyleias were beginning to get up around them.

"Can we get the cliff notes version?" Sandshifter asked.

"Stun 'em, and cover them in sand," Joe said. "Then leave the rest to me."

"Gee what a brilliant—"

"Oh, just do what he says!" Ronald snapped. He brought up his golf club and charged the Hyleia. The wolf followed Ronald into battle, bringing her staff up in a charge. The Hyleia howled and rushed the two of them. Ronald swung the club directly into a creature's mouth, sending out a spurt of blood and teeth. The Hyleia reared back in pain, and Sandshifter wasted no time in doing her part. Sand poured out of the staff and wrapped around the creature, mummifying it in a way that the Egyptians couldn't have dreamed of. Within seconds, the Hyleia was wrapped up in a ball of sand, with only its snarling head emerging.

Seeing his chance, Joe brought his staff to bear, the lion's head already beginning to glow. But before he could loose the energy, a large, furry shape suddenly darted past him and knocked the staff from his hand. As it spilled out onto the floor, the light already fading from the lion's head, the shape darted again, and Joe once again found himself on the ground with a new Hyleia above him, biting and clawing at his face.

Sandshifter and Ronald saw him fall and moved to help him, but they had no better luck. The third Hyleia shot forward and pounced on the two of them from behind, pressing them both to the floor. As they lay there, the creature unsheathed its claws and began to swipe and dig, turning their backs into raw, bloody, messes. They grunted and screamed, while Joe felt the creature's bite even through his thick gauntlets.

"Now, that's not very nice," a voice suddenly said.

Joe recognized it instantly as a familiar blade pushed through one side of the Hyleia's head and then exited out the other. It held a moment, as if relishing the shocked, pain-filled expression on the creature's face and then pulled back out, leaving two holes in the creature's head that began to leak black blood like the fountains in hell. The dead Hyleia began to fall, but a black-gloved hand grabbed its collar and threw it backward, throwing into one of the other two with a thud.

"You all right?" Stalker asked. He extended his hand to Joe, who took it eagerly.

"Yeah," Joe said. He got to his feet. "The others—"

"Taken care of," the bat said.

Joe looked over just in time to see a huge watery fist reach out and grab the creature, pulling it off Ronald and Sandshifter. Wavecrasher stepped into the store then, her watery arm holding the creature off the ground. Thunderer stepped in from behind her and dipped his finger into the water. Instantly, an electrical current shot out from the ram's extended digit through the watery arm and into the Hyleia. The creature went as stiff as a two-year-old putting a fork in a socket as the blue currents shot through its body. It let out one long yelp of pain, and then the water fist released its grip and the creature's body fell to the ground, the fur smoking and smoldering as Wavecrasher retracted her arm, transforming it back into flesh and blood.

"You guys pack some serious shit, don't you?" Ronald groaned. He tried to push himself up on the floor. He fell back a moment later, but Joe and Stalker quickly went over and helped their friends up.

"Hey, we're happy to help," Thunderer said cheerfully. He clapped the cat on the back.

The cat grinned sheepishly as Stalker glanced over at them.

"How are things going out there?" he asked.

"Not too bad," Wavecrasher replied. "Most of the Hyleias have been rounded up. Forger and Forester worked out a way to muzzle 'em, and Thunderer here figured out how to bring them to us."

"It was nothing," the ram said. He reached into his coat and pulled out a small speaker, with a wire running into his pocket. "I just boosted the power and broadcasted the sound of screams."

"And how did you get that?" Sandshifter asked.

The ram grinned and pulled a small radio out of his pocket. "Apparently, some station was using some screams to promote their big Halloween show. I just looped the screams on the radio waves and let them rip."

"Well done," Stalker said. He turned his attention to Ronald, who was having his wounds healed by Sandshifter. "You did well. Will you be all right?" the bat asked.

"Right now, I'd be happy not to have to see this place for a while," Ronald said.

"We are sorry you had to deal with that," Joe said.

"Eh, wasn't as bad as you'd think," Ronald said. "You deal with the elderly, senile, and just plain nasty all day long, all you want is to find the strength to beat and kill something."

"I know what you mean," Joe said. "You must get a lot of crazies in here—'Why don't you ever have it? You should have it! I never get what I need here!'"

"You sound like you've seen it before," Ronald said.

"Well, uh, you go to supermarkets, you see it sooner or later," Joe replied, wishing he had ended the conversation two sentences before. Thankfully, he didn't have to worry about keeping it going much longer, as he heard the sound of rattling chains scraping across the concrete.

All of them turned toward the window, holding their weapons tightly once again. The sound grew louder.

Suddenly, a Hyleia stuck its head through the window. But that was as far as it got because chains around its neck tensed and pulled it back, Forger's six arms straining to keep it at bay. The other Knights quickly drew their weapons and beat at the creature as Joe moved to stand by Ronald.

"How many guys do you have in this group?" Ronald asked, grabbing his club from the ground.

"Enough," Joe replied. He stepped in front of his old friend. "You've done all you can. We'll take it from here."

"Hey, I just helped take one of those things down. Don't pull hero crap with me," Ronald said.

"I'm not. I'm just doing my job," Joe said.

"Well, then I'm gonna give you a hand," Ronald said.

"These things can kill you without a thought."

"Screw that!"

"Listen to me. This is what we do. We don't need an unknown in the mix and—"

"Oh, somebody like me? What *I* can't handle is shit, because—"

"Oh, don't start up the racial shit, Ron. Just because you got that lady who called you the "Negro manager" to stop coming here bitching about her coupons by pretending to be part of the Black Panthers doesn't mean that it always … works."

Ronald stared at Joe with the surprise reserved only for the announcement of parenthood or neon pink socks on Christmas morning. Very slowly, he asked, "And how do you know about that?"

Joe swallowed hard, his mind racing to find an explanation for his screwup.

But Ronald wasn't going to give him the time. "Just who the hell are you? And how do you know so much about me?"

"It's … It's …," Joe stammered.

"What? Not important?" Ronald snapped. "Answer me or—"

"*Look out!*" a voice yelled out suddenly.

Ronald and Joe both looked up to see a Hyleia push through the legion of Knights and make its way into the store with a strong leap, the chains holding it snapping as it moved it. The creature landed and launched itself once again, aiming its claws at Ronald and Joe as it flew through the air.

Without thinking, Joe ducked down, hoping to get out of the creature's way. He reached his hand to pull Ronald down with him, but as his hand brushed Ronald's bloody shirt, he felt it slip through his fingers. He also felt Ronald's body start to pull to the left, as if he planned to sidestep the Hyleia. But if that was his plan, he put it into motion a second too late.

Joe turned to see the creature land on him, driving its claws into his chest. Ronald grimaced and screamed and fell fall back under the impact. They both hit the ground and skidded forward. The Hyleia bent down and dug its teeth into Ronald's neck, even as Joe screamed out his friend's name and struggled to his feet.

He ran to the creature, grabbed its furry back, ripped the creature off, and threw it into the wall, where it landed with a thud. But all Joe could see was his friend lying there, the lifeblood pouring out of his chest and throat.

"Oh dear God, Ronald, hold on!" Joe called out. He moved to his friend's side, getting ready to heal him. "C'mon, man, you can't die before you get that role with Martin Lawrence and make him funny again!"

"J-J—" Ronald stammered out, even as the blood poured from between his lips.

"Don't try to talk," Joe said. He put his hands above his friend's throat. But before he could place them down, Ronald's hands came up and grasped them. Looking up at the man who had been his friend, Ronald said, "J-J- J-Joe?"

Joe's hand moved over to his mask and slowly pulled it down, showing his friend his face once again.

"Hey," Ronald said and stopped as a choking noise started to emanate from his throat. As Ronald's body shook, Joe stretched his hand out, trying to reach the man's throat again. But suddenly the shaking stopped, and Joe could feel Ronald's grip on his hand loosen and then fall away completely.

"No," Joe whispered. He put his hands over the wounds and called upon the power. But no matter how much he called upon it, the light would not come. Still, Joe kept trying, even as the other Knights came up behind him, their faces sad and quiet.

"C'mon … work … please," Joe whispered. He continued to whisper that even as a hand came down on his shoulder.

"He's gone, Joe," Stalker said gently.

But Joe just kept going, the bat's words not even registering. Sandshifter stepped forward and gently put her hands on Joe. The Light Knight fought as the wolf pulled him away, but Sandshifter didn't stop. She held Joe's hands up, away from the body, until finally, Joe stopped fighting. The wolf let go then, and Joe's hands fell. He looked at the body that had been his friend and began to weep.

Even as the Knights stood there together, a growl reminded them they were not alone. They glanced over. The Hyleia approached, its teeth bared. Though all the Knights turned to face it, Joe rose up and pushed them away. He stared at it through eyes that could no longer show the anger and grief they felt, because they had become filled with liquid gold. And as he reached for his staff, he bared his own teeth to match the creature's savage grin.

*   *   *

Groundquake sped through the ceiling, following the king and wondering what the hell he was going to do. Now that he knew there was a Chaos Demon, part of him wanted to bail out and call the others. After all, what was he going to do? Throw rocks at a creature that could break the majority of physical laws?

But Quake wanted to see what this demon would want with the gremlin king. He wanted to see this thing that the gremlins guarded, this thing that was so incredibly dangerous. He wanted to know how the hell they had managed to get a device of such power and why they were allowed to keep it.

Looking down, he saw the king look around, as if to make sure he was alone and then he put his clawed hands onto the wall. Part of the rock glowed and then fell away, revealing a hole that the king swiftly walked through, even as it started to close up behind him. Quake knew that he couldn't reach the door in time, but that wasn't a problem. The dog pushed himself into the great stone wall, giving up his sight and allowing the earth itself to guide him to the king. It was a lot like diving into a deep trench in the ocean—complete darkness surrounded him, with only the feel of the rocks to trigger his senses.

Under their direction, he was soon able to look down and see the king enter a huge room with a huge circular door in the wall. The door was decorated with a variety of markings and symbols. Though Groundquake didn't recognize them, he knew enough of magic to know that they had to be important, especially considering how many there were. Prince Nerbino stood at the door, looking bored and unhappy as his "father" approached. The fake king grunted, and his son immediately fell to one knee before him. But the "king" waved his hand and motioned for the boy to stand up.

"Why, Father? Is there more you wish to say on my failure?" Nerbino said bitterly as he rose.

"No, my son. I've no need for that, and neither do you," the "king" replied. "In truth, you came closer to success than many of us."

"What?"

"What I said before, I said for the Knights and the populace. I too am tired of the problems caused on the mortal realm."

Nerbino listened eagerly.

"If I did not punish you, then my insincerity would be revealed."

"You truly agreed with me?" Nerbino asked.

"Yes. But Rikino was too much of a fool to put such a plan through properly. We cannot move up there so openly."

"What did you have in mind, Father?" Nerbino asked.

"They think of us gremlins as weak, ugly, stupid creatures," the "king" explained, "that we have almost no effect on the world or the balance."

"Yes," Nerbino hissed.

"Therefore, we are going to do something that will show the world the power we gremlins have."

"How?"

"Why do you think I put you down here?"

Nerbino's eyes went wide as he listened to the man he believed to be his father.

"We shall demand the power and rights that should be ours, and the power behind this door shall be our way to them. No one will ever speak against us again, be they Knight, demon, or the angels. With that power behind us, the gremlins shall be the most feared beings in all the world, as we should have always been!"

*   *   *

The Hyleia growled and snarled as it stalked its prey. Joe gave no reply, except to follow the creature in its deadly dance. The two of them circled each other, amid the broken items and the two corpses on the floor. The Knights stood back, all eager to jump in, but unable to as Stalker blocked them.

"But he can't fight that thing alone!" Thunderer insisted.

"It doesn't matter," Stalker said. "He needs to do this."

"But the way he is—"

"Just shut up and watch," Sandshifter snapped. "The bat's right. Joe's gotta do this one for himself."

"Sure, you would say that. You just wanna see him fall!" Wavecrasher snapped.

"Against that?" the wolf asked.

Wavecrasher started to reply, but before she could, a thud shook the floor, and the Knights turned to see the creature skid backward, its chest smoking as Joe's gloved hands glowed with power. The creature wheezed and groaned a bit. It started to move to the side, to begin the circling once again. But this time, Joe swung his arms to the side and unleashed a light blast right at the Hyleia.

Despite the pain, the creature managed to roll to the side, and as the light exploded around it, it managed to take another leap at Joe. It flew through the air. Joe made a running start and, in tandem with another burst of light, slid under the creature. The creature hit the ground in a heap, moaning in pain. Joe simply came to a halt and got to his feet, not noticing the black blood that dotted his clothes. He held the circular blades of light in his hands, their golden light flecked with the black of the Hyleia's wound.

"Jesus," Thunderer whispered.

"That's ... That's gotta be it," 'Crash said. "He can't go further. He couldn't."

Joe advanced on the creature as it lay there in an ever-growing pool of its own blood. Somehow, it managed to raise its head a bit at the sound of Joe's footsteps, just in time to see the light blades flash and change again. It tried to move away, but its pain was too great. As the spikes of light flew from Joe's hands into the creature's shoulder, dragging it into the wall and pinning it there, it howled, louder than any of the Knights had heard during the battle.

Joe moved up to the creature, the power forming in his hands once again. The Knights looked on in growing horror. Joe fashioned a second pair of light spikes. He raised them up to the creature's neck, held them there a moment, and then suddenly drove them in. The Hyleia screamed like a wild dog getting its spine cracked and being left to die, and even Sandshifter felt something inside her twist at the sight. Joe slowly brought out the spikes, their light hidden in the black paint of the Hyleia's blood. Then he drove the spikes in again, harder and deeper. The blood spurted out in a way that was almost orgasmic. Again, he removed the spikes, and again he drove them in.

Again.

And again.

And again.

"Dear God, why won't it die?" Thunderer asked, fighting back the urge to puke with all the strength he had. "He's stabbing it enough; why won't it die?!"

"Because he's not just stabbing it," Wavecrasher said. "Look."

The Knights saw Joe drive the spikes in. They saw the blood spurt. They saw him pull them out. And they saw the skin below the spikes close, just before Joe brought them down again.

"He's healing it just so he can stab it again!" Forger cried out.

"Not anymore," the wolf said. Joe brought them out, and the spikes finally faded away. Joe held his hand out, and the staff flew into his hands. He held it above his head, the lion's head glowing brighter than the sun, maybe even ten suns. He flipped it over, so that the top was pointed down, and raising it over his shoulders, he made the gruesome deed all too obvious.

Suddenly there was a flurry of black amid the golden light. A voice that screamed, "*No!*" A black glove closing over the light. Another flash, followed by a scream and the stench of burning flesh and leather. And then, another moan of pain to join the Hyleia's. But this one was one that Joe recognized.

"S-Stalker?" The Light Knight muttered as the gold began to drain away from his eyes. He rubbed them, still not seeing the blood that covered his hands and looked down at the black-coated figure that lay on the ground, clutching his smoking hand.

"What? How?"

"You," another voice said.

Joe barely registered Sandshifter's voice. His eyes began to drift. He saw the Hyleia before him, chained to the wall, bloody, broken, and helpless. He saw the light spikes that held it in place, and knew where they'd come from. He looked down at his clothes and saw the black blood that covered them. And then he knew it all.

"Joe," Nightstalker said, trying to get up.

But Joe just staggered away, his face as a pale as a frozen corpse. He took another few uneasy steps and then whirled around and vomited, just managing to grab on to a shelf to keep from falling into it.

Stalker tried to stand, gingerly getting up as he cradled his hand and calling out to Joe once again.

But Joe didn't hear him. As he finished emptying his stomach, he looked over and saw Ronald's corpse. Somehow, his face turned even paler and his body shook, the little strength it had leaving it again. He managed to push himself to the side, so that when he fell to his knees, he didn't land in his own vomit. Instead, he sat there, silent and horrified. His eyes went to the body of his friend to his bloodstained clothes, and back again.

"Joe," Stalker said again as he approached his friend. Reaching out, he placed his hand on Joe's shoulder. But at the simple touch, Joe shot to his feet and stumbled back, away from all of them. With a final flash of light, Joe vanished, leaving nothing behind but the bloody signs of his handiwork.

XXI.

"WILL YOU STAY DOWN?!" Groundquake snapped as he pulled Nerbino back behind the huge stone wall the dog had created.

"You expect me to sit here while that thing breaks down the door?" Nerbino snarled as he landed back behind the wall.

The Chaos Demon kept hammering with alternating blasts of white fire.

"No, but I think taking it down by ourselves ain't an option," Quake snapped back as he grabbed his hammer and used it to crack two holes in the rock. "So just help me keep it occupied!"

Nerbino snarled at the dog, but he still used one of the holes to shoot his green flame through at the creature, in tandem with the rock barrage from Quake. The two attacks stunned the demon, which staggered back. Quake grabbed his hammer and sent another message through to the Knights, wondering how things could've changed so quickly in such a short space of time.

* * *

"Father, you can't be serious about this," Nerbino said as he slowly backed away from the false king. "You have told me since I was a child that this power could never be released."

"I made a mistake, son," the "king" replied. "If we wish to strike back at those who imprison us—"

"I know, Father. But this ... this can't be the way."

"If I say it is, then it is!" the false king shouted. "This is my realm, and you are my son! You will open the door and give us the power that will lead to glory! Or do I need to find a new heir?"

Nerbino's ugly face actually seemed to pale at that, and slowly he turned to the door. Moving his hand to the symbols, the prince took a deep breath and then reached for something on his belt. Quake prepared himself to drop, slowly moving his body out of the earth and inching closer to the two gremlins.

But then, he paused in his descent. Nerbino suddenly stopped and turned to face the false king.

"What are you doing?" the counterfeit gremlin hissed. "Put in your part of the key and open it!"

"I can't," Nerbino answered.

"How dare you! You will obey your fath—"

"I can't. You told me about this because I asked you why we were allowed to survive when we make mischief and not true evil. And you told me about the power that lives behind this door—a power so great that I was sworn to secrecy for fear of it ever being discovered. I swore on my own blood, the blood that poisons everything that touches it, that I would never open it. Do you remember that, Father?"

The "king" gave no reply. He merely looked at Nerbino, dumbfounded.

And once he saw that, the gremlin prince suddenly let loose with green fire, knocking his phony father back.

"My father made me swear that oath," Nerbino said. "He would never force me to break it for anything. So who are you, creature, and what have you done with him?"

Quake watched as the "king" got to his feet and let out an all-too-familiar roar-shriek that caused Nerbino to grab his ears in pain. Then, both watched as the king's body suddenly began to stretch, becoming transparent and crystalline. Flesh became translucent and hard, and the fat face of the king fell away as the shine of the demon's scales broke through. It grew larger and larger, until the Chaos Demon stood nearly ten feet tall. Nerbino looked up with horror at the creature that had once taken the form of his father, and then started to scream as the demon's skin began to swell.

Quake pushed his way through the ceiling, falling toward the ground, but not before grabbing a piece of the rock first. As he fell, he chucked the rock at the emerging Chaos Demon, catching it right in the face. The creature roared and stumbled back as the dog flipped in midair and landed on his feet. Nerbino looked on in surprise, the demon's spell on his body broken.

"You? What are you doing here?" the gremlin prince spat out.

"Savin' your ass for one thing," Quake snapped back.

"I don't need your help!" Nerbino growled. He unleashed more green fire at the creature.

But the demon was ready this time, and as the green flames sped *toward it, it stretched out its palms and absorbed the fire into itself. The green flames spread through its body and then returned to its hands, pouring out right toward Nerbino. The prince gasped and began to return fire, but then the rock before him suddenly arched upward into a wall, blocking the flames. As they spattered harmlessly around the prince, Groundquake stomped his feet hard onto the ground, and the floor around the creature suddenly snapped up in two large square blocks that crushed the demon between them.*

"You don't need to thank me fer that either," the dog said, moving back toward Nerbino.

Nerbino started to growl and then stopped as he looked at the stone blocks. "Perhaps I do," he said, albeit through clenched teeth. "Is that thing what I think it is? A Chaos Demon?"

"Yep."

"Then you know that won't hold it."

"But it'll give us time to figure out a plan. What's behind that door anyway?"

"I cannot say," Nerbino replied. "But I can say that we have to keep it shut, which means you need to protect me."

"And why's that?"

"Because the runes that hold it sealed will only open with the blood of the king and his heir. Look out!"

*　　　*　　　*

Now, from the side of the wall, Groundquake slammed down his hammer, sending a rippling shockwave through the ground that became a huge fissure under the creature's feet. The demon fell through, crashing below to the rock as it struggled to get out. As it clawed at the rock, Nerbino unleashed another burst of green fire, hitting the creature directly in its head. The Chaos Demon staggered as Nerbino unleashed more and more flame, only for the dog to pull him back again.

"Careful! You want it to use it against us again?"

"I will not let its crimes against me go unpunished!" Nerbino snarled.

"Yeah, and if it gets you, then all it needs is your father's blood to open the door and—"

"You idiot! Don't you understand?!" Nerbino barked. "All it needs is me!"

Quake stared stupidly for a moment, and then he slowly felt realization creep into his brain. The demon had impersonated the king to lure Nerbino out. And if it needed the king's blood, what would be the easiest way to get it and open the door quickly?

"Aw crap, where are those guys?" the dog cursed. He grabbed his hammer and once again sent word to the other Knights.

* * *

"I-I didn't think he'd be the one," Wavecrasher muttered.

"Do we go after him?" Thunderer asked.

"And how would we do that? We don't even know where he went," Forger said.

"Well, we've got to do something," Thunderer said. "He's out there somewhere and out of his mind."

"Really? Could you tell that before or after he practically gutted that thing in front of us?" Wavecrasher said.

"Here's a thought," Sandshifter said suddenly. "Why don't the two of you shut up, and we'll ask our current leader what to do?"

"And what do you think that would that be?" Wavecrasher snapped.

"I don't know yet," the wolf replied. She glanced over at Nightstalker, who looked back at all of them. Though the bat could feel his concern for Joe biting at him, a cold, dark part of him said he needed to attend to things here.

"Well, leader? What's the plan?" Sandshifter asked.

Stalker's response was to turn to the wolf and ask, "Is the Hyleia still alive?"

"Our leader vanishes and you're concerned about that?" Wavecrasher asked in disbelief.

"Stalker, we've got to find him, he's not ... well you saw," Thunderer said. "What if he hurts himself? Or somebody else? Or—"

"I didn't ask for an opinion, and I'm not interested in whats, ifs, or, ors," the bat replied. "What I am concerned about is whether or not he finished the job on that thing."

The ram looked at Stalker with confusion. Wavecrasher walked over to the Hyleia and looked at its battered form. Stretching out her fingers, she felt along the creature's sinewy neck. After a few moments, she said, "Yeah, it's alive."

"Then leave it to me," Stalker said. He moved over to the creature. Kneeling down, he placed one hand on the creature's head; blackness spread out from under his palm, and wove itself around the Hyleia. But just as it covered the creature, it suddenly faded away like early morning fog, leaving the Hyleia healed.

"Now for some answers," Stalker muttered. He reached down and wrapped his fingers around the creature's neck. It gagged once and then gurgled as the bat stood up, pulling the creature up with him.

"I didn't heal you out of charity," Stalker said, looking the Hyleia dead in the eyes. "I want you to tell me something. Or else what my counterpart did to you will be nothing compared to the nightmares I will show you."

"Stalker, don't waste your time," Sandshifter said. "That thing's mindless; it's not going to answer you."

"Not ... with ... hand ... on ... throat," a wheezy voice warbled out from within the throat of the Hyleia.

"They can talk. You should really read up on your enemy," Wavecrasher said.

"All right, I'm flexible," Nightstalker said, loosening his grip on the Hyleia's throat. "Now, will you answer my question or not?"

"You ... you don't fear me," the Hyleia said, its voice like rocks twisting against each other in a mountain stream.

"No."

"Then ... I am free."

"What do you mean?" the bat asked.

"You think fear is our food. It is, but it is also our drug," the Hyleia said. "It is our everything—sustenance, joy, pride. It takes away our minds, fills us with greed and rage. That is why my kind was locked away in the realm of dreams, left only to the fear of nightmares, in a realm where we could not harm anything."

"Then who let you out?" Stalker demanded.

"You think I know?" the Hyleia wheezed. "But the word on the grapevine was that it was some sort of demon—a special one."

"And what was so special about him?"

"From what I heard, nobody gave the same description twice," the Hyleia said.

"So it was a shape-shifter," Forger said.

"No," the Hyleia replied. "A shape-shifter changes completely.

But there was something that everybody reported on—big, glowing scales."

"Are you sure?" Stalker said, shaking the creature as he spoke.

"Yeah. That's what everybody said. And they said it just ripped a hole in the dream fabric and let us out, without any magic we knew of."

"It broke the rules," Thunderer whispered. "Oh God, it's—"

"Don't," Nightstalker warned. Turning back to the Hyleia, he said, "I'm going to send you back to the dream realm. Your others are destroyed; I want you to go and tell your friends there that the Elemental Knights will be waiting for them out here. And do tell them about the Light Knight."

The Hyleia shivered and nodded as the blackness began to cover it once again. Only this time, when the shadow faded, the creature faded along with it.

"This is bad," Thunderer said as the bat turned back to face his troops. "If that thing's telling the truth, then that means we've got a Chaos Demon on our hands."

"And we're a man short," Forger added.

"Maybe. But that doesn't mean we lose our heads," Stalker said. "Think. What would the demons gain by this?"

"They keep us occupied," Forger said, "away from something else they want."

"Any ideas then?"

But before the wolf could answer, Nightstalker noticed his sword glowing with brown light. The bat touched the hilt and activated its message as Groundquake's voice suddenly echoed through the broken building.

"*What in the hell are you morons doing? Playing Parcheesi?*"

"Groundquake, what's going on? Are the gremlins after you?"

"Oh, yeah, I'm really this panicked about them! No, we've got a damn Chaos Demon down here! It killed the king and now it's going after Nerbino."

"What does it want with the prince?"

"He's half of a key that'll apparently end the frigging world if it's used!"

"What's your situation? Are you holding it back?"

"Barely! Me 'n Nerbino are workin' on it, but it ain't gonna last! Get your butts down here, now!"

"We're on our way. Do what you can until then," the bat said as the sword's glow faded. Turning back to the others, Stalker said, "You know what we need to do."

"Yeah, and how are we gonna pull it off?" Wavecrasher asked. "We need Light and Dark to stop that thing."

"True. But you aren't going to go and stop that thing," Stalker replied. "You are gonna go down there and buy time."

"So we're cannon fodder?" Sandshifter asked.

"For the moment," the bat answered. "Thunderer, go out there and call the others. You all have to go down there and give Quake and Nerbino all the help you can."

"And what do you plan to do?" Forger asked. "We could do more damage with you there."

"I still need to wipe the Hyleias from the people's minds. And we'll do more damage with me and Joe."

"But we've got no idea where he is," Thunderer said.

"Joe doesn't have a lot of places left to go. And besides, I can see the secrets, remember?"

"But—"

"Listen to him," Sandshifter said suddenly. "It's not the best plan, but it's the one that we've got to use. We don't have any other options."

"She's right," Forger said. "Even if he comes with us, he won't be enough. We need Joe."

Wavecrasher and Thunderer looked at each other and then at the wolf. And then, they both gave slow, uncertain nods. Turning back to the bat, Wavecrasher said, "We'll do the best we can."

"I don't ask for anything else," Stalker said as the cat vanished, her body breaking apart and winking out like water evaporating into the sky.

Without a word, Thunderer headed for the broken window and into the street to gather the other Knights. But Sandshifter stayed where she was, looking right at Nightstalker.

"You know where he went, don't you?" the wolf asked.

"I have some ideas," the bat replied.

"I've just got one. And I know you aren't stupid enough that you haven't thought of it yourself."

"If that's where he's gone, then I'll deal with it."

"If he's gone there, you may not be able to deal with it."

"I doubt that."

Sandshifter shrugged and said, "You know, I thought this might happen someday."

"Did you?"

"Yeah. And I thought you might be the one to keep everybody's head above water."

"Thank you."

"Don't thank me until this is over," the wolf replied as her body changed to sand and then vanished into a swirl of brown.

Nightstalker watched her vanish into the air and then, once he was alone, gave a sigh. He knew what the wolf meant, and he also knew that she was probably right. And as he looked out onto the city he still had to mindwipe, Stalker thought about what he would have to do if that was the case. He felt his heart grow sick.

*   *   *

"When are they getting here?" Nerbino yelled as the Chaos Demon released more white fire at the earth shield. The wall rumbled with the impact, and rocks rained down on the two of them.

"You think I know?" Groundquake said, putting his hands on the wall in the hope that he could strengthen it. On the other side, the Chaos Demon gathered a huge white fireball and held it between its two hands. With a roar, the creature hurled the ball at the wall. The wall shook and rumbled, and cracks spread across it. Groundquake poured more of his power into it, but the strength of the demon was too strong. As the wall came down around him, he threw his hands upward, trying to steer the rocks away from himself and Nerbino. But after putting so much power into holding up the wall, the dog didn't have enough energy left. Some of the rocks struck him from the side, but they did him no harm. In fact, he felt strength come back into his body. For a moment, he thought maybe he could survive long enough to get a plan together against this thing.

But that was not to be. A scream came from his right, and the dog turned to see the gremlin prince pinned under a large rock, even as the Chaos Demon began to advance on them.

"Goddamn it!" Groundquake swore. He ran to where the prince was trapped. Putting his hands under the rock, he said, "Can you move?"

"What do you think?!" Nerbino snapped back.

"All right, hold on," the dog began.

But then Nerbino threw his head back and let out a god-awful scream.

Quake dropped his hands, but within a few seconds, he realized what was happening. A dark red mist poured out from under the rock, moving toward the demon that needed Nerbino's blood to succeed.

Quake turned, hoping to stop it, but the mist was already speeding toward the demon, whose chest had shifted and twisted so that a large mouth had opened within it. The dog sent out a command to the earth, trying to will it upward into something that could stop the mist. But the command came too late; the mouth sucked up the bloody mist like a dog lapping up a plate of greasy sauce. The demon's scales glowed bright red for a moment and then returned to normal as it focused on the dog and the fallen prince that were now the only things standing in its way.

Quake called up the earth in another wall, but what came up was smashed to bits by the creature's fire. Nerbino's eyes went large and white as the flames reflected back in them. But then they went dark, and a shriek of pain emanated all around the caves as a white, blazing figure emerged in front of the gremlin prince, who just stared in utter horror as flames cut through flesh and cloth.

Finally, the demon stopped its assault, and both it and Nerbino watched as the figure slumped to its knees. Quake had been alternately burned and frozen. Ice covered his left arm and part of his chest. The cloth and fur on his right were burned away, the skin a pale, grimy gray, as if someone had been rubbing it with a rag filled with acid, bleach, and something even more cutting. The dog's face was just as pale and grimy, and his eyes drifted from side to side.

"Earth Knight?" Nerbino whispered, looking at the horrible wounds the dog had suffered on his behalf. But a pair of huge crunching footsteps took his attention away from that; the demon was advancing toward the door.

"No," Nerbino muttered. He struggled once again to pry himself out from under the rock. But he knew it was useless. The demon reached for the door once again. Nerbino struggled on, even as he felt his wounds twist and split under the rock. He grimaced but focused on escape. His breath was now coming out in short white bursts, and small bits of frost appeared on the rocks nearby.

Suddenly, a huge tendril of water stretched outward and grabbed the creature's left hand, while a set of chains wrapped around its right. The creature roared as the water around its hand froze and the metal flowed and wrapped around the other hand, blocking the creature from touching the doorway.

"By what power?" Nerbino said, watching the demon rage and scream in protest.

"The one that's getting you outta here, boy," a twang-filled voice said.

Nerbino looked up into Forester's furry face.

"Hold on, your highness, we'll get you out," Firesprite said. She and Sandshifter slipped their hands under the rock and pulled up. With a heave, they tossed it to the sides, leaving Nerbino's crushed body visible.

"Never mind ... the Earth Knight," Nerbino muttered as the Knights tended to him.

"He's in good hands," Sandshifter replied as Windrider moved over to the dog. The falcon dug his hand into the ground and came away with a handful of broken rocks, some of which had been crushed to powder. He sprinkled them over the dog's head, placing his free hand, glowing with white light, on the dog's chest. The effect was immediate. Quake's color returned as the ice broke away and his burned body began to heal itself. The empty look faded from his eyes until he snorted, shook, and then saw the falcon before him.

"You? You're the one sent to heal me?"

"Had to be someone?" the falcon answered glibly. "Besides, I earned it. Took down a lotta monsters today."

"Who's taking care of this one?" the dog asked.

"Take a look," Windrider said. He pointed to Wavecrasher and Forger, who were doing all they could to hold the Chaos Demon back as it pulled and pulled at their respective grips.

"What's behind the door?" Windrider asked.

"Ya got me, but we can't let it find out," the dog replied, shakily getting to his feet.

"Then we'd better put some distance between 'em. Think you can give me a sky light?"

"Up to the surface—are you crazy?!" the dog snapped. "We got enough problems without—"

"No, to the area above us. You know, where the gremlins throw their trash," Windrider said.

"Okay. Good plan," Groundquake said.

He turned his gaze to the ceiling. He narrowed his eyes, and an opening suddenly cracked and pushed its way into existence, just big enough for the creature.

"Guys, let go of it! And everybody else, hold on!" Windrider yelled, holding his arms out before him.

"Oh, brilliant," Quake muttered, but he did as the bird said, even causing the earth to lock down around everyone's feet. His eyes glowing white, the falcon used his power to spin all the air in the cavern, creating a huge vacuum. The demon snarled and bit at the winds, especially as Windrider began to narrow it above the creature's head.

"Let go!" he yelled out to Wavecrasher and Forger. Without a second's hesitation, the two Knights did just that. Without the tension from their grip, the demon instantly flew upward, sucked through the hole like dust through a vacuum cleaner. The creature's screams echoed briefly through the large tunnel and then faded as it drew farther and farther away.

"Come on, we've gotta get after it!" Wavecrasher yelled, heading toward the hole.

"Not without me," Nerbino snapped as Firesprite helped him to his feet. "That thing killed my father. It is my duty to stop it."

"Great. Just don't be an idiot doing it," Sandshifter replied. "Quake, can you get something ready so we can chase that thing?"

"Yeah. Gimme a sec," the dog replied. Soon, his eyes glowed brown. The ground rumbled briefly, and then a circular piece of earth, just big enough to hold the others and fit through the hole, pulled itself out of the ground and floated there, ready to be used.

"Ah could've done that," Forester said. "Ah woulda had a big flower, which woulda been a lot softer—"

"Kid, remember what I told you about forgetting elaborates?" Sandshifter asked, moving onto the stone platform.

"Right, right," the squirrel said, and he too moved to get on.

Once everyone was aboard, Groundquake turned his eyes toward the hole, and the platform sped upward, toward the dumps.

*　　*　　*

The blackness faded away, and he found himself on the stairwell once again. Nightstalker quickly imagined the room and ran toward it. Skidding to a halt, he reached over and pulled the door open and all but leaped inside, where he found …

"Joe?" the bat called out inside the empty room. But all he got back was the echo of his own voice.

"Damn it," the bat swore. But no anger could be found in his voice—only frustrated acceptance. This place had never really offered Joe comfort, despite all the effort he had made to change that. The killing had only been part of it; Joe had never really been able to accept the power and position that had been thrust upon him. It was why he'd clung so hard to his moral code. And now, now that he had broken that moral code, Stalker knew there was only one place Joe could go, one place that could offer him the things he truly wanted. And the worst part was, the bat didn't want to stop him.

"But I have to," Stalker sighed. He felt his heart grow heavy, knowing what he would have to do to his friend.

But he was going to do it anyway.

"I'm sorry, Joe," the bat murmured to the empty room as the shadows fell over his body again, taking him down into his element once again.

*　　*　　*

"Can't this thing go any faster?" Wavecrasher asked.

"You're in a rush to fight that thing?" Forester asked.

"Considering that the world as we know it depends on it, he should be," the cat snapped back.

"How 'bout you two quit arguing or the catfish gets out and pushes!" Groundquake snapped as he pushed the platform up.

"What are we going to do once we get up there?" Thunderer asked.

"We're gonna find it. And we're gonna do our best to kill it," Sandshifter replied.

"You know we don't have the power for that," Forger said. "Only Stalker and Joe have been able to—"

"Oh, shut up. They ain't here, so quit wishin' they were," Forester snapped. "Ah would've picked a time other than the end of the world to have a nervous breakdown—"

"Don't you dare try to judge" Firesprite yelled back, grabbing the squirrel's collar and pulling him close. "At least Joe and Stalker were trying to hold to something bigger than themselves. You just sit around complaining or making your snide jokes. You ran away in training, boy, and you know it. And I think you'd run away again, if you had to."

"Why you—" Forester sputtered.

"Shut up, kid. Or I'll shove your foot the rest of the way through your mouth," Sandshifter said. Everyone turned to face her, while Forester stared in utter shock and tried to spit something out in response. "But ... you ... Ah thought ..."

"Yeah, I thought Joe didn't buy into all this, and I didn't want him here if he didn't. And I think that bat's a self-righteous ass. But that doesn't mean I hate them for trying to do the right thing."

Forester's mouth twisted, and he tried to say something back. But before he could, the ground around them vanished, and the Knights found themselves above ground. As the air hit his nose, Forester felt his words wilt and die against the scent, something akin to rotten fruit inside a sun-dried rhino corpse covered with its own feces.

"Dear sweet Christ!" Wavecrasher swore, pulling her mask over her face.

"We have different standards than you, remember?" Nerbino said, gesturing to the huge piles of trash around them. Each one was a mix of rotten and discarded food but also various dead animals and what appeared to be trashy items from the surface world. Bits of broken toys poked out from the piles, as well as cracked phones and even a couple of refrigerators.

"How do you stand this?" Wavecrasher asked.

"You get used to it," Nerbino said as he looked around. "I'm more concerned about where the demon went."

"So am I," Sandshifter said. She drew her staff and took a couple sniffs but then shook her head.

"Too many odors. I can't focus on anything by itself."

"Just as well," Forger said. "I doubt this thing has a singular odor anyway."

"Great, another problem for us," Windrider said. "This thing's like the ultimate shape-shifter. It could be anywhere."

"Gee, that just fills me with hope and determination," Forester muttered.

"Doesn't matter. We'll have to look," Wavecrasher said. "But first, we gotta make sure it's stuck up here. Quake, you'd better seal that hole."

"Not a problem," the dog replied. He gestured toward the platform. After a brief rumble, the platform melded back into the earth.

"It's gonna have to dig to get outta here now," the dog replied. "Not that it really helps us, but—"

"Start looking," Wavecrasher said. "Keep your eyes open and be ready to fight."

"Brilliant," the dog muttered, but still he looked around as he tightened his grip on his hammer.

*   *   *

He looked on and saw the light shining from the house. He couldn't believe he'd never thought of it as anything special. This light was warm, something to beckon to those out in the dark. He saw the woman, her hair blazing in a red halo sitting in her chair, watching television. The boy was in the other room, his head down, concentrating hard on the paper that was before him. His pencil hung over it as he chewed the eraser, trying to understand the problem in his mind before even thinking of marking the paper with his pencil. The man kept watching as the boy shook his head and finally put the pencil down in frustration. He watched the woman turn to the boy now, saw her expression soften as she got up, turned off the television, and walked over to her son.

The woman looked down at the problem, her own brow furrowing as she looked it over. He smiled then as he recognized the look of intense confusion and struggle that her face always took on. It had always made him think of a cartoon banker, trying desperately to keep the bank afloat. The boy looked up then and saw his mother leaning in, her eyebrows pressed together, as though this problem held the answer to life, death, the universe, and an understanding of how to balance a checkbook. He looked at this expression, and his face split in a smile. The woman's response was to somehow intensify her look, as if she was trying to pass a gallstone while looking over the problem, and then her own face broke as she smiled and ruffled her son's hair. She spoke a few words to him and then left. He went back to looking at the problem. This time, he stopped chewing, nodded, and wrote an answer down quickly and then moved on to the next one.

This had to be the light he was destined for. He pushed through the bushes, his gloved hands still caked with blood, his clothes still awash with it. But those dark marks meant nothing. This light, this loving, wonderful light, would make it all go away.

"Your wife is beautiful. Son looks too much like you though."

Joe stopped and then turned back into the bushes to see a black-coated figure standing there, looking at him with red eyes.

"Nice trick. I would've thought you'd be too tired after mindwiping the city."

"I didn't do it alone."

"I thought Rastla couldn't interfere on this plane."

"She worked her power through me when she how big this all was. It was … a unique experience."

"What does everyone think happened?"

"A small tornado. It was the best we could come up with."

"Mm … I thought it would take you longer to find me."

"It wasn't hard. You don't have many places left to go," Stalker said.

"I only need one," Joe replied, looking back toward the house.

"Joe, you know that you can't do this," the bat said, not unkindly.

"We'll leave, start over somewhere else. They love me; they'll understand."

"Enough that they'd uproot everything they have just for you?"

Joe stopped and looked directly at the bat. "I can't go back there. I can't do this anymore. I never should've done it in the first place."

"Joe, I know what happened back there was bad," Stalker said.

"And I promise to do whatever I can to help you. But I can't let you do this."

"I'm not asking permission," Joe said. "I want my life back. And I am going to get it back. Maybe in time, I can convince myself this was all a bad dream, something I had while I was in a coma."

"It's not that simple," Nightstalker said.

"It really is. I just walk inside the door."

"Quake called after you disappeared. We have a Chaos Demon on our hands."

"What?"

"Yes. The gremlins have something down there, something powerful. The demon wants it. The others are there right now, fighting it and buying time. But we both knew that they can't hold on forever."

"No. No they can't," Joe said.

"Good. Now let's—"

"You'd better get down there," Joe said. He turned and once again started to push his way out of the bushes toward his house.

*   *   *

"Man, this thing knows how to hide," Thunderer said as the group trekked through the foul-smelling dump.

"Nerbino, is it possible that it could get out?" Forger asked. "Is there some other exit?"

"Possible, but unlikely," Nerbino replied. "This place is an alternate cave built by our ancestors. The only way in or out is through a hole in the ceiling, which locks from the other side when we aren't dumping. Everything else is blocked off."

"I can't imagine why you'd block this place off," Quake said as he grimaced and shook something off his boot. The green and orange slime slid off and then scattered away into the ground. "So what do you actually throw down here? You guys aren't exactly a wonder for cleanliness."

"It's better you don't know," Nerbino said.

"Never mind that. Everybody split up; keep looking around," Wavecrasher said.

"And who made you leader?" Quake snapped.

"Besides, Ah've seen this movie. Everybody dies after they split up," Forester said.

"We can't die," Sandshifter replied. "Looking around separately will let us cover more ground. And if we find it, I think we'll all know about it."

Forester opened his mouth and then thought better of it. "Fine," the squirrel muttered as he struck out to the left, toward a large pile of trash.

The others all began to break up as well, heading in different directions to examine the dump. But suddenly, a loud hacking sound filled the air. Everyone turned to see Forester on his knees in front of the pile, his body shaking and convulsing as he coughed and coughed.

"Oh, for God's sake," Wavecrasher muttered. "He can't even get that close to that thing before he passes out?" She turned and started walking back to the squirrel, yelling as she did so. "It smells bad, okay? Deal with it. We got a … a …"

But then Wavecrasher found herself without words as she felt her throat closing, as if something had just farted down there. She started to hack and cough, leaning on her trident as she struggled to stay upright. The cat tried to hack up whatever it was, but whatever it was wasn't a hairball. And apparently, it was contagious. Turning around, she saw the other Knights and even Nerbino clutching their throats and hacking up their lungs, most of them falling to their knees as they did so. Even Sandshifter could barely hold herself upright. Wavecrasher tried to bring in some air, anything, but the more she breathed, the more felt she felt her chest tighten and her throat close. She felt her legs go rubbery and then she was on the floor, her eyes starting to dim.

*   *   *

"You can't be serious about this," Nightstalker said, grabbing Joe and pulling him back into the bushes.

"And why not?" Joe snapped, pushing off the bat's hand. "Don't you think I deserve it? Don't you think they've asked enough of me?"

"Yes, I do," the bat replied. "But you made an oath to serve them— an oath to uphold existence itself."

"Yes. And you can have it. You be the guy who saves the world."

"It's not supposed to be me, Joe. Not alone."

"It's going to have to be for a while," Joe said. "Ralin can find somebody else to fill my shoes."

"How do you know?" Stalker asked. "He could've picked any brain-dead monkey off the streets, but for some reason he picked you."

"Then I guess even the Architects can make mistakes."

"Damn it, Joe, don't you understand this?" Stalker nearly screamed. "This is bigger than what you want, man! Your friends are down there fighting for the world, and you think you can just walk away from them? What's the point of going back home if home won't be there tomorrow?"

"It will be," Joe said, "because you are going to go back there, and you will stop that thing."

"Are you really going to bet everything on that?"

"*What do you want me do?*" Joe yelled.

"*What you were chosen to do!*" Stalker yelled. "*What I was chosen to do! What we were all chosen to—*"

A click and the sound of rusty hinges turning suddenly echoed through the air, the lights flickering on with it. Both men shut up as Jeri slowly walked out the door, glancing around for the source of the sounds. For a moment, she looked toward the bushes. But Stalker was invisible in his black clothes, and Joe was much more inconspicuous without light. She looked around once more and then shook her head and walked back in, shutting the door behind her. Both men let out a sigh of relief and then turned back to each other.

"I know this is hard for you." Stalker said. "I've felt how much you missed them—"

"You looked into my heart?" Joe asked.

"I didn't need to. It was something so strong I couldn't help but feel it. And I have nothing but sympathy for you. But you made this choice, and there isn't a get out of jail free card. You have to stick with it, no matter how much it hurts."

Joe looked at the bat, and then shook his head. "All that time, and that was all you could get from me?"

"What do you mean?" the bat asked.

"Part of me always wanted to go home, Stalker, from the very beginning."

"That's not surpri—"

"It wasn't just wanting, Stalker," Joe said. "When I took the vow, I did want to do some good. And when things started to get hard, I tried to remember that. I thought maybe I could get used to it. But part of me was always hoping, dreaming, that maybe someday I'd find my way home. There were nights when I went down to the Nexus and looked into the portal and thought about how little it would take to go home."

"What stopped you then?" Stalker asked.

"I couldn't be a hypocrite. Those things I said to Sandy and the others, about how we were dead and our lives were over, I thought I meant it. I told myself, what was I going to do anyway? Just walk back in and make my wife and son think I was some kind of undead ghoul? Or tell them that I was alive, but I couldn't see them ever again? Tell Jeri I couldn't grow old with her? Tell Cody that I was going to bury him instead of the other way around? I thought I could at least keep the world together for them. But not with the blood I have on my hands now."

"If you leave and we fail, then the blood of everything else on this planet will be on your hands."

"Do you think this is easy for me?" Joe asked. "But I ... I can't live the rest of eternity being afraid of doing ... what I did back there. I can't ever let that fear come true again."

"Joe, you lost your friend to the Hyleia," Stalker said. "You shouldn't blame yourself for losing it. Anybody would have."

"Would anybody have crucified it?" Joe asked. "Would anyone have sliced it open and jammed spikes into its neck again and again, because they could just heal it and keep going as long as they wanted?"

"You are not the first person to lose control and do something they regret. And if you go back to them tonight, if you leave us, that doesn't mean that all of that is going to go away. Something could happen, something that could make you lose it again. Do you want your family to see that?"

"That won't happen," Joe said, shaking his head. "I'm going to get so far away from all of this that I'll never have to use these powers again."

"The Architects will find you. And if they don't, the Chaos Demons will come after you. They'll find you, no matter where you go."

"Stop it."

"They'll find you and nail you to a tree for what you've done to them. And then they'll go after your family."

"Stop it."

"They'll torture them, Joe. You'll hear the screams in your mind forever. You'll close your eyes and see their lifeblood pouring out of them."

"Stop it!"

"Imagine them, cutting, twisting, branding, everything you can think of. They might decide to rape her in front of you, just so you'll die with that in your brain. And then the boy—"

"*Stop it!*" Joe all but screamed this time.

"You know I'm right. And even all your precautions won't make that go away."

"It. Won't. Happen," Joe said through clenched teeth. "Because I'm going to go in there and shut the door. And that will be the last time you'll ever see me."

Joe turned and started to walk toward the house again.

Stalker watched him walk and then said, "I know what you're going through."

Joe didn't stop walking.

"The blackout, the horrible deed at your feet afterward."

His boots treaded on the ground.

"It's happened to me too."

The boots stopped.

*   *   *

Wavecrasher could feel everything in her chest starting to close up and weaken. Her vision was blurring and growing dim. She tried to reach for her trident, thinking that maybe the power from it would be enough to get her through this. But she was already too weak to reach it. She felt her hand fall to the ground, inches from her trident. The cat tried to stay awake, but she could feel the concrete pull of her eyelids weighing her down, into the river of blackness.

And then, just as the black waters were about to close about her, Wavecrasher felt something push past her like an invisible whip. Her eyelids felt as though they were going to be ripped off, but at the same time, Wavecrasher could feel the concrete being pulled away. And more importantly, she could feel her chest and throat open up and air entering her body again.

The cat coughed and then breathed in deeply, letting the fresh, cool air back into her starving lungs. Slowly, she reached out and this time felt her hands close around the shaft of her trident. Wavecrasher felt the power flowing back into her body. She got back to her feet and turned to see what had been her savior.

Standing there was Windrider, his staff held high and his eyes glowing white. Above him, a mass of air swirled and twisted in a small, but powerful tornado funnel, its tail ending right inside the falcon's staff. As the air spun, Wavecrasher could see flashes of something glowing inside the winds.

"Somebody do something!" Windrider yelled. He tightened his grip on the staff, even as it began to shake under his hands. "I can't hold this thing forever!"

Wavecrasher looked around, praying that Thunderer or Forger was awake and on their feet. But the two Knights were only now groggily getting up.

"Wait!" Wavecrasher said. She pointed her trident right at the tornado. Looking at the falcon, she yelled, "Kid, get ready to drop it!"

"What are you gonna do?" Windrider yelled back.

"Just hold it until I say so!" the cat said, aiming her trident at the part of the tornado where the glowing flashes were coming from. The cat waited, forcing as much power as she could into the weapon and keeping her eyes focused on the glow.

"Hurry! I can feel it coming loose!" the falcon yelled. The staff shook back and forth, despite all Windrider's efforts to keep it still.

"Steady, kid … steady … *Now! Drop it!*"

With a sigh, Windrider collapsed the tornado, the staff falling to the ground as its master fell to his knees. The winds around the dump began to dissipate as the glowing section inside started to come together. As they coalesced, Wavecrasher released the power in her trident, and two streams of water shot from the left and right spikes, launching outward toward the glow, which continued to form into a solid mass. The streams came together around the glow, trapping it inside a sphere of water. The trident then held its fire as Wavecrasher held out her open palm toward the sphere and then clenched it. A huge cracking sound filled the air, and the sphere fell to the ground, the glow trapped within its icy hold.

Wavecrasher sheathed the trident and moved over to check on Windrider. She put her hand on the bird's shoulder, but Windy shrugged her off.

"I'm okay. Help the others," he said.

Wavecrasher nodded and headed over to where Forester lay, shaking his head hard as he rubbed his eyes.

"You all right, flower boy?" Wavecrasher asked.

"Ah ... will be," the squirrel said. He stopped his shaking and slowly opened his eyes. "What the hell ... was that?"

"It turned itself ... into a gas," Windrider said as Wavecrasher helped the squirrel up. "It was poisoning us. But I gathered up the air around me and trapped it inside the tornado."

"How'd you figure that out?" Forester asked.

"Had to be something in the air. I guess the rest just came naturally."

"Ya mean that didn't happen in a video game?"

Windrider's brow furrowed, and he said, "I don't think so."

"Well, that would be a hell of an obstacle, kid," Wavecrasher said, grinning at the falcon.

Windrider just shrugged, but smiled back.

"That was pretty good thinkin'," Forester said. "But Ah wanna know where the thing is now. Ah somehow doubt that was enough to kill it."

"Over there," Wavecrasher said. She pointed to the frozen sphere, the glowing bits still trapped inside.

"Cool," Windrider said, his eyes gleaming as he looked at the sphere.

"You had to say it, didn't you?" Groundquake said as he and the others slowly got to their feet and rejoined the group.

"So, what now?" Nerbino asked, coughing out the last of the poison. "Do we just keep it frozen? Is that all?"

"No," Forger said. "We need a new plan, and quickly."

"Why? It's stuck in there."

"No," the spider said, shaking her head. "We don't have the power to kill it or contain it indefinitely. We can only incapacitate it temporarily."

"What is she talking about?" Nerbino hissed.

"These things—the Chaos Demons—only light and dark can destroy them," Thunderer said sheepishly.

"What?!" the prince howled. "Then where are they? You didn't bring them with you!"

"You didn't notice until now?" Sandshifter asked.

"I thought that the rest of you were enough!" Nerbino snapped back. "I thought that only the Elementals had the power to destroy them."

"We did."

"So then, as I asked, what are we supposed to do?" Nerbino sneered.

"Stall," Wavecrasher replied.

"Stall?" the gremlin asked in disbelief. "That's your big plan? To stall?"

"We don't have much of a choice," the cat replied. "At the very least, we can keep it away from the door."

"Until what? Until your missing friends decide to show up? Of all the idiotic—"

"Uh, mates?" Firesprite said. "I think the prince is right. We'd better figure something out soon."

"See? She knows how foolish this is," Nerbino said.

"Yes, but," the lizard began as she pointed to the icy sphere. The others turned toward it, just in time to see a crack burst its way through.

"Aw, crap," Forester muttered.

"We knew it was coming out," Sandshifter said, drawing her staff. "So we deal with it."

"You guys listen to me; we keep it down here, keep it locked up, until Nightstalker and Joe get here," Wavecrasher said.

"And if we can't?" Nerbino asked.

"We will," Wavecrasher replied. "We have to succeed."

"Like the good Doc said in *Part II*, we must succeed," Windrider said, clutching his staff.

"Indeed. The consequences are too heavy for failure," the cat replied as more than a few eyebrows rose.

But then the sphere cracked once again, the glow emanating from it like a desert oil spurt in the midday sun. The Knights and the gremlin prince readied themselves as the sphere split in half and a new form began to emerge from the strange glow. It wasn't as big as the last form the demon had taken, but it was at least seven feet tall. Its body was covered in glowing scales, and it had long, powerful arms with large stumps at the end that sprouted five long claws on each one. Its feet were equally clawed, and as the group watched, two more arms, bigger and more powerful-looking sprouted from the creature's back. Slowly, a face emerged from the glowing body, a face with small, twisted eyes and a mouth full of broken teeth. It looked out at the group and let loose its low-high shriek, holding out its four clawed arms.

"Roar at this, bastard," Nerbino snarled, releasing a burst of demonfire. The green flame shot across the cave, right for the demon's face. The demon merely stretched one of its long arms across its face as the flames hit it and scattered harmlessly.

But that was its first mistake. As it held the arm there, the ground underneath its feet rumbled and then several green vines shot out and wrapped themselves around the arm, trapping it in place. The Chaos Demon snarled and tried to pull its arm free, but the vines held tight.

"Very basic, kid," Sandshifter said. "Bout time."

"Thanks. Now anybody wanna join in? Ah don't think one arm is all we can do here!" Forester said, gritting his teeth as he held his vines against the creature's pull.

"Well, far be it from me to let the bumpkin get all the credit," Groundquake said. He held up his arms, causing another rumble as two huge, stone hands rose from the earth and wrapped themselves around the demon's two left arms, holding them still as the creature slashed at them with its remaining arm.

"Nerbino, Firesprite, put the heat on that thing!" Wavecrasher yelled

Orange and green flame shot through the air, mixing together as it struck the demon, while staying far from the vines that held it down. It howled as the flames burned and scarred its glowing body.

Wavecrasher nodded and yelled out, "Windy! Forger! Your turn!"

Moving quickly, the Wind Knight stepped behind his metal sister as Forger held out all six of her hands. Windrider closed his eyes and began to gather air about him. Forger's palms split open, the flesh peeling back as spheres of metal began to sprout. The spider held on to them tightly; the winds behind her grew and grew, whirling about her in a massive windstorm. Finally the spider released the spheres, just as Windrider set the winds loose. The spheres were immediately caught up in the strong winds and, under Windrider's guidance, they shot forward like a cannonball from an overloaded cannon. The spheres slammed into the demon's flaming body. The sounds of bones cracking and splintering filled the air.

"Good work! Sandshifter, with me!" the cat yelled next. She put her hands together and unleashed a torrent of water at the demon. It struck with all the force of the spheres, nearly blowing the demon back into the wall. But the stone hands and the vines held firm, even as Sandshifter added her own power to the attack, covering the creature in a mass of wet, slimy mud.

"So what is this supposed to accomplish, tuna lover?" the wolf asked.

"Just keep going!" Crash yelled back. She suddenly cut her own stream, leaving the wolf alone in her attack.

But she stopped for only a second. The cat inhaled, brought her palms to her face, and then exhaled, her breath flying out in a blue mist that drifted toward the struggling form of the Chaos Demon. As the blue mist covered the creature, its movements slowed and a cracking sound filled the air. Sandshifter listened to the sound, nodded her approval, and stopped her stream of sand. As the grains fell around her, the wolf brought her hands together, pressing and mashing them together. The cracking sounds increased, the sands around the creature mixing together and meshing into a single coating of hard, compressed sand to go with the ice. The demon tried to move one last time and then finally came to a halt as it became trapped once again.

"Huh. Told you I had a plan," the cat said, taking a deep breath.

"Yeah. I guess you did," the wolf replied.

"Not to interrupt the love fest or nothing, but why are we not doing anything else?" Forester said. "Holding this thing didn't stop it before."

"That's why I left somebody out of the equation," Wavecrasher said, turning her gaze to Thunderer.

"Uh, well, you guys better back up then," the ram said. He stepped forward, placing both hands on his rod. Closing his eyes, Thunderer called on the power of the heavens. The answer came a second later; his rod glowed pure white, and the air around him crackled. Energy sizzled from the rod, twisting and swirling around him, even coursing through the ram himself, as the power gathered within.

The others watched in amazement; their fur and even scales stood on end. Thunderer's body began to glow and flicker, the flesh and cloth becoming invisible under the streams of white that covered the ram.

And then finally, the ram opened his eyes, even as they crackled and glistened with the power of thunder. Slowly, he raised up his rod, holding it up to the rock ceiling briefly, as if trying to get just a little more power from the unseen heavens, and then he brought the staff back down at the demon, wrapping both hands around it as he exhaled.

Krackadoooooooooooommmmmmmmm!!

The thunderclap was deafening, the sheer sound of it throwing the other Knights and Nerbino against the walls of the cavern. The piles of trash around them held a second and then followed the group onto the wall, covering them. But that was a blessing, as they were forced to close their eyes against the huge white flash that spread across the cavern—the huge burst of lighting that erupted from the rod and struck the demon with the force of a thousand thunderstorms. The ice held for a second, conducting the electricity before melting and then boiling away on the ground. The rocky sand melted into glass and then exploded, blowing all over the cavern. The demon didn't even have the time to scream as its body absorbed the tremendous energy of the thunderbolt. It followed the sand's example, exploding outward in a burst of glowing scales and mushy, almost-liquid white flesh. The lightning held the shape of its body for a second, and then it shot into the cavern wall, blackening and burning the rock face before it finally died, spent of all its energy.

And when the thunderbolt was gone, its master stood there a moment, his body smoking from the tremendous power it had held. Then he fell to the ground, breathing hard. Along the walls, the trash slowly began to fall. The Knights and Nerbino pushed their way free and back down to the floor.

"Goddamn!" Groundquake cursed, wiping trash from his face and his ruined uniform.

"He … couldn't he have warned us about that?" Firesprite asked. She pulled her hat off and used it to wipe the trash from her shirt.

"Should've asked … for half power," Wavecrasher hacked out. Something brown and rotten flew out of her mouth.

"Holy crap, Thunderer, that was amazing!" Windrider said with all the enthusiasm of a fan boy organizing the Shatner-Stewart death match for captain supremacy. He ran to the ram and clapped him on the shoulder. "I swear, that was like something from Dr. Manhattan!" he spouted. "Jesus, I didn't know you could do that. Did you even try something like that before? Oh man, was that the first time you did that? That's awesome! I got to see the first thunderclap from Thunderer. Yeah, that's what we should call it that. It'd be awesome to have a—"

"I'm … glad … you liked it. I'm … gonna try … to breathe again," Thunderer gasped.

"Oh. Right," the falcon said, trying to hold his friend up while the others approached.

"Good job, horn head," Forester said. He leaned down and placed his hand on the ram's shoulder. Green light began to spread over him, and Thunderer's breathing started to even out.

"That … that had to kill it, right?" Nerbino asked.

"I told you," Forger said. "Joe and Stalker are the only ones that could kill it. But I doubt it's gonna be able to come back from this soon."

"Even after that, it's not dead," Nerbino said.

"No, but we bought a hell of a lot of time with this," Sandshifter said. She glanced around the cavern walls, seeing the glowing scales and pasty flesh lining the walls.

"Which is hopefully all the time we need for them to get back," Wavecrasher muttered.

*   *   *

Joe stood in the bushes a moment and then turned back, while Nightstalker watched silently.

"What do you mean it's happened to you, too?" Joe asked.

"Getting mad, blacking out, and waking up with blood on my hands. Sound familiar?"

"That's impossible. I would've seen something, or the others—"

"They thought it was a part of my charming, dark personality. So did you. And I had no reason to let you think otherwise."

"Why?" Joe demanded.

"I didn't want to let you know about it until I had something to say. And besides, it was helping me."

"Helping you?"

"You know how hard it is to keep Sandy and Quake and Forester in line. Even with everything I was doing when I was conscious, I had to be harder, more frightening. And then all of a sudden, something happened that let me be just that."

"What happened?"

"It started to happen when we fought the High Chaos during training. But you brought me out of it, so I thought it was just battle rage or something."

"But something else changed your mind."

"Do you remember that priest we dealt with? The one who was killing those demons that fed on anger and keeping that little town from destroying itself during the workers' strike?"

"Yes. We held the demons in check while you went to take care of the priest. When we found you, he was ... oh, God, you don't even remember killing him?"

"He started ranting about how the monsters were destroying the town, how all those freakish beings not of God needed to die. He attacked me, pulled my mask off. When he saw my face, he screamed and grabbed a bottle of holy water. He smashed it over my head, all the while ranting about killing the agent of Satan. He was calling me a monster, a flying devil rat. And I kept thinking that this was a man of God, someone who was supposed to have a spiritual understanding. But instead he was just another panicked, angry, cowardly man. After that—"

"What?"

"After that, all I remember is you asking me what had happened, while I stood over his bloody body."

"You told us he attacked you with magic! Dear God, what you did to him ..."

"We found the rest of him."

"All over the room! Why didn't you tell us? I mean, didn't you feel any remorse about it?"

"For him? No," the bat said. "But the trio listened to me after that. And it hasn't happened since."

"How?"

"I think I know why this happens to us," the bat explained. "You've seen something similar with the others? The way their eyes glow when they're using their powers at full strength?"

"Yes. Their eyes were like flashlights. But it didn't last with them. And they never went psycho."

"But we're different from them. They draw their powers from elements. But you and I, we're powered by the heart, not the Richter scale or photosynthesis. And I think … I think things like this are the backlash. When you and I feel too much, we lose control."

"And you never shared this with anyone? Not with Crash or Forger or Windy? Not with me?"

"It wasn't anything more than a theory," Stalker said. "I didn't want to tell you something unless I was sure it was true."

"And, so what? You just waited until I spazzed out, so you could confirm everything?!"

"No! Even the Architects wouldn't tell me anything—just something about us finding the light and dark for ourselves. What did you want me to do, come to you with that?"

"You could've come to me with something! Don't you think this might've helped me?"

"Joe, how many times has this happened to you? There was that one time during training, and—"

"And I thought that was all it was, but now…. Now I know it was just a precursor to this."

"Joe, listen to me. I might have something of a handle on this, but I worry about losing control as much as you do. Why do you think I stopped you from killing that Hyliea? If we work together, we can get control. This can be a boon to us, a last resort."

"No, Stalker. I can't be afraid of doing this every time I go out there."

"And you shouldn't. This is a horrible thing for anyone to deal with. But you took down the Hyleia because of it. You injured the High Chaos because of it. And I kept the others in line, which helped us do our job. Can you honestly tell me that nothing good can come out of this?"

Joe bit his lip and then said, "No. But that doesn't make it right. Stalker, if this was supposed to happen to us, why didn't the Architects tell us? Why weren't we warned that this could happen?"

"I … Maybe—" the bat stammered, crumpling his hat as he tried to think.

"This just proves it. I need to get the hell away from these powers, and everything that goes with them."

XXII.

"ARE YOU SURE WE couldn't kill it on our own?" Windrider asked as he looked over some of the white flesh-mush scattered about the floor. "I haven't seen it move in like five minutes."

"We're plenty sure," Forger said. She watched another section of the floor, while she picked garbage off her clothes with one of her arms.

In the time since Thunderer had blown the demon to high heaven, the pieces of flesh had stayed put on the ground, not even jiggling. Even so, Wavecrasher refused to believe that they had won so easily.

Forger felt the same; all the books she'd read and even the Architects had said it would take light and dark, and light and dark alone to destroy them. Without that formula, even this would just be a temporary respite. Yet looking at the motionless pieces of flesh on the ground, even the spider was feeling some doubts.

"Maybe the kid is right though, Crash," Forger said, glancing at the cat. "I mean, maybe that much power—maybe it could actually…"

"We both know what we needed to take these things down," Wavecrasher said curtly. "And until Joe and Stalker get here and this thing is completely wiped from the earth, we keep watch."

"I know we have to be sure, Crash. I'm just making an observation."

"And I'm making sure we don't make a mistake."

"No surprise there," the spider muttered as Crash walked away. "Never looks at any new data either."

"Man, what's takin' the bat so long?" Forester muttered. He glanced around, his eyes darting across the floor too speedily to afford him any real opportunity for surveillance. "Ah woulda dragged him back here by now."

"What's the point of bringing him back if he don't wanna help?" Groundquake snapped.

"Ah still can't believe he went as far as you say," the squirrel said to the cat.

"Less talk on that, more on the job, huh?" the cat answered.

Forester grumbled but went back to his task. He turned his eyes back to the goop, even as he gripped his ax in his sweaty palms. He could still see the demon in his mind, rising up to destroy them, its strange, scaly skin all around as its body shifted and changed. The second he had seen it, Forester had remembered everything that the group had gone through during training. He remembered the horrible injuries he'd seen on the others, the ones that could've happened to him and the feeling of panic that had almost overtaken him.

He'd thought that all his time spent keeping the balance would cure him of his fear. But this wasn't a demon that could just hurt him; this was something that could truly end his immortal life. He'd stood there in horror, barely able to even think as Wavecrasher, Forger, and Quake had set the creature up. Their efforts had made it possible for him to stay unnoticed until the demon was gone, and then he'd thrown out a quip to make his absence even less obvious.

But that didn't make the fear go away. It had stayed with him even as he wrapped the vines around the creature, staying simple because he'd been too panicked to think of something better. Forester swallowed and tightened his sweaty grip as he kept watching the pile of goo, praying with all his heart that the thing was actually dead.

Gloomph.

The ax nearly jumped out of his sweat-filled palms, but he managed to hold on as he frantically looked around for the source of the sound.

Gloomph.

There it was again. Forester glanced around, looking to see which pile of goop it had come from. But all of them remained still and unmoving, looking as alive as a pig that accidentally wandered into a wood chipper. Forester started to wonder if maybe this was some kind of trick from the others or something else in the caverns.

Gloomph.

For the third time, he heard it. And this time, the squirrel knew where it was coming from. Slowly, he turned to his left, toward a large pile of the goop. He saw the way it was quivering, shaking like a Jell-O mold held by an epileptic. The squirrel's eyes went wide, and his mouth opened, but nothing came out but a squeak that would've embarrassed a mouse. The goop continued to quiver, and then, it actually collapsed in the middle, sinking down like a soufflé that came out wrong. A sucking sound began to emanate from underneath it as the goop continued to collapse into itself. Forester knew just what this meant, but all that came out of him was another squeak.

*   *   *

"Joe, you can't mean that," Stalker said as Joe turned to walk to the house.

"Why not?" Joe asked, his back to the bat. "The way I see it, you've lied to me, the Architects withheld information from me, and I became a killing machine against my will. Exactly why should I stay?"

"I know you're mad at me," Stalker answered. "But I'm asking because the rest of us need you; the world needs you."

But all the bat got back was silence. He sighed then as he pulled off his hat in frustration. Tentatively, he said, "Joe ... they ... look, if you won't ... At least think of what you're going to do to your family for God's sake!"

Joe didn't reply, but he didn't move either.

Stalker saw his chance and kept going. "Do you think you can just walk in there and they won't think you're some kind of ghost? And even if they don't, what are you going to do? Do you want to uproot them from everything they've known? It'll happen more than once. The Architects will look for you too. You'll always be on the run, always having to hide. And I know you, Joe. You don't want that for them, do you?

"You know that if you do this, no matter what they say now, no matter how much they love you, they will hate you for doing this to them. Your son will hate you for ruining his childhood. Your wife will hate you for ruining her life. And even if they don't say it, you'll know. You didn't come back before because you didn't want to bury them while you stayed the same. Do you want that to happen knowing you ruined their lives, too?"

But Joe stayed quiet.

Stalker snorted and shook his head, racking his brain for anything else.

Just as he was about to run out of ideas, he heard a trembling sigh from Joe. He looked up and saw his friend turn to him, his eyes shiny and wet. He whispered, "I ... I'm just so scared. And I miss them so much."

"I know," Stalker said gently. "But we will learn to control this. And we will use it to make this world better for them and everyone else. It's what we were chosen to do."

"Yeah," Joe said. "But is that all that's left for me? Powers and demons and everything that goes along with it. While everyone I knew withers and dies."

"Joe," Stalker began, "your family, your life, all the things you had … they're gone now. And I know you can't get them back. But that makes you … so lucky."

*   *   *

The goop began to disappear faster, pushing itself down into the earth. Forester watched with a growing horror, but all he could do was stand there, his mind racing. *It's going to come back. It's gonna be even bigger and it's going to kill us and we won't be able to do anything about it. And Ah'm just gonna …*

"Hey, fluffy tail, what the hell are you doing?" a rough voice said, breaking his train of thought. Sandshifter's voice got closer as she stomped over and said, "Look, we need to pay attention here, not … not …"

The voice stopped, and Forester knew what the wolf was seeing. It was confirmed a second later when Sandshifter screamed out *"Groundquake! Seal the ground! Close all the cracks!"*

"What the hell?"

"Do it now, goddamn it!"

The dog didn't ask questions then; he knelt and dug his hands into the ground, his hands sinking into the ground like it was water. The ground shook briefly, with a sound like a huge knuckle cracking. It stopped a second later, and the ooze halted. But as Sandshifter and Forester watched, the goo began to glow and then the sinking resumed. Within seconds, it vanished.

"What the hell is going on?!" Wavecrasher yelled. "Nothing moved."

"It did here!" the wolf yelled. "The shit just sunk through the floor!"

"But why would just one piece—"

Suddenly, there was a sound like several extremely wet farts being let loose. The group whirled around to see the piles of ooze smoking and then evaporating away in clouds of green smoke. Within a few seconds, all the piles were gone, without even a touch of residue left behind.

"What the—It hornswoggled us!" Firesprite said.

"You mean that thing was that one piece of goo?" Thunderer asked.

"It must've been. But how the hell did it get down there?" Windrider added.

"Maybe if someone had thought to seal the ground up before," Nerbino snarled.

"It doesn't matter," Wavecrasher said. "We need to beat it down there before it gets to the door."

"Then hang on," Quake said. He drew up his foot and slammed it down. The ground around them cracked, and then the group found themselves sliding back down through the earth, toward the door once again.

Sandshifter stood silent as Wavecrasher started to talk about what they should do once they got down there.

Once everyone else was paying attention, the wolf turned and moved to Forester. She reached out and spun the squirrel around and then grabbed his collar and drew him in close, so the green one could smell the spittle on the wolf's teeth.

"¿Qué en el nombre de Dios estaba pensando?" the wolf sneered, her voice too quiet for the others to hear but filled with enough venom to kill an elephant.

"Ah don't understan—"

"Not one word. You couldn't even say one little word to let us know about that thing?"

"Ah—"

"Answer me!"

"Ah … Ah … was scared … I didn't know what to—"

"Why did I even waste my time with you?" the wolf snapped. "You tell everyone that you can do such a great job at this, that you're better then all of us."

"So … So did you," Forester managed to say.

"I can also tell people that some goo is seeping through the ground, instead of standing there mute with panic."

"Ah know Ah screwed up."

"Oh, do you? Listen to me and listen good for once. If we screw this up, the world as we know it comes to an end. So either you reach up and pull 'em down, or when we get down there, you take root in the ground and turn into a frickin' tree."

"Sandy! We're almost there! You and the flower boy ready?"

The wolf gave Forester one final angry look and then turned and said, "As ready as we're gonna be."

*　　*　　*

"You actually think that I'm lucky?" Joe asked, shaking his head as if he could deny what he'd just heard. "Stalker, what do I have to be lucky about?"

"Turn around," the bat replied.

Joe's face kept its puzzled look, but he still turned, looking toward the window where Jeri and Cody stood. Joe could feel his heart ache at the very sight of them, the pain spreading through his body like stomach acid pumped into his veins. "What am I supposed to be seeing?"

"You know what," the bat replied.

"My family."

"Yes, Joe," Stalker replied. "That's why you're the lucky one, out of all of us."

Joe took that in silence, and then he let out a short, brittle laugh. "And I thought I was just going to have to worry about your killing sprees. Now, you spring mental illness on me. Tell me, did a giant talking rabbit tell you about this wild streak of luck I'm having?"

"Do you know what I see, Joe?"

"What?"

"Nothing. All I get to see is a sword and a long trail of blood that leads into the dark. And the others, they might not admit it, but that's what they see too. It's all any of us see. I've accepted that. But you don't have to."

"Oh, my God. That's what you're trying on me?" Joe said, with another brittle laugh. "The 'you have memories' ploy? Of all the—"

"It's not a ploy, Joe. It's the truth."

"Sure. Whatever you—"

"Fine, maybe it is a ploy," the bat sneered, his calmness finally fading. "But that doesn't make it any less true. Goddamn it, Joe, you have no idea how hard it is for me to even stand here and listen to you right now. You tell me that all you can do is watch them and wait for them to die so you can put a rose on their grave."

"That's true," Joe said back.

"Yeah, it is. But tell me, Joe, just tell me, how much do you think I miss my family? How much do you think the others miss their families?"

"Well ..."

"Yeah, I don't know, either Joe. And neither do they," Stalker said. "I don't know where my family is. I don't even know who my family is. I don't know my friends, my parents, my wife, my kids. Hell, I don't even know if any of those people are alive. I don't know where they would be or where they would be buried. I can't even put the damn rose on their graves. Neither can Wavecrasher. Neither can any one of us!

"I don't have a life to miss, so I don't worry and focus on the life I have now. But not you. You can look at your old life when you want to, because you have something to remember. And you stand there and tell me—me, who has nothing to remember beyond the last six months—how hard it is to look back."

Joe stood there, his face hard and stiff as the bat finished his words and looked back at him, returning his hard gaze. Joe looked into his friend's face, ready to cover it with acidic words, but no matter how hard he tried, he couldn't open his mouth. His anger did not fade, but he clenched his teeth and all but growled at the bat.

"Tell me I'm wrong, Joe," Stalker said, his voice tight and hard. "Tell me that being the only one in a group of amnesiacs to have memories isn't lucky. Tell me that."

Joe heard the words, and he took a deep breath, keeping his glare on the bat. But the longer he did, the more the glare began to weaken. Stalker kept his own gaze firm and hard as three-month-old pudding, while Joe's eyes drifted to the ground.

Finally, he sighed and spat out a response. "Fine, I can't tell you that. Are you happy now?"

"Why would I be?" Stalker said.

"But me being unhappy doesn't stop you, does it?"

"No. Do you understand why I had to do that?"

Joe ran his hand over his face but spat out, "Yes, I understand. You were right; I am lucky that way. But just because I'm 'luckier' then you guys—"

"I know," Stalker said. "I know that doesn't make things easier for you. But it does give you something."

"What?"

"You get to have clearer vision than any of us. We can talk about keeping the balance and saving people, because that's what makes things clear for us. We get a huge picture of everything we're supposed to do, and none of it has any real meaning beyond 'keeping the balance.' But you get to focus on one part of the picture, a part that means something to you. You get to picture that when you go through horrible, disgusting, and trying times. And you get to say to yourself, 'What I do, I do for them.'"

Joe turned from the bat then, his body shaking, though from anger or some other emotion, the bat couldn't tell.

"You get to fight for your family, to make the world a better place for them. You get to picture them when you do that. We get nothing, except the knowledge that it will make the world safe."

"But there's one thing you're forgetting."

"What's that?"

"What am I going to do when they're gone?"

The bat paused a moment and then gave his reply.

"You'll keep going. To be worthy of their memory."

Joe took this in silence as the words sank into his brain. He thought a few moments more and spoke. "I can't go back, can I?" he said.

"I think you knew that," Stalker said.

"Yeah," Joe said as he looked at the window again. "They've accepted that I'm gone. That's what I always worried about. If I came back, all that would change. I couldn't ever bring things back to the way they were."

Stalker stood in silence as Joe took what might be his last look at his family. Finally, he turned and said, "So I'm going to do my part to keep things this way for them."

"That's what I needed you to say, Joe," Stalker said.

"I'm going to need your help."

"And I'll give it. We'll get control of this … this fury."

"Yes we will. But that's not what I need you for now."

"What do you mean?"

"Before I go to deal with the Chaos Demon, there is one thing you are going to do for me. And I'm not leaving here until you do it."

The rocky ceiling glowed briefly as the goo that had once been the Chaos Demon pushed its way through. Slowly, it floated down to the ground, unhinged by gravity or any other earthly constraint. It stretched and twisted in air, expanding as if it was being given power by some unseen force. Long, spiny arms sprouted out as the goo itself seemed to dry and harden, forming into a body as it reached the ground.

Six crystalline legs touched the ground and drove the creature up. The rest of its body began to inflate and harden, forming a huge shape like a crystal spider with a pair of arms sticking out of its back. But even then, the goo began to push upward, and a new shape began to form out of the spider's back. The shape stretched upward, taking the arms with it as it inflated and changed. A chest soon began to take shape, along with a head that pushed out from it—a pointed head with several eyes and a hole in its center that seemed to be a mouth. Large tubes emerged from its back. Finally, the creature's transformation stopped, and it stood there in its new form—a huge, crystal spider-centaur, its scaly skin glowing all the while.

The Chaos Demon skittered toward the door, its legs clicking along on the stony ground. Its huge mouth pulsed in and out with each step as it came closer and closer to its goal. Its arms began to change color, the white fading away to be replaced by dark red—the color of gremlin blood. The demon channeled all of the stolen lifeblood of Nerbino and his father into its arms as it came to the door and saw the symbols that held it closed. It placed its huge hands on top of them and closed its eyes. The blood in its arms began to drain out. It began to fill in the symbols, moving through them like water through pipes. The blood swirled through the door, filling more and more of the symbols as a creaking sound began to emanate from the door.

The Chaos Demon's mouth twisted into a horrid, toothy grin; the end of its plan came closer and closer. Within seconds, this door would be open, and the plague inside would wipe over the world above.

But that grin, that plan, faded away as the ceiling began to rumble. The demon didn't stop pumping the blood into the door, but it turned its head just in time to see Groundquake's platform pop out from the bedrock and hit the ground. The demon snarled but turned back to the door and gave no other response. It didn't need to, not when its goal was so close.

"*No!*" Nerbino howled. He hurled his demonfire at the creature. But the green flames just bounced off the demon, which didn't notice the impact.

"You can't kill it, remember?" Forger said. She pushed the gremlin aside and stepped to the front, her arms all unfurled and pointed at the demon. Forger clenched her fingers and six long chains shot toward the demon, each one armed with spiked tips. The demon, completely absorbed by its work, didn't even hear the chains whistling through the air until the spikes had driven into its body. At that point, the demon let out a scream of pain and pulled its arms away from the door, trying to grab the spikes. But Forger gave the chains a mental command, and the spikes popped out into three long hooks that dug into the creature's "flesh", locking in tight as the monster screamed.

"C'mon, you ugly doppelganger," Forger growled, yanking the chains and pulling the demon back. Its legs skittered and dug at the ground, but Forger still managed to pull it back, inch by inch. The demon growled and snapped at the air, digging its legs into the ground and reaching for the door. Forger pulled hard, but the demon had just as much strength as she did. Sweat rolled down her face as she strained and cursed. But slowly, the creature made its way back to the door, inch by inch.

Then, it stopped dead in its tracks. It whirled around to see Wavecrasher, Sandshifter, Groundquake, and Nerbino pulling at the chains along with Forger as the other Knights drew their weapons and prepared to attack.

The demon turned its head back as the tubes on its back began to vibrate.

"Um, should it be doing that?" Windrider asked.

"It's a Chaos Demon spider-centaur. Ah was kinda hoping you'd know what the hell it does," Forester replied.

"No, this is new for me. God, I wish this had been a game. Woulda been awesome," the falcon muttered.

"You and me—*Holy shit, duck and cover!*" Forester yelled as the tubes stopped vibrating and large, white, cottony goo balls flew through the air toward the Knights. The squirrel immediately moved out of the way, and the others did the same. But some didn't move fast enough.

With a yelp, Thunderer and Windrider found themselves wrapped up in the goo. Before the remaining Knights could react, the remaining goo balls suddenly splattered onto Nerbino and Wavecrasher, knocking them from the chains and pinning them to the wall.

"Bloody hell!" Firesprite cried out. "Are you guys all right?"

But the only response was sounds of struggle and shouting.

"What the hell is that stuff?" Forester yelled.

He looked at Thunderer, who was writhing in the silky goo if he was being dipped into boiling oil.

"Don't waste time with questions!" Sandshifter yelled. She grabbed three chains in one grip and held them all together, pulling against the demon. "Firesprite, Forester, get over here and help me! Patty Parker and I can't hold this thing by ourselves!"

"But the others—"

"There's no point in freeing them if that thing gets to the door!"

Firesprite paused a moment and then ran over to the chains, grabbed as many as she could, and pulled back with Sandshifter. The lizard then turned to see Forester coming toward them, with hesitant, nervous steps as he glared at the demon.

"What are ya doing? *Move!*" Firesprite yelled.

"What ... the hell?" Forger managed to get out as she and Sandshifter looked toward the squirrel.

"*Dios te damn it mierda sin valor!*" Sandshifter spat. "*Get your furry ass over here now, or so help me I'll—*"

"Ah'm ... Ah'm comin'."

"*Shut the hell up and get over—*"

But that was as far as the wolf got as the tubes vibrated and then the gooey web shot out once again. Forger and Firesprite let out a yell, but it didn't matter as the webbing shot into them and knocked them to the ground, along with Sandshifter. Forger hit with a sickening thud, her head striking a heavy rock. She let out a groan and then the chains snapped from her hands, going slack as they left the spider's body. The demon stumbled forward, surprised by the lack of strain. As it fell to its knees, Forester stood there, too surprised and frightened to move.

"*Las cadenas! Get ... the chains!*" Sandshifter yelled from her webby prison.

"C'mon ... Forester! Before it ... gets up!" Forger yelled through the pain.

The squirrel gave a short, quick nod and started to move toward the chains. But then the demon stirred. Forester's eyes went right to the creature, and he froze in his steps; the creature got back to its feet, each leg clicking on the ground. The squirrel could only watch as it stretched its arms forward and began to move toward the door once again.

"Forester! Get the chains, for the love of God!"

"Goddamn it, you stupid little—Do something!"

But those words did nothing for the squirrel. Forester just stood there as the demon crawled ever closer to the doors, ever closer to the end of the world. He tried to think of something, anything he could do to stop this thing. But nothing came into his mind. He'd always been so sure that his way was the right one and that he wouldn't need anyone's help in proving it. But as he watched the creature advance on the doors, Forester knew that this would be his legacy. The wolf had been right; he was nothing more than a waste of ...

Yes. Yes, that's exactly what he was. And with that, Forester knew exactly what he had to do. The squirrel sheathed his ax and pointed his hands right at the Chaos Demon's back. The skin on his palms began to squirm and then the "mouths" opened up once again. Forester took a breath, gathered his power about him, and then sent it out from his open palms. But he didn't send vines or flytraps this time.

"Is he ... is he shooting seeds at it?" Forger asked in disbelief as thousands of small, dark particles flew from the squirrel's palms toward the demon.

"What?" Sandshifter snapped. "What the hell is he—Huh?"

The wolf halted her words as she realized that Forester was directing the seeds directly into the tubes that sprouted from the Chaos Demon's back. All those thousands of seeds shot directly into the demon, who had halted in its tracks and begun to roar anew. But they were not roars of pain—more like roars of annoyance. The attack was nothing more than a distraction but enough to get the thing to turn from the door and turn its angry gaze on Forester.

"Run, Forester!" Forger yelled as the demon began to skitter toward the squirrel. *"You can't beat it on your own!"*

But even as sweat dropped from the squirrel's face, he didn't move from his spot. Instead, he slowly rubbed his fingers together as the demon came closer. The creature kept advancing, but just as it was about to take the final step toward Forester, the squirrel stopped rubbing his fingers and pointed them straight down toward the ground. As soon as he did, the demon stopped moving, its legs still and lifeless. It pulled and prodded at its lifeless legs as it tried to take another step, but it just stood there, paralyzed as Forester and the others watched.

"What … what did he do?" Sandshifter asked.

"The seeds—dear God, of course," Forger said.

"What?"

"That's why he fed it the seeds. So he could make it take root!"

"Huh?" the wolf asked as she took another look at the monster. She saw it struggle to pull up its legs, and one leg managed to come up a bit. And that was when she saw the long roots that had dug their way into the ground.

"He finally got it," Sandshifter whispered. She turned her gaze toward the squirrel, who stood there watching the creature with the amazement of a man finally marrying his high school sweetheart.

"Nice job, kid," the wolf said.

"Thanks for the idea," Forester said, turning back around.

"If ya got us out of here, we could give some even better ones."

"Oh … right," Forester said. He grabbed his ax and ran over to where the wolf and spider lay. The blade glowing green, Forester slowly lowered it onto the bottom of the poison webbing covering the wolf and then, with the speed of a man ripping off a Band-Aid, sliced through, letting it fall from the wolf's body.

"Couldn't have cut it a little closer?" Sandshifter asked, slowly getting to her feet.

"Must you always find something to criticize?" the squirrel asked as he turned his attention to Forger.

"How are you ever going to get better if I don't?" Sandshifter replied.

Forger emerged from the webbing.

"Right. Ah … aw, crap."

"What?" Forger asked.

"Ah just felt one of the roots snap."

"Oh, shit," Sandshifter said. She turned her gaze back to the demon.

The creature was pulling even harder at the ground, with one leg already freed. As it pulled and heaved at the ground, the roots heaved and stretched.

Forester stepped forward and placed his already-glowing hands on the ground, as if he was trying to strengthen the roots. But whatever he was doing wasn't enough. Three more cracks echoed through the air as the demon broke free from its earthbound chains and glared at the squirrel with hate in its eyes.

"Forester, go free the others. We'll hold it off," Forger ordered.

She and Sandshifter stepped forward, drawing their weapons. But Forester didn't move back; instead he came forward, walking past both of the other Knights.

"What are you doing?" Sandshifter asked as the creature began to advance.

"Ah ain't done yet," the squirrel replied.

"What do you mean?"

"How many seeds did Ah feed into that thing?" Forester asked.

"What the hell does that have to do with—"

"Watch and learn."

Forester brought his arms out, held them together, and then pulled them apart. The second he held them out, the creature stopped and began to scream in pain. For a second, Sandshifter and Forger stared at it in confusion, not seeing anything different about the demon. But then, Forester's second attack was revealed as the branches erupted out of its sides, poking through the strange flesh as if it was nothing more than air. More branches sprouted from the monster's body, and pieces of flesh began to rain down on the ground. Vines emerged from the tubes in its back, long ones with green spikes at the end. They writhed around and swiftly began to stab the demon; it screamed with each cut. And every time a cut was made, more vines and branches would slither out. Its head reared back in agony, and then it grabbed at its eyes. As the Knights watched, a popping sound filled the air. Small white orbs littered the ground as the demon pulled its hands back to reveal flowers blooming where its eyes had been.

"*Sainte* ... holy," Forger said as she looked on in disbelief at the sight.

"I am never calling you flower boy again," Sandshifter said.

But before Forester could finish, a horrid screech filled the air. The scales on the demon's body glowed brighter and brighter, with all the intensity of a thousand decked-out Christmas trees on the receiving end of a lightning storm.

"Oh, what now?!" Sandshifter yelled, throwing her coat over her eyes.

"Spider, any ideas?" Forester yelled back.

"Bright lights and screaming like this usually lead to an explosion!" Forger screamed.

"We have to get behind something! Forester, free Groundquake! Forger, chain the others and drag them all together!" Sandshifter yelled.

Without a word, the two Knights ran off to follow their orders, while Sandshifter shut her eyes as tightly as she could. She held out her hands, and sand began to flow from her sleeves. It whirled around her as the light and screams grew brighter and louder.

Forester leaped across the stone floor as, behind him, Forger's hooked chains flew through the air, locking onto a different web-covered Knight. The squirrel paid them no mind though as he came to the webby mass that held Groundquake. Forester pulled out his ax and cut through the webbing that held his friend. The dog groaned as the webbing fell from his body, barely moving on the ground.

"C'mon, ya damn Yankee! We need your help!" Forester yelled. He grabbed the dog and heaved him onto his shoulder.

"Hate … Yankees," Groundquake moaned.

"You're not that out of it," Forester muttered as he tried to make his way back to Sandshifter, with only the sounds of shifting sands and the clank of Forger's chains to guide him.

"Come on, people! Move your asses!" Sandshifter yelled. She continued to collect the sands around her.

"*vous tenter … ce faisant glisser de nombreux corps,*" Forger panted as she pulled the bodies near them.

"English! Where's the squirrel?!"

"Ah'm coming! He's goddamn heavy," Forester yelled, stumbling into the grouping. Dumping the dog onto the ground, he yelled, "Ah don't know how much help he's gonna be."

"He'll be help enough!" the wolf replied as she dropped her hands, though the sands continued to swirl around them. Putting her hands onto the dog's hammer, the wolf forced her power into the weapon. The orange light swiftly filled the air. Quake's ragged breathing started to steady as the hammer began to glow with its own brown light. The second it did, Sandshifter pulled away her hands; the dog's eyes popped open, and he sat straight up.

"Huh—*Jesus Christ, what the hell is that?*" he yelled as the light from the demon shot into his eyes.

"Never mind!" Sandshifter yelled. "The demon's gonna explode. We need protection."

"Right," the dog said. He dug his hands into the ground, and the earth suddenly rose up around them, like a hand closing its fingers. Within a few seconds, it had become a hard shell, encasing them inside its protective cover. As it shut around them, the sands that whirled in the air began to coat the earth-shield, like frosting covering a cake. And as it covered the earth-shield, it began to gather and harden itself, until it was completely coated, doubling the shield's strength. The creature's roar filled the room.

"Dear sweet God, why won't it die?" Forester asked as he shifted inside the dark inside of the shield.

"Just pray to *Dios* we survive when it does," Sandshifter said. The screams echoed even through the rock shield.

"But it won't," Forger said. "Nothing we can do should be able to—"

"Do you hear it screaming out there?" Groundquake snapped.

"Maybe Forester's seeds did more damage than we thought," Sandshifter said.

"Huh. Who'da thought flower boy would actually get the job done for once?"

Sandshifter would've said something else, but the screaming outside suddenly rose at least five octaves in the space of two seconds. The ground around them shuddered, like a giant hand was shaking it. Slivers of light poked through the shield, and the layers of earth and sand began to crack all around them. The Knights stopped their arguing and covered themselves and their comrades as the world outside their shelter seemed to end.

And then, just as soon as it had started, the shaking ended. The Knights looked around their small shelter, caught between being glad that the explosion had ended and wondering if it was safe for them to leave just yet.

"Do you think it's dead?" Quake asked.

"You remember what happened the last time we blew it up?" Forger asked. "But I'm sure we bought ourselves some time."

"Yeah. Or maybe it turned into something else, and it's just waiting for us to come out so it can gut us," Sandshifter said.

"We won't disappoint it then," Forester said, his ax glowing in the darkness. Led by its glow, the squirrel quickly sliced through the bondage that held the other Knights and Nerbino.

"Now Ah just need some help with the healing and—"

"Leave that to me," Forger said. She moved into the center of the structure. Turning toward the bodies of her friends, the spider reached out, guided by the light of the ax. Five of her six hands found a body and laid themselves upon the bodies' weapons and chests; the sixth held her mace. As the Knights watched, a gray light began to fill the small space, matching the green. Moans and mutterings sounded in the air as the Knights and Nerbino began to regain consciousness.

"Can't be said that having an arachnid around never came in handy," Forester said as Forger continued to pour on the light. After a few more seconds, she finally pulled her hands away, and they all began to pull themselves up.

"What happened?" Firesprite muttered. "Is it dead?"

"If it's not, I think we are," Nerbino said. "Where the hell are we?"

"A big, sandy pile of earth," Quake said. "And it's a good thing too. Otherwise you'd be a buncha little bones on the ground."

"The demon pulled something big, didn't it?" Wavecrasher asked. "What's our status?"

"Not too bad," Forger said. "Forester can tell you about it. He's the one responsible for us being here."

"He—Oh God, what did you do now?"

"Ah got big and ugly to explode, thank you very much," the squirrel snapped.

"He fed a bunch of seeds into it, and then he made it take root," Sandshifter said. "Then he did some ... exfoliation."

"Huh?" Windrider asked.

"Think Poison Ivy killing somebody by getting them to eat a salad," the wolf said.

"Oh. *Oh!*" the falcon exclaimed. "Oh God, that's awesome! Was it all creepy and nasty to watch?"

Sandshifter cleared her throat and said, "Yeah, that's one way to describe it."

"And I had to be unconscious. Goddamn it!"

"Okay, but why are we in this thing?" Wavecrasher asked.

"Something he did made that thing go nuclear," Sandshifter explained. "We got everybody together and woke up Cujo to make shelter."

"Forester decided to wake everybody up before we went outside to check on it," Forger said.

"Good move," Thunderer said. "Let's crack this thing and see what the hell it is we have to deal with. After all that, I can't believe it's at full power."

"But we still don't know what might be out there," Wavecrasher said. "We should have a plan."

"Ah think we all know the plan by now," Forester said. "Stall the damn thing. And 'sides, we ain't gonna know what to do until we get out."

"I agree. Pop this thing," Nerbino snapped.

The dog glanced at the two of them and then nodded. He twirled his wrist, ending the motion by extending his index finger and pointing it downward. Immediately, the stone walls fell into the earth, leaving only the casing of sand around them, standing about them in a thick blanket. Sandshifter simply took a deep breath and gently let it out. The sand then went off in the winds, traveling about and then returning to the wolf's body. Within minutes, the sands had vanished, leaving the room open around them.

Slowly, the group looked around. When they had destroyed the demon before, there had been broken, gooey pieces all about them. But now, the cave was empty. All that stood there was a pile of roots and branches from Forester's seeds. The Knights saw no trace of the Chaos Demon anywhere.

"Do you think Ah actually killed it?" Forester asked.

"No," Wavecrasher said. "We fell for this before, remember?"

"She's right," Forger said. "Windrider, you'd better create an air pocket around us. If it's turned into gas again, it won't be able to poison us."

"Right. How do I do that?" Windrider asked. "Wait, I think I can figure it out."

"I hate it when he says that," Groundquake muttered as the falcon stuck his hands out and breathed in. The group felt a breeze pass by them and then each felt his or her ears pop. Then the air stopped moving once again.

"Okay, we're good," Windrider said, bringing his arms down. "The air pressure's holding around us. If it comes in, I'll feel it."

"Good. Everyone, get around the door," Wavecrasher said. "Above everything else, we have got to keep that thing shut."

"Tell us something we don't know," Quake muttered.

The group quickly leaned up against the massive doors, putting all their power in front of it.

"Let's hope this works," Firesprite said. "God knows how many other ways there are for it to attack."

"God knows nothing."

"Who said that?!" Nerbino snarled as he whirled about.

"I think we can guess," Forger said.

"It can talk?" Windrider asked in disbelief.

"Apparently," Forger replied. "I suppose something like this would be too delicate an operation to leave to a mindless animal."

"Great. It can think and it's invisible," Quake muttered. "Wait. Forester, can you get some pollen and—"

"And where do you want me to throw it?" the squirrel asked.

"Everybody, stay alert," Wavecrasher said.

The Knights gripped their weapons tightly as the gremlin prince called out to their mystery voice. "I am the king of the Gremlins! In the name of my father, I demand you show yourself!"

"Your father is dead. His fat neck snapped easily. His disease-ridden blood was rich and thick."

Nerbino snarled, the demonfire already burning in his hands. But before he could unleash it, he found Firesprite's hand on his shoulder.

"Hold on," the lizard said. "This is what it wants. It wants you mad and trigger-happy, ready to make a mistake."

"Chaos Demon!" Wavecrasher yelled back. "We are the—"

"We know your names. Servants of the builders. Extensions of their power."

"Then you know what we are capable of," Wavecrasher responded. "We've destroyed you twice already. And we will continue to do so until you leave this place."

"Death has no power over us. Life has no power over us. We existed before both. And we shall exist long after both."

"Big words for an invisible man," Sandshifter said.

"Man is nothing. Man is a piddling of the Alpha, of the stupidity that caused existence."

"The Alpha?" Forger asked. "What the hell are you—"

A hacking laughter, wet and loose like flesh being ripped from the throat filled the chamber. The Knights grimaced at the sound, even as it faded away and the demon's voice returned.

"They didn't tell you. You sacrificed so much, and you don't even know the true power you serve."

"What do you know about it?" Forger asked.

"Perhaps everything. Perhaps nothing."

"Why should we believe you?" Wavecrasher asked.

"Because we desire peace. We desire the end of the struggle that you and your foolish masters have tried to keep upon the universe."

"No you want to create a whole new struggle!" Nerbino yelled. "As much as I despise the balance they strive for, I would take it over your madness any day."

"We do not desire madness. We desire freedom."

"Everyone is free!" Wavecrasher yelled. "Everyone has the choice of good or evil; they can be whatever they want."

"They have but two choices. And once they make their choice, you and others like you force them to stay with it. Everyone must be good or evil; no one can be both. Everyone must fall into a category because there must be a balance. We have seen man fall under the weight of the stupidity that the builders and the Alpha made. But for us, it means nothing. Left or right, good or evil—none of it matters in chaos. One can be good. One can be evil. One can even make the choice to be neither or both. We offer the freedom to be anything one desires, not to be confined to a single role. And you spit in our faces for it, even as you hunger for it."

"We don't hunger for anything you offer!" Wavecrasher said back. "You want to destroy everything we had because you didn't like it. You tried to force your way upon us and … uhh … heekk."

"Crash?" Sandshifter said as the cat stopped talking and began to grasp at her throat.

"He's doing the Darth Vader choke," Windrider cried out. "Dear God, the Force is real!"

"Forget the Force! Help her!" Thunderer yelled, running over to Wavecrasher, who had already fallen to her knees, her hands clutching at her throat. But as the ram came close to his friend, he suddenly stopped, grabbing at his own throat as gurgling noises began to emit from his mouth. As the Knights watched, Thunderer rose, still clutching his throat and then kicking his legs as he hung in the air. Suddenly, the ram flew backward, heading for the wall, but before he hit it, the ground cracked open and a large bush suddenly grew out of it. The ram landed right into it as the branches and leaves began to shift forward, lowering him to the ground, where Firesprite was there to meet him.

"You all right?" the lizard asked as she caught the ram and slowly brought him down.

"Awkk … what … was—"

"I think you've got your answer right there," Firesprite replied, looking over to where Wavecrasher was still kneeling.

The air around the cat began to shimmer. As everyone watched, crackling noises could be heard as the air solidified around the Water Knight. The first thing to form was the hand, knitting itself around the cat's neck like invisible sewing needles were weaving a scarf around her. The fingers were long and sinuous, ending in sharp, pointed tips. They had no skin; rather they seemed to be formed of a purplish crystal. And slowly, more and more of the demon became visible. A long, thin crystal arm weaved into existence, and a pair of birdlike, three-toed feet appeared by Wavecrasher's knees. They continued upward, stretching in long, thin legs, forming in tandem with similar arms, which were covered in purple crystal spikes. A thick, body, covered in the demon's scales formed as well. Muscle outlines were chiseled into it, with more spikes popping out of its back and a line of them running across its chest. And then, the last piece came into place; a squat head with a large, crown-like forehead that sloped back across its head appeared. A single green eye in the center of its head appeared, with a large hole below it. The eye moved over the group, one by one, as the hole contracted and expanded, like a mouth.

The voice echoed through it. "We will give the universe the freedom it desires," the demon whistled through its mouth hole.

"Not while we're here," Sandshifter snarled, gripping her staff as the others stood behind her.

"That can be corrected. In fact, one of you will be taken out of the equation rather soon," the demon said, tightening its grip on the cat's throat.

"Let her go, you twisted piece of crap!" Sandshifter yelled. She unleashed a huge sand ball at the demon.

It watched as the sand sped toward it and then waved its free hand across the air just before it struck him. The missile exploded harmlessly, raining sand all around the demon and Wavecrasher. Sandshifter's eyes widened in disbelief.

"Your power means nothing to us. Did you think you could hurt us when all the laws of this universe mean nothing to us?"

"Thought it was worth a try," Sandshifter growled. "But hey, there's still a few elements to go through."

"Damn right," Firesprite said, the tip of her spear bursting into flame as she glared at the monster. One by one, the others activated their own powers, creating mini-windstorms, writhing chains and vines, crackling thunder, floating rocks, and fires, both demon-enhanced and normal.

"There is no need for such power to be wasted," the demon sneered. "If you desire your watery friend, then by all means, have her."

With that, the demon picked up Wavecrasher and hurled her at the Knights. Firesprite doused her flame and moved to catch the cat, who landed on her with a heavy thud that knocked the lizard down.

"Wasn't ... expecting that," Firesprite grumbled as she pushed Wavecrasher off.

"It doesn't think it matters how many of us—*Gaahhkk*!" Quake began to say, screaming as the demon suddenly appeared behind him and brought its clawed hands down across his back. The dog fell to his knees in pain.

Windrider and Thunderer moved to attack, both raising their weapons high. But the demon caught them, and before anyone could react, it shot its white fire into the weapons, which erupted into flames that quickly spread to the two Knights. The falcon and the ram howled in pain. The demon reached across, grabbed them both, and then slammed them together, creating a huge burst of the white flame before their smoking bodies fell back to the ground.

The demon had no time to celebrate though as blasts of red-hot fire came streaking across the air at it and Firesprite pressed the attack. But the demon merely dodged the fires and, as it had with Sandshifter's ball, it spread out its hands in an arc and cancelled out the flames all around it.

But as it did so, Sandshifter suddenly leaped behind it, pulling her staff across its neck and holding it back. It struggled to escape.

"Now, Forger!" the wolf yelled.

Without a second's hesitation, Forger unfurled her arms and shot eight large, pointed metal spikes at the creature. But as they flew through the air, the demon suddenly dug one of its feet in and whirled around, putting Sandshifter right in the path of the missiles. Forger's eyes widened as she tried to call them back, but it was already too late. The spikes impaled themselves in Sandshifter's back with a meaty thud and a huge scream of pain. In her agony, the wolf released her grip, and the demon whirled about again and using the momentum, threw the wolf right at the arachnid, sending both crashing into the wall.

"And we thought you might still be a challenge," the demon sneered. It turned in the direction of the door.

Firesprite started to draw up her flames again, but the demon absently pointed its hand at her and released a stream of white energy. The lizard started to shape the flames into a shield, but the white slipped through the orange and hit the Knight dead on.

The demon let out its wet laugh once again and turned to walk to the door. But as it did, there was a flash of green, and then the creature let out a scream, turning to find Forester's ax buried in its back.

"That … hurt … but not … enough," the demon snarled, turning toward the squirrel.

"Then let's see if this does," Forester replied. He suddenly bent down to reveal Nerbino standing behind him. The gremlin let out a burst of demonfire that caught the demon right in the face. It screamed and then brought its hands to its burned face, staggering about as Nerbino and Forester began their next attack.

The prince continued his rain of green flames, each one exploding against the Chaos Demon. Forester swiftly brought up his hands and then unclenched his fists, shooting a wave of small, tipped missiles that impaled themselves into the monster's back.

"Thorns? That was the best you could come up with?" Nerbino snapped.

"Just wait," Forester said. Sure enough, the demon started to move about like it was disoriented, even drunk. Its arms flailed about bonelessly, as if the creature had forgotten how they worked. Its head lolled from side to side, and then with a groan of pain and confusion, the monster collapsed to the ground with a thud.

"What … what did you do to it?" Nerbino asked.

"Those thorn were covered with about fifty plant-based poisons," Forester said as he walked over to the monster.

As Nerbino moved to help Firesprite up, the squirrel put his hands around his ax's shaft and, with a grunt, pulled it out.

"Nice one, mate. Now stand back," Firesprite replied. She drew up her flaming spear. But before she could use it, Nerbino grabbed the shaft of the spear and pointed it away.

"This monster killed my father. By honor, it is my duty to kill it," the gremlin sneered.

"And as an Elemental, it's my job ta take care of it for the safety of the world," Firesprite replied. "How 'bout we both end this for him?"

Nerbino glanced at the fallen demon for a moment and then looked at Firesprite as she ignited her spear. Seeing that, Nerbino said "Fine." He pointed his blazing green fire at the monster, while Firesprite brought up her spear again. The two of them let loose, their flames swirling together as they flashed through the air and struck the demon. The monster went up faster than a cigarette in the mouth of a two-month deprived smoker, its body consumed by red and green flames.

Forester watched the monster burn. But as he looked at the monster, he immediately desired to be struck blind. The flaming mass twitched once and then sat straight up, burning all the while. Forester whirled around, words of warning on his lips, but he was already too late. Even as Firesprite and Nerbino saw the monster and began to bring up their weapons again, the demon raised its burning hands and released two blasts of white flame that streaked across the cave and hit the two of them right in the chest, knocking them back into the wall with a meaty thud.

Forester gulped and brought his ax back over his head. He ran toward the creature, thinking that maybe he could still end this nightmare. But the demon turned its head toward him, and as it did, the flames on its body suddenly changed to white and then vanished, revealing a completely unharmed Chaos Demon in its place. The demon's chest rippled, and two impossibly long arms twisted out of its white body and slithered toward Forester. Before the squirrel could react, one snuck behind his back and grabbed his collar, pulling him up and over even as the other one grabbed his ax and pulled it out of his hands. As he hung there helplessly, the arm began to twist itself around the squirrel like a living rope, trapping his body in a mass of white, squirmy flesh.

"You really thought you could do it," the demon said, getting to its feet. "You truly thought that flame and some rancid tree sap would be enough to stop us. There is only one power in the world that can stop us. But we knew what the builders had planned. They have considered it for eons—ever since the great wars that formed your world. And yet, they still selected a weak fool to hold the light—a fool that we knew could break with a few simple deaths."

"H-How?"

"We can watch the worlds from our prison. We saw the builders and their plans come to fruition. We studied you as you trained, through the eyes of the false demons. And in him, we saw our salvation. We knew it was only a matter of breaking him and then, using the ambitions of the foolish gremlin, to lure the rest of you down here so that we could crush you, one by one."

"The ... harem ... girl."

"We knew it would make you Knights suspect. But even then, we were releasing the Hyleia and taking away your great weapons. And without them, you have no chance of stopping us."

"You ... you ... haven't won ...yet."

"No, not yet. But after we destroy you and open this door, after we release the plague inside and the world has fallen into chaos and disrepair, when the Chaos Father is finally strong enough to emerge from his prison and return creation to the glory of the nothingness—then we will win.

"But you will only be around long enough to see it begin," the demon added as it turned around, toward the door. As its eyes fell upon the door, they went wide and then narrowed. It let out a roar of anger. The space where the door had been was still there. But the door itself was gone. All that stood there now was a smooth pike of rock wall, which still bore markings as if it had once held a door.

The demon snarled again; it marched toward the body of Groundquake, who was still on the floor, his body slowly healing the wounds from the creature's claws. It grabbed the dog's collar and pulled him up, holding him up face to face.

"What did you do? How did you hide the door?" the demon screamed at him.

"Wha—what're ... ya talkin' ... about?" Quake mumbled.

"Do you take us for fools?" the demon raged as it spun Quake around so that he could see where the door had been. "The earth is your power. We command you to bring the door back!"

"I don't ... know ... what ... you're talkin' ... about," the dog replied. "I'm ... barely ... alive ... after ... what you ... did."

The demon hurled the dog to the ground, his body hitting with a thud and a groan of pain. Whirling around, the demon started to walk to the door space, its free hands beginning to change form once again, growing larger and wider.

"If the door cannot be brought to us, then we will bring it ourselves," the monster snarled. It knelt down by the doorframe and brought its hands up, ready to press them down into the earth.

"But that'd ruin all the work I had to put into your little surprise."

"What?!" the demon screeched as it stood up. "Who speaks to us?"

"Someone who rather enjoys existence," the voice replied, echoing all over the cave.

"We do not have time for games! Bring back the door, so that we may end this pitiful mistake called creation."

"Oh yeah, that's real incentive for me to do that," the voice replied. "But tell you what. Being the nice, reasonable guy that I am, I'm just gonna throw some more gas on this fire, okay?"

"What are you—" the demon demanded. But then there was a flash of blackness, and when it faded, the demon and Forester stood in the center of the cave.

But that wasn't the only change. The door stood across the room from them. But it was also to the side of them. And behind them.

The door repeated itself across the walls, doubling over and over like a wallpaper pattern, creating at least a hundred doors all around them.

"Enjoy the scavenger hunt," the voice replied.

The demon grated its teeth and looked about. Turning its head to the ceiling, the demon yelled, "What are you? We demand you show yourself to us!"

"Black flashes, doors that appear and disappear and replicate. Doesn't that tell you something?"

The demon stayed silent.

And the voice answered, "How did stupid little nothings like you ever become a threat?"

For a few moments, nothing happened. And then, a black fog swirled up in front of the monster, twisting and turning about in the air. It solidified, taking on a form. The demon's eyes narrowed, and Forester looked on in utter relief as the fog finally vanished and the black-coated Nightstalker stood before them.

"We should've known," the demon sneered. "Another of the pathetic illusions your power lets you create."

"Yeah, but you aren't gonna be alive long enough to see through it," the bat replied. He drew his sword. "Now let my friend go and get back to whatever dimension you came from."

The monster just laughed. *Darkness alone cannot destroy us. You are only delaying the inevitable.*

"Now when did I say I was alone?" Stalker asked with a grin.

At that, the demon's face filled with fear, but it was already too late. Suddenly, its face filled with pain as a beam of golden light shot out from the side, slicing through the arms that held Forester. The squirrel fell to the ground as the demon screamed and staggered about in pain, its white flesh dissolving and bubbling where the light had hit. Slowly, it turned to see the Light Knight standing there, his staff drawn and glowing, pointed right at the monster's face.

XXIII.

"You ... you two weren't supposed to be here," the demon spat out, it's voice changing, growing darker and angrier as it spoke.

"I can imagine that's what you wanted," Joe said, holding his staff steady as he spoke. "Now, I'm going to give you one chance. Leave now, or you won't leave at all."

"We ...we aren't frightened of you," the demon said. *"We know your weakness, Light Knight. Your love, your caring—that is what makes you weak. And that is why you are unfit for the destiny you were forced into."*

Joe gave no answer, only held his staff and stared at the creature.

The demon's face broke into a twisted smile as it slowly got to its feet. *"Come now, Lightrider. Prove to us that we are wrong. Show us that you are the master of your destiny, not that thing that beats inside your chest. Destroy us! Return us to the nothingness from whence we came. Or do nothing and let us release the great plague and bring chaos back to your world."*

"Why isn't he doing anything?" Forester whispered as Stalker burned off the last of the creature's arms.

"Don't worry. He made a promise," Stalker whispered back. "He has a plan."

"Will you do nothing more?" the demon taunted as Joe stood there. *"Have you only the strength to point and pretend to defend? We would expect more from the representative of light. Or perhaps that is not who you want to be, is it?"*

"I'm not the one with a power staff pointed at him," Joe answered, his voice tight. "Now get the hell out of here before I do blast you to oblivion."

"And then what?" the demon asked. *"Will you continue to find things like us? Will you blast them to oblivion as well?"*

"Yes."

"For eternity? Do you not see the foolishness? You think this will give you 'purpose?' Bah! Purpose is stupidity that man and the builders invented. If life must have meaning, why shouldn't you be the one to choose it?"

"I chose to stop things like you from ruining the world. I chose to protect the people I care about, even if I have to do it without ever seeing them again."

"You were tricked into believing that the builders truly embrace free will? What choice did they offer you? To be their servant or die? Yes, even now I can smell the stink of death upon you. You were forced into choosing a life of keeping an order in a way that sickens you.

"But there are many ways to exist. We desire freedom—to be and do what we want, not what is expected. Can you truly say the world would be better with the order of your masters? Can you say that you are better because you 'chose' to embrace it?"

"Was it that great freedom that let you release the Hyleia? That let my friend be killed?" Joe asked angrily, his face hard and angry.

"The Hyleia moved of its own will. But even so, would we have let them loose there had you not chosen to embrace the light? We desire escape, freedom for ourselves and our father."

"At the expense of innocent lives?"

"Do innocents not die because of the balance?" the demon countered. *"Does evil not claim innocent lives? Do not the good die to stop it? And what do the builders do to stop the deaths? Throw you in the middle and force you to endlessly balance the scales until this wretched existence comes to an end? You, who desired no more than to exist and live the life you wanted.*

"But we can change that. We can offer you an end to the killing. We can let you live your life on your terms, with those you desire. Will you throw such a choice away, or will you slay us, for the continuation of the pointless, destructive balance?"

Joe stayed silent as both the Knights and the demon looked on. He simply looked at the demon as he held his staff up.

Finally, he spoke. "I told you before; I made my choice."

With that, Joe loosed a burst of light at the demon. The light struck the creature in the shoulder, and it howled in pain.

"And I'm sticking with it. Get away from the fucking door and goback to hell."

"You will die for this!" it screamed. *"You reject us for what? So that you can return to a life of killing and endless violence? So that you can lose those you care about?"*

"There is nothing you or anyone can do that will make me go back. And I will not let you destroy what remains of what I used to be."

"By leading a life of violence and killing?" the demon sneered.

"Not when I can help it," Joe answered. "And even if I can't, I would rather lead this life than hand the world over to nothingness. I can get through the killing because there's still one thing that separates me from monsters like you.

"I try really hard not to enjoy it."

"A pity we don't feel the same," the demon said, its twisted smile back on its face. It took a step toward Joe.

But the Light Knight gave no ground, only shook his staff once again. The demon smiled again, and then its body began to ripple. Joe stood his ground, waiting for the demon to attack, but instead, it rippled once and then faded away.

"That … was unexpected," Stalker said. Both he and Joe looked about in confusion.

"Ah wouldn't be so surprised," Forester replied. "The damn thing did the same to us. Turned into gas and tried to poison us."

"How long can we hold our breath?" Stalker asked.

"As long as we have to," Joe said.

"Good," a voice said from behind. The trio turned to see Sandshifter staggering toward them, with Forger and Wavecrasher holding her up, their bodies finishing the healing process. Firesprite, Windrider, Thunderer, Groundquake, and Nerbino trailed along as well, their bodies still smoking from the demon's attack.

"Looks like you guys had a hell of a fight," Joe said.

"Yeah, we did," Quake snapped. "And what were you doin'?"

"Not now," Thunderer said.

"Yes, now," Sandshifter said. She marched up to Joe. As she approached, the wolf reached behind her back and grasped something within the folds of her coat. She grunted in pain, and then pulled her arm back, drawing out one of Forger's spikes, now red with blood. She held it out to Joe and then dropped it at his feet.

"We took a lot waiting for you," the wolf said.

"I know," Joe said.

"We got the hell beaten out of us, more than we ever have before because you had to run away from all the ugliness of this job, like I always thought you would," the wolf continued, her voice sneering and cutting.

Joe gave no reply, except to watch as the wolf finished.

"And now, after all that—"

"Yes?"

"You still came back."

"Yes."

Sandshifter looked at Joe. And as her eyes burrowed deep, she said, "You got any ideas, fearless leader?"

"Maybe. Forester mentioned something about a gas?" Joe said.

"Yeah, but I doubt it'd try the same thing twice," the wolf replied. "It knows we can stop that."

"Then what are we going to do?" Windrider asked.

"What, Mega Man never had this problem?" Wavecrasher asked.

"No. Superman might've though," Windrider replied.

"Here is an idea."

The group whirled about, trying to find the source of the voice. But before they could, it spoke again.

"You can die!"

With that, the ground beneath them shook, and then Joe suddenly rose up into the air, his arms pressed to his side. Surprised, he dropped the Light Staff to the ground as he shook in the air above.

"Put him down!" Stalker swore. He hefted his sword and swung out toward the spot where Joe was hovering. But the blade, instead of hitting flesh, cut through only air as the demon's laugh filled the room. Stalker turned for a second attack, only to be hit by an invisible force and knocked into a nearby stalagmite, smashing it to bits.

Sandshifter and Quake immediately stepped forward, launching twin streams of sand and dirt directly below Joe. But as with Stalker's, their attacks hit nothing, shooting past Joe and splattering against the wall. And just like Stalker, they suddenly found themselves on the wrong end of a battering ram as they rose up and shot out to the wall, striking hard enough that when they fell, their outlines were cracked into the wall.

"Goddamn it … let me … go!" Joe spat out, struggling against his invisible bonds.

Below him, the remaining Knights and Nerbino danced about, firing their attacks in an attempt to locate the demon. But every attack, be it water or fire or thunder, shot clear through the wall, causing dust and broken rocks to fall all about.

The attacks were revealing something, though. Joe would constantly move around in the air from one spot to the next as the attacks splattered around him. The demon was right in front of them, but with the invisibility, it was able to move about with ease and attack and dodge at will.

Joe knew that if he didn't figure a way out soon, the Knights wouldn't stand a chance. He glanced down at the ground, where his staff still lay. Concentrating with all his might, he willed the staff to fly to his aid and free him. The wooden weapon trembled and then slowly began to rise and move toward the call of its master. But it suddenly halted and slammed back to the ground, pushing itself deep into the rock as Joe was swung from side to side. He tried to hold his concentration, but without seeing the staff, he was forced to submit to the constant motion and halt his efforts.

Joe's mind whirled as he thought of the skills, all the tricks that he'd learned from Ralin and his experience as a Knight. He thought of the ways to bend light, form it into shapes, call it to him in even the bleakest darkness—all these and a hundred more tricks flowed through his mind. But none of them told him how to make the invisible visible, to see that which was hidd—

"Stalker!" Joe yelled. "Stalker, get up. You can see things that are hidden in the dark; you can stop this thing. C'mon, man, move your furry ass!"

The bat nodded, and his eyes went black, looking about in the shadows. He looked about in confusion, as if he saw nothing. And then a great force threw the bat to the side of cave. Thunderer and Wavecrasher followed across the cavern, while Forger's wave of spikes slammed into a wall.

"Shit," Joe muttered. It was all up to him now. But no matter how hard he racked his brain, Joe could think of nothing that could help him. All the things he had learned from Ralin flashed through his mind as he searched for just one that could help him.

Seek the answers in the dark.

That's what I'm trying to do! Joe thought. *But apparently there aren't any answers there ...*

Joe stopped his thoughts then as his eyes opened wide. He smiled and took a second to ready himself.

The Knights and Nerbino continued to battle the invisible demon; none of them noticed the way that the torches around them were beginning to glow brighter, their light slowly filling the cavern.

But what happened next did catch their attention. The torchlights increased once more and then seemed to explode in bursts of light, making the room almost perfectly white in its brightness. The full brightness only lasted a minute, and then the room fell into total pitch-blackness, save Joe's body, which now glowed with golden, painful light. Everyone was forced to cover his or her eyes, but even with their coats pressed over their faces, they couldn't escape the brightness.

Had they been able to see, they would've witnessed Joe's body changing as the power filled his bones and veins. It coursed through him; golden waves washed over the Knight's body, coating him in a coat of pure golden light. It was more light than Joe had ever called to himself before, more then he'd thought he could've survived. But he felt no pain from it. No, in the grasp of this power, Joe felt ... utter and complete joy. All the darkness in his heart had been pushed to the very farthest corners. Joe reveled in it, letting the memories, the love, and everything else wash over him. It was better than anything else he had ever experienced before—not from the Architects, not from Jeri, not from any kind of joy that he'd found in either of the lives he'd led.

All these thoughts rushed through Joe's mind. And then they left as he released all the power he had gathered to him. The result was a burst of color that the world had never seen before. The caves were turned into a mad painter's canvas as every single color in the spectrum flashed across the walls, brighter and harder than any light ever produced by man, demon, or anything in between. The gremlins in the city saw it rush out through the ground under their feet, and even in the city above, the concrete began to glow and shimmer as the light penetrated everything it came across. And then as quickly as it had come, the light vanished.

Even as the light faded inside the cavern, one thing came to replace it—a scream of ungodly pain.

"What ... what in the name of heaven did he do?" Sandshifter asked. She slowly lowered her coat, blinking her eyes rapidly.

"I don't know," Forger said, her own eyes blinking as each hand took to rubbing a different one. "I never thought ... that he could do something like that."

"So much light. Holy shit! Stalker!" Thunderer said. "There's no way he could've survived all that light! We gotta—"

"No, we don't," the bat groaned. He slowly got to his feet, without a single mark from the light upon his body.

"How the hell did you survive that?" the dog spat out in disbelief.

"I'm not sure. All I remember is—*Jesus Christ!*" Stalker yelled, pointing behind the Knights.

"Oh, I'm gonna hate turning around, ain't I?" Groundquake said, even as he did so.

Joe's attack had worked; he'd been freed from the demon's grasp and was dragging himself up to his feet. He regained his footing and saw the group staring behind him. He turned around. As he'd expected, the burst of light had forced the demon from its invisibility. But after looking at it now, Joe almost wished he'd left it there.

The demon had taken a form similar to a giant squid. Eight long, fleshy arms were spread out all over the cave. Each one was covered in hundreds of suckers, and inside each sucker was a long, sharp barb. The tips of the arms ended in barbs as well. The arms all linked up to a large, central body, which consisted of a large mass of flesh and an opening in the middle, with a long beak inching out of the bottom. And above that, breathing in rapidly, was a human-esque body, covered in more of the sucker-barbs and topped by a slimy looking, tentacled face with glowing scales on the sides.

But despite the fierce appearance of the monster, Joe wasn't afraid.

"Why does it always go after the eight-legged? Aren't there other kinds of monsters?" Forger asked.

"Dude, it's a coincidence. Let it go," Quake said.

"Sure, but if it had fur and a muzzle—"

"Not now, guys," Stalker said. He turned to Joe. "What in the hell did you do to it?"

"I figured out where it was hiding," Joe answered. "It's funny really."

Stalker raised an eyebrow and asked, "Okay. How?"

"It actually changed its body so that light wouldn't reflect off of it," Joe said. "And without that, well, you saw nothing."

"Then how'd you bring him back?" Windrider asked. "What did that lightshow—Hey, that's a great name for that trick!"

"It's not bad at all," Joe replied. "I gathered up all the light in the room and then shot it through the entire spectrum. And if something doesn't reflect light—"

"It passes through it," Forger finished. "And a dim room like this, the demon could handle, but that much … brilliant!"

"Yes, it is," Stalker said. "But how did you get it to leave me alone? I should've at least gotten some kinda burn outta that mess."

"I told it to avoid you," Joe said simply.

"You ... told it to?" Stalker repeated.

"Yeah. We Knights can command the elements, you know."

The bat grinned and said, "Yeah. I guess we can do that, can't we?" "I'll have to remember that if I have to drop a shadowbomb one of these days."

"Oh, dear God, please stop before the kid wets himself over naming these moves," Groundquake muttered.

"Ah'm sorry Ah doubted you," Forester said.

"Oh, come on, you really thought I'd go with the squid over there? What kind of loser teams up with a giant squid to destroy the world?" Joe said.

"Ozymandias," Windrider replied.

"Who the hell—Why do I even ask?" Sandshifter said, shaking her head.

"How sweet. The Knights are finally together again," Nerbino said with a touch of sarcasm. "I'd feel all warm and fuzzy if—"

"You weren't a gremlin?" Groundquake asked.

Nerbino didn't reply. Instead, he simply dove to the ground as a loud, angry roar filled the air. The Knights followed his example as the demon swung one of its massive tendrils just above their heads. They quickly rolled to the side as the demon's tendrils continued to swing around them. But despite the massive amount of slimy, pale flesh swinging through the air, the Knights managed to get just out of its reach. The demon retracted its tendrils and pushed itself up.

"We do not care if there are ten or eleven or even a thousand of you!" the demon screamed. *"We shall plunge this world into the nothing, and you shall all go with it!"*

"There'll be nothing left for one of us," Joe replied, holding up his staff as the others drew their own weapons.

The demon let out another roar and launched two of its tendrils directly at Joe. The Light Knight immediately rolled forward, dodging the tendrils. The remaining Knights split apart, with a group leaping to either side. As they avoided the tendrils, Thunderer and Firesprite snapped back up and fired their weapons in sync. The demon leaped up as the fire and lighting impacted the wall below it.

But then it screamed as Joe, seeing the creature's exposed belly and mouth, fired off a light burst that shot directly into the monster's beak and spread through its body. Joe brought up his free hand and pushed his palm open. The demon stopped moving down, and its body splayed out, as if steel rods had replaced its bones. As the light flowed through its body, the white skin flashing gold, Forger brought her mace up and then swung it back down. As the weapon came up through the air, some of the ridges on it loosened and flew through the air. As they flew, the ridges grew larger and sharper, until they reached almost eight feet in length. The demon saw the spikes coming and tried to move its light-infused body. But Joe held the light steady as the spikes flew into the two tendrils that the demon had tried to use against them. The tendrils flew back and then the spikes drove them into the wall, nailing them into place.

The demon snarled and tried to bring more of its tendrils around to attack. But then it halted and let out another snarl as it looked down. On one side, a huge stone hand had wrapped around a pair of tendrils, while two more were covered in sand and ice. Still, the demon saw that at least one tendril remained free and it stretched that one around toward the only figure it could reach—Nightstalker.

The bat stood quietly as green demon flame suddenly slammed into the tendril and exploded around it. It held there free for a moment, the tendril shaking back and forth in pain as the fire flickered out. But as it swung around, the ground underneath it cracked open, and long vines shot out and wrapped themselves around the tendril, pulling it down to the ground.

"You think this will stop us!" the demon screamed. *"We will break these bonds and destroy you all!"*

"Actually, we do think it will stop you," Nightstalker said.

The bat walked over to Joe, with Firesprite, Thunderer, and Nerbino behind him, their weapons at the ready.

"Let's hurry," Joe said, his face strained. "It's getting harder to keep this stuff pumping through it."

"You will never be rid of us! Others will follow!" the demon screamed. *"We will never stop!"*

"Actually, I'm pretty cool with that. Because we will never stop being here to send you back to hell," the bat replied.

The demon sneered and then turned its glance to Joe. *"This is what you have chosen! We will haunt your every waking moment, Light Knight! Your life will be nothing more than destruction and killing, for a pointless, selfish balance that you don't even believe in! Is that worth throwing away everything you once believed in? The freedom we offered?"*

"I'm not throwing away any kind of freedom," Joe replied. "And I'm not throwing away what I believe in either—because even now, I'm sorry that I have to do this. But it isn't going to stop me. Now Stalker, if you would be so kind?"

"With pleasure," the bat replied. His sword glowed with black fire, which he sent out toward the monster. The dark flame struck its body and instantly pushed its way inside, melding with the golden light that Joe continued to pump into the creature.

The demon's howl reached a fever pitch as the two opposing elements filled its body, ripping its pliable form to shreds both inside and out. And even as the shadow and the light tore the creature asunder, the other Knights held their weapons high and unleashed their own might. Flames and water, earth and sand, spikes and thorns, lightning and winds, and even demonfire shot into the creature.

It let out a final scream and then fell silent as what passed for its throat fell away, evaporating into a pale, yellowish steam, like rancid piss being boiled away. As its body began to fall away, the steam began to pour out of it, along with a strange light of the exact same color.

Joe saw it, and turned his head to tell the others to hold. But by then their combined powers had already done their job. The last of the Chaos Demon vanished.

When its body faded away into steam, though, the strange light radiated outward, covering the cave and the Knights, growing brighter and brighter until none of them could see.

XXIV.

"Hey."

"Uhh ..."

"Hey! Is anybody dead? Gimme a yell here!"

"Huh? Quake?"

"Joe? You okay?"

"I think so," Joe said, shaking his head and rubbing his eyes. He slowly pried them open a bit at a time, until he could finally open them all the way. For a second, the world around him looked pale and watery, with a yellow tinge all over it, and then he blinked and the world eased back into normalcy. Joe shook his head a final time and then felt a pair of arms grasp his shoulders and gently lift him to his feet.

"You sure you're all right?" Groundquake asked, gingerly bending down to pick Joe's staff up from the ground.

"Yeah," Joe replied, taking the staff. "How's everybody else?"

"All here and accounted for."

Joe turned to see Sandshifter standing behind him and the other Knights and Nerbino standing behind her. Most seemed winded and tired (Sandshifter was leaning heavily on her staff, while Forester was holding Wavecrasher up) but they all still stood there as best they could.

"That ... was ...*awesome*!" Windrider all but howled, shaking his staff in utter joy and clenched his fist at the ceiling. "We really did it, you guys. We saved the world from a Chaos Demon. Man, this is ten times better then killing Ganondorf. This is better than the Joker and Batman in a death match!"

"Now that's high praise," Forester said with a smile.

"It isn't important what we're better than," Wavecrasher said. "What matters, is that we just took down a Chaos Demon."

"Exactly," Joe said. "All of us."

"And maybe it can stay that way?" Sandshifter said, casting an eye at Joe.

"Absolutely," Joe said.

"Then I'd better stick around to make sure you actually keep that promise."

"Me too," Forester said. "Y'all showed some serious nads today. But don't think Ah'm gonna roll over for ya."

"I wouldn't waste my time trying," Joe replied.

"Then let's all swear to it," Stalker asked. He stuck out his hand. "All of us in this together, no more questions, until the world ends."

One by one, the Knights stepped up and placed their hands down onto the pile. And Joe knew that, as long as they all kept that loyalty, he would ...

"By the First Gremlin, you people are sickeningly sentimental."

"Something bothering you, prince?" Joe asked, turning around to face Nerbino.

"You truly need to ask?" the gremlin replied. "When my people succeed, we simply say 'good job,' pat each other on the back, and get back to life. No wonder you humans enjoy those romance novels we find in the trash."

"You know, there might be a way to bring big, tall, and world-ending back," Stalker said. "I mean, we go back home, we find a spell book or two, come back here, tear another hole in the dimensional fabric, and then—"

"Oh, for hell's sake, I didn't mean you didn't do well!" Nerbino answered. "I suppose it is better to have a sentimental group of Knights who can work together then one who cannot function."

"You bet you need that," Groundquake said. "After all, you're king now, ain't cha?"

"I doubt I can do as well as my father," the gremlin said sadly. "But I will have to try. And I will make you this promise; I will uphold all the laws and balances that you and the Architects give me."

"Glad to hear it, Your Majesty," Joe said, bowing his head. "But first, can we ask a favor of you?"

"What do you wish, Lightrider?"

"A bit more protection for this door," Joe replied. "Stalker, drop the illusion."

The bat nodded and waved his hand. The multiple doors wavered and then faded completely, leaving only the true door remaining. Joe walked over to it, looking up at the massive door and the intricate carvings within it.

"You said that only the gremlin king and his heir together, can open this door?" Joe asked.

"Yes. So it has been since our kind was given these lands by the Architects," Nerbino replied.

"I see," Joe said. "And there is no other way to open it?"

"None that I know of."

"Good. Quake?"

"Yeah, Joe?" the dog answered.

"I want you to encase this door. Bury it in the rock as deep and as thick as you can."

"Not a problem," Groundquake replied. He held his arms out, his fingers curled into claws. The dog stared hard at the door, focusing all his power and concentration upon it. As he did, the ground began to rumble and the door appeared to shake inside its framework. Quake brought his hooked hands together in a great clap, and the stone around the door stretched outward, as if it had become a great stone imitation of the ocean waves. As the group watched, the stone then wrapped itself together, forming around the door in a great stone seal, burying it forever inside the cave walls.

"Very nice," Forger said.

"You expected less?" the dog replied.

"It is impressive," Nerbino agreed. "But mere stone will not be enough."

"Oh dear God, am I gonna get any compliments outta this job?"

"It's good enough for what I need," Joe said. He raised his staff, the lion's head glowing. He pointed it to the stone and a beam of light shot from it, striking the stones. The earth glowed like pure gold for a moment and then faded back to their gray normalcy.

"I've charged it with light," Joe said, before anyone could open their mouths to ask. "That'll keep out gremlin and Chaos Demon, along with anything else that might come around here. And with that, I think it's time we leave you to your kingdom, King Nerbino."

"Indeed. I give you my thanks, Elementals."

Joe nodded, and he and the other Knights raised their weapons. In a flash of multicolored lights, the Knights vanished, leaving the new gremlin king to announce his rule.

*　　*　　*

"He has made his choice."

"As I knew he would."

"Even as I questioned and feared what he would do. But your charge has shown understanding and a ... compassion that I had forgotten. Perhaps the simple devotion and care he showed were enough ... *are* enough for a leader."

"I accept your apology."

"But I hear resignation lingering in your voice."

"I chose Joseph for his kindness and devotion, because they were qualities that I wanted. And I knew that they would make him struggle with the needs of being an Elemental and how to use the power of light."

"And you know that there is still much for him to overcome—still much that could darken his uniform, as mine was long ago."

Ralin's eyes narrowed, as he replied, "Yes. And that is something we cannot allow."

"It was what needed to be done. Do not forget that."

"I do not. And yet—"

"Ralin, as our brother would say, a great sword must pass through much flame and shaping before it can be made strong. Lightrider has shown that, for now at least, he can weather it."

"Yes, Rastla. But what will keep him in the flame, to take the punishment?"

"If you seek an answer, then look here, and remember the lesson we both learned."

* * *

The being once known as Joseph Hashimoto and now known as the Lightrider sat on his bed, gazing upon his staff, as it gave off a faint glow.

"This is what I get for eternity," he said aloud. He looked at the staff, seeing the golden tinge upon his desk and his chair. "Make the world shine. I suppose I could've done worse."

Still, a thought lingered in Joe's mind, echoing even as he spoke. *What does it profit a man to create a utopia, if he can never see it?* Joe heard the thought and shook his head, because there wasn't an answer for him. He would have to make his own.

Then a sharp, quick rap upon the door came, breaking Joe from his inner monologue. Pulling the staff away, Joe called out, "Come in."

The door swung open, revealing what appeared to be nothing more than solid black. But then the blackness shifted as Nightstalker entered the room.

"You did it?" Joe asked, getting off the bed.

"You expected less?" the bat replied with a smirk. "It took a little digging, which took longer than usual—Wavecrasher is boning up on magic again—but I found the spell."

"You're sure she didn't see you?" Joe asked.

"No. I came when I knew she'd be asleep. They weren't in her treasure box though. Apparently, Jeri chose to keep them closer."

"She would," Joe nodded. Stalker reached into the folds of his coat and into a secret pocket. He fished around a moment and then drew out a small golden chain. He handed it to his friend without a word. Joe took it with trembling hands, his fingers gently touching the two gold rings the chain held.

"These are … the originals?" he asked.

"One is," Stalker replied. "I used the duplication spell to make the copies and then put them on the chains. She kept your ring. And you have hers."

"Good," Joe replied. He took the chain and placed it over his head, hearing the clink as the wedding rings touched.

"You know, when you said there was one thing I had to do for you, I didn't think this would be it," the bat replied.

"Why?" Joe asked. "What did you think I'd ask?"

"Something a lot harder," Stalker said. "Bringing them here or making the Architects give them immortality or—"

"And would you have done it?"

"Well, the fate of the world was at stake, so I would've taken my chances with bending cosmic rules and laws."

"Hmmph," Joe chuckled. "No, Stalker, I know they can't be part of my life anymore. But I can still fight for them, even when they're gone."

"You still have a family, Joe. We just have fur and some of us drool. And have mandibles. And tails. And wings. And—"

"Please, Stalker, it's depressing enough that I can't see my wife again," Joe said. "You don't have to remind me I'm captain of Noah's Ark for all eternity."

Both Knights broke out laughing at that, until Joe stopped and said, "I can't do this alone. Thanks for being there to help me."

"Always. Because I know you'd do the same for me," Stalker replied. He stuck out his hand.

Joe nodded and took the hand. Sparks literally flew between them. And as light and dark swore their eternal brotherhood and friendship to one another, Ralin and Rastla watched from above and knew that the balance of the universe would be in good hands.

EPILOGUE

The pen crossed its final letter and then came to a halt. He placed it down next to the book. Flexing his hand, he reached over and flipped through the pages, marveling at the amount he'd been able to fill. He still had so much left, about how he had gotten to this place and how he had changed again. But that was for another time. Now that he'd put those days down and seen them once again, what he did think of them? Did he regret them? Did he embrace them? Did they even matter anymore?

As he looked at the book, he reached up to his collar and pulled out a chain. The rings were dulled a bit now but could still shine well enough for him. As they glistened in the dim light, he remembered the words he had said long ago. That had been what had pressed him into the Knighthood—the desire to make the world better for the people he loved.

"And I did, didn't I?" he asked aloud.

He had done things that were terrible. And he had done things that had filled him with joy. He looked at the rings that united him and his wife. Once, everything he'd done had been for his family. And in the end, it still was.

He would never forget his terrible deeds or stop regretting them. But now, he could remember why he did them.

To protect the world.

To keep the balance.

To be the person his family could be proud of.

To be a person he could be proud of.

And to do his duty—so that the world could be a little brighter.

He nodded then and shut the book. But he left the pen and ink on the table as he opened the desk drawer to put the book away. He could still feel the weight of the words left to write. Perhaps when he put them to pen and paper, he would feel them lifted. And then, he would have something to remind him of why in the times he felt confused and unsure of what he had become.

But he knew he could not leave it like this. He looked at the unadorned cover, wondering what he could do to improve upon it. And then it came to him. He waved his hand over the cover, and as he did, golden letters emblazed themselves into the cover. He looked at the newly titled Lightrider Journals *and he knew that this would be a fine title for his life. Opening the drawer, he placed the book inside and closed it, until the next time. As he shut it, he paused a moment. He heard the voice of the Obelisk, his charge, in his mind telling him that his friends had returned home. He would need to greet them and hear what had happened on their new mission. And he wanted to check on his replacement.*

Joe turned from the desk and headed toward the door to the stairway. He reached the door and paused to look back at the desk, where the first chapter of his second life lay. He wondered briefly how long it would take him to write the other chapters. Then he shrugged and moved through the door. It didn't matter; he had eternity.

ACKNOWLEDGEMENTS

My parents, who kept nagging and pushing, while helping me and keeping me around long enough to get this book done.

Derrick Fish for his amazing skill at bringing my dreams to life and Jed Soriano for his vital early work on the Knights.

Carol Lombardo, for all her long hours editing this book and reminding me how much I need to learn the difference between *then* and *than*.

The people at Walgreens—managers, coworkers, and customers—who gave me the material I needed to bring Joe's human life into reality. I especially must thank Ronald Brown, who was crazy enough to become a character here, Christina DeMarco for making me look good in a photo (no easy task!), and Darren Poree, who read the manuscript and helped trim the fat off it.

Stephen King, Terry Brooks, Brian Konietzko, and Michael Dante DiMartino, whose collective works gave me the vision and the tools I needed to shape my own world.

Everyone who read my drafts and heard my ideas; told me what was right and wrong; and, most importantly, told me to keep writing. You all know who you are.

And Colin James Maher, my cousin, who's up eating PEZ with God after years of bravely fighting Ewing's Sarcoma. I miss you, but I hope this book does you justice. (Please visit http://www.friendsofcolin.org/home.)